THE SOUL THIEF

S L HOWE

One More Chapter
a division of HarperCollins*Publishers* Ltd
1 London Bridge Street
London SE1 9GF
www.harpercollins.co.uk
HarperCollins*Publishers*
Macken House, 39/40 Mayor Street Upper,
Dublin 1, D01 C9W8, Ireland

This paperback edition 2024

1

First published in Great Britain in ebook format
by HarperCollins*Publishers* 2024
Copyright © S L Howe 2024

S L Howe asserts the moral right to
be identified as the author of this work

A catalogue record of this book
is available from the British Library

ISBN: 978-0-00-869581-1

Samantha Lee Howe began her professional writing career in 2007 and has been working as a freelance writer for small, medium, and large publishers ever since. She is a multi-award-winning screenwriter and a *USA Today*! bestselling author. She is the author of over 27 novels, more than 60 short stories and two screenplays. Her back list includes Thrillers, Horror, Fantasy, SF and Steampunk.

An ardent supporter of charities, Samantha is Survivor Ambassador for domestic abuse charity IDAS (Independent Domestic Abuse Services) which is based in Yorkshire. She also supports Anna Kennedy Online as sponsor, judge and presenter for the Autism Hero Awards and Autism's Got Talent as well as breast cancer charity, Pink Ribbon Foundation.

Samantha lives in South Yorkshire with her husband, historian, writer and publisher, David J Howe, and their cat Skye. She is the proud mother of a lovely daughter called Linzi.

<u>www.samanthaleehowe.co.uk</u>

samanthaleehowe.co.uk

facebook.com/samanthaleehowe

instagram.com/samanthaleehowe

threads.net/@samanthaleehowe

tiktok.com/@samanthaleehowe

Writing as Samantha Lee Howe

The Stranger in Our Bed

The House of Killers

Kill or Die

Kill a Spy

For Linzi and Olivia - the future is in your hands (no pressure!)

Part I

Prologue

Dr Warren Carter made his way across the ward. It had been a long week, and the day itself, full of family-related issues, had been a trying one. Sleep would be welcome and he was looking forward to climbing into the uncomfortable narrow cot in the doctors' courtesy room.

A small lantern cast light over the desk near the door where a young nurse was writing observation notes into a thick ledger.

'Good evening, Dr Carter,' said the nurse.

Warren recognised her, but couldn't remember her name. It was Rosie or Daisy, or some such name. He looked around the ward, noting how quiet it was.

'How are the patients this evening?' he asked.

'Mr Stanwick has been restless. He seems to be in a lot of pain but Dr Hardy didn't want to prescribe any more laudanum today. He said he's had his quota and the hospital couldn't afford to give the medicine unless it was necessary.'

As if on cue, Stanwick began to moan.

'We can't let the man suffer. I'll prescribe it for him. How is his leg?'

'Gangrenous,' said the nurse. 'I can smell it from here.'

Warren sighed. 'What did Dr Hardy say he was going to do about it?

The nurse shrugged. 'I shouldn't really be saying this, doctor, but...'

'Please speak freely,' Warren said.

'Dr Hardy will probably leave him until it's too late. I believe that Mr Stanwick will die if someone doesn't remove that leg soon.'

'I'll take a look.'

Warren walked down to Stanwick's bed. The bed covers lay over a metal frame that arched over the man's legs. Warren lifted the blankets and pulled away the frame. The smell of rot wafted up from the man's right leg and Warren could see that the bandage was already turning black with the poison that seeped from the wound. As the nurse had indicated, infection had set in and only amputation would save Stanwick's life. The man was in a state of delirium. He moved his head from side to side, an expression of abject pain on his face.

'Prepare him for surgery,' Warren said. 'We're doing this now.'

Stanwick lapsed into a quiet doze after Warren fed him a dose of laudanum. They wheeled the bed away into a side ward and the nurse put on a large white apron over her long black uniform, ready to assist him. Warren put his surgical tools onto a small table beside Stanwick's bed. Then he stripped off the rotten bandages and took a proper look at the damage.

What had started in Stanwick's foot had now spread to below the knee.

'I'll cut from above the knee to make sure we have it,' Warren said. 'You aren't squeamish are you, girl?'

'Rosie. My name is Rosie, and no, doctor, I can assist you without fainting.'

Warren lifted one of Stanwick's eyelids and looked at the man. 'He's under. He shouldn't feel anything now.'

He picked up his saw and began to cut through flesh and bone. Stanwick barely groaned. Blood splashed over Warren's apron and onto the floor as he vigorously worked his way through the leg. Sweat poured down his face with the exertion. Rosie wiped his brow without being asked. She was the perfect assistant: the room was awash with the man's gore, but Rosie never turned away. She worked as instructed, passing Warren the instruments and taking away the used and bloody saw, which she dropped into a bucket along with the severed limb.

After he had sewn up the wound, Warren sloshed more surgical spirit over the stitches. Stanwick was quiet – so much so, that for a moment Warren was concerned they had lost him after all. He placed his stethoscope against the man's heart: he could detect faint beating and sighed with relief.

'He's all right for now, but the next twenty-four hours will be crucial.'

'Well done,' Rosie said. 'I think you saved his life, Doctor.'

Rosie helped as he cleaned Stanwick up. They turned him sideways, removing the soiled bedding, and placed on a new nightshirt that covered the neat and clean bandage around his thigh.

'He will be much more comfortable now. Thank you. You have a good soul and a compassionate heart,' Rosie said.

Warren took the compliment. It was why he'd become a doctor and, unlike some of his colleagues, whose egos were bigger than their empathy, he wanted to save lives and help people.

After they wheeled him back onto the ward, Rosie made a quick check on the other patients. They were all sleeping soundly and now that the surgery was complete, and the laudanum dose was still in his system, Stanwick was peaceful too.

'He'll be in shock when he learns he's lost his leg,' Rosie said. 'But better that than his life. Don't you think, Doctor?'

Warren nodded. His hands were submerged in a tepid bowl of water and he scrubbed at his nails to remove the traces of blood and gore that clung to them.

A few minutes later, another nurse arrived to take up Rosie's post. It was now around one in the morning. Warren felt overtired; he remained while Rosie explained to the nurse that Stanwick needed to be watched.

'The side room will have to be cleaned when the orderlies come on duty,' she said.

They left the ward together and Warren turned right to head to his room.

'Doctor Carter?' said Rosie. 'Perhaps you would care for a nightcap?'

Warren looked at the girl, really seeing her for the first time. She was pretty. Her dark hair was escaping from her nurse's cap. She had removed the soiled apron and replaced it with a clean one, though Warren didn't know when or how she had achieved this without him noticing. She was wearing a black dress underneath it: something all the nurses wore, simple with fluted arms. The dark colour barely showed the stains, but still the dress appeared to be as spotless as the new apron. In the gaslight her eyes were dark, but Warren wondered what colour they really were.

'I have some French brandy in my room,' she said. 'It helps me sleep, after a long hard day.'

Warren was a little shocked by how forward she was, but he turned and followed her down the corridor and out towards the back of the hospital where the nurses' quarters were: a place that was always off-limits to any young doctor.

'What if your matron finds out?' Warren whispered.

'It's only a drink,' she said.

Rosie took his hand. Her fingers were icy to the touch, but he found he couldn't pull away. Despite his better judgement, he had the outlandish compulsion to go with her.

In her room, Rosie drew the curtains and lit a lamp that was on a small table beside her bed while Warren stood by the door, his hands clenched together as though he were afraid to touch anything.

Rosie opened her wardrobe and retrieved a bottle of brandy and two glasses which she placed on her dressing table. She opened the bottle and poured a small amount into each glass, then she held one out to Warren. He stared at the glass for a moment, wondering what he was doing there. Then he took it and sipped the contents. The brandy burned his throat in the way that good liquor does. It was delicious and warming. Warren hadn't realised how cold he was until that first sip slivered down his gullet.

Rosie sat down on the edge of the bed. She had removed her cap and her black hair was tumbling over her shoulders. Warren looked away. He wasn't used to women being so bold.

Even so, he wanted to sit beside her.

'Why don't you then?' said Rosie, as though reading his mind.

Warren found himself sinking down onto the edge of the bed.

'Can I ask a favour of you, Doctor?' Rosie said.

Warren nodded.

'I've admired you for a while. I'd like to draw you. Would that be okay?'

'Draw me?'

'It's a hobby of mine…'

Rosie laid back against the headboard, one leg raised up, the other draped down to the floor. All she was wearing was a white cotton shift. She now had a small piece of paper and a stick of charcoal in her hand. She was sketching rapidly. Warren closed his eyes. He couldn't remember giving her permission, nor could he recall when she had removed her uniform. It was as though time skipped by every time he blinked.

Warren experienced the oddest stirrings as he watched her. Her eyes flicked up and over him, as her hand moved rapidly. It was as though she were stroking him with every touch of the charcoal on the paper.

'Almost done,' she said.

'What time is it?' Warren stood up. 'I really should return to my room. Get some sleep.'

Rosie stopped drawing and met his eyes. 'Soon, Warren. I've *almost* captured you.'

He felt the life seep from his limbs and he slipped back onto the bed. Rosie was above him. She gazed down at him with those mysterious dark eyes that rarely blinked. They stared into him as though they could see his very soul.

Time blurred once more. Warren blinked again.

Rosie didn't look as though she were enjoying herself. She was lying on the bed crying.

'What have I done?' Warren gasped.

Rosie turned into the pillow and cried, 'Doctor … why did you…?'

Warren felt confused. He backed away. Pulling his abandoned clothing up from the floor, he dragged on his trousers and shirt, while the girl pulled the sheets around herself. He couldn't take his eyes from her tear-streaked face. Her expression changed. It became lascivious again and then it began to look just like…

Warren looked away. It had been an awful day! A trying day. Surely, he could be forgiven for losing his mind? This wasn't real. He was probably asleep in his room, dreaming it all.

On the floor he noticed the pad of paper. His image, a smiling kind face, was now smudged. He looked like a distorted monster.

The room was small and claustrophobic. The walls appeared to shift; the ceiling scooped down. The corners were full of shadows. Warren knew he had to get out of there.

'I'm sorry,' he said. 'I thought this was what you wanted.'

Rosie didn't answer.

Warren backed towards the door. There was a darkness, a blurred shape in the corner of the room. He hadn't noticed it earlier, but now it moved towards him as though herding him out and away from the girl.

In the dark corridor of the nurses' quarters laughter followed him. What had he done?

The guilt at hurting an innocent girl hounded him from the building into the night. He ran through the streets of Manchester. A half-dressed madman, tearing at his hair and clothing as the wind whistled past his ears, screaming obscenities.

Chapter One

'Miss Carter still won't see you?' Major John Mainwaring asked.

'No. For the past six months all my letters have been returned unopened. I don't know what to do.'

'I've never understood the whims of the fairer sex,' Mainwaring said.

'You never wanted to remarry then, Uncle John?' Mitchell asked.

'I'm a career man,' said Mainwaring.

Mitchell knew that this wasn't strictly true, as Mainwaring's career had been cut short when he was severely injured, during an uprising in 1883. A bullet wound to the spine had forced his early retirement and brought him home from his beloved India. Now, wheelchair bound, he lived in comfort, with a modest income from his pension and a small subsidy that was paid to him from Mitchell's estate – a trust set up by Mitchell's father for Mainwaring's continued care of his godson.

Mitchell was grateful to have Mainwaring in his life. With

or without the financial support, Mainwaring had always taken his role as godfather seriously. He had been close to Colonel Damien Bishop, Mitchell's father, and had been there when his mother caught the cursed malaria fever – a sickness that killed her after many troubled months. Mitchell had been very young at the time and didn't really remember her. He had grown up in a house full of Indian servants who doted on him, spoiling the boy while Bishop had been too busy 'doing his duty for Queen and country'. Mainwaring had been there for him, though. He took an interest in the boy, never having had a son of his own, and enjoyed bringing him treats and spent many hours playing cards and reading stories to him.

After his injury, when he knew he needed to return home, Mainwaring had suggested bringing Mitchell home too. He couldn't bear the thought of never seeing him again. By then the boy was thirteen, and had rarely spent any time with other British children. He was smart and educated – his father had seen to that at least. And the small colony school had boasted of solid education, if nothing much else.

Much to his surprise, Mitchell had been more than willing to come to England. He had been born in India and had never seen what was still, technically, his homeland. It wasn't much of a wonder that Damien Bishop agreed, however, as he barely saw his son, and found the boy's looks to be a constant reminder of his beloved wife.

At Mainwaring's suggestion, Bishop had promptly organised an appropriate boarding school. Mitchell had returned with Mainwaring and his manservant Neeraj, and took up residence in the school. Any colonial rough edges were soon smoothed away and the boy fitted in with remarkable ease. And, during school holidays he spent his time in the company of his godfather and Neeraj.

Now, twenty years on, Mitchell behaved as though he had always lived in England, but Mainwaring knew that deep down he was still as unconventional as he had always been. Boarding school had taught him to hide it, though, because Mitchell had soon learnt that it didn't pay to be different.

Mainwaring's relationship with Mitchell had changed several times over the years. When Mitchell's father died in India, Mainwaring had taken on the role of parent full-time. As Mitchell grew into a man, Mainwaring remained in the distance as his benefactor and friend; always there to advise. He offered unconditional love, and for this Mitchell was always grateful.

'You have to face it, my boy. It's over. She believed her sister too quickly above you. Strange, after the love the two of you shared,' Mainwaring said. 'But women are notoriously capricious.'

Mainwaring was sympathetic but he hated to see Mitchell suffer so much at the hands of the fickle sex. He had tried to see the girl himself, but her servants had turned him away at the door. At that time, he had also seen the culprit, Sara Carter, Laura's younger sister, smiling from the window of one of the rooms upstairs. Her strangely satisfied smirk made Mainwaring think of the proverbial expression, 'The cat that got the cream'. He wondered if the sister's deliberate interference – and obvious lies – which led directly to the break-up, had some deeper significance to the girl. He didn't tell Mitchell any of these thoughts, though, as he could not think of any way to put right the wrong that had been done. The family would not hear that the sister was deceitful. No matter how hard they had tried. Forcing Mainwaring to conclude that the situation was, at least for now, best left, in the hope that it could be later resolved.

'I know. I can't reconcile it in my mind. Uncle John, I just don't know what to do. Laura loved me. I know she did. I can't understand why she wouldn't at least give me an opportunity to explain.'

'Time is often a healer,' Mainwaring said. 'Laura may one day realise the truth, but until then you have to move on. You liked your detective work. Why not look for a new mystery to solve?'

Mitchell grew thoughtful. 'I know you're right. I just find it so difficult to accept that I may never see her again.'

Mainwaring placed a hand on Mitchell's shoulder. 'Time to return to society, perhaps… There are other beautiful women out there. And who knows, you may cross paths again and find some common ground.'

Mitchell shook his head. 'I've been shunned from social circles. Although the family hasn't publicly decried me, our sudden separation is being blamed on me, in private. Socially, I'm ruined.'

Mainwaring laughed. 'My dear boy, if every young man who had overstepped the mark with a lady was blacklisted, there would be no marriageable men around. You have been hiding away like the guilty. Maybe it's time to attend a public event and start to mend those bridges you think have been burned. I think you might be surprised.'

Mainwaring was right, of course. Mitchell had not been shunned. He had merely avoided public engagements for fear of ridicule, and eventually, those invitations had stopped coming.

'I received an invitation to a garden party at Heaton Park. The new Earl of Wilton is giving a party in honour of the birth of his second son. I think you should come along,' Mainwaring said.

At that moment Mainwaring's manservant, Neeraj, came in. He placed two tall tumblers on the table beside them.

Mitchell exchanged a few pleasantries with the ageing butler. He had spent many hours with the man during the years when he had lived with his godfather. Until, that was, his twenty-first birthday, when Mitchell had moved into the family home left to him by his mother.

Seeing Neeraj now, reminded Mitchell of his own hopes and dreams. Although he was happy in his own home – a beautiful townhouse in the centre of the city – he missed Neeraj and Mainwaring's reassuring company. He had a butler, a house-keeper, a cook and a scullery maid. It was all that any single man might need. He had hoped, though, that Laura would make the house more of a home, simple though it was.

'I'm well. Thank you for asking,' answered Neeraj as Mitchell queried his health. Indeed, the man did look healthy and strong. He never appeared to age. 'How is your good self?'

Mitchell said he was well, even though he didn't really feel happy or content. He didn't want to worry Neeraj.

'Gin and tonic, dear boy?' Mainwaring said, holding out one of the tumblers as Neeraj left. 'The sun is over the yardarm, after all.'

Mitchell smiled. Old habits die hard. Mainwaring had never quite given up taking quinine in the form of the tonic water. The gin, of course, was the added kick. Mitchell had heard that malaria could recur even without the bite of a mosquito, and he wondered if Mainwaring had ever suffered the affliction.

'Just making sure,' Mainwaring said, as though reading his thoughts. 'So, you'll come to the party with me, then?'

'Yes,' Mitchell said, despite his instinct to hide away. 'I think I will.'

The garden party began at 2.30pm and Mitchell arrived with Mainwaring in the major's carriage. On arrival Neeraj and the driver lifted Mainwaring out of the carriage and placed him into his wicker wheelchair. Neeraj then wheeled him towards the rear of the house.

The party was taking place in the grounds and within the orangery. There was an expansive ballroom, with large French windows that opened out onto the gardens at the back of the house. Around the long room, several staff served canapés and wine. Mitchell and Mainwaring accepted a glass of champagne from a butler in formal uniform, who was wearing gold brocade on his shoulders especially for the occasion.

As he walked through the room, Mitchell recognised vases and statues, the type he had seen filling the houses of some of the wealthy colonists in India. He glanced at Mainwaring.

'Was the new earl ever in India?' he asked.

'He may have visited. But I know he does have a fondness for the artefacts.'

'I suppose he has *you* to thank for finding a few?'

'*Me?*' Mainwaring said. 'I don't really know the new earl. Though I was a good friend of his father…'

Out in the garden, Mitchell recognised a lot of his former social acquaintances, all of whom had been quiet since his disgrace.

'Bare face it, dear boy,' Mainwaring said behind him. 'Let's speak to Wilton. That will stop the wagging tongues. He will be a good contact for you to have.'

Neeraj pushed Mainwaring's wheelchair towards the earl as he stood with a group of young women.

Arthur George Egerton, the fifth Earl of Wilton, was only a

few years older than Mitchell, but he was already married, with two small children. He had recently inherited the title of earl, and the house, following his father's death at the beginning of the year. Even so, the earl and his Italian wife, Mariota Thellusson, were trying to keep up the traditions that the late earl had established. Inviting the local gentry to the house once a year, would ensure their own acceptance in Manchester's social circles.

'Arthur,' said Mainwaring. 'Have you met my godson, Mitchell Bishop?'

Arthur had spent most of his youth in London, and Mainwaring knew full well that Mitchell and he hadn't met. They shook hands and Mitchell was soon being introduced to the gaggle of young, eligible women surrounding the earl. Mitchell couldn't help wondering if this had been set up from the beginning. As he listened politely to the chatter of one young woman, he noticed Neeraj discretely wheeling Mainwaring away.

'Mitchell. Nice to see you,' said a voice behind him.

Mitchell turned to see Warren Carter, his ex-fiancée's twin brother extending his hand.

He rapidly excused himself from the girls and took Warren aside.

'Thank you for coming over. How is Laura?'

'I need to talk to you,' said Warren. 'Shall we find somewhere quieter?'

The two men strolled away from the gathering, round the outside of the house and down towards the lake. As soon as they were out of earshot, Warren began to speak.

'Mitchell, I don't know how to tell you this … I think I may be in a spot of trouble.'

'What kind of trouble?'

Warren swallowed. 'It's hard to explain. There have been some very strange occurrences, since that night.'

'Warren, please believe me, I love Laura … I would never hurt her.'

'I know.'

Warren paused, then rifled in his pockets until he found a pipe, tobacco and matches. He lit the pipe, puffed on it for a few moments and then began walking again. He led Mitchell to a bench overlooking the lake. Though it was difficult, Mitchell remained quiet, patiently waiting for Warren to tell him what was happening. Warren took out his pocket watch, flipped open the cover and looked at the time.

'By now I reckon the doctors will have institutionalised my sister Sara,' Warren said.

'Good heavens! What do you mean?'

'I will explain. But first I want you to tell me what happened between you.'

Chapter Two

December 1897: six months earlier

'Mr Bishop to see Miss Laura,' announced the housemaid, Alice, as she led Mitchell into the drawing room.

Laura Carter put aside her needlepoint and stood to greet Mitchell. She waited for the maid to leave before she threw her arms around him and planted a firm kiss on his lips.

'Darling…' Mitchell said.

Laura was petite and pretty, with dark blonde hair, and a smile that always warmed Mitchell's heart because it was full of genuine love. He pulled her close, hands around her tiny waist, and kissed her until he noticed the slow flush of embarrassment colour her cheeks. He loved the way she reacted to him. Always passionate, but still so shy. All of which he hoped would never change when they were married in six weeks' time.

A cough from the doorway made them jump apart.

'Mitchell, dear,' said Elena Carter, his future mother-in-law. 'I'm so glad Alice told me you were here.'

Mitchell's smile was warm and held a small apology for his enthusiasm, but he saw the vague twinkle that told him Elena was amused by their romance. He realised that Elena knew how much Mitchell loved her daughter and how much that was reciprocated.

'And how is my other favourite lady?' Mitchell said, planting a kiss on Elena's cheek.

'I'm well, thank you,' she said. 'Please sit, dear boy. I've ordered tea.'

As if on cue, Alice returned with a tray containing a silver teapot, three china teacups and saucers, and a tiered sandwich plate containing cucumber sandwiches and small cakes.

'Really mother,' Laura said. 'I will never fit into my wedding dress.'

Mitchell laughed. Laura had the appetite of a bird and her tiny figure reflected that. It was a family trait. Elena Carter, even after having three children, had retained her youthful figure, not much wider than her young daughter.

'Laura, you be mother today. You need the practice,' Elena said.

As Laura began to pour tea into the cup, Sara, Laura's younger sister, came into the drawing room. 'Mother, I can't possibly wear that… Oh hello, Mitchell.'

Sara's tone changed as she noticed Mitchell perched primly on the sofa beside Laura. She smiled at him. Her expression was somewhat predatory and it always made him feel uncomfortable. Unlike Laura, Sara was particularly outspoken. He found her bold. Too much so on occasion, and her change of tone now worried him. He could never tell if Sara approved of him or not. One minute she was polite, the next she would make some gibe about his hair, and about her poor sister being married off to a 'pretty boy'.

'Mitchell is taking me to the opera later,' Laura said. 'But first, we plan to take a stroll in the park.'

'In this weather?' Sara said.

'Whatever do you mean? The weather is glorious for December,' Laura replied.

They were having freak weather. An 'Indian summer', their father liked to call it.

'That lovely pale skin of yours will go all freckly. Not a good look for a bride… Oh, but maybe Mitchell will like that … being born in India and all.'

'Really!' Elena said. 'Many respectable people were born and raised in the colonies, Sara. I think it's rather exotic and exciting, myself.'

'Of course, Mother. I wasn't implying otherwise. Just that Mitchell may be a little more broad-minded than most people.'

Elena gave Sara a look that warned her not to pursue whatever peculiar train of thought she had right then.

Sara's smile widened as she sat down next to her mother and looked straight at Mitchell. 'Oh, I could think of far more interesting things to ask about India. But of course, I am only … teasing. You know I can't help myself.'

Mitchell looked down at the cup Laura offered him and pointedly ignored Sara's lascivious expression.

'Really, Sara!' Elena said, her good nature finally giving into exasperation.

Mitchell sipped his tea. It was a little weaker than he preferred it, but he said nothing. He placed his cup down on the ornate table before him and took Laura's hand.

'Ah. Young love,' Sara said.

Mitchell and Laura ignored her.

'Sara, you said you had a problem with your new dress?' Elena said.

'It's the bridesmaid dress I have issue with,' Sara snapped. 'You know green isn't my colour.'

Elena stood. 'Come, let's go and look, shall we?'

Sara stood reluctantly and Laura met her mother's eyes, nodding quickly to acknowledge her gratitude. Then, Elena led her wayward daughter out of the room, leaving Mitchell and Laura alone.

Mitchell raised her hand to his lips and kissed her fingers.

'Sorry about Sara,' Laura said. 'I don't know what's got into her lately.'

'It doesn't matter. It's probably some phase she's going through. Is that your new photograph?' asked Mitchell, his eyes falling on a framed picture placed on the wall above a tall yucca plant in the corner of the room.

'Why, yes! We went to the new shop on the high street. Warren suggested it. He had this thing that he wanted us to have a siblings' photograph before the wedding. Mister Naylor, the owner, was very obliging. It turned out well, didn't it?'

Mitchell stood and walked across the room to look closely. He saw a picture of Laura and her twin brother Warren with Sara. Warren was sitting in a chair looking very serious as Sara and Laura stood behind him. Laura was wearing her slightly embarrassed, modest smile, whereas Sara was smiling broadly. As he looked at the picture, Mitchell almost imagined that smile changing to the expression she had worn just moments earlier. A slightly rapacious gleam in her eye, as though she knew more about the world than an unmarried woman should.

'Lovely,' said Mitchell. 'You look particularly beautiful, darling.'

He turned and looked at her. She really was beautiful and he could barely wait for their wedding, to have all the time in the world to spend with her – with no interruptions to their kissing. His eyes ran over her figure. He couldn't imagine anything but loveliness beneath the formal day blouse and skirt she was wearing. He could barely wait to touch the bosom he had caught glimpses of when she wore the low-cut evening gowns. Especially the first one he had seen her in. A gown of dark purple velvet, tight across her waist, it had emphasised the curve of her breast, and the flow of her hips. The large bustle at the back had swayed provocatively as she walked, but Mitchell had noticed immediately that this was not deliberate on her part – merely the enforced movement caused by the restrictive gown and the bulk of fabric behind her. She was petite in height. Barely over five feet, whereas Mitchell stood over six feet, a good foot taller.

Sometimes she wore heeled boots under her skirt, which gave her added height, but also made her walk sway even more. He loved it. And loved her so much, sometimes it hurt. Laura was still an enigma to him, modest but strong, loving and generous in a way he had never encountered in women with breeding and money. Though that could have been down to the fact that her family were technically 'new money'.

Her father had a thriving business. A mill on the outskirts of the town. He had inherited it from his father, but, with the industrial boom in the area, the family were now independently wealthy. Of course, Laura's money, her dowry, meant nothing to Mitchell. He would have married her even if she had been a pauper.

'I got a new case today,' Mitchell said, changing the subject. 'A case of missing persons.'

'Oh Mitchell, I thought you weren't doing that detective stuff anymore!' Laura said. But she smiled. It was a quaint quirk of his and there was something so attractive and modern about him being a gentleman detective.

Mitchell didn't need to work, of course. He had his own wealth in the form of an established trust fund left to him by his late father, and controlled by his godfather. He wanted for nothing. A situation that had often left him bored, until he met Laura. She knew that he had fallen into doing investigations to fill his time. Since they had met, though, Mitchell had spent most of it with her. They read in companionable silence; went riding together in the park; walked; talked; enjoyed the opera; shared so many things that his days had become full in a different way. If he did take a case, which was rare, it was never for money, more for interest.

'Come. Sit beside me again and tell me all about it. You know I love to hear of your investigations.'

Mitchell hurried to her side and sat down. But not before he placed a soft kiss on her lips. She really was unique and her generous interest in his hobby pleased him.

'A young man has gone missing. His parents are worried that he has somehow fallen in with the wrong crowd.'

'What does he look like?' Laura asked.

'Actually, I have a photograph of him. I'll bring it next time, so that you can see. He's rather ordinary, I'm afraid, though.'

A few hours later Laura and Mitchell returned from the opera. Laura wanted tea, and so she left Mitchell in the study with a glass of her father's port. She had rung the bell several times, but neither Alice, nor their butler, Stevens, had responded.

'It is rather late. They probably retired, but I will go and find someone,' Laura said.

Mitchell sipped the port – a good vintage with a full-bodied taste – while he waited for Laura to return. He expected Elena to appear anytime, as she usually did in her role as chaperone, but the house was quiet. Then he remembered that Laura's parents had been invited to play bridge, an evening that was guaranteed to be late. Mitchell was pleased. Time alone with Laura was just what he wanted. They had kissed a lot in the carriage on the way back; she had even let him run his fingers over the soft bulge of her bosom as it showed above the tight evening dress.

He closed his eyes, sank back into the sofa, and took another sip of the port.

'All alone, I see.'

Sara stood beside him. She slowly sat down on the sofa, closer than she should have. Mitchell sat upright.

'Laura has gone to find the maid,' he said. 'She will be back soon.'

Sara smiled. She licked her lips in such a way that Mitchell felt uncomfortable. 'Did you have fun this evening?' she said.

'Yes.'

'I really don't know what you see in her. A man like you could have anyone.'

'I don't want "anyone". I want Laura.'

Sara looked down at her hands. 'You know … I've always held you in high regard.'

Mitchell laughed. 'You do have a funny way of showing it.

But I'm sure we will get along eventually. I always wanted a little sister. I am an only child, you know.'

He realised he was babbling. Then admitted to himself that this was because Sara was making him feel nervous.

'Is Warren home?' he asked.

'Working at the infirmary, I suspect. We hardly see him these days. He loves helping the poor.'

'Admirable. But a shame that you miss him.'

Sara leaned forward. 'I didn't say I missed him. Anyway, I don't want to talk about Warren. Or Laura.'

'Sara, what are you doing?' Mitchell said, his voice firm now as he grew tired of her game. 'I love your sister.'

'That's only because you haven't tasted me yet…'

With that Sara placed her mouth over his, pushing her tongue between his lips. He tried to push her away, but she had unbelievable strength and she wrapped her arms around him, pulling him to her.

China smashed as it hit the floor. Sara and Mitchell fell apart. Mitchell used the distraction to stand up and move away from the girl.

'Laura, I'm sorry you had to see this,' Sara said. 'Mitchell and I have been having an affair.'

Mitchell laughed. Her words were so absurd, but the laughter died in his throat as his eyes met Laura's. She *believed* it.

'Laura, darling. Of course we haven't… Sara was just…'

'Get out,' Laura said. 'I don't ever want to see you again.'

'Laura, you can't believe…'

'I said leave.'

Laura removed the ring from her finger and held it out.

'Sara. Stop messing around and tell her the truth.'

'She knows the truth,' Sara said. 'Why hide your feelings for me anymore? She saw us kissing.'

'I didn't kiss you. You kissed *me*.'

Sara shrugged.

'Laura…' Mitchell said. His heart was breaking. He couldn't believe that Sara could lie about this. She was evil, vile. It was all so cruel and uncalled for.

'I love you, Laura. I could never even…'

Laura's eyes were cold. 'Take this thing. This offering of your supposed love. Don't ever come back here.'

She placed the ring down on the coffee table in front of him as though she couldn't bear the thought that they might accidently touch, and then turned and walked out of the room.

'How could you?' Mitchell asked, turning on Sara. 'You've ruined everything!'

Sara's eyes were the blackest he had ever seen them. Darkness filled the irises, swarmed the white. Mitchell drew back, revulsion and fear coloured his cheeks. She was a demon – something viler than he had first imagined.

She was lying on the sofa now, pulling up her skirt like a street whore. 'You know you've always wanted me.'

An abhorrent odour seeped into the room, a smell as though someone had turned on the gas but was too slow to light it. No … burning matches…

Mitchell picked up the ring and hurried to the door. He hoped to catch up with Laura. He hoped he would force the truth from Sara. But at that moment Elena and Harold Carter arrived home. Laura threw herself into her mother's arms, crying, and Mitchell knew that no matter what he said, no one would believe him. He would always look like the rake who had seduced her younger sister.

Pushing the engagement ring into his jacket pocket, he hurried past the cluster of Carters, out to his waiting carriage.

Only when he was in his carriage did he consider how bizarre the whole episode had been, not least Laura's overreaction. How could she possibly believe this of him? How could they go from being so in love to becoming estranged within the space of a few minutes? He couldn't understand her sudden coldness, the unwillingness to listen to his side – the truth – and how she had so easily given up her ring. Maybe the love she'd felt for him hadn't been real at all?

Chapter Three

W arren Carter entered the house feeling relieved that Sara would be gone. The last few months had been a tremendous strain on the family. Not least Laura. But he hoped that by talking to Mitchell that day he had resolved something. That maybe their relationship, so unfairly ruined by his younger sister, could, in fact, begin again.

'Warren! I'm so glad you are home,' Elena said, coming out of the drawing room. 'I really don't know what to do.'

'Now, Mother, this is going to be difficult for all of us. But Sara is in the right place. The doctors at Greenfield are the best in the country. If they can't help her, no one can.'

'I feel so…'

Warren took her arm and led her into the drawing room. He glanced over at the library door, saw it closed, and knew that his father had shut himself away again for the evening. He was disappointed that Harold had left his wife in such a state, but it was typical of him. A former colonel, his father had an aversion to displays of emotion and much difficulty in accepting that one of his children had some kind of mental sickness.

Warren placed Elena on the sofa by the fire. 'Where's Laura?' he asked.

'In her room. She barely leaves it these days.'

'We will have to get her out of that habit. I've invited Mitchell round for supper on Saturday.'

'On no! Why have you done that? It's finished, Warren. Let's leave it that way. Laura is a lovely girl. She will find someone else without the history…'

'What history, Mother? Mitchell has done *nothing* wrong. You know that, don't you?'

Elena pulled a silk handkerchief from the pocket of her skirt and dabbed at her eyes. 'The shame … oh, the shame…'

Warren sat down. He was ill. He had been feeling this way for months, ever since Sara had begun to exhibit her eccentric behaviour. His mind slid back to the days after Mitchell and Laura's split, to how Sara had stopped him on the landing upstairs. To how she had pulled him into her embrace and forced her tongue into his mouth. He had pushed her away. Horrified. At the time he had thought, like everyone else, that somehow Mitchell had corrupted the girl. It was the only explanation for such odd behaviour. She wasn't acting like his young sweet sister anymore.

'What is wrong with you?' he had asked.

'I want you, Warren,' Sara had said. 'Come to my room. No one needs to know. It will be our little secret.'

He had backed away from her, down the landing to his own room, her horrible, mocking laughter following closely behind.

The next day she had behaved as though nothing had happened. But a few days later she had tried once more to kiss him when they were alone in the drawing room. After that he had avoided being alone with Sara. But sometimes he had found her looking at him and her expression was so lewd, that Warren had begun to fear, even then, that her sanity was in question.

But what had started it? He just didn't know.

Working at the infirmary had kept him away from home most nights. He had buried himself in his work, avoiding any conflicts or issues at home, and on the rare occasions he ate dinner with the family, Sara was quiet, Laura reflective and his mother and father polite and formal, as though they, too, knew that all was not well in their household.

Then one night, Warren had returned home early from the infirmary. He went into the study, poured a nightcap, and sat in the dark, crystal glass in hand, as he gazed at the dying embers of the fire. Warmed by the whisky, he dozed a little in the huge leather armchair that was twisted away from the room, facing the fire. He was roused by the sound of female laughter. Jerking awake, Warren realised that he was no longer alone in the room. He remained still for a while, thinking he had caught the servants doing something wrong.

'Now, Benjamin, I didn't say you could do that … *yet*,' said Sara.

Warren was shocked and embarrassed. He did not know how to make his presence known. Though he had to stop whatever his sister was doing and throw out the man, Benjamin, who had no right to be in their home.

'Stop teasing me, you little tart,' said Benjamin. 'You brought me back here for one fing. I ain't stupid.'

Sara giggled again. 'Show me what you have first.'

Warren could stand no more and stood up. He saw that Benjamin was standing, back to him, as Sara sprawled across the couch. Warren coughed as the stranger dropped his breeches and exposed himself to Sara.

Sara laughed, noticing Warren for the first time.

'Ah. My dear brother. Want to join in?'

Warren's face filled with rage. 'Get out of here!' he ordered as Benjamin pulled up his trousers and held them in place with one hand.

'Look 'ere. What game you playing? She in-v-v-vited me in,' stuttered Benjamin in confusion.

Warren could smell alcohol on his breath as he grabbed him by the collar. He hurled him out into the hallway, opened the front door, and pushed him half-dressed out onto the front steps.

'Don't come near her again,' Warren warned. 'Or I'll have the police on you.'

'Slut!' shouted Benjamin, pulling up his wayward breeches. 'She's a slut. A teasing whore!'

Warren reached for a walking stick from the stand by the door and proceeded to beat Benjamin with it. By then the whole household was awake and lights were going on in other houses either side and across the street. The butler, Stevens, came running from the servants' quarters, still in his nightgown and cap.

'Sir! Should I call the police?'

'No,' said Warren. Then he closed the door on the interloper and returned to the study.

He shut the door, leaving Stevens in the hallway.

'What the hell do you think you're playing at?' Warren asked through gritted teeth. He had no intention of letting the butler, or the serving staff, hear any more than they already had.

Sara was still lying on the sofa. Her blouse was open, and

in the dull light remaining from the fire, Warren saw her bare breasts.

'Cover yourself up!' he commanded.

But Sara just smiled. 'Don't you like what you see?'

'That man was right. You are a whore. And from this day, you are no longer my sister!' Warren said.

'If that is the case, then there is no reason why you can't have me. You know you want to, Warren. You know you've *always* wanted to.'

Warren was appalled by her words. 'There's something deeply wrong with you…'

At that moment Warren heard his father and mother coming downstairs to find out what the commotion was.

'Cover yourself,' he warned again.

Then Warren opened the study door and dealt with the situation by sending the servants away.

'Mother, take Sara to her room and lock her inside,' he said.

'But … what's…?'

'Do it now, Mother, please. I need to speak to Father.'

Sara went reluctantly, ignoring her mother's shocked expression when she saw the state of undress the girl was in. After they left, Warren poured out to his father the whole sorry tale of her strange behaviour. And her attempts to seduce him, her own brother.

'I can't believe it!' Harold said.

'She needs to see someone. It's like she's lost her mind…' Warren explained. 'I'm no psychiatrist, but I have seen patients like this. Lewd behaviour, lapses in memory. There's a medical term for it. I believe she is suffering from schizophrenia.'

'Oh, dear God.' Harold sank down onto the sofa his daughter had just vacated.

'She can't be left like this. She's a danger to herself and others,' said Warren.

'What can we do?' Harold asked. Warren had never seen his confident, military father so helpless.

'I'll give her laudanum tonight. It should make her sleep and, hopefully, remain in her bed. But until she has seen a doctor, she's not to be let out of her room.'

After that there were more weeks of hell. When she wasn't drugged, Sara behaved as though demon-possessed. The servants were afraid of her, and for this reason, only Laura and Elena ever entered her room with food and fresh clothing.

The house turned into an infirmary for a while. Warren saw his mother's fragile nerves become more and more frayed. Each day became harder. They brought in various medical professionals, and even once, on the insistence of Elena, Warren sent for the local priest.

After a half-hearted exorcism, Warren realised that there was only one course of action: Sara had to be committed, or her illness would drive the entire family insane.

He took time off from his work and went to visit several different institutions, finally settling on a private home, just outside Manchester, in a place called Alderley Edge. It was run by a Christian doctor specialising in schizophrenia. The home was exclusive and contained many ailing wealthy patients who, Warren noted, were well cared for. His biggest fear had been that Sara would be mistreated. Greenfields, though, was run by kind people who understood her condition.

'We are making advancements all the time,' Dr Greenfield said. 'All hope isn't lost. We will do our best to help your sister.'

Warren arranged that the hospital would collect Sara. It was the easiest thing for the family, and the doctor recommended that they didn't visit for at least a week in order to give the girl time to settle in, and then time to assess the level of her sickness. Warren agreed to all of this on behalf of his parents because they were incapable of making the final decision.

Now, after she had gone, he had to deal with the aftermath too. The house was oddly quiet, and his mother, he knew, would take some time to recover from the upset.

He hugged her now, and instead of fetching tea, he poured her a large sherry.

'I can't believe how horrible this has all been,' Elena said.

Warren listened as his mother poured out her fears and phobias. She was worried about Sara; afraid of scandal; concerned that life would never be the same again for all of them.

Warren held her hand and with his best bedside manner, reassured her as much as possible.

'All hope isn't lost,' he said. 'Sara may be cured.'

'How did this happen?' Elena said, giving way to tears again. 'How did my lovely little girl turn into this awful monster?'

'I don't know,' said Warren and he really didn't. His medical mind insisted there should have been some early signs. But there just hadn't been.

Just then, as though she knew he needed her, Laura came into the drawing room. She sat down on the other side of her mother and both she and Warren hugged Elena as she cried. It was the first step to their future recovery – which would still take many months to reach.

Chapter Four

Mitchell returned to his home to find it in complete darkness. He passed through the hallway, turning on the gas lamps, driving away the oppressive shadows. It had been a warm day, but he could feel the cold as he entered the house. It was Sunday. Normally, by this time, the housekeeper, Mrs Dalton, had returned from her family visit, and there was a large fire blazing in the hearth. Mitchell was a little perturbed that there was no sign of her, or the fire.

'Strange,' he murmured to himself as he opened the door to the drawing room.

He walked through the darkness to the mantels beside the fireplace and turned the lights on. They flickered briefly, and then steadied. The room lit up with a warming glow.

Mitchell turned and took in the familiar surroundings. Brocade silk with white swans on a black background covered the walls. Decor left over from the days when his parents lived here. That was before his father was posted to India, and the young newlyweds made their way to the adventure that would result in them never returning to England. The furniture was the same too. There was an ornate mahogany writing desk, and a matching bureau that rested against the wall near the door opposite the fireplace. The fireplace itself – tall, with dark wood painted black – boasted an intricate design in red; an exotic bird repeated at intervals around the frame. Two cumbersome sofas, covered in plush red velvet, faced each other either side of the fireplace. There was a low mahogany table between them, and on the end of the sofa closest to the door was a small round table, on which stood a potted plant that had seen better days.

The room wasn't very large. Mitchell felt it was cluttered but was loath to dispose of anything left by his parents. It needed a woman's touch. He had once hoped that Laura would sweep inside, like a new broom, clearing away the old-fashioned style, making the place theirs, rather than a house that still belonged to the dead.

He considered taking a seat on the sofa, but the room was too chilly. Instead, he left the room, passed the staircase leading upstairs and headed to the stairs that went down to the kitchen.

Downstairs he found the kitchen in good order, though he rarely ventured there. In the middle of the large oak table the cook, Mrs Maybury, had left him a plate covered with a clean cloth, as though anticipating his early return. He lifted the cloth and saw a platter of cold meats. The meat looked appetising, but he had an urge to visit the gentlemen's club he had shunned in recent months instead. He'd had a strange day and still hadn't assimilated all that Warren Carter had told him about his family's troubles.

He sat down at the table. It was warmer downstairs than up; the coals still smouldering in the back of the oven warmed the room. He removed the cloth and picked at the meat with a fork that the cook had left for him beside the plate. He was rarely home alone and it was peculiar, but of course the staff all took Sunday off to visit family, go to church, or rest.

At that moment he heard the back door open and recognised the steady tread of Mrs Maybury as she came downstairs. Mrs Dalton was with her.

'Oh, Mr Bishop, sir!' said the cook. 'You're back early!'

Mitchell smiled at them. 'I was wondering where everyone was. But you're right. I am back sooner than usual.'

'Mr Bishop,' nodded Mrs Dalton, 'I'll get Aggie upstairs now to relight the fire in the drawing room. We all had a meeting at church that went on a little longer than normal.'

'No need to explain,' Mitchell said. 'Your time is your own.'

At that moment a loud ringing heralded that someone was at the front door. Mrs Dalton and Mrs Maybury looked at each other. The butler, Mr Jenkins, wouldn't return to work until the following morning. He had a wife and family, a place of his own and didn't stay on the premises at all after his working hours.

'Aggie will answer it,' Mrs Dalton said, but she went back upstairs to make sure.

Mitchell finished the meat, as Mrs Maybury placed a kettle on the stove. 'Some tea to warm you, sir?' she said.

Mitchell became aware how awkward the cook was feeling because he was in her personal space. He realised he would find it odd if she came into the drawing room and sat down.

'Yes... I'll take it in the drawing room, please, Mrs Maybury.'

Back upstairs, he found Warren Carter in the hallway with Mrs Dalton. The man looked dishevelled and shocked.

'Warren, whatever's wrong?'

'I need to speak with you,' Warren said.

Mitchell led him into the drawing room. Aggie was using a pair of bellows on the fire, and the coal and paper were catching nicely.

'Aggie, can you tell Mrs Maybury that it's tea for two now, please?' Mitchell said.

Aggie curtsied and hurried from the room as Warren collapsed down onto the sofa.

He covered his face with his hands and pushed back his untidy hair.

'Something dreadful has happened,' he said.

'Is Laura all right?' Mitchell said. His heart lurched with anxiety as he sat down on the sofa opposite Warren.

'It's not Laura.'

'Sara then…'

'No. At least … as far as I know she is fine in the sanatorium.'

'Dear boy, whatever *is* the matter?'

There was a brisk knock at the door and Mitchell stood and opened it, to find Aggie with the tray of tea. He stepped back and let the girl bring it in, then quickly dismissed her before Warren lost his nerve.

Once the girl had gone, Mitchell ignored the tea and went to the bureau and poured two large glasses of whisky from the decanter there.

'Here.'

Warren took the glass and swigged the contents so quickly that the fiery liquid caught in his throat. When the coughing fit ended, he took another sip, this time with more care.

'After we talked yesterday, I called home briefly. We haven't heard anything more from the sanatorium, but all was fine. Sara went meekly, as expected. Then, I had to go into the infirmary. It was a difficult night, I had to amputate a patient's leg and the nurse on duty was … very helpful.'

'So, you've come straight from the hospital?'

'No. I've been walking around. Since the early hours. I daren't go home. I just don't know how I'm going to face everyone.'

'Warren, for the love of God, what's happened?'

'I think … I hurt someone. I didn't mean it. I just misread the signs…'

Mitchell placed a hand on Warren's shoulder. 'Tell me,' he said.

Warren told Mitchell about the nurse, Rosie, and her bold familiarity. How what appeared to be an open invitation turned into a horrible misunderstanding. When he finished his story, Mitchell sat back on the sofa and thought.

'You say the girl invited you back to her room? Then undressed herself?'

Warren nodded.

'I'm no expert, but that sounds like an invitation to me,' Mitchell said.

'I thought so … but then, things went all strange. She was crying and her face kept changing…'

'Changing? How?'

'I was … was with her … and suddenly she looked different. She wasn't this bold chit of a girl anymore – she was scared, shocked. Then her face turned to me and she smiled. She looked just like … *Sara*.'

Mitchell sighed. 'I know what's going on here, even though I'm not a doctor. You've been under rather a lot of strain recently. Sara was clearly on your mind, especially since she was only just taken to the sanatorium. You're feeling guilty about making that happen.'

'No. I'm not,' Warren said firmly. But his eyes looked less afraid.

'As for this girl … what you describe is moments of missing time. As though you blacked out. Maybe the drink she gave you contained some substance.'

Warren's eyes lit up. 'If only that were so! Do you think that may have happened?'

'She won't be the first nurse to try and catch herself a doctor,' Mitchell said. 'I investigated a similar thing some time ago. A doctor's receptionist who accused him of trying to molest her. In that case she was after money to keep it quiet. I soon had the police on to the girl, especially when we disproved her accusation because the doctor in question had an iron-clad alibi. She was part of a ring of extortionists.'

'Good heavens! Was she arrested?'

'Unfortunately, no. She got away, but the man's reputation was safe. Tell me what this girl looked like.'

Warren described Rosie.

'Could be the same girl,' Mitchell said. 'But then, it could be a coincidence.'

'Will you look into this for me?' Warren asked. 'I thought I was losing my mind.'

'Yes. For now, I'd like you to stay here,' he told Warren. 'I'll have Mrs Dalton make up a bed for you.'

Warren drained his whisky glass as Mitchell stood and rang the bell. When the maid returned, he gave instructions to fetch his coat and to make up the guest room.

'Where are you going?' asked Warren.

'To the hospital. Do you remember the girl's room number?'

'Twenty-two,' Warren said. 'She was new but I had seen

quite a lot of her over the last few nights. She was always on the late shift.'

'You don't know her second name?'

'No, just Rosie. That's all I know.'

Mitchell left Warren and went once more to the kitchen below the house.

'Mrs Dalton,' he said. 'I have to go out and leave Dr Carter for the moment. I wonder if you can see to it that he has a hot bath and a change of clothes? Take whatever you need from my wardrobe.'

'Of course, sir,' Mrs Dalton said. 'Is Dr Carter all right, sir?'

'He has had a trying time. A little kindness would be most welcome.'

The housekeeper nodded, and Mitchell went back upstairs and out into the night.

The entrance to the hospital was busy when Mitchell arrived. Visiting hours had just ended and the relatives and friends of patients were leaving en masse as the ward sisters ushered them out.

'Visiting is over now, sir,' said the guard on the door.

'I'm a friend of Dr Carter,' he said, gambling that the guard didn't know that Warren wasn't at the hospital. 'I'm supposed to meet him inside.'

The guard stepped aside and let him pass. He didn't want to get in trouble with one of the doctors. The matron had power in the hospital, but not as much as the gentleman doctors did.

'Thank you,' said Mitchell.

He made his way down the main corridor, looking for the

ward signs, until he found the one pointing towards Ward Eight. If anyone asked, he would tell them he was visiting the man whose leg had been amputated, Mr Stanwick. It also gave him a perfect excuse to seek out Rosie.

As he passed the women's ward a young woman came through the doors. She was wearing a dark-brown coat, long hair tied up at the front, but left down over her shoulders. Mitchell glanced at her, took off his hat and smiled. The girl nodded, then turned away as though embarrassed.

Mitchell walked on. He found the ward in question on the next corridor and as he entered, he saw the duty doctor doing his rounds.

'Can I help you?' asked the nurse at the desk near the door.

'I'm Mr … Smith. My uncle, Mr Stanwick, had his leg amputated last night. I would just like to see the nurse who was on duty.'

The nurse frowned and looked down at the ledger on her desk, flipped the sheet over and looked back over the reports.

'Oh yes. Dr Carter was on duty, but he's not here tonight. We don't know where he is…'

'I said I would like to see the duty nurse. To thank her… I believe she brought the problem to the doctor's attention. She saved my uncle's life.'

The nurse frowned again. 'Strange. There's no signature on the report. I don't know who was on for the early part of last night.'

'I believe her name was … Rosie…' Mitchell said to prompt the girl.

The nurse shook her head. 'I don't think so. We don't have a nurse by that name…'

Mitchell looked up and noticed that the matron and doctor were walking back down the other side. He decided that they might be more inquisitive than the nurse, who had failed to ask any questions or to confirm the details of his enquiry.

'Never mind,' he said. 'I'll ask again tomorrow when I visit.'

Mitchell hurried out of the ward and back down the hospital corridor. Then he followed signs to the back of the building where he knew the nurses' quarters were situated.

He found the main door locked.

Mitchell retrieved a small pouch from his pocket and began to pick the lock. He had learned the trick after an old school friend had enlisted his help some years before. His first case, in fact – one of stolen identity, in which the young man had found himself relieved of all his personal documents, and indeed his very name.

At the time, Mitchell was only twenty-two, and his friend, Barnaby Reynolds, newly arrived in the city, had been suckered in by a wayward landlord who stole his possessions while he was out looking for work. On returning to his lodgings, Barnaby had found himself locked out. After a row erupted, the unfortunate young man, lacking identity, found himself arrested when he tried to pick the lock. The landlord promptly produced someone claiming to be the real occupant of the room.

Barnaby remained in prison for a week before he remembered that Mitchell lived in Manchester and with the only coin remaining in his pocket, he bribed the gaoler to send Mitchell a message.

When he arrived at the prison, Mitchell learnt of his friend's plight and offered to help, not knowing that this was the start of a hobby that would lead him into more adventures than he perhaps would want. But he was bored, and he had always liked Barnaby.

Of course, proving the theft had been difficult, and it had taken Mitchell down a slightly illegal route when he forced the lock on his friend's old room. The landlord, feeling himself aggrieved, called the police, but Mitchell was able to prove he was working for Barnaby and persuaded the attending bobby to search the lodging-house premises.

Barnaby's possessions were found, along with a photograph of him with his parents, and the landlord promptly, and rightly, had his own collar felt.

After that, Mitchell had practised opening locks of all kinds. He even paid a locksmith to teach him how, and bought the tool kit from the man.

Now, some six years on, he heard the lock of the nurses' quarters click and he pushed open the front door to the building. Then he skulked down the corridor, hoping that none of the nurses would choose that moment to leave their room.

On the second floor he found room twenty-two. He knocked softly, but got no response. He turned the handle. As expected, the door was locked. He began to work on the lock, pausing only when he thought he heard someone open a door further down the corridor. He heard the chatter of two women, then realised it was on the floor below. The front door opened and their voices receded as they exited the building.

Mitchell began work once more on the door. He heard the satisfying click, then quickly turned the handle, opened the door, and went inside.

The room was completely dark. Mitchell found his way to the window and opened the curtains, letting the gaslight from outside spill into the room. He looked around. In the gloom he could see that the room was devoid of any personal effects. He considered for a moment that Warren had been mistaken; that the girl was in some other room and he had given Mitchell the wrong number. However, there was no way of finding out unless he knocked on every door and asked the names of the occupants. This, of course, was not an option. His presence here had to remain a secret, for Warren's sake and his own.

The bed was unmade. Fresh sheets and blankets were folded and left on the mattress, as though they were waiting for a new occupant to make them up. His hand fell on the top of a chest of drawers. There was a washbowl and a jug – devoid of water. He opened the first drawer, found it empty, and then looked through the others to discover the same result.

Aside from the bed and the chest of drawers, there a small wardrobe on the other side of the tiny room. Mitchell went around the bed and opened the door. It creaked from lack of use. Inside, as he suspected, he found nothing. By this time, he had discovered the gaslight on the wall. He lit it and the room illuminated. He glanced around. Dust on the window ledge and on top of the chest of drawers showed him that the room had not been used for some time. He was sure now that he was in the wrong room.

He turned back to the gaslight and switched it off, then decided he should leave the room as he had found it. He quickly went back to the window. He looked outside onto the back street – nothing stirred – then closed the curtains. As he turned, his foot brushed against something that was sticking out from under the bed. The room was now in darkness. He couldn't see what it was, but he bent down and scooped up what felt like a piece of paper.

He made his way back to the door. At that moment he heard the steady tread of someone coming up the stairs. He waited until he heard the person pass before he opened the door slightly and looked down the partially lit corridor. He saw a nurse in a black-and-white uniform open her door and go inside her own room further up. Then, stuffing the paper inside his jacket, Mitchell left the room and hurried back down the stairs and out of the building.

He was relieved to be out and back on the road. He removed the paper from inside his jacket and under the nearest streetlamp, he studied his findings. The paper contained a charcoal sketch of a man, half-dressed, hair wild, looking for all the world like a madman. Even in this portrayal, Mitchell could tell the likeness. It was clearly Warren Carter.

Mitchell folded the paper and returned it to his inside pocket. Then he hurried back to the main road and hailed a hansom cab to take him home. Already, he was beginning to believe that something very strange was afoot, and he now knew that Warren had not been wrong when he told him the room number of the nurse. But where was she? The room looked as though she had never been there, but the drawing confirmed that she had.

Chapter Five

Warren removed his watch from his inside pocket, unclipped the chain that connected it to his waistcoat, and placed it on the bedside table. Then he slipped off his tarnished clothes, dropping them to the floor, and submerged himself in the copper tub. Mrs Dalton and Aggie had filled the tub with hot water, before leaving him to his privacy. The water was a little too hot, but he enjoyed the sting. It made him feel cleaner. He closed his eyes and slipped into a half-sleep. He was confident that Mitchell would help him and allowed himself to rest.

As the water began to cool, Warren woke. For a moment he had forgotten where he was. The room temperature had plummeted even though the fire in the hearth was blazing. He reached for a towel and wrapped it around himself as he stepped out of the tub. Shivering, he went to the fire; the heat was wonderful and it warmed him as he dried his skin. Then he dressed in the clothing Mitchell had left for him.

Mitchell was shorter than Warren and the trousers were a little tight. He didn't mind, though. It was only a temporary loan, and Mrs Dalton had promised to wash and dry his own clothes, to return them to him as soon as possible. He tucked in a white shirt and buttoned up the collar, then placed a velvet smoking jacket over the shirt, and tied it at the waist.

The wind outside his room started to pick up. The window rattled and Warren went over and pulled back the curtain to look out on the street. It was lit by a row of gaslights, and the few trees that lined the road swayed in the brisk breeze. Otherwise, all was quiet and still.

Warren closed the curtain again and turned back to the room. He stopped moving. The room had changed. The tub was gone, yet he had not heard Mrs Dalton and the servant girl, Aggie, come back for it. He glanced back at the window. Time had slipped away from him again. Time. He remembered his watch on the table beside the bed and he walked across the room and picked it up. He flipped open the cover and noted that it was two hours since Mitchell had left him. The time felt right, he hadn't lost a moment, even with his short doze in the bath. He turned back to look at the room. The copper tub was back in place, just as he had left it.

Warren shook his head. He couldn't have *imagined* it gone, surely?

At that moment there was a light tap on the door. Warren opened it to find Mrs Dalton and Aggie there.

'Shall we clean this up for you now, sir?' said Mrs Dalton.

Warren stepped back and let the women in.

'There's a light snack for you in the dining room,' Mrs Dalton said.

Warren placed his watch in the pocket of the smoking jacket and went out onto the landing, down the stairs, and found his way into the dining room.

A little later he was in Mitchell's study. He found a decanter of port and poured himself a glass, knowing that his friend wouldn't mind.

'Remember what happened in Daddy's study?' said a voice behind him.

Warren turned quickly. Out of the corner of his eye he thought he saw Sara, but as his eyes darted around the room, he found he was alone. He put his glass down on Mitchell's large oak desk. His hands were shaking. A white blur ran across his peripheral vision. He turned his head quickly. Nothing. He found himself fumbling for his pocket watch again. He looked at the time. Mitchell had been gone almost three hours. Not such an unreasonable time, since the journey to the infirmary was at least a twenty-minute carriage ride away.

'Why did you do it?' said a voice.

Warren looked up to find Rosie standing by the door.

'Did Mitchell bring you here?' his face flushed with embarrassment. The girl was standing in her shift before him.

Rosie rubbed away the tears in her eyes. 'You raped me, Warren.'

'No. You invited me … you…'

He stopped talking as he saw the smile spread across her face. It was so like Sara's provocative expression that he backed up into the desk.

Rosie's smile grew wider. Her teeth blackened; and became sharp points. It reminded Warren of a stuffed shark he had seen at a museum once.

'Why did you do it, Warren?' she said again, moving towards him.

'I didn't! I don't … remember exactly what…'

'But you had me locked up and I didn't remember.' The

voice changed and so did Rosie; before his eyes she turned into Sara. She was now wearing the clothes she had worn when he found her with the rake, Benjamin. Warren closed his eyes. He didn't want to see his sister like this.

'Warren? Warren? Are you all right, man?'

Warren opened his eyes. He was sitting on a leather sofa facing Mitchell's desk.

'What?'

'I thought you had gone to bed, then I heard a noise in here,' Mitchell said.

'I … must have been dreaming.'

'Yes.'

'Thank God!' said Warren, sitting up. 'Sorry, was I talking in my sleep?'

'More like moaning…'

Warren rubbed his eyes and pushed his unruly hair back from his face. 'What time is it?'

'A little after ten. Are you all right?'

Warren nodded. 'Did you see Rosie? Is she all right?'

Mitchell sat down on a leather footstool. 'No. She wasn't there.'

'She's left the hospital?'

'Warren. Rosie's room was completely empty. It was as though she was never there.'

'You are saying I imagined her?' Warren said. His frown deepened. This idea reminded him of the doubts he had about his own sanity.

'I thought for a while that this was the case. Then, I found this.' He pulled the piece of paper from his jacket and unfolded it.

Warren stared at the sketch. 'Rosie did this.'

'It fits in with what you said, but it doesn't explain where she's gone. Or indeed who she is.'

'I never knew her last name. I should have, but there are so many nurses. I have an appalling memory for names.'

Mitchell patted Warren's shoulder. 'Don't beat yourself up, old man. After I found this I went back inside the hospital. I was just going to catch a cab back here, but then changed my mind. The nurse I'd seen said there weren't any nurses called Rosie. So, I went to see the duty matron. She was reluctant to help, but when I told her I was a private investigator and I might have to bring the police in, she became more cooperative.'

'What did she tell you?' Warren asked. 'Did she give you Rosie's last name? Did she know where she had gone?'

'Warren, there never was a Rosie working at the hospital. In fact, the girl on duty with you was called Deirdre. She was the one who told you about Stanwick's leg. She assisted you.'

'I got her name wrong, then?'

'No. I spoke to Deirdre. She remained on duty long after you had left. It was she who instructed the orderlies to clean up the side room where you operated on Stanwick,' Mitchell explained. 'She also had red hair, not dark brown.'

'No. She invited me back … she…'

'Not Deirdre, Warren. Whoever the girl was that invited you back to the nurses' quarters, it wasn't her. You see, there were two nurses on duty that night, and the other girl, Mary, backed up everything Deirdre said. They aren't allowed to be on duty alone in the men's ward. There always has to be two of them.'

Warren thought this through. It was true, that was the rule, but he didn't recall seeing another girl, not until later. After Rosie or Deirdre helped him operate.

'Maybe they were lying,' Warren said. 'Maybe Mary had been absent for some reason.'

'I thought that, but … the Matron told me she had done the rounds while you were operating. She checked in with Mary, and at one point looked into the room where you and Deirdre worked on Stanwick. It was all as the girls said.'

Warren shook his head. 'Then I'm going insane. Just like Sara.'

Mitchell picked up the drawing and studied it. 'I don't think so. But I don't know what is going on yet. You see, I think Rosie does exist. I think she duped you as you came out of the ward. You were tired, you said yourself you can barely tell the difference between the young nurses. Rosie was there. She led you back to room twenty-two and she drew this.'

'But why?' asked Warren. 'Why pretend to be a nurse? Why … *seduce* me?'

'I don't know. But when we find this girl, we may have some answers. I need you to describe her to me in as much detail as possible.'

Warren went home the next day, after Mitchell had convinced him that he had been the victim of a scam that had failed. With Mitchell's reassurance that they'd find Rosie, he was less afraid. Mitchell would help him now, and he was sure he'd get to the root of it. Then he came face to face with Elena and his mother's panic-stricken face brought back that surge of anxiety he'd managed to shake for a short time.

'Warren! Thank God you are home!' said Elena. 'We've been worried sick. Someone from the hospital came to enquire where you were. You weren't on duty last night.'

'I'm sorry, Mother. I've… I just needed some time alone.'

Warren followed Elena into the drawing room. She said nothing about his ill-fitting clothing. She was nervous and uptight and Warren knew his mother was struggling to understand what was happening in their family.

Stevens knocked on the door and when invited, he entered holding a silver tray. On the tray was a calling card.

'Who is it, Stevens?' asked Elena. 'I don't want to be disturbed.'

'Dr Greenfield, madam.'

'Greenfield? It must be about Sara. Send him in,' Warren said.

'Warren, don't you think you ought to…' Elena said, nodding her head at his clothing, which she had finally noticed.

'Oh. There's no time for that, Mother. I want to hear how Sara is.'

Stevens led Greenfield into the drawing room, and after the offers of drinks and the formal exchanges were made, Greenfield sat down on the sofa. He appeared to be in as much of a state as Warren had been the previous day.

'Whatever is the matter, man?' asked Warren. 'Are you ill?'

Greenfield's obvious pallor had both Elena and Warren sitting on the edge of their seats. He appeared to be struggling to tell them why he was there.

'Is Sara all right?' asked Elena.

And when he took a breath and still didn't answer, Warren said, 'For heaven's sake, spit it out, man!'

'I have to ask you to come to the sanatorium,' Greenfield said. 'We have a problem. Sara has somehow managed to … lock herself into her room. We can force the lock but would prefer to try and talk her out. She has proven much more … *difficult* than we imagined she would be.'

'Doctor, I thought you *knew* what medication to prescribe,' Elena said. Distress made her voice rise an octave.

'I do. I mean … I thought … the medication isn't working. In fact, even laudanum has no effect on her. It's as though…'

Greenfield gulped.

'As though what?' asked Warren.

'It is as though she is *possessed*. I need one of you to come to see her. I need permission to … exorcise her…'

Elena said nothing and so Warren decided not to mention that the local priest had already tried to do this without success. He had picked Greenfield because he was a Christian. Some instinct had made him feel unsatisfied with the medical explanation of Sara's sudden deterioration.

'If you can give me a few moments, I will change and come with you,' Warren said.

'I'll get my coat,' said Elena.

'No, Mother. I think you should stay here,' suggested Warren.

As Warren hurried up the stairs, Laura came out of her room. 'What's going on?'

Warren's harried expression concerned her immediately. 'Mother's been worried about you. Good grief! Is that Mitchell's jacket you're wearing?'

Warren looked down at the green tweed day jacket and nodded. 'I was with him yesterday and last night.'

Laura's face was blank. 'How … is he?' she asked.

'As upset as you are. I don't know why the two of you don't talk this through.'

Laura shook her head. 'I can't. It's too … complicated.'

Warren took her hand. 'Get your coat. I need you to come to the sanatorium with me. Mother is in too much of a state to be of any help.'

Warren turned away and hurried down the landing to his room to change before Laura could question him further.

Laura waited in Greenfield's carriage as Warren tried to reassure their mother that they would help Sara as much as they could. She was wearing a long brown coat over her day blouse and skirt. Despite the early spring, the weather had turned bitter and so she also wore a pair of kid gloves and a fur-lined hat. Around her neck was a luxurious fox fur.

Warren and Greenfield finally came out of the house and climbed into the carriage. What Laura didn't know was that Greenfield had tried to persuade Warren to leave her behind with his mother. But Warren had insisted. He didn't admit that his own nerves were frayed by recent events and he needed the support.

'Laura's tougher than she looks,' he told Greenfield. 'Perhaps she's the strongest of us all.'

Greenfield looked over his glasses at the young woman. He realised with a start that their likeness was more than familial. He recalled Warren mentioning they were twins on his first visit to Greenfields. The doctor had wanted to know something of the family history before he agreed to observe Sara. It had taken him a moment to recognise the close similarity between the two. Laura was indeed very composed, unlike her brother, who twitched and twisted in his seat as though he were sitting on pins. This was a far different man than the one Greenfield had first met. Surely Sara's ailments had not affected him so much more since she was removed from the house? Greenfield would have expected some form of guilt to create cracks in the peace of the family. But the relief of placing Sara at Greenfields should have overcome that quickly.

'Dr Carter,' Greenfield said. 'How are you feeling? You seem … upset.'

Laura looked at Greenfield, then glanced at Warren. Of course, her brother wasn't himself at all. Why hadn't she noticed it? Warren looked tired and drained. He had been under a great deal of stress, but hadn't they all? Laura felt a surge of guilt. She had been so wrapped up in her own misery. The loss of Mitchell hurt so much, and each day did nothing to improve it. But now she looked at Warren, really looked, she could see how exhausted he was.

She took his hand, just as she had many times when they were children. Warren held it for a moment and then pulled away as though the contact were something unpleasant or inappropriate.

Greenfield saw the sadness in Laura's eyes, but said nothing.

'We've had a very difficult few months,' Laura said.

Even though the driver pushed the four horses leading Greenfield's carriage, the sanatorium was still an hour's drive away. When they finally arrived, Warren's nerves were shot. The bumpy ride made his already aching muscles feel battered and bruised. Laura appeared to be fine, and even though he had rejected the comfort she had offered, he was glad she was there. The truth was, he was still shaken by the mysterious encounter he'd had with Rosie, and the night spent at Mitchell's had been haunted by dreams in which he had merged Sara and Rosie, and on one occasion he'd imagined himself in bed with Sara. For this reason, he really didn't want to be alone with her. He was unnerved by the incongruity of the last few months. The dreams had been buying into some dark part of himself that had wanted to respond to Sara's seduction, but he couldn't admit this, even to himself.

The driver opened the carriage door and Warren climbed out. Then he held out his hand and took Laura's as she stepped down.

They followed Greenfield into the main entrance of the sanatorium. It looked just as he remembered it. A large house at the front, leading into a big reception area. Consultation rooms on either side. Warren had been shown the rooms that the patients slept in. Each had a private room, fit for a private hospital of this calibre. But he was surprised when Greenfield turned left, away from the central staircase and the rooms upstairs he had previously seen.

'We don't put patients in the open area at first,' Greenfield explained. 'Not until we've assessed the level of … sickness.'

They walked down a dark corridor, which Warren realised was an extension on the back of the house. This was a part of the place he hadn't seen, and it horrified him to realise that the doors either side of them were covered in metal. They were, in fact, not so much rooms as they were cells.

'What is this?' asked Warren.

'She would have been moved to the better rooms, in time,' Greenfield said.

'It's why you didn't want anyone to visit her right away,' Laura said. 'I thought that was odd.'

'It's a necessary part of the settling-in process. It does, however, upset relatives to think that their loved ones are locked up like this. But some of the people here are a danger to themselves and others.'

Greenfield said this kindly and Laura nodded as though she understood. She had seen the state that Sara had been in prior to her being committed.

'You lied to me, Greenfield,' said Warren. 'This isn't what I wanted.'

'You wanted us to cure her. We have to do that the best way we see fit,' Greenfield said. He stopped outside one of the cells. 'She's in here.'

'Well open it, man,' Warren snapped.

'I can't,' said Greenfield. 'I told you. She's locked herself in.'

'How on earth did that happen?' Laura asked. She was annoyed now. The outer calm she had so far displayed had been held together with extreme effort.

'Sara!' she called, banging on the door. 'Open this door right now and let us in!'

There was no response.

'Sara!'

'Hello, Laura. Is Warren with you?' said a voice from behind the door.

'Sara? Let us in. Please,' Warren said.

'Did she like what you did to her, Warren?' Sara said. 'Did that dirty little slut of a nurse enjoy you?'

Warren grew pale. He began to feel the sick panic rising up like bile in the pit of his stomach. There was no way that Sara could know about Rosie. It wasn't possible.

'Sara, we are here to help…' Laura pleaded.

A scream pierced the air. The door rattled from the inside, as though Sara was attempting to open it. Laura was jolted back as the metal-plated door grew burning hot to the touch.

Sara screamed again.

'What's happening?' Laura cried.

Something smashed against the door. The sounds of a

battle, as though the girl were fighting off the very devil himself, issued from the room. A sickening thud, the sound of breaking bones.

Warren yelled, tearing at his hair as though the screams were sending all sanity from his mind.

'What the devil is going on? Greenfield, do something! Get this door open, now!' Laura said.

'I feared this,' Greenfield said. He hurried down the corridor, yelling for the orderlies, and two big men came running around the corner, followed by a female nurse.

'Get this door open,' Greenfield said.

The sounds from inside were those of someone being tortured. The smell of burning flesh wafted under the door. They could hear Sara crying tears of terror, madness and pain.

Laura banged on the door but one of the orderlies pulled her aside. He was carrying a large hammer and he smashed at the lock, over and over until it cracked and split. Then the two orderlies threw themselves against the door simultaneously.

'It's hot!' said one of the men, rubbing the singed shoulder of his white uniform.

'Good Lord! She must have set the room on fire!' said Greenfield.

They all stared in impotent shock as the metal plating buckled and cracked with the heat issuing from inside. Greenfield crossed himself.

'Smash the hinges!' he ordered.

The first orderly picked up the hammer again and attacked the hinges. They heard the wooden frame crack, punctuated by a grotesque scream from inside the room, and the door finally gave.

'Be careful!' Greenfield said. 'We'll have to contain the fire she's started.'

The orderlies strained the door open. Half off its hinges, lock smashed, it was dragging on the floor and required massive effort. This close to getting into the room, Laura and Warren were galvanised into action. They threw themselves against the backs of the men, and the last bit of weight forced the door to give way.

All four stumbled forward into the room.

Instead of flames and smoke, the temperature had plummeted to below freezing. As Laura recovered, she noticed that the air was steaming when she exhaled. The cold air inside burned her lungs as she breathed heavily from the exertion.

Sara lay partially across a low cot and half onto the floor. Laura stared. She couldn't make sense of the twisted and broken limbs. The girl's face was a bloody pulp, as though she had been repeatedly beaten by some unknown attacker.

The room, however, was completely empty other than the girl and the bed. There was only one small, barred window that even a cat would have had difficulty passing through.

Greenfield rushed over to Sara. He knelt down, checking her pulse. Then he stood, stooping once more to close her eyes.

'No!' Warren said.

Laura grabbed and held him before he could hurl himself further into the room and over to the obviously murdered body of their sister. Warren fell into her arms and sobbed while Laura looked around the room in shock. She couldn't cry. All she thought about was the state the room was in. She took in the huge claw marks on the walls, the smeared blood on the floor and the broken body of her sister.

Looking back at the wrecked door frame, she saw that the wood was charred, all evidence that fire had been in this room. But where was it now? Why was the room as cold as a tomb?

'She didn't do this to herself,' Laura said.

'You're incompetent, Greenfield,' Warren said. 'I will bring the police in to learn what evil happened here.'

'I assure you she was alone!' Greenfield said. 'The room was locked from the inside. This is self-mutilation. There is no other explanation.'

'There has to be. She *didn't* do *that* to herself,' Laura said, gazing in horror at her sister's destroyed face.

Part II

Chapter Six

December 1897: six months earlier

Toby Naylor turned the sign on the door over so that 'Open' was showing to prospective customers. He glanced down Market Street at the stall holders slowly setting up their wares for the day. He waved to the grocer as the man looked up. The man nodded and looked back at his wife as she stacked a pile of oranges into a neat pile. Each of the stalls were set up on carts, which the sellers wheeled in every day to sell their produce. There was a baker, a butcher, a stall that sold linen, and even a local farmer sent one of his milkmaids out to sell mugs of milk from large canisters, as she sat pertly on a wooden milking stool.

Manchester city centre was a thriving place and Toby was glad he had chosen here to set up his photography shop. As he walked away from the door, his assistant, Artie, rushed inside, late as usual.

'I know, boss,' he said. 'There was a carriage overturned on Deansgate…'

Toby said nothing. He had heard all of Artie's excuses and he believed none of them. But he was a smart boy and worked hard when he was there. This was why he often turned a blind eye to some of his exploits, especially his eye for the local female traders.

'Help me set up,' he said. 'We have a family coming in for a portrait this morning.'

Toby went to the back of the shop, lifted the blackout curtain that covered the developing room, and opened the door. While he went inside to bring out the developed photographs that had hung drying overnight, Artie rushed away to gather the negative plates from the stock room. He was setting up the camera when a young woman entered.

'Hello, miss,' Artie said. 'Can I help you?'

'I'd like to see Mr Naylor,' said the woman.

She was a pretty girl. Young, perhaps in her twenties. Artie put down the plate he had been about to load into the back of the camera and went into the back room to find Toby. A few minutes later Toby returned.

'Can I help you?' asked Toby.

'I was told that … I could help *you*.'

Toby flushed slightly. She wasn't the usual sort. Not an obvious doxy, like Doris and the girls that hung out around Sackville Street.

'I'm not sure what you…?' he said, checking her intention wasn't a mistake. He had to be careful. The local pigs had been sniffing around. Inspector Stream in particular liked to keep reminding him that he had come from the slums. That he would always be the Salford scally he was born and bred to be. But Toby had raised himself up. Money talked now, and he had money.

Maybe the girl was a set-up.

'You need models,' the girl prompted. 'Models, who … need money.'

Toby looked over the girl. She was modest-looking, wearing the sort of dress his own sister did when she went to church. He felt it a little strange that she would want to take her clothes off and pose for 'gentlemen's photographs'. She was pretty, though, and she had that shy look which might sell well.

'Come in the back,' he said, despite his reservations.

They passed through the stock room and out into another room. It was a studio, set up with another camera. He pointed to another door at the side.

'In there is a dressing room. You'll find all the things a girl needs to make herself pretty. I have customers, so stay here until I get back. All right?'

The girl nodded.

'What's your name?' Toby asked as an afterthought.

'Rosie,' she said.

Toby went back into the front studio just in time to see the customers arrive.

'Mr Carter,' Toby said. 'And these must be your two lovely sisters.'

'Yes,' said Warren. 'Miss Sara Carter. Miss Laura Carter. This is going to be a present for Laura, who is getting married in a few weeks' time.'

'Yes. I remember you saying. Congratulations, miss. Perhaps we can interest you in our wedding photograph package? We can bring the camera to any church in the area.'

'What a wonderful idea!' said Sara. 'I think that would be a lovely surprise for Mitchell.'

'So do I,' said Warren. 'In fact, if you want it, Laura, I'll be happy to pay for it and make the arrangements.'

'Why not,' said Laura. A small flush of pleasure coloured her cheeks as she thought about her wedding day. 'How exciting!'

'Well. Let's see how this session goes, shall we?' suggested Toby. 'The picture will be ready tomorrow for you to collect, Mr Carter. My assistant Artie will help you now.'

Toby left Artie to take the picture and he heard the excited chatter of the two sisters as Artie directed them into the standard pose.

In the back room, Toby found Rosie wearing a dressing gown. She had applied make-up but it was way too much and showed a total lack of experience.

'You're new to this, ain't you?' Toby said.

Rosie nodded. 'It's not my first choice of making a living.'

'When did you first go out on the streets?' Toby asked.

'On the streets?'

'You know … when did you … get your first … customer?'

Toby was used to dealing with whores; they didn't like to be called that, though. And they hated people to be too blunt about their careers. It was as though they liked to pretend to themselves that they had an ordinary job. Some of the girls he knew had husbands and kids back home, but walked the streets to pay the bills and feed their families. Though these ones were rare. Few men would let their wives sell themselves to keep a roof over their heads. If indeed they even knew what their wife did when she was 'out at work'.

'I don't have customers,' Rosie said.

'Oh!' Toby said. But, he believed her – she *really* wasn't the type. 'What you doing here, then?'

'My mother is sick. We need money.'

'Well, it's as good a reason as any. Women come to me when they need money. Doesn't really matter why, I suppose.'

He placed her on a chaise longue and moved the dressing gown to reveal one leg. At the last minute he gave the neckline of the dressing gown a tug, and it fell off her shoulder, revealing bare flesh down to the top of the curve of her breast.

'Don't worry, the way *you* look, you won't have to show too much.'

Rosie wasn't sure if that was a compliment, but she tried not to dwell on it as she listened to Toby's instructions. She felt a flush creep up into her cheeks as she threw back her head and looked straight into the camera.

Toby bent down, lifted a curtain up from behind the camera and then muttered something about watching a bird. It was all so surreal that Rosie tried to make herself believe she wasn't there, doing this awful thing.

There was a loud whirring sound and a bright light almost blinded her. She blinked and rubbed her eyes.

'Never had your picture taken before?' said Artie from the doorway.

Rosie looked at him through blurry eyes. She pulled the dressing gown back over her leg and shoulder quickly.

'Don't worry yourself,' Artie said. 'It blinds everyone the first time. You'll get used to it.'

'Where is Mr Naylor?' she asked.

'Rushed out to develop you, I shouldn't wonder. He'll want a few more before he pays you, though.'

'Really?' asked Rosie. She had hoped it was all over and done. She didn't even want to see the finished picture.

'Let's get started then,' said Artie, loading another frame into the back of the camera.

'Right. What do you want me to do?'

'Sit forward, knees together. Then look straight into the camera.'

Rosie took up the pose.

'You're a natural, you are,' said Artie. 'I reckon we could make regular use of you.'

'Oh no,' said Rosie. 'I probably won't do this again. It's just…'

The flash exploded.

As Artie left with the frame, Toby came back. He was clapping his hands in delight.

'You photograph very well,' he said. 'I'd like to take a few more. Different poses. Perhaps a different outfit. And let your hair down over your shoulders.'

Rosie went back into the dressing room and looked through the racks of clothes that were there. Mostly they were underwear, corsets, pantaloons, all dressed up with feathers and jewels to make them appear exotic. She took off the dressing gown and kept on her own corset and pantaloons, then she picked up a long thin dress of sheer fabric. She slipped it on over her underwear, but as she looked at herself in the mirror, she realised that the dress was see-through and the underwear beneath didn't look right.

She removed it again. Then quickly loosened her corset, removed her chemise and pantaloons and slipped the dress back over her naked body. Then she let her hair down.

When she came out, once more, Toby was struck by how beautiful she looked with her hair down. It was long, hanging past her bottom, to the top of her legs. As Toby loaded a new frame, Rosie removed the dressing gown. She stood before the chaise, and positioned her hair so that it covered the see-through areas over her breasts. Toby looked up and caught sight of her. His breath caught in his throat.

'I don't want to reveal myself too much,' said Rosie. 'Is this all right?'

'Yes…' Toby said, swallowing. 'Lovely.'

Already the price for her photos was going up in his mind. Rosie was new and innocent-looking. In fact, despite the circumstances that had brought her here, Toby suspected this was the most adventurous thing she had ever done.

'You married?' he asked casually.

Rosie shook her head.

'I can't think why. You're bloody gorgeous…'

Rosie blushed again. Then she looked to the side and back again as he directed. The camera whirred. The flash exploded. And Rosie learnt that Artie was right, her eyes didn't sting anymore. In fact, she was beginning to enjoy herself.

Chapter Seven

April 1898: present day

Mitchell Bishop flicked through the newspaper as he ate his breakfast of boiled eggs, ham, bread and cheese. It had been a few days since he had heard from Warren Carter and so far he'd had no luck at all finding the fake nurse, Rosie. He was beginning to wonder if she would ever surface. Usually, her sort wanted something. Probably it was a scam to extort money from the young doctor, knowing that a breath of scandal, certainly an accusation of rape, could ruin his reputation, and may even result in him being arrested. It would certainly stop him working at the infirmary.

His eyes ran over the births and marriages page out of boredom and he tried not to think about Laura, Warren's twin sister, and the wedding that they should have had. It was six months since he had seen her and it still hurt the same. His heart ached and he felt sick when he recalled the awful incident with her sister Sara. Even though Sara was now institutionalised and her mental state was being assessed, still

Laura hadn't contacted him. He wondered whether this was just stubbornness on her part, or whether she still blamed him for what had happened.

Warren was on his side, though. He knew what Sara had done, and Mitchell had to hope that his friend would help him repair the damage, and that he and Laura could rediscover the trust they once had. It would be a two-way street, the way he saw it. Her lack of faith in him had done as much damage to his trust in her, as her sister had done to Laura's trust when Sara had lied about him. Both sides would have to work at it if they could ever rebuild and move on.

Mitchell's mind went back to Warren's invitation to the Carter home. It was Saturday tomorrow, but because he hadn't heard from Warren, he was loath to just turn up to dinner. It crossed his mind to send a note to reconfirm, because he was desperate to see Laura.

At the top of the obituary page, as though willing it, Mitchell's eyes fell on the name 'Carter', printed in capitals and in bold. He read the piece quickly. Then put down the paper. Sara was dead. He felt shocked and nauseous.

Now Sara would *never* admit the truth. That is, if Laura was still unprepared to listen to his side.

He stood up and paced the dining room, hands behind his back. What to do? The piece mentioned the funeral was taking place at the end of the week. Mitchell wondered if he should go, or if such a thing would be considered poor taste under the circumstances. He wasn't sure what to do. The urge to pay his respects was driven by his need to see Laura. He felt guilty about this, though. Especially as his first thought had not been sympathy for Sara, but a regret that she couldn't now tell the truth.

He stopped pacing. *Of course! Warren!*

He would have a message sent to Warren immediately, but instead of reconfirming dinner, which would be tactless, he would send his condolences and ask permission to visit and pay his respects to the family before the funeral. He was sure Warren would welcome this.

He left the dining room, and his unfinished breakfast, and went down the short corridor to the drawing room. At his writing bureau, he sat down and began to write. Once the letter was finished, he sealed it in an envelope and rang the bell.

'Sir?' said Jonah, his butler, at the open drawing-room door.

'Please take this urgently to the Carter residence. For the attention of Mr Warren Carter.'

A few minutes later, Mitchell heard Jonah leave to carry out his request to deliver the letter and to wait for a response from Warren.

Mitchell went up to his room, and changed clothes. He needed to get some fresh air. He felt the urge to clear his head, and strangely, a walk into town might just do that.

He put on his light overcoat and picked up a walking stick from the stand near the front door. The one he chose had a silver handle, carved into the shape of a wolf's head, and Mitchell favoured it because it was ergonomic and sat nicely in his hand. But as he opened the front door, he found Laura Carter standing there, hand raised as she reached for the bell pull.

'Laura!' His arms opened in welcome, half expecting her to run into his embrace.

'Mitchell,' Laura nodded, her eyes meeting his briefly before dropping to the floor.

He noticed how sad her eyes were, yet her stance was

formal and held none of the warmth he was used to when she greeted him. He dropped his arms down to his sides.

'May I come in?' she asked after a moment's awkward silence.

'Of course.' Mitchell stepped back. He dropped his cane back into the stand and then helped her to remove her coat, which he hung up next to his own.

He led her into the drawing room.

'Tea?' he asked, moving towards the bell pull to call Mrs Dalton.

'No, thank you,' she said, but she sank down on the red velvet sofa as though she was exhausted.

'I saw the obituary. About Sara. I'm so sorry, Laura. As it happens, I had just sent a note with Jonah…'

Laura looked at him as though the world was water in which she was drowning. Then, Mitchell saw her eyes fill up, watched her swallow down the tears, and compose herself. All of this happened in a few seconds, and he turned away and rang for Mrs Dalton in order to give her a moment.

'I could do with something myself,' he said.

'Tea would be nice, then,' she said.

Mrs Dalton appeared a few moments later. 'Oh, Miss Laura! How wonderful to see you!'

Laura greeted the housekeeper. They had always got on well, which had pleased Mitchell, since the two women would have been living in the same house together if the marriage had gone ahead. He hadn't wanted to lose Mrs Dalton; she kept the daily household chores running to perfection, and Mitchell had hoped that wouldn't change when Laura took over as lady of the house.

'She's looking well,' said Laura when the woman left.

Mitchell said nothing. He didn't want polite small talk. He

wanted to talk about what had gone wrong between them. He wanted her in his arms and, above all, he wanted to feel her warm lips against his once more.

'Laura … I…'

'I came here to enlist your help,' she said. The firm formality in her voice stopped him in his tracks. 'Warren is dead.'

Mitchell couldn't comprehend her words for a moment. It felt like a black fog fell between them, that she was as insane as her sister had become.

'Mitchell, did you hear me? Warren is dead.'

Mitchell sank down onto the sofa opposite and looked at Laura's hands. They looked bare without his ring on her finger. Wrong, somehow.

Her words sank into his brain, and he shook his head involuntarily.

'How did it happen?' he said.

'Ever since Sara died, he has been behaving … oddly. We suspect… Well, the police think he killed himself.'

Laura began to tell him about how Warren and she had found Sara.

'They had locked her in this … cell. Somehow, she had got the key from one of the orderlies and then locked herself inside. It's still a mystery how that happened. When they broke down the door, we found … we…'

'My God Laura, you were there too?'

Laura swallowed again. 'She was like a broken doll. And I still can't get the echo of her screams out of my head.'

'The doctors have no explanation?' Mitchell asked, his voice soft.

'They believed she was so insane that she smashed herself against the walls of the cell until she shattered her bones and

died. Mitchell, you should have seen the room. There were …
claw marks on the walls, which were smeared with Sara's
blood. It was as though … something had been in there with
her. But there wasn't anything. I saw for myself that she was
quite alone.'

Mitchell listened as Laura poured out the story of the days
that followed. How Warren had organised everything because
their parents were too distraught to act.

'Warren took on the whole burden of organising the
funeral, the obituary, even the flowers. He did this in a quiet,
calm manner and when it was all done and there was nothing
else to think of, he just retreated into himself. Then, last night, I
heard the most awful noises coming from his room. I thought
that perhaps he was crying. At last, the grief had reached him.
Because I knew he couldn't hold it in forever. So, I went to his
room to try to comfort him. As I was about to knock, I heard
him talking to someone. Then I heard a woman's voice
replying. I was a little shocked, but didn't know want to do. I
couldn't just go in and embarrass them both, and so I slipped
quietly away and back to my room.'

She halted her story as Aggie brought in the tray of tea.

'Thank you, Aggie. That will be all,' Mitchell said.

Then he poured Laura a cup and held it out to her. She took
the china in trembling hands, but didn't drink.

'I wish now that I had disturbed him. If I had gone in there,
then maybe Warren would still be alive.'

Mitchell poured his own tea and added two lumps of sugar.
He stirred and sipped, then added another lump.

'So, you found him dead this morning?' Mitchell prompted.

'No. About six in the morning the servants were up lighting
the fires, and we were disturbed by a loud knocking. Knowing
that my parents were in no fit state to deal with anything, the

butler, Stevens, came to my room and asked me to come downstairs. He said the police were there. Obviously, I pulled on my dressing gown and came down immediately. I found a tall man in our drawing room, wearing ordinary clothes, and a uniformed police officer. The tall man told me his name was Inspector Stream. He was investigating, he said, the death of Sara. Then they told me that Warren was dead. That a witness had seen him, running as if pursued by hounds. That he had thrown himself into the Manchester Ship Canal. The witness ran to fetch help, but when he returned with a local bobby, it was too late. Warren was dead.'

Mitchell mulled over her story. He found it difficult to believe that Warren would kill himself, even though he had seen him last in a state of agitation. Was Sara's death enough to tip him over the edge? He'd never known Warren to be so highly strung.

'My parents are in a terrible state, but I left them when your letter arrived for Warren. I'm afraid I rushed over here and left Jonah behind. It seemed important to talk to you, to find out what you know.'

'I don't know anything at all,' Mitchell said.

'But your letter. It mentions an investigation. It names a girl: Rosie.'

'I'm not sure that Warren would have wished me to speak of this to you. I'm sorry, Laura. But that tale will go with him to the grave.'

'You don't understand. That was who was with him last night,' Laura said. 'She was in his room. I heard her. He called her Rosie.'

Chapter Eight

December 1897: three months earlier

Toby Naylor placed the photographs side by side on the table. He was expecting his first customer any time and he had developed more photographs of Rosie than any of the other girls. She was rapidly becoming a phenomenon and although he didn't know where she lived, and had no way of contacting her, she had turned up of her own accord at least six times in the last three months. On average, twice a month.

Naylor was delighted. His sideline, of producing provocative pictures, which he reproduced onto cards – the type you found in cigarette packets – was doing a roaring trade. So much so that he had been able to pay off more than half of the loan he had taken out from Sean Gallen, a local thug-cum-loan-shark he had used to help raise the capital to buy his cameras and set up the photography studio in the first place.

'Waiting fer someone?' asked Gallen, as though summoned from thin air by thought.

Toby looked up and saw the man, dressed in an expensive dinner suit, standing by the back door.

'Mr Gallen!' Toby said. He hurried to the door to try and prevent Gallen coming inside. He didn't want him to see the pictures. He knew instinctively that this would be a very bad thing.

'I heard there was something interesting going on here,' said Gallen, pushing past Toby as he stepped into the room. 'This is *very* interesting indeed.'

'It's just a hobby,' Toby said, trying to bluff his way out of the situation.

Gallen walked around the table admiring the photographs. 'These are real arty,' he said. 'Didn't realise you was such a talented boy.'

Toby didn't answer. He wrung his hands nervously.

'I know these girls. They all work for me, one way or another. But not this one...' Gallen picked up a picture of Rosie. 'Who is she?'

'I don't know,' said Toby.

'You don't know. Looks like you know her very well to me.'

Over the past few months, Rosie had become bolder. Toby had pictures of her fully nude, as well as semi-clad. In all of them she retained a pose of quiet indifference. She never showed the lasciviousness of the whores, and even though Toby had tried to make a move on her, Rosie had made it clear that other than posing, she was completely off-bounds.

'I only know her first name. She's not from round 'ere,' Toby said.

'And yet, she's working my patch.'

'No, Mr Gallen. Rosie isn't a street girl. She's just some poor kid who needs money for her mother, who's sick.'

Gallen looked at Toby and chuckled. 'And you believed

that line, did you? They all have a relative that's sick, or a baby that's dying. That's the standard line of a whore to excuse the fact that she likes selling herself.'

Toby didn't know what to say. It was difficult to explain, but he knew Rosie was different. She wasn't a whore. She wasn't like any girl he had ever met. Of course, he knew a man like Gallen wouldn't understand anyway, so he didn't try to explain.

'You see … this offends me,' Gallen continued. 'That you use my girls like this, without my permission.'

'Mr Gallen, I'm sorry. They never said they worked for you. You know what whores are like.'

'Yes, I do. I also know what conniving little chancers are like too. Is this what my loan paid for?'

Toby didn't answer. He didn't know what to say.

'Only, I think that you should have done the right thing, Naylor. You should have come to see me. This is a dangerous game you're playing, and one that needs protection.'

The penny began to drop. So Gallen wanted a cut of the sideline, for which he would give protection. Protection, that was, from his thugs, who would no doubt find Toby alone one night and teach him a painful lesson, if he didn't pay up.

'Sure. Of course, Mr Gallen. I think protection is a good idea,' Toby said quickly. 'Shall we say five per cent?'

Gallen tutted and shook his head. 'Now you see, I always thought you were a smart lad. I'm thinking more like fifty-fifty. Plus, you still have to pay off the loan I generously gave you.'

Toby's eyes hardened then he quickly smoothed out his expression.

'Well, I'd be happy to oblige, Mr Gallen, except it's the cost of everything. The materials take up a lot of expense. If we could agree to something a little less, then I'm sure I will enlist your services for – protection.'

'This isn't a time to haggle,' Gallen said. 'One of my boys will call round later for the first instalment – after your customers have been, that is.'

Gallen swaggered out of the back door, leaving Toby in a complete panic. He closed the door and sat down at the table. His hands were shaking and sweat streamed down his face as though he'd been caught outside on a hot day. Pulling out his handkerchief, he mopped the sweat from his brow. Then looked down at the photographs. One of the pictures of Rosie was missing, and he realised that Gallen had taken it. He would probably have his men look out for her now. At that moment, he hoped the girl never returned. He would hate for her to fall into the hands of a thug like Gallen. Whether she wanted to or not, he would have her on the streets, and Toby had been paying her more than the others, just to avoid that happening. If the girl was desperate enough, and Gallen stopped her working for Toby, that would probably be the only course of action she could take.

There was a discreet rap on the door. Toby looked up and saw his first customer waiting outside. It was the butcher from the market, a regular. He stood up and opened the door again, ushering the man inside to choose from the new photograph cards. After that there was a stream of regulars. Most of them came to get Rosie's new cards. She was rapidly becoming everyone's favourite girl.

By the end of the evening, he had a new stack of money in a tin. He divided it in two, then took out the making costs of the pictures from the second pile, and added it to the first. He went upstairs to his quarters, lifted up the rug by his bed and raised the loose board there. Here he hid the larger pile with the rest of the money that he had stashed so far.

As he came back downstairs, he found two of Gallen's men waiting at the door. He let them in and asked them to wait. He went into the developing room and found an old frame box, and put Gallen's money inside. He didn't want the thugs to see how much was there. It was double a normal instalment, and he didn't want them getting any ideas about trying to rob him.

'This is for Mr Gallen,' he said. The parcel was tied up with string and the two men looked at it as he held it out.

'Yeah. This better be what Mr Gallen was expecting,' said one of the men. He was a big man, with a square jaw and a boxer's nose. Toby didn't want to meet him in a dark alleyway anytime soon.

'Everything is as Mr Gallen wanted,' Toby said.

The second thug took the box, weighed it from hand to hand, and then, satisfied, they left.

Toby locked the door behind them. He was sick and worried. The last thing he wanted was Gallen on his back. He would have to do twice as many photographs now to make up the shortfall. And Gallen would probably have his pimps monitor how much he paid the girls now, too. Ensuring that the greedy bastard got a cut of that. Toby hated Gallen and his ilk: he wished he would get his throat cut…

Chapter Nine

Present day: April 1898

'Y ou wanted to see me?' said Inspector Stream.

Mitchell introduced himself as a friend of the Carter family. 'I'm also a detective,' he explained. 'I've been asked to look into the deaths along with the police, and was wondering if we could come to some arrangement on information sharing?'

Inspector Stream laughed. 'The best thing an "amateur" detective can do is stay out of our way. We are doing everything we can to find out what happened.'

Mitchell produced the letter Laura had given him, stating that he had permission to act on the family's behalf.

Stream sneered at it. 'We are not obliged to answer to the family. A policeman's job is a civil duty and we answer to our superiors. We will, however, inform them when we have any new evidence. There will be an enquiry hearing next Tuesday in which we will explore the evidence. The family may attend but are not required to do so.'

'I'll be there on their behalf,' Mitchell said, stressing again that he was the liaison. 'I would like to see the witness statement regarding Warren's death.'

'That information is confidential.'

~

Mitchell left Stream's office realising that he needed to pull a few strings. He hailed a hansom outside the station and set off to see his godfather, John Mainwaring.

It wasn't long before he was sipping gin once more with Mainwaring, and he poured out the tale of recent events.

'Laura has asked me to deal with the police, but they are being reluctant. Inspector Stream is particularly obstructive.'

'Mmmm. I know his superintendent, helped him acquire a very rare ornament from Asia,' Mainwaring said.

Mitchell didn't ask, but he had a feeling his godfather's modest income didn't quite stretch to the ostentation on display in his large townhouse. He'd long suspected that Mainwaring dealt somehow in artefacts, but wasn't sure how deeply involved in importing he was.

'It's a pity you don't have a likeness of the girl,' Mainwaring said. 'There may be a way of tracing her if we knew what she looked like. I suspect that young lady may have some answers.'

'All leads went cold. Everyone at the hospital denied any knowledge of the girl,' Mitchell explained. 'I wish Laura had seen her, but she has at least heard her voice. We know she exists and is not, as I feared at first, a figment of Warren's imagination.'

His godfather rang a small bell by his side and Neeraj appeared.

'I need some writing paper. Let me send Stream's superintendent a letter introducing you. I'll get you on that investigation, and access to the witnesses. Stream could do a lot worse than have someone with your sharp brain helping out.'

'You'd do that for me?' Mitchell said.

'Of course.'

In the afternoon Mainwaring always took a small nap. It was a habit he had got into to help combat the heat in India, and after his injury returned him to England, he had found that he still needed the rest, even in the cool climes of his home country.

Neeraj wheeled Mitchell's godfather away, and when the tall Indian servant returned, Mitchell followed him down into the kitchen, and they sat and talked as they had when Mitchell was young.

'Uncle John seems well,' Mitchell said.

'He is a man very strong of character,' Neeraj said.

Neeraj made them some fresh lemonade.

'Do you miss India?' Mitchell asked suddenly.

'No,' Neeraj said. 'There is nothing for me in India, but sometimes my old bones would enjoy a little more heat.'

Mitchell realised he had never asked about Neeraj's family. He had always assumed he was part of their family. Over the years Neeraj had cared for him as much as he had Mainwaring, with the same loyalty and unwavering dedication.

'We are in evil times,' Neeraj said. 'The peace of our city is being disrupted.'

Mitchell was used to Neeraj's superstitions but he hadn't heard him speak this way for a long time.

'I'd like to tell you a story,' the old Indian said. 'It is a tale brought down from my father, from his grandfather, and has been told father to son across the centuries.'

Mitchell settled down. He loved to hear Neeraj's fairytales. They always had a significance in the present that he later understood. He was like a wise uncle who imparted knowledge with strong morals. Morals that Mitchell had always tried to adhere to, even in his darkest moments, but with varying levels of success.

'There was once a man who sought the truth. He felt there was a secret that only he was not a part of, and when his wife denied it, and said that he was imagining things, he began to look around and ask others what they knew. But everyone he asked said they knew no secret, and behind his back the man believed that they talked about him. Eventually he had asked everyone in the village about "the secret", even the children playing in the dirt by the well. But every one of them shook their heads and said they knew nothing. Still, he couldn't accept it. He began to watch the villagers in silence, looking every day at their routines, and trying to learn everything he could about their personal lives. He watched the women washing clothes down by the stream and listened to their gossip. When he tired of this, learning nothing more than mundane things, he began to track the men. Some of them who liked to hunt for food in the nearby forest let him come with them. Again, he was silent and just watched and listened. Eventually he spent time listening to the children playing. When he was convinced that there was no secret to find, he returned to his home.

'His wife was strange with him. "Where have you been all these days?" she demanded. "Learning secrets," said the man. "What secrets?" asked his wife. "There are no secrets," said the man.

'The wife was confused and she began to imagine that the man had a secret that he wouldn't tell. She began to think he had another woman. Eventually the idea became so big in her head that she threw him out of the house. "That will teach you to keep secrets from me," she said. And she refused to let him return until he told her what he had heard and where he had been.

'Eventually the man made up a story. A wild adventure, and a secret held in another village. He created a whole world that did not exist, just so that she would let him come back into the house.

'Satisfied, the wife eventually let him in. Their marriage was different after that. The wife felt they shared a secret that no one else in the village knew. It bonded them together and they lived for the next few years in a state of happiness that they had never had before. During that time the man never learned that his wife did have a secret she never told. It was something she kept inside her until the day she died, still young and beautiful, and very much loved by her husband.

'After her death one of the villagers finally admitted that they had known, all along, that she had been unfaithful to the husband. The rumour spread through the village, reaching the ears of the man through a well-meaning friend.

'At the funeral pyre the man reflected on the happiness he had shared with his wife for the past few years. He wished that the villager who had revealed the truth had never spoken, because it made a lie of that happiness and undid all the good things they had shared. The truth he had once desired so badly, now led to pain. One night, soon afterwards, he left the village and never returned.'

Mitchell was quiet. 'That is a sad story, Neeraj. What does it mean?'

'Sometimes the truth is not what we want to hear,' Neeraj said. 'I have something for you. It was given to me by my father when he told me this story. And I did not know what he meant or why this was important to me.'

Neeraj removed a chain from around his neck. It was of yellow gold, and hanging from it was a round flat gold disc. Painted on the disc was a vibrant blue eye.

'This is a talisman. It wards away evil. I feel you are entering a period of dangerous times.'

'Neeraj, I can't take this from you.'

'My father always said I was to pass it on. That I would know the time. This protected me during the battles. It also helped me protect your godfather, when he was hit by the bullet. I have no sons. I have no daughters. But I hold you in my heart as I might a child of my own. This is now for you.'

Mitchell took the chain and examined the emblem. The gold was still warm and it held Neeraj's clean musky scent. It was ostentatious, but he had never noticed it around Neeraj's neck before, which surprised him, because after all these years, he thought he knew everything about the man.

He slipped the chain over his neck and loosening his collar he dropped it down under his shirt. Even though he didn't believe in Neeraj's superstition, he couldn't refuse the gift, for fear of insulting someone who had played a huge part in his life since the day he was born.

'Keep this close to you in the coming days,' Neeraj said. 'This is all I ask.'

Mitchell nodded but said nothing, keeping his cynicism to himself. But the charm warmed against his skin and despite his lack of belief, it did give him some comfort.

Chapter Ten

Laura Carter held her mother's hand as the coffin was loaded onto the funeral carriage. She was wearing a long black coat over a formal black dress, and a hat with a black veil to cover her anguished face. Her mother, Elena, leaned on her arm, tremors shuddering through her as though the warm spring air couldn't break through the darkness of her black funeral clothes.

As the doors on the carriage carrying the coffin closed, Laura, with the aid of her father, Harold, turned Elena towards the small black carriage behind. Then she climbed inside herself, grateful to shut out the neighbours who had come out of their homes to watch the procession with mawkish fervour. Men removed their hats as a mark of respect, women shed tears, but nothing helped to remove the feeling that the world was falling down around their family.

They had considered postponing Sara's funeral, and burying her and Warren at the same time, but the police had told them they were holding Warren's body and the funeral directors advised them not to wait. As it was, the coffin had to be closed. A choice that hadn't sat well with her mother, who despite being told it was not possible, had wanted to take one last look at her daughter. Laura thought that this was because she couldn't believe Sara was gone. It was hard for all of them to accept, but Laura had seen Sara's mutilated body, and it was an image she was trying hard to forget.

Laura looked out through the open window as the carriage began its slow journey to the cemetery. She caught sight of Mitchell holding his hat against his chest, head bowed, and fought the urge to cry again. She wished he could have been in the carriage with her. She felt drained of tears and emotion, blank mostly, but then the silliest acts of kindness found some more water lurking and ready to spill. She pulled out her handkerchief and dabbed her eyes quickly under the sheer black veil.

Her mother was staring at the other side of the carriage as though she had been transported into a strange and alien world. She had said nothing since the coffin arrived that morning. Just stared at the black wood as though it was the only real thing in the room. When the bearers started to lift it, Elena had flown into a panic, and it had taken all of Laura's strength to prevent her mother from throwing herself onto the coffin.

Her father had completely withdrawn. Any sign of his usual stiff-upper-lip resolve had vanished in the catatonic vacancy that was the only expression he could make. This same expression had been present when he heard of Sara's death, but since the police visit, and the discovery of Warren's apparent suicide, her father had barely said a word. Laura had become the strong one, and she was bowing under the strain, but looking after her parents was the only thing that had kept her going. She was afraid to fully give in to her own grief, in case it overwhelmed her too. One of them had to be in charge, and she knew that task had fallen to her.

The carriage came to a halt as they reached the graveyard a short time later. Harold Carter's father had bought a family tomb, and now the doors would be unlocked for the first time since his parents' death. Sara – and Warren when they could bury him – would at least be laid to rest with family. It was a small comfort to Laura that the burial site was already chosen, for this was at least one thing she had not been required to decide on.

The carriage door opened and the funeral director held out his hand to help Laura and Elena to climb down. The coffin was quickly removed and the bearers were already taking it into the church.

Laura looked around and saw Mitchell and several of her friends gathering outside. The family followed the funeral director and he positioned them behind the coffin. They entered the church, walking down the aisle behind the coffin. Laura couldn't help recalling that she should have walked down this very aisle on a day of happiness. The irony that this was now happening – probably the worst day of her life – was not lost on her.

As the family sat in the front pew, she glanced back to see Mitchell taking a seat two rows behind. She wished he were sitting next to her, but didn't like to go and ask. Her eyes scanned the rest of the people present. Friends of Sara, Laura's own friends, and a few of Warren's had gathered to pay their respects. Her eyes went back to Mitchell. Just behind him she noticed a woman that she didn't recognise, with long hair, pulled back at the front in the style of a much younger girl. But this one was in her early twenties. The woman wasn't dressed in black. Instead, she wore a dull, washed-out brown coat. She was so unlike any of Warren or Sara's friends that she stood out.

Laura turned to face the front as the service began. She made a mental note to approach the stranger after the service. Then she forgot the girl entirely, as she was lost in a wave of grief that she felt would never end.

Back at the house, the servants had prepared a buffet for the invited mourners. After she had settled her mother and father down on the sofas in the drawing room, Laura went off to search for Mitchell. She passed through the dining room, then glanced into the study. She was surprised to see that he hadn't arrived. At that moment she saw him coming upstairs from the kitchen and servants' quarters. He was carrying a notebook and was still writing when he looked up and saw Laura.

'I was talking to Stevens,' he said. 'I wanted to know all that the servants observed over the last few months.'

'Investigating? Even today?' Laura said.

She sounded tired and drained. Mitchell fought the urge to put his arms around her. Even though she had invited him back into their lives, it was only as a friendly detective. He had no right to touch her and to do so now, when she was feeling at such a low ebb, was completely inappropriate.

'Sorry. It's an opportune moment. Perhaps I should...' Mitchell put the notepad and pencil into his jacket pocket.

The doorbell rang and in lieu of the servants, who were all

occupied with the guests, Mitchell went to the front door while Laura stood in the doorway of the drawing room.

'Mr Bishop, what a surprise to find you here,' said Inspector Stream, his voice heavy with sarcasm.

'Inspector,' Mitchell nodded. 'Do come in. We are in the middle of a funeral wake, as I'm sure you are aware.'

Stream stepped inside and Laura closed the door of the drawing room to prevent her parents from seeing him. She nodded to Mitchell, who then led the inspector away from the mourners and into Harold Carter's study.

'A drink, inspector?' Mitchell asked.

'No, thank you. I was hoping to see Mr Carter.'

Laura followed them into the study. 'I'm Miss Carter, inspector. My parents cannot deal with this right now. But as you know, I have instructed Mr Bishop to deal with you on our behalf. I believe you weren't very accommodating last time he visited you.'

'Miss Carter, I have come here to tell you that we have no further evidence. We are now convinced that both your brother and sister committed suicide. I have been ... *instructed*,' he said this word through gritted teeth, 'to help Mr Bishop and give him access to any and all witnesses to interview. I can only hope that you will then accept my findings and let your brother and sister rest in peace.'

Laura's eyes were like steel as she looked at the inspector, and Mitchell was impressed with the way she faced him down.

'Inspector Stream, if Mr Bishop finds the same as you, then that is exactly what we will do. If he does not, then I expect the police to be willing to pursue any evidence he finds to the contrary,' Laura said.

Stream's arrogant expression dropped for a second. 'You *really* think he will find something else, don't you?'

'I know my brother. He wouldn't kill himself. Certainly not right now, when we all need him so much. Something else was going on. I just don't know what.'

Stream grew thoughtful. 'Suicide is something that many family members find difficult to accept. There is usually no sign beforehand to indicate a problem. I have seen some terrible things done in the name of depression, anxiety and loneliness, Miss Carter. However, I have a strange feeling about this, despite our own inability to find anything more. This is why, despite my better judgement, I have agreed to let Mr Bishop in. I hope he does find something we can work with. But if he doesn't, then I hope you will let this go and move on with your own life.'

Stream's tone was kind, but strong, and Laura just nodded. The strength she had displayed flagged again.

'After the funeral I'd like to come over to the station and read the witness statements,' said Mitchell.

'Certainly,' said Stream. 'And now I wish you…' his mouth hovered over the expression 'A good day', as he realised it would be inappropriate, 'all the very best. My condolences, Miss Carter. To you and your family.'

Mitchell led Stream out and Laura sank into her father's leather sofa, taking a deep breath. She didn't know if she had the strength to go back out and face family and friends, who were working their way through the buffet. When Mitchell returned, he saw how exhausted she was.

'Leave it all to me,' he said. 'You expect too much of yourself. Have you eaten today?'

Laura shook her head. 'I couldn't.'

'Then I'll fetch you something. Eat, no matter how little, or you won't have the strength you're going to need.'

Laura nodded. Mitchell turned away and headed for the door.

'Mitchell…' she called. He looked back. 'Thank you. Thank you for everything.'

Mitchell's smile was tight and sad as he left Laura to her grief.

Chapter Eleven

While Artie tidied away the equipment Toby took the money out of the till in the front of the shop and retired to the back room to write up the daily takings. Removing Artie's wages first, he stored the cash in a small metal box. They had become busier lately. A whole bookful of orders was lined up for the coming weeks. This meant, that in order to keep up with the demand for his sideline, Toby had been forced to give Artie more responsibility. The boy was turning into a good photographer now and had taken on most of the legitimate clients. He even turned up early to work in the mornings, and was so organised that he had the photography frames set up, ready to take one picture after another, without delay. It was obvious that Artie was enjoying the work more.

Artie came into the room a little while later.

'All done in there, and I'm set up for tomorrow too. We've an 'usband-and-wife photo first thing, and then I've to go out to do a wedding party at St Jude's. Should take all afternoon.'

'Thank you. Artie, here's your wages for the week. I've

given you extra. Ta so much for all the effort you've put in this week.'

'No trouble,' said Artie. 'I love taking the pictures. Think it's me callin'.'

Toby nodded. He remembered having the same enthusiasm when he discovered the new art of photography too.

'Beats drawing any day,' said Artie. 'Will you lock the door after me?'

Toby stood and followed Artie to the front door, then locked it behind him as he left. He returned to the back room just as someone knocked on the door.

He glanced through the glass panel to see Doris, one of the local street girls, standing by the door. He sighed: he wasn't really in the mood to take pictures of her tonight. He wished that Rosie would appear again, but also hoped she wouldn't, as he feared that Gallen's men were still watching his premises to see his movements. Already Gallen had returned to query the latest 'profit-share'. Now Toby had taken to keeping accounts for some of the cash as a way to 'prove' the sales. Of course, his customers weren't to be named in the ledger, which made the faking of the totals far easier. He also wasn't stupid enough to create a real accounts book. He didn't trust Gallen's men not to try and search his place one day. Which was why the only other book was the one he had for his legitimate shop sales.

He turned the key in the lock and opened the door.

'Hiya, darlin',' said Doris as she slipped inside. 'Wondered if you needed some extra photos today?'

Toby shrugged.

'I been finkin' all about what your punters may want. Maybe they would like to see a little "real" action. You know what I mean?'

'No. I don't,' said Toby.

'Well … Gallen told me pimp that he …'

Toby opened the back door again. 'Leave, Doris.'

'Why? Wassamatter?'

'I have to pay Gallen as it is. I'm not having him and your pimp tell me what the pictures should contain.'

'They are just trying to 'elp yer.'

'They are trying to make more money,' Toby said. 'There is a certain artistry involved in this for me. And I won't have it ruined by smut.'

'Aw. Don't be like that, Toby, love,' said Doris. 'Tell you what, why don't I take care of those frustrations o' yours. No charge. Something on the 'ouse?'

'No … I …'

Doris was dancing gracefully around the room in a way that Toby had never seen her move before. It was beautiful. Flowing. He suddenly wanted to photograph her. But didn't know how he could show that movement without the plate blurring.

He closed and locked the door. Her hair tumbled down; it reminded him of Rosie. And suddenly her face had changed too. She was no longer the rough street girl. She was young, breasts firm and pert, hair gleaming in the gaslight with auburn lights. The stained, tawdry red dress was replaced by a pure white shift with long sleeves that dropped down to the floor. She was Guinevere as her hair tumbled down over her shoulders, down past her waist.

'Rosie…' he said. 'You're here…'

'Yes, dearie… I'll be anyone you want. All on the 'ouse.'

She knew exactly where his bedroom was and Toby followed her upstairs. He watched the sway of her full but youthful hips. The white dress flowed like spilled milk as she lay back on the bed.

He must be dreaming: no way would Rosie ever offer herself like this. She was too clean, too pure. But Toby knew that this impression of her was all an illusion. No pure and decent girl would take off her clothes for him to take photographs of her, would she?

The dress was gone now, it lay in a heap over the rug that covered his hiding place.

'Rosie,' gasped Toby as she opened to him. 'That's it, Mr Naylor, you know you always wanted it,' said Doris.

Then the face before him changed. He saw rouge-smeared lips, over-red cheeks, frown lines and wrinkles that shouldn't have possessed the face of the woman he desired. He began to pull away until Rosie was before him again, her mouth clamping on his, tongue pushing between his lips that felt and tasted like a live slug. He drew back from the kiss. Vile breath that stank of cheap gin and unclean teeth wafted into his face as the mouth moved, yelling vile obscenities.

Toby heaved away, yanking the sheet back with him, to cover his naked bottom half. He stared down at the writhing horror of sagging breasts with shrivelled nipples that looked like rotting prunes.

'What are you?' he cried.

'I'm Rosie, or Doris, or Susie, or anyone you want me to be.'

The thing on his bed laughed.

Toby screamed. Sickness pulled at his insides. His trembling knees could barely support him as she opened her mouth and waggled a blackened tongue.

'Come on, lover. Let me show you what I can do with this.'

She crawled across the bed, hand reaching for the sheet that covered him. Toby watched it, unable to move, paralysed by fear. The hand, nay claw, was dried and shrivelled, like the hand of a body rotted and dried out in an ancient grave.

He looked back at her face. Flashes of Rosie and Doris danced across the horrific features.

'Leave me alone,' he begged. 'What do you want?'

Grotesque laughter, a deep cackle, came from withered lips in a shallow hiss.

A loud banging erupted from below. Toby felt as if the whole building was being attacked by the hounds of hell.

'Mr Naylor! Mr Naylor!'

He heard his name yelled over and over. The creature before him still came on. Its form solidified now into Doris and stayed there.

'Mr Naylor! Are you home? Please let me in. It's Rosie.'

Toby looked at the door of his bedroom, then back at the bed. The thing that had been there was gone. There was no sign of the clothing she had discarded. He looked down at the sheet he was gripping. His own clothing was still firmly in place.

He glanced over to the window and caught sight of his dishevelled state in the dressing-table mirror. He dropped the sheet and on trembling legs, staggered downstairs.

He was confused. Sick. As though he were waking from an alcohol-fuelled sleep.

'Dreamin' … musta fallen asleep.'

But the nightmare was so real!

He reached the back room and looked out at Rosie. She looked scared. The door was locked, just as he had left it.

'Please, Mr Naylor, can I come in?'

He hesitated. If he hadn't been dreaming, then some changeling had been here and it had taken Rosie's form. He shook his head. He must have been asleep; nothing so hideous could possibly exist.

He turned the lock and opened the door. Rosie ran inside and threw herself into his arms.

'Thank you. Thank you!'

'What's the matter?' he asked, shaking away his own fears as he pushed her back to look into her frightened eyes.

'Something was following me,' Rosie said. 'I thought…'

Toby led her to the chaise and she sat. But she was trembling so much that he was afraid to leave her.

'Lock the door,' she said.

He turned and complied, feeling the sense of her urgency.

'It's probably the local thugs,' Naylor said. 'They've been looking out for you.'

'Why?' she asked.

Toby shrugged. He was embarrassed to tell her about Gallen, and how he couldn't stand up to him.

'I wanted to warn you, but you never left me any contact details.'

'This wasn't a … thug,' Rosie said.

'Then who was it?'

'I couldn't see them properly.'

Toby didn't know what to say or ask. He was trying not to look at her. The dream, or whatever it had been, had been so vivid. Being around Rosie now made him feel guilty and dirty. He didn't like to admit to himself that he had been fantasising about her. Every bit as much as the men who bought the pictures he had taken of her. He shuddered as the Doris-thing appeared behind his eyes. That would teach him for having lewd thoughts about this sweet girl, wouldn't it?

'Should I help you get home?' Toby asked. 'I can call a cab, come with you all the way if you like?'

Rosie frowned. She looked over at the door and Toby could see that she was very afraid. 'Could I ... stay here?'

Toby looked around, confused. He didn't know what she was saying. It was obvious to him that she wasn't just some girl off the streets. There was a certain amount of breeding evident in her features, that were not just pretty, but were in fact, strikingly handsome. Maybe she was the bastard daughter of someone important. Toby could only imagine. Whatever it was, the dull-brown dress she was wearing had seen better days and was at odds with her refined bone structure.

'That's all right. I'm sorry I troubled you...' Rosie said. 'I'll leave. I'm sure it's all my imagination, anyway.'

Toby was even more confused. Why was she leaving? Then he realised that he hadn't answered her.

'No, you can't go out alone. Of course you can stay. You can use my room. I'll sleep down here,' he said, pointing to the chaise.

'I don't want to put you out. I'll sleep here.'

Toby wouldn't hear of it. Besides, he felt odd about returning to his room. If he had been dreaming, he didn't remember going to bed, and it was unusual that he would do that fully clothed. He went up to the room and lit the lamp by the bed, then straightened the sheets to hide the evidence of his strange episode. After that he went downstairs again to find Rosie putting the kettle on the stove.

'I hope you don't mind,' she said.

'No. Good idea,' said Toby. 'Might calm our frayed nerves.'

Rosie looked at him sharply. She had noted the beads of perspiration that left his forehead and face damp as he opened the door to her. He was obviously in some kind of trouble too.

'Tell me about these thugs,' she asked.

'Local protection racket. They got wind of my little sideline.'

'Wanted a cut of it, huh?' she asked.

Toby nodded.

'Sean Gallen – he runs it. I borrowed money off him to open the studio. He turned up, saw the pictures, and noticed you weren't one of the…'

'No. I'm not a street girl,' Rosie said.

'He assumed you were, though. Thought you were working the area without his permission.'

'I see.'

'So, it's just not safe for you to come around here no more,' said Toby. 'I'm sorry to say that. You're my best seller.'

Rosie nodded. 'I'll be out of your way tomorrow. When it is light.'

'I'm sorry about this,' Toby said again. He felt guilty to be turning her away like this. She came to him because she needed money. He was worried about what she would have to do to earn the income she got from modelling for him.

'I'll be fine,' she said. 'Things always look better in the morning. I'm tired now. Are you sure you will be all right on the chaise?'

'Yeah. Upstairs on the right. That's me room. The one opposite is the stock room. Full of photograph stuff.'

'Thank you.'

Rosie left him and Toby stared at the kettle. She hadn't made tea after all, and the water was just starting to boil.

Chapter Twelve

Sean Gallen liked death. He liked the smell of it on his hands. And the blood that was spilt in his name always felt like it was there too. He never let his guard down and regularly struck terror in the hearts of his own personal guards, showing them he was just as capable of taking any of them out, whenever they displeased him. That evening he had proven himself again. One of the guards had failed to come back with enough money from his rounds of the local pimps. Gallen knew that the man wasn't at fault, but he couldn't let himself be seen as 'understanding'. It would be misconstrued as a sign of weakness. A sign that he was going soft. And someone was always waiting to take advantage of moments like that…

So, he beat the man with his bare fists, until he could barely walk. The others, his most trusted guards, dragged away the failure, knowing that this could happen to any of them, at any time. It was a reminder that Sean was strong, Sean was dangerous, Sean was not to be trifled with.

Years ago, Gallen had worked for a man called O'Leary, a

thug who had run all the organised crime in Manchester. O'Leary had grown fat and lazy. He was an easy mark, the way Gallen saw it. He had believed in his own invulnerability and had let his guard down once too often. Gallen had started working for him as an errand boy at the age of twelve and he had watched and learnt. He killed his first whore, on O'Leary's instruction, at the age of fourteen. It was to be a message to all the street girls and their pimps, that they had to pay into the organisation, or they would all find themselves dead in a dark alley: face slashed open, throat slit – just as the whore's had been. But Gallen, for all his casual taking of orders from O'Leary, knew the man's weaknesses and bided his time. One night, when he was just fifteen years old, he broke into O'Leary's house, walked into the man's bedroom while he slept and slit his throat. That night signified a change of regime and he took over the organisation. But it wasn't as easy as taking out O'Leary. Sean had to take down all the men that guarded him, and bring in his own, showing that anyone who dared challenge him would wind up dead.

Now, sitting in his expensively furnished bedroom, his bruised fists soaking in a bowl of soapy water, Gallen thought back on the effort it had taken, and how O'Leary's main guard, who could have easily taken him, hadn't even attempted to fight back. He had just taken the beating because he was afraid to challenge the new leader. The guard was smart enough to know that if he challenged Gallen and lost, then he would be killed, not just beaten.

'Here's your gin, boss,' said one of the other guards, coming into the room.

'I said whisky, you moron!' Gallen snapped.

His mood hadn't calmed with the beating he had given, though. In fact, it had worsened.

'Get me one of the girls. That new one,' he said. 'Sally. She ain't all used up like the others yet.'

The guard quickly returned with a petite blonde girl and a decanter of whisky. Gallen dried his hands, smearing blood on a white hand towel. He held out the bowl and the guard took it away as the girl stood awkwardly in the corner. She was nervous; she had heard about Gallen's exploits that night and she was afraid she had done something wrong.

'Get your clothes off,' Gallen ordered.

She said nothing as she started to strip. Naked, she was too thin. Gallen liked his girls with a little more meat on them than that, but he couldn't be bothered sending for another one. She would have to do. He ordered her to lie on the bed, then he climbed on top of her. His eyes fell on the picture beside his bed, of the girl that Naylor called Rosie. He imagined her under him instead of the scrawny Sally. She had the sort of curves he liked. It was a source of frustration to him that his men hadn't found her yet, and that Naylor didn't know who she was.

When he was done, he rolled off Sally.

'Get out,' he ordered.

Sally scrambled from the bed and began to dress as quickly as possible. Then she left the room, relieved that she had only been the outlet for Gallen's lust and not his anger.

Gallen lit a cigarette, then lay back on the spot the girl had just occupied. He looked around the room, feeling relaxed for the first time all day. He took a drag from the cigarette and picked up the photograph card of Rosie. The card was small and it was difficult to make out her features that clearly. She was wearing a see-through dress, the breasts were well-developed but firm. His eyes ran down the curve of her hips and took in the dark triangle he could just make out between her legs. His impression of her was that she was pretty. She had that innocent look that none of his whores had, at least not after their first week on the job. Lying on your back, taking one guy after another did that to a girl. It aged them, used them up, which was why Gallen and his guards were constantly looking for something young and fresh to earn the best money.

Looking at Rosie, Gallen felt himself hardening again. He regretted sending Sally away and considered asking for her return. He could tell why Naylor's little sideline in cards was so lucrative. There were a lot of men out there that couldn't afford whores, but buying a card was within their means.

He took a long drag from his cigarette and let the smoke sit in his lungs for a moment before blowing it out into the space above him. The room was rapidly filling with his expelled smoke. He turned, sat on the side of the bed, stubbed the remains of the cigarette in an ashtray by the bed, then lit another one.

The room stank of blood, smoke and sex. He dimmed the light beside his bed, then, naked, he walked across to the window, opened the curtains and looked out into the street. He took another drag and blew out smoke. He turned the lock above the window and raised it up to let the smoky air out and the cool night air in. He breathed in the fresh air, mingled with another lungful of nicotine. Then leaned out of the window to look down the street.

It was late. Maybe two or three in the morning, Gallen wasn't sure and didn't care. He was more alert at night. All was quiet. The street was empty, except for…

He could hear heeled boots click along the street. He saw a girl walking towards his house. She looked up at him and waved. Then she disappeared into the shadows between streetlights. At the next gaslight she reappeared, then silence fell as she passed into the darkness again. Gallen frowned as the girl appeared again, closer this time. He could make out that she was smiling now. When she reached the streetlamp under his window, she stopped and looked up. He looked at her, feeling strangely pleased: he was certain now that she was the girl from the postcard.

'You've been looking for me,' she said. Then she placed her fingers against her mouth in a 'shh' pose. Gallen was intrigued.

'You saucy minx,' he called.

'Come down,' she laughed. 'Alone. Or I might disappear again.'

Gallen turned, grabbed his dressing gown, and pushed his feet into his slippers. He stubbed out the cigarette in his hand, then hurried out of his room. Downstairs he passed the half-open door of the kitchen. His men were playing cards, drinking his whisky, and a few of the girls were sitting around, half-dressed. For a moment he felt angry. They all thought he had retired and they could do what they liked in his absence. Then Gallen simply ignored them; he had bigger fish to fry. That little slut was outside and she wanted to see him. She wouldn't be the first whore who thought she was better than everyone else. He would get out there and show her just what she was.

He walked down the corridor and opened the front door: the slut was standing by his front gate.

'Come on,' she said.

He approached the gate. There was something ethereal about her, as though she were a creature he had dreamed up. She was certainly a stunner. It would be a shame to mess that up. He might even want to keep this one all for himself for a while.

'Where to?' he said, responding to the sexy curve of her smile.

'This way.' She began to hurry away before he could open the gate. She was light on her feet, dancing like a nymph across the road and off down the street.

Without thinking, Gallen followed.

He almost caught up with her at the end of the street, but once he turned the corner she was nowhere in sight. He hurried on, eyes darting everywhere until he was halfway down the next street. He stopped. She had gone. She was taunting him. He began to feel angry.

'Here,' she said.

She was standing beside him, then she took his hand and led him through a gate and into the garden of another house. The front door was open. She took him inside and up the stairs.

'You live here?' he asked. 'Right around the corner from me?'

She said nothing as she pulled him into a bedroom. A large master suite, not unlike his own.

'Cigarette?' she said, holding out a pack of his favourite brand. He took one while she struck a match, lighting the end before blowing out the flame.

'Who are you?' he asked.

She didn't answer, but she took the cigarette from his fingers, then pulled him over to the bed.

He fell into the sheets, suddenly alone in the bed. She stood by the bed looking at him. Then she pulled on the covers, throwing them over him. He pushed them away from his face, tried to get up, but the linen gripped his arms and legs like the tentacles of an octopus. He struggled, but every movement made the problem worse. The sheets wrapped around him, and the more he twisted and turned, the worse it got. He was completely entangled in the bedclothes.

'What's going on?' he said, his voice rising in panic.

He saw Rosie standing above him, cigarette in one hand, a decanter of whisky in the other. She smiled. Then sprinkled the contents of the decanter over the sheets.

'What are you doing?' he asked as the smell of whisky filled the room, mingling with cigarette smoke.

The sheets tightened, cutting off his oxygen. The room was as smoke-filled as his own bedroom had been. It obscured his view of the girl. He heard the striking of a match, and the flame lit up her face for just a moment. It was the most monstrous face he had ever seen. Coal-black eyes reflected the flame. Warped, lined cheeks and an awful sneering mouth. Then the lit match fell onto his sheets. The fabric caught with a whoosh as though the flames were fanned by the breeze coming through the still-open window.

Gallen tried to scream as fire burned through the sheets and his dressing gown caught fire. The blaze bit into his flesh, but somehow the sheet was stuffed into his mouth, pushing his tongue back into an uncomfortable position that almost forced it down his throat. He struggled and tugged, twisted and turned, but the sheets wouldn't come free, even as they burnt away. He smelt his scorching flesh, even as the smoke-clogged air choked the last bit of oxygen out of his lungs, and the pain sent all traces of sanity from his mind.

At the last minute he turned his head and saw the picture of Rosie at his bedside catch fire. But his crazed mind couldn't make sense of it. He felt as though he were dying in his own bed, his own room, though he knew he had left the house to follow the girl.

As Gallen died he reflected on his own demise. It wasn't

another gang rival, nor was it one of his own men that was responsible. It was only a girl. A mere chit of a thing who had made him lower his guard. He had grown slow and stupid, just like his predecessor.

~

'It's cold in 'ere,' said Sally.

She was sitting astride one of the guards who had fallen into an alcohol-induced sleep halfway through. Sally pulled herself free, then went to retrieve her clothing from the floor. As she slipped on her dress, she glanced over at the partially open door into the hallway. She walked through the smoke-filled room and looked out into the corridor.

'Someone's left the front door wide open,' she murmured as she wandered down the corridor to the door.

One of the other guards, head down on the table, roused as she spoke. 'What?'

He pulled himself up. As he came out of the kitchen he glanced back at the staircase. A billow of smoke was coming down the stairs from the boss's room.

'Jesus! There's a fire!'

He ran up the stairs, taking them two at a time, until he reached the door. He tried to open it, but the handle burnt the skin from his fingers. He stepped back, kicked hard until the frame gave way. Fire rushed out, knocking him backwards as the flames exploded over him.

Sally was standing at the front door looking outside into the small front garden and the street when the blast knocked her through the doorway. She landed on the path as screaming and yelling erupted from inside the house. As she struggled to her feet, it occurred to her that Gallen was dead. Instead of going back to see if she could help, she staggered down to the gate, opened it and hurried out onto the street.

She was gaining confidence now. She didn't care if the house burnt down, or if all of the guards died trying to put the fire out. All she knew was that it would take months for those survivors to decide among themselves who their new boss was. There would be fighting, murders, gangland wars. They would have so much to think about that they would forget all about her. Why would they even care about one missing whore? They would probably think she'd died in the fire too.

Picking up her skirt, she began to run barefoot down the street. She was free!

Toby woke in the middle of the night. He threw back the blanket, stretched his cramped legs and looked around the dark studio/kitchen. All was quiet, but there was a smell. At first the odour reminded him of cigarettes, then it grew stronger, and he suddenly became afraid that a fire had started somewhere in the building. He stood up quickly: the developing liquids in the darkroom were highly flammable. *Damn!* This was all he needed. He hurried through the door towards the shopfront and darkroom, glancing up the staircase as he went. As he opened the door to the front studio, he discovered all was as it should be. The scent of smoke wasn't present there at all. He checked the darkroom, just to be on the safe side. Nothing was out of place; the prints he had developed earlier were dry now and ready to be framed. All was well.

As he passed the stairs again, he became aware that the smell was concentrated there. He crept upwards, sniffing the space, but the smell disappeared by the time he reached the top. He stood outside his bedroom, wondering if he should check on Rosie, but he didn't want to disturb her, or to have her think he was trying to molest her while she slept. Eventually, he went downstairs again, and curled up once more on the uncomfortable sofa. It took a while before he fell back to sleep, but he could no longer smell smoke and had begun to believe he had imagined the whole thing.

As he drifted off to sleep Toby imagined that a dark shadow had gathered around the studio. It held a stifling miasma that smelt of burnt flesh. He woke up again, coughing the awful smell out of his lungs. He looked around the room, but it was still in pitch dark, as though the night had barely even passed. Or as though the vivid dream he'd had was merely seconds, not hours long.

He sat up, rubbed his eyes, and looked around the room in a confused daze.

Something moved. He turned to looked directly at the space. There was a kind of blurring in one of the corners of the room. He shrugged: it was just a trick of the light.

Something streaked across the room. He even felt the air stir.

Then Toby remembered his awful dream before Rosie had turned up; that dreadful thing he had seen that looked like her and Doris, and his mind reached back … someone else he knew was in there too. Like something had swallowed them, and could call their essence forward, projecting it like an overlapped negative image. He recalled the face changing before his eyes.

He shook the image away. But the thing was so real. *Shit!* He had always had an overactive imagination. When he was a child he had often cried out in the night, convinced that his room was stalked by some evil thing not of this world. His mother called it the night terrors; Toby had hated the dark.

Toby closed his eyes again and tried to encourage sleep, but he *felt* something nearby, as though someone were in the room watching him. He opened his eyes again, pulling the blanket up, reverting to his old childish belief that the covers were some form of ward that would protect him from the darkness inside the room. He could see nothing, then the blurred outline of a figure appeared before him, standing so close to the chaise that he could almost reach out and touch it.

Toby shrank back, trying to get away. He felt the same paralysing terror he had felt as a boy.

Evil emanated from the figure in a cold, dark rush. There was a hiss like an intake and expiration of breath, and a foul stench permeated the air. It was as though the breath of the dead had been blown deliberately into his face. Something reached out towards him. He couldn't move. A dry husk, that made him think of a sharp tree branch, brushed against his face. An old, rotten, dried-out, mummified hand cupped his chin with loving affection. He imagined that black, slug-like tongue protruding between yellowed teeth as the hand pulled him closer. He tried to resist, but couldn't. The strength had completely evaporated from his limbs. His breath was shallow, heart pounding in his ears, and the skin the thing touched felt as though it were turning to ice.

Dry lips pressed against his mouth as he tried to scream. He felt himself choking on desiccated flesh as it crumbled to powder in his mouth. Somehow Toby managed to pull away. He heard the snap of bone, and felt the dry fingers fall away from his face. Feeling returned as his skin began to warm again. But it hurt, as though he had severe frostbite.

The thing was swaying before him, a crumbling, skeletal

mass. His eyes had adjusted, or maybe it was purposefully showing itself to him now. Toby felt rotted rags brush against the side of the chaise. Then the thing climbed onto the chaise and crawled on top of him. It was heavy, and strong, as it held him down, pinning his struggling legs and arms to the couch. He tried to twist, felt the agony of his muscles straining against what should have been rags and bones. But it had supernatural strength, and now Toby could see eyes – red, monstrous, blood-filled eyes – that were so full of rage, he was forced to look away.

He tried to scream again. But the thing laughed, clamping a decayed palm over his mouth, as it pressed down on his chest. The air rushed out of his lungs, and as Toby tried to heave it back, the thing on his chest began to throttle him. He struggled harder, panicking as he became more oxygen deprived, but the monster was too strong. It squeezed and squeezed until finally Toby felt the darkness crowding into his limited vision and his consciousness closed down.

Part III

Chapter Thirteen

There was a strong odour of burnt flesh, which somehow managed to overwhelm the smell of burnt wood and furnishing. Sean Gallen's house was still smoking as Inspector Stream and his men picked through the destroyed bedroom. One of Stream's officers had opened the window wide to help expel some of the cloying fumes.

'Looks like a straightforward case of smoking in bed to me,' said Sergeant Grimes, pointing to the charred remnants of a packet of cigarettes.

Stream looked around the room, down at the floor. The mattress was burnt through. Sean Gallen was a murky mass of blackened bones. It looked as though molten lava had been poured over his body. Stream used his walking stick to push aside some of the debris around the bed. Bits of fabric had somehow survived but looked like crispy bits of burnt paper which crumbled to ash when touched.

Somehow the fire had blown itself out. Stream couldn't see how. A fire of this intensity should have burnt through the house long before the fire brigade arrived and might easily have spread to the houses either side. Stream thought that the neighbours should thank whatever God they believed in that this had not happened. As it was, one of Gallen's men had been killed when he opened the door – probably to save his boss. The other people in the building were suffering from smoke inhalation. Two of the women had been taken to the infirmary for medical treatment, but the men, being the tough guys that they were, had refused any help.

Stream saw an empty decanter lying on its side under the bed next to a crystal tumbler. He picked up the decanter and sniffed at the top. There was a faint trace of scotch whisky, mingled with smoke, remaining inside. He picked up the tumbler. A piece of paper was stuck to the side. Stream pulled the paper away. At first, he thought it was a cigarette card. He was about to discard it when he noticed it was the picture of a woman. And the card was, in fact, photographic paper. Half of the picture was burnt, but the face and chest were still visible and Stream could see that the girl was wearing a sheer dress, showing her breasts.

'Looks like Gallen was into more than his usual racket,' Stream said. He held out the picture for Grimes to see.

'She's a looker,' Grimes said. 'Too nice for it, really.'

'Yes,' said Stream. 'Not the type.'

They searched the room for more of the postcards.

'Something this arty would take a professional,' said Grimes.

'Yes. And there's only one shop around here that does photographs,' said Stream.

'Naylor's?' Grimes said. 'He always keeps his nose clean…'

'Doesn't mean he wasn't strong-armed to do this for Gallen, though.'

'Still,' said Grimes. 'There's only the one picture, not a

stash. If he were into a pornography racket, then surely there would be more of 'em about.'

'So, he was a punter?' Stream said. 'Interesting thought, when he had a stable full of his own whores.'

'Yeah. But none of 'em look like her, do they?'

Stream said nothing, but he was curious about the girl. There was something about her. He felt as though he had seen her before but couldn't recall where. He placed the burnt photograph into the pocket of his overcoat.

A few minutes later Dr Barker arrived. Stream left Barker with Grimes to examine and wrap up the body to send it to the mortuary for a post-mortem. He made his way downstairs and into the back kitchen. Here was a den of iniquity. Empty bottles, semi-clad whores, and the surly remains of Gallen's gang, sat waiting to be interviewed.

'Anybody see anything?' Stream asked.

No one answered. Two of the whores sat huddled together at the kitchen table, a blanket pulled over their thin shoulders. One of them had singed hair. The other, a smoke-blackened face. One of the thugs stood behind them. Stream met his eyes, but the man looked down, all signs of arrogance blown away with the death of their boss.

'So, he just died in his sleep, then?'

Another thug coughed smoke out of his lungs, then reached for a half-empty bottle of whisky. He took a large swig – enough, Stream thought, to reduce anyone to another coughing fit. But it settled him, and after clearing his throat once more, he began to speak.

'He was up there alone. We dunno what happened. One minute we were all sleeping, the next we are coughing our lungs up.'

Stream nodded. 'Nothing unusual then? No late-night visitors?'

'Sally said the door was open,' said a whore in the corner. Stream recognised her as 'Doris', one of the Sackville Street girls.

'Which of you is Sally?' asked Stream.

The girls looked around, noticing for the first time that one of their number was missing.

'She ain't here,' said Doris. 'Ain't seen her since the blast that killed Ronnie.'

Realising he wasn't going to get anything more, Stream turned away, and then remembered the photograph in his pocket. He took it out and walked over to Doris.

'Is this Sally?'

Doris stared at the print. Her eyes flickered away, then back at it. 'Nah. That ain't her.'

'Do you know *this* girl?'

Doris shook her head. 'Never seen her before.'

Stream stared at her for a moment. She was hiding something, but he was sure she told the truth about not knowing the girl in the picture. He walked around the room, holding the photograph out. The thugs weren't talking, and the girls said they didn't know her. Stream was pleased that he had been right about the girl. She wasn't one of them, unless they were protecting her, and Stream didn't think they were. But it didn't help him with his investigation to have even one loose end. And the photograph was indeed a loose end.

The thugs and the girls were in a state of shock. Too thrown off kilter to have any real guile. They knew nothing, Stream was certain of that.

The smoke in the house was too unpleasant and Stream's lungs were beginning to hurt.

'Take all their names and addresses,' he said to one of the bobbies in the hallway. 'Then let them all go. I don't think there's much to go on here.'

Stream walked down the corridor and looked outside onto the garden and the street. Without realising it, he had perfectly mimicked the actions of the young prostitute, Sally, who had decided to take Gallen's demise as a sign to leave the control of the pimps and thugs.

Stream stepped outside onto the path. He found a piece of torn cloth snagged on the broken pathway. He picked it up, placed it in his pocket with the picture, then walked up to the gate. He looked up and down the street. The neighbours had returned to their homes. Now that the firemen had gone there was nothing more to see, but as he looked down the street, Stream thought he saw a young man loitering at the corner. He looked twitchy and nervous. A thin wisp of a lad, probably older than his impoverished frame made him look. As he saw the inspector looking at him, the boy slunk away, hurrying off in the direction of the town centre.

Stream frowned. The lad had been familiar but he couldn't think where he had seen him. *Some petty criminal*, he thought.

The front door opened wider behind him. Stream looked over his shoulder. He saw the doctor and a few of the bobbies bringing out the body. Stream stepped back from the gate, allowing them to exit, then he followed the body as they loaded it onto a horse-drawn cart. He looked around the street, noted the twitch of curtains across the way, then he took his notebook out of his inside pocket and began a door-to-door interview with the neighbours.

By noon Stream was no further on. It appeared that everyone had been in bed sleeping while Gallen's gang were drinking and partying in the same street. He reached the final house at the end of the street and knocked on the door.

'Good afternoon, sir. I'm Inspector Stream and I'm investigating the death of Sean Gallen at number 33,' Stream said as a man in a string vest opened the door.

'Wondered how long it would take you to get to me,' said the man.

'Did you see anything suspicious last night?' asked Stream.

'You mean apart from Gallen chasing some doxy down the street in just his dressing gown and slippers?'

Stream looked closely at the man.

'Can I take your name?' he said.

'Sure. Pete Simmons. I'm a dock worker. Was on a late shift last night.'

'You saw Mr Gallen?'

'Yeah.'

'Chasing a girl, you say?'

'Well … it was hard to miss him, really. He was shouting like the drunken scum that he was. Yelling at the girl to stop running.'

'She was running from him?'

'Yeah. In that "catch me" sorta way. If you get my meaning…'

'I do. Had you seen her before?'

'Well, that's partly why I noticed her, really. She didn't look like … the others he has around there. And it was a bit weird, the way they ran round the block then… Well, they came back and she was leading him like a dumb animal.'

'Can you describe her?'

'Not really. Clothes were like any girl you might see – brown coat, a hat pulled down over her face. Young, I'd say, but definitely not a street girl. At least, not by her dress.'

'You didn't see her face?' Stream asked.

'No … except…' said Simmons.

'Yes?'

'She passed under the streetlamp there. I had the door open, was having a smoke on the doorstep, as the missus doesn't like it inside the house. I thought the girl looked at me. But I couldn't… It was a trick of the light, really. Her face looked peculiar.'

Stream stopped writing on his notepad and looked back at Simmons. 'What d'you mean?'

'It was all sorta fuzzy, like…'

Stream probed Simmons a little longer but could get nothing more from him. As he closed his notepad one final question occurred to him.

'You say the girl led him back to the house? And you saw them go back inside?'

Simmons nodded. 'That's right.'

'Did you see her come out again?' asked Stream.

Simmons frowned for a moment while he thought about the question. 'I was still out here when the blast happened. It fair shook the street. Then I seen one of those girls, one of the tarts, running out like the devil was after her. I got me boy up and he was the one what ran for the fire brigade. After that they all came out. But no. I never saw that girl. She never came out at all.'

'Thank you for your help,' Stream said.

'Not a problem. Just hoping that means we can now have a nice street again. When that scum moved in, the neighbourhood went to shit,' said Simmons.

Stream nodded and left.

He went back inside the house and asked his men to do a

thorough search of every room. If the girl in brown didn't come out, then she must still be inside somewhere.

Chapter Fourteen

Toby Naylor woke with a start. His head hurt, as though he had been drinking cheap ale all night, and his throat was sore and parched. Light streamed through the back door window, and he threw back the blanket as though it were choking him. His body felt feverishly hot. His lungs burned as he heaved in air. For a moment he forgot where he was. And then, as his bleary eyes adjusted to the daylight, he looked around the room and recalled that he was sleeping downstairs because he had given up his room the night before for Rosie.

His mind was a blank after that, though he recalled the remnants of a horrible dream. He felt a terrible sense of dread as he remembered the dream. His chest hurt. His muscles felt sore and strained, as though he had tried to lift some excessively heavy weight. Vague images of trees and branches, dried-out wood, flittered through his mind, but he couldn't make sense of them.

He tried to sit, and the room spun until he closed his eyes again.

At that moment he heard the steady tread of small feet on

the stairs that ran just outside the room. Rosie came in a few seconds later. She looked fresh and lovely, as though she had slept well.

'Oh! I'm sorry!' she said, seeing Toby still lying on the chaise.

'That's all right. I'm awake.' His voice was hoarse. His throat hurt. A lot. It was bruised inside. He forced himself up into a sitting position, but his ribs felt sore.

'Thank you for letting me stay,' she said.

'Did you sleep well?'

'I completely blacked out. Don't think I've ever felt that tired before. Or scared.'

'What was it that really scared you last night?' Toby asked.

Rosie shrugged. 'Told you. Thought something was following me.'

'Some*thing*?'

'Yeah. Couldn't see it properly, but it felt like…' She shrugged again. 'It's silly, really. Like you said, things look better in the light of day. Now I'm sure I imagined everything.'

Toby didn't pursue it further. He stood and walked gingerly over to the sink. There he pumped water into the bowl, swilled his face, dried it on a towel and filled the kettle. When he turned, Rosie had lit the stove and she took the kettle from him.

'If you need to freshen up, I can make tea,' said Rosie.

Tea was brewing in the pot and a fire was in the hearth when Toby returned. He had changed into a fresh suit, ready to face his clients for the day. He felt better after washing and changing, but he was still very tired.

Rosie sat down at the table and poured tea for them both.

'I ought to go,' she said. 'Need to change my clothes before I see my mother.'

'How is she?' asked Toby. 'You never said what was wrong with her.'

'Still very sick. The doctors don't know what's wrong. That's part of the problem.'

'Rosie, I want to help you. Let me give you some money.'

Rosie looked up over her teacup and smiled. 'That's kind of you, Mr Naylor, but I can't take your money. I have to earn it. Maybe I can do a few photographs for you today. Then we will both be square with each other.'

'You don't have to do that. I know you're not that type of girl, really. In fact, I think I may destroy all the negatives of you. Let me help you.'

Rosie shook her head. 'No. And that would be silly, considering you earn money from them. I have to *earn* the money. You understand that, don't you?'

Toby didn't understand.

'If you give me the money, then I will *owe* you. I don't want that kind of pressure. It's hard enough as it is.'

'You won't owe me anything. I told you, it's a gift. No strings.'

Rosie put down her cup and stood. She went into the back room and returned after a few moments wearing a pink satin dressing gown.

'Take some pictures,' she said again. 'Then I can take your money.'

Toby sighed. Then he stood and began to set up the camera while Rosie moved the blankets from the chaise. When he was ready, she removed the dressing gown. She was wearing nothing but a pale pink ribbon tied around her throat.

'Want to make some real money?' she said, and he was shocked by how similar her words were to those spoken by the dream Doris/Rosie. Her words sent a sick feeling into his stomach as they echoed around his memory.

'What do you have in mind?' he said finally.

'This…'

Rosie sat back on the chaise and spread her legs. He could see her sex. But still her expression was sweet, innocent. The flash went off and she didn't move. It looked as though she had been caught accidentally. It was just the type of photograph that his voyeuristic clientele would really enjoy. Toby changed the frame in the camera as Rosie changed position. As she bent over the chaise, he had a perfect view of her beautiful bottom. At the last moment, before he exposed the frame, Rosie looked back at the camera. Her expression was coy. Toby knew this one would be a winner too. As the flash exploded, the images and poses were burned into the back of his eyes. She stood now, back to the camera, head slightly turned, and just one piece of silk draped over her hip, to highlight the nudity of the rest of her body. At some point Toby realised that she had taken up the role of 'director'. He was no longer suggesting poses, she was naturally doing them; and every one of them was natural, beautiful and very arousing.

Frame after frame was used until Toby depleted his entire stock.

'Enough,' she said as they took the last one. She pulled the dressing gown back over her naked body. She looked tired, drained, as though the poses took everything she had, and all that freshness was sucked dry by the energy it took to create them.

Rosie said nothing else as she returned to the dressing room and put on her clothes.

The business day hadn't started yet, but Toby heard the

steady knock on the door in the front studio. He picked up the last of the used frames and took them into the darkroom. Then he made his way to the front door. Artie stood there, smiling.

'What you looking so happy about?' asked Toby as he opened the front door.

'All your troubles are over,' said Artie. 'At least for now!'

'What do you mean?'

'There was a fire on Church Street last night.'

'So?'

'You really don't know, do you?' Artie laughed. Toby had never seen him looking so happy.

He locked the door again and Artie all but danced into the back room. 'Gallen's dead. I was just on the street. Saw the inspector who is investigating. It'll take months for Gallen's goons to work out who's in charge, and you know what? I'm banking that they won't even remember the racket he had going with you.'

'My God! What happened? Was it a gang war?' Toby asked.

'Nah. Don't fink so. But the police are over there now. Looks like he set himself alight while smoking in bed!'

At that moment Rosie came out of the dressing room. She was fully dressed again in her own clothes. She nodded to Artie as she passed to the kitchen table.

'What's going on 'ere, then? Early session?' Artie asked.

'Yes,' said Rosie.

'We've run out of frames,' Toby said, trying to change the subject.

'Better go and make some up for the next clients, then,' said Artie. He winked at Toby as he left.

Toby was bemused by the presumption that more was happening between him and Rosie than had occurred. He shrugged as Artie went into the main studio, then he turned to find Rosie looking at him with an expectant expression.

'Oh. Sorry. You need to be paid!'

He went to fetch money from upstairs, coming back quickly with much more than usual. 'You earned it,' he said when she frowned. 'I can charge a lot more for those new pictures.'

Rosie nodded and took the money. Then she leant over and kissed him on the cheek. As she pulled away, Toby thought he smelt the faintest traces of smoke clinging to her clothes. It made him feel peculiar.

'Gallen's dead,' he told her, trying to gauge her reaction.

'Who?'

'The thug I told you about? The one that had his men watching me so he could find you. You should have no problem now. Come back whenever you like.'

'That's good, Toby.' Rosie smiled then went to the back door, slipped the lock and hurried out before he had time to react.

'Toby, eh?' said Artie from the doorway.

'What?' Toby said, confused.

'She's stopped calling you Mister Naylor.'

Toby said nothing. Smoke still clung to his nostrils and the strange thing was, he suspected Rosie didn't smoke. He went to the back door and looked out. There was no sign of her now. She had gone, disappeared, and he still knew nothing more about her. If it hadn't been for the stack of frames, he might well have imagined the whole thing. She was like a mysterious fairy that came into his life, gave him a glimpse of magic, and then completely disappeared.

'Aren't you happy, then?' Artie asked.

'Happy?'

'About Gallen. Jesus, you ain't wiv it today, are ya?'

Toby mulled over what he felt. There was a feeling of dread in the pit of his stomach. A sick darkness that spread into his gut. He hurried out back and into the outhouse, his stomach griping. He felt strangely afraid. More so now that Gallen was dead than he had when the greedy bastard was alive. Something was wrong, every instinct told him so, but he just didn't know what.

'I am pleased,' he said later as Artie put a frame into the camera.

'I should bloody fink so too. You ain't never been this lucky.'

Toby nodded, but he felt a tingle of guilt. It was so horrible to gloat over someone's death – even if the person in question was evil.

Chapter Fifteen

'Who's that?' said Elena Carter as she sat down inside the carriage and turned her head to look outside.

The second funeral was over and had been a quiet family affair which included Laura and her parents, with Mitchell and a few close cousins only. They had decided not to do a wake. Not because they didn't respect Warren or didn't want to honour his life; it was more that they just couldn't face another one so soon. After the service, after Warren was placed in the Carter tomb with his younger sister Sara, they climbed back into their carriage to drive home.

'What?' asked Laura, sitting down beside her mother.

'A girl. A girl drawing.'

Laura leaned across her mother and looked out over the gravestones. Sure enough, a young girl with long brown hair, wearing a brown coat, stood with a sketchpad. As Laura looked out, the girl began to swirl a piece of charcoal over the paper in her hands. Laura had the distinct impression the girl was drawing her.

'How peculiar,' Laura said, sitting back from the window. 'She seems to be sketching us…'

Mitchell was only halfway into the carriage when he heard the exchange. 'Girl? What girl?'

He stepped back and walked around the horses to see the girl. 'There's no one there.'

'Of course there is. Mother and I… Oh. She's gone.'

'Never mind the confounded girl,' said Harold Carter. 'Let's get back to the house. Mitchell, you'll join us for dinner, won't you?'

'Of course,' said Mitchell, climbing into the carriage.

As they drove away through the cemetery, Mitchell turned his head to look out of the carriage window. He scanned the row of tombstones, looking for any sign of the girl that Elena and Laura had seen, with no success.

She couldn't have just disappeared like that, he thought. Then, as the carriage turned onto the main road, he caught a glimpse of a brown coat, as someone turned the corner down the street. It was so fleeting that he thought he may have imagined it. By the time they arrived back at the Carter residence, he was the only person who had not dismissed her as unimportant.

'So, what did this girl look like?' Mitchell said as Stevens poured red wine into the crystal goblet beside his dinner plate.

'I think I've seen her before,' said Laura. 'She had long dark hair, loose down her back, but tied up at the front in a ribbon. To be honest, I thought it odd that she wore it like a girl half her age…'

'How old must she be?' said Elena. 'I got the impression of

youth, but you may be right, dear. It could have been the hairstyle.'

'At least twenty, I should say,' Laura said.

'You said you've seen her before? When?' asked Mitchell.

'Last week. At Sara's funeral. She was sat in the pew behind you. I'm sure it's the same girl.'

Laura continued to describe as much as she could recall about the girl she had seen. 'She was wearing the same clothing as last time. I remember the brown coat.'

Mitchell sipped his wine as Stevens and one of the servant girls began to serve food onto their plates.

'Strange thing to do, if you ask me,' said Harold Carter. 'Hanging around cemeteries and drawing the grieving family. Very odd indeed. Think I might have to speak to the chaplain about it. Can't have that kind of thing.'

Mitchell was relieved to see Laura and her family pick at the food on their plates. Warren's funeral had been traumatic, but they were bouncing back better than he might have expected after the loss they had suffered in the past few weeks.

'So how is the investigation going?' Laura asked as Stevens and the maid left the dining room.

'Slow. Stream is reluctantly passing on information. But I managed to get the name of the witness that saw Warren...'

'Oh good. So you'll talk to them?' Laura asked.

'Yes. Already arranged for tomorrow.'

After dinner they retired to the drawing room. Mitchell found himself sitting opposite Laura, with Elena by his side, but after sipping half-heartedly at a glass of sherry, Elena excused herself.

'I'm so very tired. I hope you don't mind,' she said. 'This has all been so...'

'No need to explain,' Mitchell said, standing up to take her hand.

Elena wished them both good night and took her leave.

'I should go…' said Mitchell.

'No. Please stay a little longer. I'm not tired. I feel … rather wound up. I can't explain why,' said Laura. 'And we aren't really alone, if that is your concern. Father is still smoking in the study.'

Mitchell sank back down onto the sofa. There was a moment of awkwardness and his eyes scanned the room, looking for something to talk about.

'Oh!' he said as his eyes fell onto the photograph of Laura, Sara and Warren. It was half obscured by the yucca plant that had grown excessively tall since it was placed there.

Laura looked towards the point that drew Mitchell's gaze. 'What is it?'

Mitchell stood. He walked towards the picture and pushed aside the leaves of the plant. 'The picture? Oh … you had two of them taken?'

'What are you talking about?'

'This is a different one…'

'No. There's only ever been one photograph…'

Mitchell stared at the photograph. It was impossible. This had to be a different picture. But the frame was the same. The image identical in size. Now, though, Warren and Sara had moved. Mitchell recalled that Warren had been sitting in a chair, facing the camera, as Sara and Laura stood either side of him. Sara had been smiling broadly, but Laura had only a discreet curve to her lips. Warren had appeared formal and sincere. Now Sara also had her hand on her hip, and she appeared to be laughing at the camera. Her eyes held a strange and sinister gleam. She looked dishevelled. She looked insane.

Warren was the biggest shock of all, though. His calm, sincere expression had altered. He looked worried, afraid, harried. His hair was unruly, clothing crumpled. Just as he had been the night he appeared at Mitchell's home, asking for his help.

Laura's face was the same. Serene, beautiful, and just the hint of a smile.

'Good lord!' Laura said as she came up behind him. 'That isn't the picture we had taken.'

'I knew you'd still be up,' said Mitchell. 'Can I come in?'

'Of course,' said Neeraj, bowing his head as he stepped back to allow Mitchell entrance. 'The Sahib is asleep.'

'That's fine. I came to see you.'

Neeraj closed the door and they went into the conservatory at the back of the house.

'Can I get you some refreshment, Mitchell-Sahib?

'No. I don't need anything except some advice.'

Neeraj lost his public formality, and they sat together like the old friends they were.

'If I can help, I will.'

'Something happened tonight. Something I can't explain.'

Neeraj nodded.

'I need you to tell me a story, Neeraj. One that I recall you shared when we first moved here from India.'

Neeraj frowned. 'I have told you many stories, Mitchell-Sahib.'

Mitchell tried to cast his mind back to the moment that had sparked Neeraj's words of wisdom. He remembered he had come back from school with a passion for art. Proudly he had begun to show Neeraj his drawings. The Indian admired the sketches of the family corgi, the vase of flowers in the hallway, and the most interesting one of all, the exterior of their house. But as Mitchell sat at the kitchen table and attempted to sketch his Indian companion, Neeraj covered his face and refused to let him continue.

'Whatever's wrong with you?' asked Mitchell. 'It's only a sketch. I just want to capture you.'

Neeraj took the charcoal away from Mitchell's keen fingers and placed it and the half-drawn picture aside.

'Don't you remember the story I told you? The day Bhakti died?'

Mitchell felt a pang of sadness as he recalled his Indian nursemaid. But the day had been traumatic and he could barely remember anything beyond finding her dead.

'Once there was a man who lived in a village far from the sea,' Neeraj prompted, and Mitchell knew that one of Neeraj's unique stories was to be told. They all took place in some nondescript village, as though it were a blank canvas to hang every moral on.

'The man liked to create images,' Neeraj continued. 'Using a fallen branch, he would copy still objects that he saw around him. Animals. Plants. Buildings. Just as you have done, Mitchell-Sahib. But these images became too easy to copy, and the wind always destroyed them, or children playing outside would trample and crush his efforts. He never felt that he could truly preserve the images. After a while he began to experiment with different materials. He charred a branch and drew black outlines on stones and pebbles, but the colourless images didn't satisfy him. Then he made himself a brush using hair taken from the tail of a horse. He mixed spices with water, mud, egg yolks. Creating colours and textures to give the images depth and warmth. And he began to daub this on small smooth rocks that he found around the outskirts of the village.

'He captured once more the goat tied to the well, or the bloom of a flower outside the window of his hut, or the rise of a mountain in the distance. But this time the colour made them special, interesting, and soon the villagers were admiring his skills. He gave away the small rocks and they placed them around the insides of their homes. The colourful pictures brightened the huts of his friends, and so they began to call him the Image-Maker.

'One day the Image-Maker found a long piece of bark in the woods as he searched for more flat stones, and he began to see the possibility of putting images on the wood. By then he had exhausted the surrounding landscape, the huts in the village and the animals he commonly saw. And so, he created his first image of a person. She was the sister of his friend. A sweet, quiet girl, soon to be married, and the Image-Maker thought that this might make a suitable present to cheer the home of the newlyweds. Secretly he copied her as she drew water from the well, or sat milking the goat in the field beside the village, until he devised an image that captured her fresh sweetness perfectly.

'On her wedding day, the Image-Maker presented the bride and groom with the bark. It was a beautiful picture. He had captured her well and his friend, the girl's brother, was also pleased with the Image-Maker's kindness.

'After that many of the villagers wanted their images drawn on bark, and soon the Image-Maker was overwhelmed with requests that he tried his best to fulfil. He was much loved by them for his talent and vision.

'Many months passed and the Image-Maker created more and more bark drawings. The bride, in the meantime, began to change. Rumours abounded that the marriage had proved to be a bad match and this was the reason for her obvious unhappiness. She was missing the sparkle she once had. She was no longer the happy, sweet girl she had been. Instead, she turned into a mean-spirited shrew. Constantly challenging her husband. She was slovenly, the home they lived in soon fell into decay, and sometimes her husband would come home and find no food prepared.

'Time passed and a holy man came to the village. He was travelling to a sacred shrine in the mountains. As with all holy men, the villagers were glad to see him. They gave him food. They invited him into their homes, and the man whose wife was a shrew invited the holy man to visit them, in the hope that by showing him hospitality they would receive a blessing. You see, the man loved his wife. He wanted to be happy, and to make her happy, but was unable to do so. The holy man accepted the invitation and as he walked into the home of the couple, he was shocked to find it in such disarray. The wife was particularly angry that the husband had brought someone home without telling her, but she served the holy man, saying nothing shrewish at all. The holy man, however, knew that something was wrong with her. She was so normal, so ordinary, but there was no kindness in her eyes. The holy man asked to look around the house. The wife objected. She became irritable and afraid. Eventually the husband took her arm and led her outside, leaving the holy man within.

'After a few minutes the holy man came out. He held in his hands the piece of bark containing the woman's image. The husband looked at it. "That is not the same picture!" he said. And indeed, the image had changed. The sweet and vibrant girl once captured there was now the shrew. She had around her a strange white sheen, a ghostly figure of herself. As though her spirit had become disembodied and was trying to get back inside. "We must destroy this image," said the holy man. "But first we must place your wife's soul back into her body."

'The man was horrified and afraid. "But how did she lose it? How is this possible?" he asked. The holy man explained that he didn't know, but he knew that the wife needed to be tied down. The empty vessel would do anything to stop the soul returning.

'The villagers gathered as the holy man performed the ritual. The wife screamed and fought, but they overpowered her and she was tied to a chair near the well. Water was poured over her head in an act of purification and the piece of bark was placed by her feet. The holy man sat crossed-legged before her and prayed and chanted. Hours later the holy man was still searching for the woman's spirit. He felt it nearby but couldn't call it from the prison in which it had been captured. "But where is it?" asked the husband.

'The holy man looked at the bark image once more. He noticed that the white ghost around the woman had moved. It pointed to the hut of the Image-Maker. "There!" said the holy man. The villagers and the husband looked around. The Image-Maker was the only person not among them. Murmurs of confusion went up around the crowd. Where was he? Why had he not appeared to support the holy man and help the young couple? Surely this was not his fault? They couldn't believe it. He was such a kind, caring man.

'A group of them gathered by his door and knocked. But

the man did not come out, and so they opened the door and went inside. They found the man sitting unmoving in his chair by the stove. When they spoke to him, he did not respond. The young wife began to yell that they should "leave him alone". That he had nothing to do with this, but the holy man asked them to bring the man out immediately.

'They led him towards the tied-up wife. But the Image-Maker made no sign of recognition. "What have you done to this woman?" asked the holy man.

'"Nothing," replied the Image-Maker. "I don't think I have ever seen her before."

'The crowd murmured in confusion. They had stones, bark drawings and all manner of trinkets from the Image-Maker that each of them valued. But now he was a shadow of his former self. The holy man was in a dilemma. The man did not appear to have committed any crime, but the woman was clearly possessed. As the man approached and saw the bark drawing, a strange change came across him. "Give it back to her! Give it back!" he yelled. He became so agitated, that several of the villagers had to hold him to prevent him from throwing himself at the holy man.

'The holy man looked around the village. "Who else has allowed this man to draw their image?" he asked. Several of them nodded and murmured. "Bring all of the images," the holy man said. 'I want to see them.' The villagers complied and soon all the bark drawings were at the feet of the holy man. He looked at the images. Some of them were clear and simple, but a few of them showed signs of a faint white shadow slipping away from the figure, but unlike the wife, they were all half over the original image and not completely separated. "We must destroy these," said the holy man, and despite the objections he piled the bark up in the centre of the village and set them alight.

The Image-Maker pulled free of the villagers that held him and ran away into the forest. He screamed as though the fire that burnt was burning him also. He was never seen again.'

'What happened to the wife?' Mitchell asked.

'She became kind and loving again,' Neeraj explained.

Now in the present, Mitchell recalled the details of the story. He didn't know why but he felt he had to show Neeraj the image of Laura, Sara and Warren. He placed the thing he was holding down on the table, then peeled away the blue velvet fabric wrapped around it.

Neeraj saw the brown wooden frame first, then he noticed the images in the centre.

'What is this?' Neeraj asked.

'It's a photograph,' Mitchell said. 'It's all the rage at the moment. All my friends have been having them. Laura and I planned to have one for our wedding.'

Neeraj picked up the frame as though he thought it would burn his fingers. 'The Image-Maker,' he said as he studied the picture. 'But how?'

'You remember the story?' Mitchell asked.

'Of course.'

'I need to know, Neeraj. Who told you the story and why?'

Neeraj nodded as he studied the picture. 'There is white around Miss Laura,' he said finally.

'Yes,' Mitchell said. 'What does it mean?'

'It means that they were captured. All of them.'

'Of course the image of them was captured in the photograph? I know … but…'

'Not just their image, but their spirit,' Neeraj said.

Mitchell picked up the picture. 'I don't believe in all of that hocus-pocus. I do think someone has done something to this picture, though, to make us believe that they have lost their souls,' Mitchell said. 'I just want to know where the story came from. It might explain who would do something like this.'

Neeraj stared at Mitchell in surprise. 'You don't listen, Mitchell. They have been caught by the Image-Maker. He will control them like puppets. Make them do things, and they may never even remember doing them.'

Mitchell thought back to Sara's behaviour. How she had lied about her relationship with Mitchell and how, the next day, she had denied all knowledge of the event to her brother Warren. But why would this happen? Who would do this? He couldn't believe it was possible.

'You need to find the person who captured this image,' Neeraj said. 'Then you have to destroy it before their eyes.'

Mitchell blinked. He was torn between what Neeraj said and his own lack of belief in the supernatural.

'Why?'

'Because this thing, this demon that takes men's souls, cannot hold onto them if the image is destroyed. It has to be by fire, and the picture has to burn until it is completely destroyed. Then you must scatter the ashes to the four winds.'

'It's probably all a coincidence. Surely if this … soul thief … could do as you say, then why is Laura fine? Why hasn't it used her too?' Mitchell said, trying not to offend Neeraj by outright denial of his beliefs.

Neeraj looked down at the picture.

'He hasn't used her *yet*; it doesn't mean he won't.'

'How do you know that?' Mitchell said, annoyed with himself for continuing the conversation. It was just superstitious nonsense. Why was he even listening to it? Why had he come here anyway? *I don't know,* he thought. *I needed reassurance.* But what Neeraj was telling him was far from reassuring and it threatened everything he wanted to believe about the world he lived in.

'Here,' said Neeraj. His brown finger traced a faint white glow that shone around Laura's head. It looked like an artist's impression of a female saint.

Mitchell frowned at the picture. He couldn't imagine Laura losing her mind as Sara and Warren had in the end. But as he looked closer, he could make out a faint white shadow behind the two dead siblings, and the shadow made no contact at all with the figure in front.

'It's not too late,' Neeraj said. 'But you must act quickly!'

Despite himself, Mitchell felt the urgency that Neeraj was trying to convey. He tried to fight against the certainty he could see in his old friend's eyes. A cold dread filled his heart with fear and no logical explanation could dispel the anxiety.

Chapter Sixteen

The photograph on the wall was tilted sideways slightly, as though the person who had hung it didn't like straight lines. It was large, in a basic oak frame that had been varnished with a dark wood stain. It was the cheapest frame that the shop offered because Sophia and Stephen hadn't been able to afford more. As it was, it had taken several months to save up for, and Sophia had forgone a lot of small luxuries to own her very own photograph.

Married life hadn't been exactly as Sophia had hoped. Stephen's expected promotion at the law firm hadn't happened and the meagre salary he brought home as a mere clerk was barely enough to live on, let alone allow her to have all the fine things she had hoped she would have. It got worse when she had learnt about his addictions. He liked to drink too much and, she suspected, gamble. Sophia had learnt early on to make sure she got the week's housekeeping every Friday before Stephen went out to the gentlemen's club. She never understood why he went to the club, but when asked, he made some vague references about how it was good for his career to mingle with colleagues. 'You wouldn't understand, Sophia,' he told her in a dismissive and often patronising tone.

It was difficult for Sophia, especially when Stephen came home drunk. She soon began locking the bedroom door on those nights. She couldn't bear the smell of the ale on his breath, nor the awful, rough fumbling that happened if she let him in. The next day he would be contrite, but it didn't help to mend the slow deterioration of their relationship. Then Sophia had seen the photography shop appear on the high street. She had spent many market days gazing into the window, looking at the framed photograph examples. This was something that she could have that would stop her friends from casting her pitying glances during their weekly tea mornings. It would be something she could show when it was her turn to have everyone around. It would make her dingy home so much brighter.

It hadn't been difficult to persuade Stephen to come with her. She told him that they wanted free models, but really she had made a deal with that nice man, Mister Naylor, paying a little every week until she had cleared the cost of the photograph and frame. Naylor and his assistant were sworn to secrecy. Sophia got the impression she wasn't the first wife to tender this lie. So when they turned up for the session, she and Stephen posed in their best Sunday clothes, a picture of marital bliss and sincerity.

The next week, picture framed and in place over the fireplace, Sophia had grandly shown her friends.

'Stephen treated us because he's getting a promotion soon,' she had boasted.

Of course, the promotion never materialised and as the weeks went on, Sophia had become convinced that it was obvious to everyone that her husband was a wastrel. She just didn't know what to do about it.

But the picture still gave her pleasure. It was the only thing in life that she felt she truly deserved. And she looked so pretty on it. So much more so than the pale, pinched creature she saw in her looking glass every morning these days. In fact, she was convinced she was coming down with something. She felt so weak and wan, not like herself at all. Like she was lacking something.

She stared at the picture now. She loved the pristine blouse, with the expensive lace collar, which was part of her trousseau. And the expensive brooch she wore at her throat; an item passed down from her grandmother. Not that she would be getting many new and nice things from now on unless Stephen's promotion happened soon.

'Where's dinner?' Stephen said.

Sophia jumped as he entered. He was home early, and dinner wasn't quite ready.

'It won't be for another hour,' she said. 'You're home early.'

'Thanks for stating the obvious,' he said. 'I always knew you were a clever girl, Sophia.'

Sophia wasn't sure how to respond, even though she heard the irony dripping from his words.

'I'll go and check on everything in the kitchen,' she said.

'Do that and hurry it up. I need to go out again.'

Sophia put the pan of prepared vegetables on the stove, then opened the oven to look at the meagre piece of meat she had acquired from the butchers. The small piece of beef was almost cooked. It would just be a matter of waiting for the vegetables now.

She returned to the drawing room and found Stephen staring at the picture.

'You don't look anything like that anymore. You've turned into a hag, barely a year of marriage passed.'

His words stung, but when Sophia looked at the picture she felt better. Nothing mattered if she had this. Her beauty had been captured there and it would always be perfection.

'I've been a little under the weather,' she said.

'How long will dinner be?' he said.

'Not long now. Shall I make us a pot of tea?'

'Port would be nicer,' Stephen said as he continued to look at the photograph.

Sophia glanced over at the empty decanter, a present from her parents. 'We … don't have any.'

'What do you do with the money I give you? I get no comforts at all!' Stephen said. He didn't turn but his voice was angry, accusatory. Sophia wondered if he had somehow learnt that she had paid for the photograph after all.

Sophia felt the tears welling up in her eyes. 'I can barely afford to feed us on what you bring home.'

'Well, you can expect even less from now on. I've been fired.'

Sophia stared at Stephen's back. She couldn't believe what she was hearing. No job. How would they live? What if her friends found out? They would have to ask her parents to help, and the shame that would bring on her was unimaginable.

'What … happened?' she asked.

'I was sick of them. Sick of their lies and promises. So, I asked for a rise and they laughed in my face. Said I wasn't worthy and that I was being paid too much already.'

'That's awful!' she said, feeling genuine sympathy for him. 'After all the hard work you've put in for them.'

Sophia placed a hand on his arm, trying to comfort him, even though she was in a complete state of panic.

Stephen turned around. His expression was so unpleasant, Sophia looked away. She saw hatred in his eyes and not just for his former employers, but for her also.

'Give me that brooch,' he said, pointing back to the photograph.

'Why?'

Stephen's hand lashed out, the back connected with Sophia's face, and she crumpled to the floor, shocked rather than hurt by the slap that echoed around the room.

'I said give it to me. We need money. I know someone who would buy it.'

The tears came then. She expected his sympathy, hoped for his regret, but the only response he gave was more dark anger.

She scrambled up from the floor and hurried from the room. Her brooch was in her jewellery box in the bedroom. She was shaking, knees weak as she climbed the stairs, his voice ringing harshly in her ears.

What had happened? He had been so nice, so kind before they married. But since then, Sophia had experienced nothing but deep disappointment. She reached the bedroom and stumbled inside, hurrying to the dressing table. There she found her jewellery box. She picked it up, opened the lid and gazed down at the brooch. It was only jewellery. It didn't matter really, did it? As long as they had money to live on until Stephen found a new job. She glanced at her face in the mirror on the dresser. Her face was red, evidence of the slap. Tears burst down her cheeks once more. She had never been hit before, certainly not by her husband. It was all so horrible and unfair. She didn't know what to do. She could leave him, return to her parents, tell them everything. But the thought of it made her feel such deep, dark pain and shame. She couldn't possibly do that. It would be a scandal and her mother would never allow it.

She looked down at the brooch. It was the only thing she had of her grandmother's. She had loved it ever since she was a child and the thought that this would go to a stranger, that she would never see it again, made her sad and angry. She bought into the anger, pushed back the sadness and fear. Her heart became a rock of stone sitting in her chest.

He had done this. Stephen was a failure. Why hadn't she seen that all along? Better that he made her a widow, than he shamed her with his failings. No one, not even her mother, would object to her going home again if Stephen died.

A smile formed on Sophia's lips. That was the answer. An accident, or … her mind stuttered over the thought, the smile dropped briefly from her face. How? How could she make this an accident?

Then the smile returned; a new cunning lit up her now dry eyes.

She walked to the top of the stairs.

'Stephen? I'm searching for more things for you to sell. I think there is a bottle of wine in the cellar. One father gave us to start our own collection. I'm sure we both need a drink after all of this bad news.'

She heard Stephen come out of the drawing room and then she crept downstairs. She went into the drawing room, picked up the crystal port decanter and walked along the hallway to wait at the top of the cellar stairs.

Stephen was almost at the top by the time she got there. He was holding a candle to light his way. 'Where is it? I can't find it.'

Sophia smiled. 'Turn around and light the way. I'll follow and show you.'

As he turned Sophia swung the decanter as hard as she could. It connected with Stephen's skull, a resounding crack echoed in the stairwell and he dropped the candlestick as he began to fall. She watched him roll down the stairs. It was almost in slow motion, as though time was standing still so that she had the best view of his demise. He hit the bottom: head smacking down on the hard-tiled floor.

Although the candle had gone out, Sophia could still make out the shape of Stephen's prone body. It didn't move. She closed and locked the cellar door. Then took the decanter she was holding into the kitchen. Surprisingly the expensive, thick crystal hadn't broken. There were blood and clumps of hair in the grooves of the cut glass. She pumped water into the sink and submerged the exterior, rinsing away the hair and blood until the crystal shone again. Then she patted it dry, returned to the drawing room and placed it back in its pride of place on the black inlaid wooden sideboard.

She glanced over at the picture above the hearth. Her once sincere self was now smiling. Sophia frowned. Was it possible that the photograph had changed? Her eyes fell on the figure of Stephen. In the picture there was something wrong with his head. She reached up, pulled the photograph down so roughly that she accidentally tore out one of the hanging clips.

The more she looked at it, the more she felt the evidence of her guilt was there for all to see. No longer did she see herself as beautiful. Now her face looked mean, grotesque. She hated the picture and all it represented.

Sophia looked around the room. No one must see this. She had to hide it – but where? Her mind ran through the possibilities. If she hid the photograph anywhere in the house, it may be found when she packed up to move back to her parents. And she knew they would insist on helping her, despite her protestations.

All she wanted to do was go home. She looked down at the weak fire in the hearth. There was barely enough coal to keep it going during the day and so she had suffered the cold, only making it up an hour or two before Stephen's return.

Her eyes ran over the photograph again. She had loved this. Really loved it. Now it was a monstrosity. It was the only thing between her and the possibility of living a peaceful single life as a widow.

She opened the back of the cheap frame, pulled out the thick photographic paper from inside, then she crumpled the picture and threw it into the fire. The paper was highly flammable and it caught immediately. Sophia stepped back and watched it burn. She felt sick, queasy, as though some evil thing was squirming inside her, trying to get out. She staggered back, falling into the chair by the hearth. Her hands and face began to burn, as though she was in the flames and not the photograph. She screamed, slapping at the imagined flames as they licked up over her face and hands. She felt her hair catch; burning ash coughed out from the fire and died on the tiles. Sophia watched the embers smoulder, and the sensation of burning diminished.

She stared blankly at the weak fire. Her mind emptying of all the bad things that had happened that day. Then she stood up, looked at the clock on the mantelpiece and realised it was almost time for Stephen to return home from work. She went into the kitchen and turned off the vegetables in confusion. She didn't remember switching them on.

She looked around the kitchen. All was in order, yet she felt the strangest sensation, as though something had changed. As she walked back to the drawing room, shivering from the cold of the house, her eyes fell on the closed cellar door. She was sure she had some wine down there, left over from their wedding. Something her father had given her for special occasions.

Sophia felt a strange compulsion. Today there would be reason to celebrate. She picked up a candlestick from the hallway table, lit a match and waved it over the candle. She wondered where the matching candlestick had gone. Strange, because she hadn't moved it.

The cellar door was locked. Sophia turned the key and pulled the door open. Her foot was on the top step when she noticed the body at the bottom. She stepped back, fear and anxiety clutching at her chest. Then she let out a heartfelt scream.

A few hours later, Sophia watched as Stephen's body was removed, and the mortuary cart drew away. They'd questioned her, of course, but she didn't know anything. Now she was a widow. Penniless. Her only course was to return to her parents. She'd probably have to sell her grandmother's brooch to pay for the funeral, too!

But a sense of relief came over her at the thought of never having to see Stephen again.

'What happened to your face?' her mother asked as Sophia came into the drawing room.

Her mother had made tea and was now pouring it into the china cups she'd given Sophia as part of her wedding dowry. For a few seconds, Sophia couldn't remember why her mother was there. Then she recalled that one of the neighbours had sent word to her parents while she waited for the authorities to arrive.

Her father was now taking care of everything with the police inspector outside.

Sophia glanced at her reflection in the wall mirror. She saw the blossoming bruise on her cheek but didn't answer.

'No need to explain,' her mother said. 'The brute! I'm sorry … but this *accident* was probably the best thing that could have happened. We should have stopped you marrying him when we heard of his habits…'

'Habits?' Sophia asked, even as the truth dawned on her. She felt a surge of resentment, even anger towards her mother.

'Of course, you must come back home while you grieve,' her mother said.

Sophia took a sip of the tea and sank into her own world of deceit, hatred and contempt. It was then that she began to plan what she would do to her parents. After all, as an only child, she would inherit everything. Then, she would never be poor again.

Sophia caught herself. *What a hideous thought!* She placed her teacup down on the table and stood up. Looking at herself in the mirror, she smoothed her ruffled hair. Her eyes fell on a shadow that lurked above her, and then, just as suddenly, it disappeared.

Sophia felt a sense of release, as though something evil had held her in its thrall, taking what it needed, and now had passed on, as though it was as bored with her pathetic life as she was.

Chapter Seventeen

Inspector Stream was in his office when Mitchell arrived early the next morning.

'I'm glad you've come in,' said Stream. 'I'm investigating a case that I think you could help me with.'

Mitchell sat down opposite Stream without being asked. 'Really?'

Stream opened the folder on his desk, removed the picture he had found at Sean Gallen's house and placed it down on the desk in front of Mitchell.

'Found near the body of a local thug, Sean Gallen. Heard of him?'

'Yes,' said Mitchell. 'And I suspect you already know that I had dealings with him last year.'

'Quite so,' said Stream.

Mitchell had come across Gallen twelve months ago on a missing-person case. Gallen's gang had snatched a young girl and put her out on the streets. A nasty case. One which Mitchell was able to solve, returning the poor girl home to very grateful parents.

'You said "body"? Gallen's dead?'

Stream filled him in on the case.

Mitchell looked down at the photograph of the girl. She looked familiar somehow, but he was sure he didn't know her. 'Street girl?'

'No. At least not in Manchester. We don't know where she came from. But I think there's a link to this card and the fire that killed Gallen.'

Mitchell handed back the picture. 'I want to come to Naylor's with you.'

'Mmmm. I always knew you were a bright one,' Stream said. 'I'm going there now. But don't get under foot. Have you spoken to the witness yet that saw Warren kill himself?'

'No. With the funeral, I hadn't quite…'

'Well, you're going to kill two birds with one stone today. Artie Weddon works with Naylor. He's his assistant.'

'That's interesting.'

'I also spotted him at the end of Church Street when we were bringing out Gallen's body. I didn't recognise him at first … but … he has form, even though he's been keeping his nose clean since he's been working at the photography shop.'

'You think there's a connection?' Mitchell asked.

'I don't believe in coincidences. Something is going on at Naylor's. Whether there is a link, I don't know. But we have to explore every avenue. Personally, I don't really care about Gallen. The world is a better place without that Salford scum in it. But pornography, that's a different matter,' Stream said.

A young family consisting of a woman, a man and two small children were posed before the camera as Mitchell and Stream entered Naylor's photography shop. There was a high-pitched whirring sound and the flash exploded, lighting up the room, blinding everyone with its hot brightness. The smallest of the two children, a little boy, burst into tears as the light stung his eyes.

'I'm sure we will have it,' said Artie, lifting his head out from underneath the camera cloth.

He saw Stream and Mitchell, and nodded. 'I'll just take this into the back,' he said, removing the used frame from the camera.

Immediately afterwards, Toby came in, having been alerted by Artie that the inspector was there.

'If you can wait a minute, gentlemen,' he said. 'I just need to give Mr and Mrs Grahams a receipt for their photograph.'

The couple soon left, taking their unhappy children with them, and Stream wasted no time, or subtlety, on his interrogation of Toby.

'How can I help you, inspector?' said Toby.

'Sean Gallen is dead.'

'Yes, I heard,' Toby said. 'Don't know what it has to do with me, though.'

'We found something rather interesting in the ashes,' Stream continued.

'Oh yeah?'

'A photograph,' said Stream. 'And I believe you took it.'

'I take lots of photographs,' said Toby. 'Doesn't make me a criminal.'

Mitchell said nothing as Stream talked to Toby, but he wandered around the shop, looking at displayed copies of photographs.

'Looking for anything in particular?' said Artie.

He had appeared beside him, and Mitchell realised that

Stream and Toby were still in the thick of a fencing-match discussion about his possible involvement with Gallen.

'How often do you change your displays?' asked Mitchell.

Toby shrugged. 'When we need to.'

Mitchell looked back at the pictures. 'Why? Do they fade? Or warp, perhaps?'

Mitchell didn't see the frown that appeared on Artie's brow, because he was still looking at the display photographs. When he glanced back at the young man, his features were strangely serene.

'We do good quality 'ere,' said Artie. 'You only have to ask some of our customers.'

'I intend to. But I'd like to talk about someone who was here six months ago.'

Mitchell watched Artie's face closely as he mentioned Laura, Sara and Warren's visit.

'Don't remember 'em,' Artie said.

'Strange, only I'd have thought you would remember them, since you witnessed Mr Carter throwing himself into the canal.'

Artie narrowed his eyes. 'That was an awful fing to see. Been trying to blank it from me memory ever since.'

'Tell me, do you keep copies of all the photographs you take?' Mitchell asked. 'I'd like to see the oldest ones you have.'

'I'm afraid not,' said Toby, overhearing the conversation.

'What do you do with them?' asked Stream. He darted a glance at Mitchell, wondering where this line of questioning was going but he was willing to follow it, since his attempts to browbeat Toby had failed miserably.

'We burn them,' said Artie.

'We only like to have current photographs on display. But we usually keep the best ones up for a few months. Sometimes it encourages the customer to buy another one,' explained Toby.

'Why would they need another picture?' asked Stream.

'Sometimes relatives want a copy. Especially grandparents, when children are in the pictures. Reprints are quite popular now.'

'Reprints?' Mitchell asked.

'Yes. We don't make a copy of every single photo, but we do keep the negatives,' Toby explained.

'I see. Can I look at these negatives?'

Toby shrugged. 'If it will help you with your enquiry… Artie, can you get the negative box and bring it into the shop?'

Artie gave a surly nod and went off into the back of the shop. He soon returned with a box and Toby took it from him. 'That will be all, Artie. Why don't you tidy up in the back, please?'

Artie left but Mitchell noted that he didn't appear too happy to do so.

Toby led Stream and Mitchell to a table near the door. He placed the metal box on it and took off the lid. The sun was streaming in through the glass door. Toby showed Inspector Stream and Mitchell one of the negatives held up to the light which streamed through the strange transparent paper. Mitchell could make out the picture of a young couple. The next one was of a small child sitting on a rug. Stream and Mitchell glanced through each of the negatives in turn, but neither of them spotted anything out of the ordinary.

'What do you hope to find?' asked Toby.

'A girl,' Stream said.

'There are many girls in there,' Toby said.

'I'm looking for a particular girl.'

Stream reached into his pocket, pulled out his notebook

and opened it. Inside was the picture card. He held it out to Toby, who took a sharp intake of breath before he could stop himself.

'You know this girl, don't you?' said Stream.

Toby shook his head. 'No. I was just shocked. She's half-naked!'

'You see, Sean Gallen was involved in something very seedy. I mean, what respectable girl would pose for something like this?'

'I wouldn't know,' Toby said.

'It strikes me that you would know,' Stream continued. 'That you are the only man capable of producing something like this in the area.'

At that moment Artie came back into the front studio. 'All clean and tidy, boss,' he said.

Toby met Artie's gaze and Mitchell noticed some signal, or code, pass between them as Artie winked one eye.

'Inspector, why don't I show you my darkroom?' Toby said.

'Darkroom?'

'It's where I develop all of the negatives and turn them into pictures.'

Toby walked towards the back of the shop and Stream began to follow. He paused and then looked back at Mitchell. 'You coming?'

'I think I'll continue looking at these,' Mitchell said. He had the feeling that if there had been anything to hide in the back, Artie would have removed it already, which meant there was nothing to see in the back rooms. He thought that his time would be better spent looking in the studio that hadn't been touched or 'cleaned' since they arrived.

Stream followed Toby and Mitchell remained under the watchful eye of Artie. He finished looking at the final negative and returned it to the box. Then he held it out to Artie.

'You can put these back now. I don't think we can learn anything by looking at these,' Mitchell said.

Artie took the box and stood with it as though unsure what to do. He clearly didn't want to leave Mitchell alone in the shop, which made Mitchell all the more convinced there was something there that might be of interest.

Mitchell walked away from the counter and browsed the room, wandering over to the camera and the area set up to take the photographs. A chair, a chaise longue, and a love seat were stacked behind a folding screen. Set up in front of the camera was a two-seater sofa and a small round table with a plant on it. Behind the sofa was a pair of fake curtains draped on the wall, which was all clearly used as a backdrop to create the picture. To the side of this 'set' were a few rolled-up rugs and a couple of cushions which had obviously been discarded on this occasion.

'You recreate a home environment,' Mitchell said.

'As best as we can,' said Artie.

Mitchell glanced around the floor once more but could see nothing obvious that might confirm suspicion on Toby or Artie. He was just about to turn away when he noticed an artist's sketchpad on the floor near the camera. He picked it up and began to leaf through the pages. There were rough sketches of people posing for the photographs, even one of Toby taking a picture.

'These are good,' Mitchell said. 'Whose are they?'

Artie flushed with pleasure, rapidly losing his surly pose. 'D'you fink so?'

'You did these?'

'Yeah. Little hobby o' mine.'

Mitchell looked through the pad, admiring the drawings and commenting on the style. Artie was sketching in charcoal but they were very realistic. The idea of the 'soul thief' described by Neeraj came back into his head, but he dismissed it. He couldn't have faith in an ancient superstition, no matter how sincere Neeraj's beliefs were. There had to be something else at the heart of Sara and Warren's death. However, what was familiar was the sketchpad used by Artie. The paper was like the one used by the mysterious Rosie who had sketched Warren at the hospital.

'Where did you buy this paper?' Mitchell asked. He suddenly thought he might have a way of finding the girl he was looking for. 'I have a friend who draws. She'd love one of these, I'm sure.'

Artie went to the reception desk, tore a piece of paper out of the back of a ledger and wrote down the name and address of the shop that supplied the pad. As he was about to hand it to Mitchell, the boy gave him a confused look, as though he didn't know where he was. The colour drained from his face and he began to stagger, as though drunk.

'Are you all right?' asked Mitchell, helping him to the sofa in front of the camera.

'Sorry about that. Came over all queer then.'

'What's the matter?' asked Stream as he returned with Toby.

By this time Artie's colour was rapidly returning to normal.

'He just felt dizzy,' explained Mitchell.

Toby went to fetch a glass of water and returned with it. Artie took the glass with trembling hands.

'Dunno what was up… Sorry…' he said.

'Just rest,' Toby said.

Once they were happy that Artie was fine, Stream and Mitchell left.

Chapter Eighteen

As he undressed for the evening Mitchell considered the strangeness of the day. He recalled the picture of the girl he had seen, the artist's sketchpad and the piece of paper that Artie had held out to him. Mitchell realised that he had forgotten all about both the pad and the piece of paper. It was only later that he remembered he hadn't taken the address for the shop after all. He cursed himself for being distracted and decided he would return to the photography shop the next day.

He hung up his smoking jacket on the back of the bedroom door, then slipped off his trousers. Strange how the day had promised to reveal so much, and yet he felt he knew nothing at all. It bothered him that Artie had taken ill at precisely the moment when he was about to give him information that might have led somewhere. It was all a little convenient. Maybe Artie was smarter than Mitchell had taken him for, which was why the images in the sketchpad bothered him so much.

He slipped on a dressing gown and went downstairs to his

study. There he opened the top drawer and pulled out the sketch of Warren. He looked at the charcoal strokes. They were different, and in no way related to those he had seen in Artie's pad. In fact, all the pictures Artie had drawn showed happiness. People smiling as they prepared to be photographed. It didn't add up that this would have any bearing on this picture, which was horrible, really: Warren looked like a madman, just as he must have looked seconds before he threw himself into the canal.

Mitchell brought the picture back upstairs to his room. He placed it on his dresser and then went to his washstand, poured cool water into the bowl and swilled his face. He pondered the sketch as he dried his face and hands before turning off the gaslight.

As he climbed into bed his mind went to Laura. He had seen much more of her recently. She had even taken a walk in the park with him that afternoon and, despite everything, was recovering remarkably well from the losses the family had suffered in the past few weeks. Out of tragedy had come hope. The irony was not lost on him.

He placed his hands under his head and stared up at the dark ceiling above his bed. A small filter of light was leaking into his room from the gaslight outside. The light flickered, casting strange shadows over the walls and ceiling. Mitchell closed his eyes and felt himself drifting into sleep. But he felt the glimmer, as though it could reach into his closed eyelids. A warmth went into his limbs which had nothing to do with the warming pan that Aggie had placed in the bottom of the bed. Sleep came into the corners of his eyes, pushing aside the lambent light, and he drifted in that halfway place where dreams and reality merge. He felt a slight pressure on his bed. In his half-conscious state, he imagined it was Rufus, his father's old hound, climbing up on the bed, trying to look for some morning warmth and attention. His mind drifted into thoughts of those times, and then the dreams came.

It was India, some fifteen years earlier. Mitchell was playing out in the yard while his father was working. He was with the regiment on some kind of official business and had been away for a few days. Bhakti, the housekeeper, was singing inside. Mitchell loved her like a mother; indeed, he had often been mistaken for her son, and he could have been, with his dark hair and eyes, and skin turned brown from the sun, as he played outside so much.

Bhakti called him for tea, but he was engrossed in his game. He had a strange urge to draw images in the dirt with a thin stick. Bhakti came out looking for him. She was wearing a sari that was a brighter yellow than the sun itself. By then, he had created a drawing like a floor plan of the entire house, with flat staircases seen from a bird's-eye view.

'What are you doing, Mitchell-Sahib?' Bhakti said. 'You must come inside. Your dinner is ready.'

Mitchell began to draw Bhakti inside the house. It was a dark place, a British mansion – the type he had never seen, since he had been born and raised in India, but somehow he knew about it. Maybe he had seen drawings in one of his father's many books at some time. Or maybe he had heard tell of such places as he sat playing at his father's knee. It didn't matter, really. Mitchell knew this place for certain. He had seen it many times in his mind's eye.

Bhakti tutted at him, calling once more from the step. It was the hottest part of the day and she knew the colonel wouldn't thank her for letting Mitchell darken his skin any more than he already had. Sometimes she would clout him for disobedience. Mitchell always took it good-naturedly. He was a tough little boy, always fending for himself since his mother's death, but Bhakti loved him. Everything she did was for his own good. She saw potential in the boy. He had something special that shone through, and sometimes she saw a dark-purple smudge appear on his forehead, as though his third eye was trying to open. That kind of sensitivity was rare in a *sahib*. But she couldn't tell him about it, or encourage it, though she would have, had he been her own son.

Mitchell drew Bhakti standing behind a door. A dark shadow loomed behind her. He frowned at it. He didn't remember drawing the shadow; it had appeared there on its own.

'Mitchell-Sahib, this is the last time I call you…'

Then suddenly Bhakti was quiet. Mitchell noticed the silence more than when Bhakti was shouting or singing. He stopped drawing. The shadow in his haunted mansion had blotted out Bhakti. Feeling strangely guilty, he scrubbed out the drawing.

He wandered back into the house. All was … too quiet.

In the conservatory his lunch was laid out and covered with net domes to keep the flies off. Mitchell sat down, lifted one of the domes and began to pick at the food underneath. It was a vegetable curry and he mopped it up with a thin chapatti taken from another plate. When he'd finished another chapatti, he swilled his fingers in a bowl of cooling boiled water, wiped them on a napkin and drank from a glass containing warm lemonade. The heat was stifling inside. Mitchell noticed the fan had stopped turning and went to wind up the mechanism. He turned it several times and the fan above his head began to turn, moving the hot air around the room, but barely making it any cooler.

'Bhakti?' he called.

Usually she joined him for lunch, but her place remained empty. He made sure the covers were over the food, then went looking for her in the kitchen.

Down below ground, in the coolest part of the house, Mitchell noted that Bhakti had left the pantry open. He crossed the room and began to close the door but discovered there was something blocking it. He looked into the pantry: Bhakti was lying on the floor inside. She was looking up at him, but her face was wrong.

'What are you doing, Bhakti?' Mitchell said.

Bhakti didn't move. She lay still, eyes shining with unshed tears.

'Are you ill?' asked Mitchell.

He bent down to touch her skin, then he saw the snake. It was coiled around Bhakti's waist and up around her throat. Mitchell backed away. He understood, even then, that it was too late.

He ran back upstairs and out into the yard and began to yell. It was the time of day when everyone went inside, trying to catch up on the sleep they couldn't get in the hot evenings, and his frightened calling for help wasn't answered quickly.

Mitchell fell to the dirt and sobbed his loss into the ground.

A hand fell on his shoulder.

'Mitchell-Sahib, what is wrong?' Mitchell looked up at Uncle John's servant, Neeraj.

'I drew a picture,' he cried. 'And the darkness appeared in it. It swallowed Bhakti.'

Neeraj sat and listened as Mitchell poured out the story, then he went inside to find Bhakti's body, just as Mitchell had described. Within an hour she was removed from the house and the snake, a boa constrictor, was killed.

'It was a snake,' Neeraj explained. 'Nothing you did made this happen. But I must tell you a story about someone who did have that kind of power. They called him the Image-Maker, but really he was a thief, who stole the souls of men…'

~

In her dream Laura had drifted into a realm of potential happiness. She was walking with Mitchell, her arm linked in his, and she heard the steady tap of his cane as they walked through the park. It was a glorious day. Bright, but not too hot. Laura was wearing a pale-yellow day suit, which consisted of a small jacket that was fitted closely on the body but flared at the hips to allow room for her bustle at the back. The skirt matched, but underneath the jacket she wore a cream chiffon blouse, high at the neck, and a small cameo brooch. Mitchell looked so handsome and smart in a light-cream jacket and trousers.

The tap of the cane changed rhythm. Laura looked down but noticed that Mitchell wasn't carrying it after all. He was holding the photograph of Sara, Warren and herself. It looked different, though. Sara and Warren's images were so faded, they looked almost see-through.

'Why do they look like that?' Laura asked.

'Because I have their souls,' said Mitchell, but it wasn't his voice. Laura looked up at the person whose arm she was linking with. She saw a familiar face, but it wasn't Mitchell's. She couldn't remember who this man was, though she felt she should.

She tried to pull her arm free, but the man grabbed it. 'No. You can't get free that easily. You're mine now.'

'No,' Laura said, and she pulled harder, but the energy drained from her, the more she struggled.

'Who are you?' she gasped.

'I'm a thief of souls. Your image is mine.'

Laura felt exhausted. She slipped down to the floor, a faint or swoon, something she wasn't given to, overcoming her. As she looked up at the figure above her, she watched its face change. Slowly it became *her*. The cream suit changed to pale yellow; the creature was even wearing her clothes!

She heard the hard rap again, as though the cane she had thought Mitchell was carrying had slammed once more onto the pavement. She stared up at herself, seeing that wolf's-head cane held aloft in her own hand, and then it swung downwards towards her.

Chapter Nineteen

Mitchell jerked awake. Sweat peppered his brow and he pushed back the covers from the bed, letting the cool air dry the sweat from his body. He hadn't felt this hot since he left India many years ago. It was almost as though he had brought the heat out of his dream and into his room. It was suffocating.

His mind went over the dream. It was horrible, really. For the first time in years, he thought of Bhakti and that awful day, recalling every detail in his dream, as though the memory was important somehow. Even now he experienced an overwhelming sense of guilt that somehow Bhakti died because of his drawing. But it was insane to even consider it, for that would mean Mitchell was evil and the darkness he sometimes thought was inside him was, indeed, real.

'No,' he said aloud, denying it once more. *I'm not a bad person. I wasn't responsible.*

He turned his legs over the side of the bed and sat on the edge. The dark was the same as when he had first gone to sleep, as though it were only minutes before.

He reached for the lamp beside his bed and lit it. The room sprang into view and Mitchell breathed deeply. The light, somehow, made him feel less vulnerable.

He reached for his pocket watch and looked at the time. He had only been in bed for an hour, yet it felt as though an entire lifetime had passed. He stood up, and walked across the room. Throwing back the curtain, he raised the window, letting the cool night air rush inside. Then he reached for his dressing gown, put it on and opened the bedroom door.

The landing was dark; everyone in the house was now in bed and Mitchell didn't want to disturb them. So, he crept across the landing and made his way downstairs in the dark. He had walked through this house many times without light and knew every step, every corner, every placement of furniture. At the bottom of the stairs, he turned right and opened his study door. Dull embers were still alight in the fireplace. Mitchell made his way across the room and lit the gas.

He looked around. Everything was tidy and undisturbed. He crossed to his drinks cabinet and poured himself a large brandy in a crystal balloon glass. He sipped the drink, then turned the light off again before heading back upstairs.

The bedroom was still illuminated by the small oil lamp beside the bed. Mitchell placed his glass down beside it and removed his dressing gown. Then he climbed back into bed. The stifling heat had left the room, but he kept the window open. Across the room on his dresser, Mitchell could see the drawing of Warren lying face down.

It didn't take a medium to understand that the dream he'd had was somehow caused by the questions the sketch raised in his mind, and was fuelled by Neeraj's story of the soul thief.

Mitchell put it down to his overactive brain, but somewhere inside him, he began to question his own logic. What if Neeraj was right?

He turned the lamp down, but not completely off. A dull light took away the total darkness, but left some of the corners in shadow. Mitchell felt oddly insecure about the darker corners – bizarre, since he didn't believe in monsters hiding under the bed. He pulled one of the sheets over him and lay back. There was a cool breeze wafting into the room and it comforted him. He closed his eyes.

He felt that strange sensation again; as though something had crawled onto the bed with him. His eyelids were heavy, too heavy for him to bother opening them; and when he felt the faint tickle of hair against his cheek, he thought of Laura.

Soft lips pressed against his cheek. The kisses could have been those of his mother, or Bhakti, or Laura… It all came down to her. His beautiful love.

A deep sadness leaked into his half-dreaming state. They were walking in the park, Laura in a pale-yellow day outfit, just as they had earlier that day. He thought of the warmth in her eyes as he felt arms wrap around him. He turned towards the body next to him, snuggled and accepted a shower of kisses.

The buttons on his nightshirt opened. A long-nailed hand slid inside and he felt cool fingers stroke his warm skin. It was an astonishing sensation. The sheet lifted; he felt the cool body spread over him. It was wonderful.

His eyes slitted open. Dressed in nothing but a shift, Laura was above him. Her lips were warm as they found his mouth, kissing him in a way they had never done before. He pushed back the feeling that it reminded him of the intrusive kiss Sara had tried to place on his lips, that awful day six months ago. He kissed her back. Letting her tongue explore his mouth, as he pushed his own into hers. How he wanted her…

Laura … *his* Laura. He had dreamed of being this intimate with her. Laura as his wife. The only woman he could ever truly love.

Her mouth left his and he felt the absence in his sleep, but the kisses continued down over the skin, now exposed by the fully-open nightshirt. Her breast brushed against him. Mitchell groaned. He turned his head into the pillow as her cool hand stroked his chest.

'Darling…' he groaned again. Hands reaching down, he pulled her up and into his arms, taking her mouth as he rolled her under him.

Somehow Laura had lost the chemise. She lay naked and vulnerable beneath him. He wished this wasn't a dream, wished he could truly make her his wife. She opened her legs, wrapped them around him, and the disappointment he felt was palpable. This was a dream. Laura, his virgin love, would never know how to do that – not until he taught her, anyway.

'This is what you want. This is what we both want,' she murmured against his lips.

He tried to open his eyes again but the dream wouldn't let him go, and he ached to be satisfied, even if it was only in his imagination.

He pushed against her, felt her tense a little in fear, or excitement, he wasn't sure which. But it felt so real to be pressed up to her like this, the excitement became too much. He pulled away, fearful of letting go too soon and ruining the moment.

'What's wrong, darling?' she whispered. 'Don't you want me?'

'Let's slow down a little.'

She continued to stroke his chest, the coolness in her hands never warming. Mitchell lay on his back and pulled the sheet between them.

'I need a moment,' he explained.

Laura backed away. He felt her pull one of the covers over herself.

'What … am I doing here?' she asked.

Mitchell opened his eyes. The room was still glowing with the dim oil lamplight. Laura was sitting up in the bed, looking confused.

'How did I…?'

'Oh my God! This isn't a dream,' Mitchell said.

Laura looked at him, her expression bemused, as though she were waking from a walking sleep.

He reached for her. Found warmth in the skin now. Her cheeks flushed.

'How did I get here?' she asked again.

Mitchell pulled his nightshirt closed, climbed from the bed and found her chemise. He handed it to her and turned away as she slipped it over her head. For the first time he noted the pale-yellow day skirt and jacket thrown over the chair by the open window.

He picked up the pile of clothes and placed them on the bed without turning around.

She dressed as though in a daze, while Mitchell reached for his dressing gown and pulled it on over his nightshirt.

Once they were both decent, Mitchell turned around and found Laura stood awkwardly beside the bed.

'I don't understand what happened,' she said.

'We … were … making love.'

'No … I understand that part … I just don't know how I got here.'

Mitchell had no answer for her.

'I was dreaming and suddenly you were there,' he explained. 'I don't know how you got in or when.'

'I came to you?' Laura bowed her head. 'I don't remember arriving here or anything until…'

'Until we were naked together?'

She nodded, cheeks still flushed, head still bowed. She couldn't meet his eyes. 'Did we…?'

'No. I stopped. But we almost…'

'Oh God. This is shameful!' Her hand flew to her mouth, in horror of what she had almost done.

'No, Laura. Not shameful. We loved … *love* each other. It's what people do to express that love.'

'But we aren't married. My parents… Oh my God, what am I going to tell them?'

'You don't have to tell them anything, darling. Nothing happened. Well … not the ultimate thing, anyway.'

'I have to go home, sneak back in. Mitchell, I don't know what was in my mind. I saw myself, but had no control … I thought I was dreaming too.'

'There's nothing to be ashamed of. Maybe you were sleepwalking… A psychiatrist might say it was your subconscious telling you that you wanted to be with me.'

Laura sank onto the edge of the bed. 'I do. I mean … that's certainly true.'

'Then it's all fine. We will set the ball rolling for our marriage again. Nothing would make me happier!'

Laura looked at him blankly for a moment, as though trying to shield her real thoughts. 'Yes. That's what should happen between us, but Mitchell … what if…'

'Yes, darling?'

'What if I'm losing my mind? Like Sara. Like Warren…' She cast her eyes back over the confused bedding, blushing as she recalled her own forward behaviour.

Mitchell couldn't answer. He really didn't know what to say. He was worried too.

Part IV

Chapter Twenty

Toby Naylor was worried: Inspector Stream, bumbling though he was, might well be able to pin something on him. Of course, he'd had nothing to do with the death of that thug, Sean Gallen, but he was responsible for the pictures. It would only take one of his regulars to spout off at the mouth, and he was sure he would get his collar felt.

'That was Mitchell Bishop with him,' Artie had explained after Stream and Mitchell left.

'So? All cops look alike to me.'

'He ain't no cop. But he's a gentleman and a detective. He's the bloke what pulled a girl right from under the nose of Gallen last year.'

'What girl?'

'Don't you know nuffink? Rumour was, Gallen's gang kidnapped someone. Bishop got her back. Took some balls to take on Gallen and live,' Artie said.

'That Gallen was a bastard. Can't say I'm sorry to hear he's dead,' Toby said.

Artie nodded.

'That Bishop bloke is smart, though,' Artie continued. 'He's one to watch. He never stops looking once he's on a case. Not like Stream, who will probably just chalk Gallen's death up to accident eventually. Or good fortune for the local beat. Whatever…'

'It was an accident, though, wasn't it? Artie, what do you know?'

'Nuffink. Honest.'

Toby looked around the room at the back. Instead of a second studio, it now looked just like any kitchen would. Artie had cleverly hidden the changing room, that contained all of the lingerie and costumes worn by the models, including the see-through shift that Rosie was wearing in the picture Stream had. He had moved a tall, thin cupboard over the entrance.

'Well, it was genius making sure everything looked normal back here,' Toby said. 'Let's move that cupboard back where it was. I'm expecting Doris and Enid over soon for some photographs. Good job Stream came when he did and not when we were in the middle of it all.'

Artie dragged the cupboard away from the door. It made a loud scraping noise.

Toby noted the noise and wondered how Artie had managed to move it so quietly earlier. He had heard nothing in the front room of the shop, which was just as well. He opened the door and glanced in. There he found the piles of boxes containing the negatives of the girls, and a box of the postcards.

'Hopefully, we'll have some new ones to sell tonight,' said Artie.

'Artie, I think you deserve a bonus,' Toby said, pulling out a wad of cash from the pocket inside his jacket. It was money he had taken out to pay the girls, but now that Gallen was off his back and Artie had used his initiative, he felt inclined to share some of the profits. He held out the money without counting it.

'Seriously? For me?'

Toby nodded. 'You know, I only started this venture to help me pay off Gallen. Now, I suppose that doesn't matter so much. The thing is, I always planned to stop once the debts were paid. But I like taking the pictures; they give me a sense of freedom. Do you know what I mean?'

Artie nodded. 'It's art. That's what it is!'

'Exactly!'

They hurried to set the back studio up again, and as Artie returned with some new frames, Doris and Enid arrived at the back door.

The girls looked happier than usual, and Toby got some of the best shots he'd ever had from either of them. Then he left Artie to take some while he went into the darkroom, carrying the frames.

In the back of the room, he placed the new frames down, then picked up a box of negatives. These were the ones he had taken of Rosie on her last visit. Toby had not had the chance to create the cards from them yet. He held them up to the light, looking at her beautiful face, while completely ignoring the exposed body parts. Toby felt strange about possessing them. Part of him didn't want to sell the pictures. He tried not to think about the men who bought them, or what they would do with them. It was a terrible thought, and one that didn't sit well with his Catholic upbringing. But Toby knew that these pictures probably prevented those same men from cheating on their wives with the local whores. Although there was no question that some would still do that, and the postcards were just a new titillation for them.

He began to develop the negative that contained Rosie lying back on the chaise with her legs open, dark triangle of pubic hair revealed. He exposed the negative onto one large piece of paper several times and placed it into the developing tray. The pictures burst into life as he moved the picture into the next tray. Twelve small, postcard-size images began to settle on the sheet. He removed the page, hung it up and went on to the next one.

Tonight he had open house. He would have several locals traipsing in to buy the cards, and he wanted enough new ones of Rosie to keep their interest. He quickly moved on to process the negatives of Doris and Enid. The girls were posing naked together, arms around each other. In some of the shots they even kissed.

'Damn!' he murmured as he placed a sheet full of Doris and Enid into the second tray. There was something wrong with the picture. Doris's face just didn't look right. 'We'll have to take these again.'

He hung up the single ones of Enid. All of these were fine, and one of Doris at first appeared all right. Then he hurried out to the back studio/kitchen.

'Where are they?' asked Toby. 'Doris's haven't come out right. We'll have to do them again.'

'They're getting changed,' Artie said. 'Here, try these. I'm sure some in there are pretty good.'

'Take them into the darkroom, will you? I have to pay the girls and send them on their way,' Toby said.

Artie took the frames into the room. He paused to admire the cards of Rosie drying on the line, then looked over Doris's picture. It had finished developing and looked as though her face was smeared with something.

Toby came in as Artie began to process the new frames.

'Bit blurry, that one,' Artie commented.

'Yes, all of them of her came out like that. I think she must have moved as the flash went off. I will have to talk to her about it for next time.'

Doris stood on the corner of Sackville Street, the front of her gaudy orange dress pulled up to reveal a thin ankle. It was a quiet night but she wasn't too worried. She had earned a good amount at Naylor's that day, and it had been added to the stash of money she had hidden behind the sink in her meagre quarters. The local pimps were too busy arguing amongst themselves about who owned who, and so all the girls were hiding everything they could, now that Gallen wasn't calling the shots anymore. Doris smiled as she thought about the expression, 'organised crime' she had heard once. 'Organised' certainly wasn't the term she would use for the state of things right now. It was one of her regulars who had used the words. He was a local magistrate with a fetish for oral sex, but he liked to have her bottom half naked so he could watch her buttocks move as she worked. He was all right, though. Not like some of the Johns who were rough with her, or wanted the other hole instead of the regular place. Something she didn't particularly care for.

Doris lifted her skirt higher as an open-top carriage full of toffs went by. The men were drunk and some of them yelled and jeered at her.

'What about it, gents?' she called. 'I can take you all on.'

The carriage rattled away and Doris dropped her skirt again as she noticed a peeler rounding the corner.

'All right, Doris?' said the policeman.

Doris laughed and waved when she noticed it was someone she knew. She had taken care of him a few times before he got married, but he didn't need it anymore.

'All right there, lovely,' she said. 'How about a little action for old times' sake?'

The bobby laughed. 'Not tonight, love, but I'm sure someone will take you up on that offer.'

He walked on, truncheon in hand, as though he were expecting trouble.

'Chance'd be a bleedin' fine thing,' Doris murmured.

It really was a slow night. The gin in the local pub was calling. She could go there tonight, spend a little; she could certainly afford it now. She weighed up the possibility of doing any trade. Then, making up her mind, she turned and began to walk towards Piccadilly.

'Hey!'

Doris stopped. She turned to see one of Gallen's ex-bodyguards standing at the end of the street.

'Shit!' she murmured under her breath. 'Hello, me lovely.'

She walked back towards him. Bruce was his name. It always reminded her of the word 'brute'. And Bruce suited his name, more than anyone she knew. This didn't look good for her tonight.

'Why weren't you over at the house last night?' Bruce said.

'I didn't know I was supposed to be,' Doris replied.

'We need to sort out who's doing what. Or the March Brothers will move in, and believe me, you won't like that.'

'You putting yourself forward for leader?' Doris asked.

'Maybe.'

'Oh.'

Doris couldn't think what else to say.

'And I'd like you to be one of me girls.'

Shit! Doris thought but didn't say aloud. 'Oh,' she managed.

'So, you better be over at Gallen's old house later tonight. There will be gin in it for ya, and maybe we can find a room to get cosy in.'

Doris nodded but she hated the thought of spending any time with Bruce, or of him owning her. She thought about the money hidden in her house. The last few days had been more lucrative than the last year. More nights like that, where she didn't have a pimp creaming most of it off, would mean she could get out of Manchester. Possibly even retire. She was sick of the game. Sick of the thugs and the insecurity of their lives. Most of all, she was sick of Johns and their perversions.

She watched Bruce walk away. The craving for gin was stronger than ever, but dare she go out and ignore the order to go to the house? Nothing had been decided. She knew at least three other thugs who wanted to take Gallen's place. By tomorrow Bruce might even be dead. But if she went, showed any allegiance, she'd suffer for it from whoever did take over.

'Caught betwixt the devil and the deep blue sea,' she murmured, recalling her mother's favourite expression.

It was no fun being a whore sometimes. Although, when she was younger, Doris quite enjoyed the sexual freedom it gave her. Mostly, in those days, she chose who and when. It was easy when you were young and fresh: everyone wanted you. She had made more money on the streets than most. But those years of heavy drinking and abuse of her body had taken their toll. At thirty, Doris was no longer youthful. Still, it would be nice to find a husband sometime. Maybe one who didn't mind her worn looks, especially when he learnt how interesting she was in the bedroom.

Making a decision, Doris turned away from Sackville Street

and headed off towards the High Street. All the shops would be closed now, but she knew who might help her to avoid the gangs and being pulled into their wars: Toby Naylor. He was a decent sort, and he paid well. She could offer some very indecent poses for him and maybe the next payment would be enough to get her out of Manchester until everything was settled.

If he wouldn't help, she could always use her knowledge of that 'other girl'. She had recognised her immediately when Inspector Stream flashed the picture the morning after Gallen burned to death. Rose, she thought she was called. She had seen her leaving Naylor's once, and knew she didn't walk the streets. She wasn't the type. Odd that she took her clothes off for Naylor's little sideline, though. They had all been told to look out for the girl once Gallen got the picture of her. Doris knew how much he would have loved to get his hands on a sweet-looking kid like that. He had specialised in deflowering the innocent ones. After him, anything was preferable.

Doris turned off the main strip, away from the lit areas, and hurried into the back alley behind Naylor's. A few knocks on the back door should do it, and Naylor would either help or he wouldn't. But Doris was certain she could get some money out of him, one way or another. One thing was for sure, by asking him she wouldn't be making her plight any worse. Bruce, or his ilk, had no allegiance with the photographer. She thought they had forgotten about him now, too. No one had mentioned the photos or Naylor since Gallen's death, which Doris had considered strange, until she realised they were all so focused on the idea of being the next 'boss'. It was only a matter of time, though, that one of them would remember collecting from him, and the photographer would be in the same situation as the street girls, paying all his profits for so-called protection.

The lid from one of the dustbins in the alley ahead fell to the ground with a loud clatter. Doris froze, then backed up into the dark to avoid being seen. A cat hissed and ran out from behind the bins. Doris almost laughed at her own jumpiness. She had passed through these alleys many times without any problem. She smiled, moved out from the darkness, and then noticed the shadow that stood beside the bins. It moved, turning its head to look at her. She knew she was being watched even though she couldn't make out the features.

'Who's that?' Doris called. 'I ain't scared o' ya! And if it's raping you're after, then I got the clap…'

The shadow moved. Doris assumed it was male, but couldn't tell who it was. Maybe it was Bruce, watching to see where she was headed. She would cop for it if he cottoned on that she wasn't planning to go to Church Street at all, despite his instructions.

'Is that you, Bruce? I was just going to a … a customer. Then I planned to come on to yours. Gotta make me living, an' all.'

Doris began to walk forward. Even though the silence frightened her, she knew she had to appear brave if she was going to face down whoever was there. She wasn't going to let some stupid man stop her getting to Naylor's, and if she had to fuck her way out of a bad situation, it wouldn't be the first time.

She was almost at the bins when the figure stepped forward from the shadow.

'Oh!' she said. 'What *you* doing 'ere?'

The light from the streetlamp filtered down from the bottom of the alley. It reflected on something silver. Doris barely recognised the top of a gentleman's cane as it came down on her head, smashing her between the eyes. She fell back, blinded by fright and blood. But her assailant was relentless. The cane-top struck again and again. Through bleary, blood-streaked eyes, Doris saw the vicious wolf's head (pure silver, if she wasn't mistaken) descend on her one final time. Many blows later she was feeling no pain. But by then her face was a bloody pulp, so smeared and distorted, that it looked almost exactly like the faulty photograph still hanging in Toby Naylor's darkroom.

Chapter Twenty-One

Mitchell had taken Laura home, hailing a cab, and picking the lock of her front door to help sneak her back inside. He had been too shy to attempt a kiss, even though the evening had taken them further than they had ever attempted to go before.

After she went inside, the blush still glowing on her cheeks, he had walked home to clear his head. It had been quite a turn of events, one that he didn't care to repeat until after they were married, for Laura's sake and the sense of respect he had for her. He was still confused and concerned about how she had come to be in his house, in his bed, but he couldn't see this sudden change in their relationship as a bad thing. Though it was certainly true it raised concerns about her state of mind, if she were walking in her sleep.

Now, the most terrifying thought of all was her walking alone through the streets at night. Anything could have happened to her. It was fortunate that it hadn't.

On his way home he passed the photography shop and paused, looking in the window at the pictures he could still make out in the gaslight. The happy couples, the family portraits, the small children playing with wooden toys, all looked so posed and formal. Mitchell wondered why anyone would even want to make such an effort to be immortalised on a piece of paper. It was common practice that some people even had pictures taken of their dead. Especially lost children. Mitchell had seen such grotesque pictures of parents with their dead infant, or widows posing with their late husbands. He didn't think this was a sideline of Naylor's, though. Not that he expected to see death photographs in the window. For the most part those were deeply personal, but he realised that he hadn't seen any in the box of negatives he had been given earlier. There were still so many unanswered questions, and Artie's sudden illness had prevented him from asking further questions about Warren's death, which Artie had witnessed.

Mitchell walked on and rounded the corner at the bottom of the high street with the idea of cutting through the back alley behind to make his way home. But, as he turned down the dark lane he saw a small female boot protruding from behind the dustbins. He paused, scrutinised the boot, then moved closer. He could now see a foot and a leg, the hem of a dress, and an exposed thigh.

He pushed aside the bins and the light from the bottom of the alley spilled over the body.

'Oh God,' he said.

Bile rose into the back of his throat. The girl was a mess. Her face was so severely battered that her nose was smashed, her lips split to reveal shattered teeth. Her forehead was caved in like an overripe melon that had been dropped. One eye was wide open, staring up at the clear night sky; the other was so swollen, he couldn't tell if it even remained in the socket. He placed his fingers to her throat to try to detect a pulse, but it was obvious she was dead.

Mitchell stood up, hurried to the end of the alley and back up the high street, calling at the top of his lungs in the hope of attracting attention.

It wasn't long before one of the beat bobbies heard him and came running.

'What's the matter?' asked the bobby.

'A body!' Mitchell panted. 'I found a body.'

Mitchell led him to the alley. By now the noise had roused those living above the shops and in the houses that backed onto the alley. It wasn't long before people emerged from the buildings to see what was going on. Mitchell glanced over the sleepy men and women, mostly gathered in slippers and nightclothes, with thick blankets wrapped around them for warmth and decency. They loitered at the end of the alley, talking in whispered tones.

Another policeman appeared, responding to the piercing call of the first one's whistle. Mitchell stepped back and let the police do their work. A mortuary cart was sent for and the area was cordoned off.

'You found the body?' asked another bobby.

Mitchell noted the pad and pencil the man held, and so he explained what he had found. He gave his name and address for future reference.

'Thank you, sir. You may go home now,' said the officer.

He was about to turn away when he saw Toby Naylor standing at the entrance to his backyard. He looked pale and shocked, as though he recognised the girl the police were trying so hard to hide from the voyeuristic locals.

'Is she dead?' Toby asked as Mitchell made his way over.

'Yes. Did you know her?'

'One of the local street girls. I've seen her around.'

'I knew her too. Doris was her name,' Mitchell said, watching Toby's expression carefully. 'I interviewed her last year on a missing-person case I was working on.'

Toby didn't answer. He gazed blankly ahead as the mortuary cart arrived and the body was loaded onto the back.

'This is horrible,' Toby said. 'Used to be safe at night around here. The area's going to the dogs.'

'Found something!' called one of the bobbies as he scoured the area where the body had been. 'Looks like the murder weapon.'

The policeman held a walking stick up horizontally, his hand clasped in the middle of the wood. From his vantage point nearby Mitchell could see the blood-caked ergonomic handle. He knew the design well. It had been made to fit his own hand, and despite the blood and bits of hair and skull clinging to the weapon, Mitchell knew without a shadow of doubt that it was his walking stick.

He held in a gasp, but gave an involuntary shake of the head. He couldn't remember where he had last seen the cane. He didn't recall using it at all the day before. And he hadn't been carrying one tonight, in his haste to ensure that Laura was returned home safely and without scandal. He watched the policeman wrap the cane, then slipped back into the now-dispersing crowd. There was not much for them to see once the body had been moved.

Walking away, Mitchell experienced a growing fear and concern. His heart rate jumped back up to the speed it had been when he first spotted the body.

Why would Doris be murdered, and who would use his cane to do it? The fact that the weapon had been left there to be found suggested that someone was possibly trying to frame him. But who and why? He would have to go into the station in the morning and talk to Stream. It was obvious that someone wanted him out of the picture. Maybe he was closer to solving this mystery than he had first thought? Or at least, the killer thought he was important enough to knobble.

He thought through the day's events. Nothing unusual had happened. His visit to the photography shop had been odd, but nothing so extreme that he could blame this on, or point the finger at Toby. Of course, the girl had died at the back of the shop, which might be enough to make Stream look at Toby a little closer.

At the next corner Mitchell turned into his street and walked down the left-hand side until he reached his house. He took his keys from his pocket and let himself inside. Then glanced at the grandfather clock in the hallway. It was 3.30 in the morning, and he felt drained and shocked.

He walked quietly up the stairs and into his room. The oil lamp was still lit and the glass of brandy he had poured earlier was still on the table beside the bed. A small comfort that would probably help him sleep.

Mitchell undressed, pulled on his nightshirt, and climbed back into the bed, before he recalled the open window.

As he pulled back the curtains to close the window, he glanced down into the street. A girl was standing beneath one of the streetlights. She looked up at him and nodded. There was something very familiar about her. He watched her walk away from the light and disappear into the darkness. He considered calling after her, but after the night's drama, he felt incapable of taking any more. All he wanted to do was curl up in bed, drink his brandy and sleep.

Mitchell closed the window, pulled the curtains, and returned to the bed.

As he lifted the brandy glass to his lips, the smell of almonds assaulted his nostrils. He looked down into the glass. The brandy had been stood out in the open, but it shouldn't smell differently after just a few hours. He put the glass down, but the smell was under his nostrils and he couldn't shake the feeling that it was familiar. He lifted it again. Then he recalled a case he had come across some years ago, when a man died under mysterious circumstances. The room he was found in stank of a strange chemical that had the disturbing odour of almonds. On further investigation, arsenic was discovered in the man's whisky decanter. His wife was later charged and hanged for his murder.

Mitchell was now certain that his brandy was poisoned. He pushed the glass aside. He had sipped from the glass earlier and all had been fine. This left only two options. Either someone had come into his house and poisoned his glass while he returned Laura to her home, or Laura had tried to kill him. But no. It wasn't possible. Laura loved him, and he dismissed this notion as insane almost as soon as it bloomed in his mind. After all, any determined thug could have picked his lock, taken the cane and left something in his glass, without his servants knowing.

The more he thought about it, the more likely this scenario was. It was another thing he needed to put before Inspector Stream tomorrow.

He glanced over to the dresser, noting that Warren's picture was still where he had left it. That was a relief, at least.

He turned the light off, rolled over onto his side, but no matter how warm and comfortable he felt, sleep was slow to come.

Chapter Twenty-Two

'Thank you for coming with me,' Laura said as they climbed the few steps up to the entrance of Manchester Royal Infirmary. 'I couldn't face going through Warren's things alone.'

Mitchell opened the door and nodded to the security man.

'We are looking for Dr Glenister's office,' Mitchell said.

A passing orderly was asked to lead the way and Mitchell found himself walking the corridors of the hospital once more, only this time with a legitimate reason. They reached Glenister's office a short time later and the orderly, a surly chap who was better suited to dock work than to the care of the sick, waved his hand rudely in the general direction of the doctors' offices, which were all housed in the same corridor.

Mitchell read the signs on the doors, Glenister's was third along on the right.

He knocked on the door.

'Come in,' called Glenister.

'Dr Glenister?' Laura said.

'Yes indeed. Miss Carter, do come in. I'm so terribly sorry for your loss.'

'This is Mr Bishop, he's … a friend of the family.'

After the pleasantries were exchanged, they sat down in two leather chairs that faced Glenister's desk.

'Dr Carter is sorely missed here,' Glenister said. 'He had a special way with his patients, and the nursing staff were very fond of him indeed.'

'Thank you,' said Laura. 'I'll convey your words to my parents. It may give them some small comfort.'

Glenister nodded. 'I do hope so.'

'You have some of Warren's possessions, I believe?' Mitchell said.

'Yes. We took the liberty of packing his office up for you. Obviously, patient records are confidential and we had to make sure that they were kept private, and any that were on his desk have now been locked away.'

'Of course,' Mitchell said.

'But we've left his things in his office. It's next door and has been kept locked since … Dr Carter … well. Perhaps you'd like me to show you?'

Dr Glenister retrieved a large ring full of keys from the top drawer of his desk, and Mitchell and Laura followed him back out into the corridor.

'Take all the time you need,' said Glenister as he searched the ring for the right key. 'Just let me know when you're ready, and I'll send for some orderlies to carry everything out to your carriage.'

'Thank you. You are most kind,' Laura said.

The key turned, the door opened and Glenister gasped when he saw the room. 'What the devil!'

The room was in total disarray.

'We've had a burglary,' Glenister said. 'Those filing cabinets were locked.'

Glenister hurried into the room and pulled the call rope by the fireplace.

'We will have to get the police. I'm so sorry, Miss Carter. I can't imagine why or how this happened.'

Mitchell looked around the room. He noted the strewn paper over the floor, the boxes of Warren's possessions that had been tipped up, as though the thief had been looking for something specific.

'I'm so sorry,' Glenister said again.

The same orderly who had directed them to Glenister's office arrived a few moments later. He stepped back in surprise when he saw the state of Warren's office.

'Go to the telephone room and have them call the police station,' Glenister said.

Back in Glenister's office, Mitchell and Laura were brought a tray of tea. Left alone, there was an awkward silence.

'What … what is happening, Mitchell?' Laura said finally.

He took her hand and held it. 'I don't know. I wish I did.'

Glenister returned. He looked flustered. 'It seems the thief was … looking for something among the patients' records. It's all very odd. There's an empty wallet, papers gone from inside, and the name tag removed. I have no way of knowing whose records are missing, or why. Not until we actually require them, that is.'

Mitchell squeezed Laura's hand. 'Will you be all right if I go and look around Warren's office?'

Laura nodded.

In Warren's former office Mitchell closed the door behind

him, shutting out the corridor. He had no idea what he was looking for but suspected he would know it when he found it.

He began to pick his way through the bits of Warren's life that none of them had really known about. His doctor's bag was tipped over; the stethoscope, bottles of laudanum and a small scalpel were on the floor underneath it.

The drawers of his desk were pulled out and discarded, contents spilled over the polished surface. There were pens and bits of paper. A leaking ink-well had fallen sideways over the blotting paper; ink had seeped through until some of it had dribbled over the edge of the desk. Spots of blue stained the wooden floor. And there, Mitchell spotted a footprint. It was the pointed toe of a lady's boot.

'You!' said a voice behind him. Mitchell turned to find Inspector Stream at the door of the office. 'Grimes,' Stream continued, 'arrest this man.'

'What for?' asked Grimes, surprised.

'Suspicion of murdering Doris Leyland. We found your cane, Mr Bishop. Did you think I wouldn't recognise it?'

'You are telling me someone tried to poison you?' Stream said, his voice full of indifference. 'Who did you upset?'

'No one. At least, I don't think I did. There is also my cane,' Mitchell said.

Stream sighed. He had been over Mitchell's explanation and it didn't fit in with his view of the previous night's events. Especially when Mitchell refused to explain why he was out alone that late at night.

'You're a single man. I assume you took Doris to the alley

for some fun,' Stream said. 'She tried to rip you off and you got angry. It happens all the time.'

'Certainly not! I told you. I passed the alley. I saw the body. If I was guilty, why would I run to find one of your men? And why would I leave my cane for him to find?'

That was the part in the scenario that just didn't add up to Stream either. Mitchell could have quietly gone away, left the girl to be found by someone else, and then declared his walking stick stolen when asked. Or if he'd had any sense – taken it with him. No murder weapon meant no connection to him. He was too smart to have done something as stupid as this, but Stream wanted an easy resolution to the murder. He was tired of having to work too hard to solve cases.

Grimes came into the interview room. 'Someone to see you, inspector. Says it's urgent.'

Grimes gave Mitchell a meaningful look.

'Stay here,' Stream said. Grimes floundered, unsure if Stream was talking to him or Mitchell, and so he waited inside the interview room, looking around awkwardly until Stream returned.

'You can go,' said Stream to Mitchell. 'It seems you do have an alibi. Miss Carter is outside. You should have told me you were with her last night, and we could have resolved this sooner.'

Laura was waiting for him outside near the front desk. She took his hand as he came out.

'You didn't have to tell Stream about last night,' Mitchell said once they were alone inside a hansom cab. 'Not that I'm ungrateful. I just don't want your reputation to be ruined.'

'He was sworn to secrecy and I was rather sketchy about the details. You don't honestly think I could leave you in there, do you? Knowing you've done nothing wrong?'

Mitchell leaned across the carriage and kissed her. 'I love you, Laura. Let's get married. There's no reason why we can't go ahead with the plans we once made.'

Laura smiled. 'It would make my parents happy. Give them something nice to look forward to.'

'But what about you? Will it make *you* happy?'

Laura kissed him back. 'You know it would. Wasn't it obvious last night, how I feel about you?' she said, her cheeks flushing.

They stopped off at Mitchell's house and Laura waited in the sitting room while he changed his clothes.

'Let's forget all this photograph business. I've a mind to concentrate on our future and put these terrible circumstances behind us,' Laura said when he came into the drawing room more formally attired.

'I agree. But don't you want me to find out what happened to Sara and Warren?'

'Not if it means you keep getting into trouble. Or if it delays us all moving on and being happy again. I want to be happy again, Mitchell.'

He sat down next to her and took her hand. Then he took something out of his pocket. Laura looked down as Mitchell pressed the engagement ring onto her finger. She glanced at her hand, admiring the ring, then she kissed him softly on the lips.

'We can be happy, Laura. I truly believe it,' Mitchell said. Then he kissed her back.

～

In the mortuary Dr Garner removed the clothes of the whore known as Doris Leyland. The fabric reeked of sweat and gin, but he folded them neatly onto a chair beside the body. When he reached the pantaloons, and began to pull them away, he found a money pouch. He put it aside, but didn't look in. That would be something to inspect later. For now, he had to see the damage that had been done to confirm his report for the hearing tomorrow. There was no doubt in his mind though that they were looking for a killer.

Garner swilled water over her remains. Blood and clumps of hair washed down the drain. He noted her arms were covered in bruises consistent with defence wounds, but not as many as he might have expected. Possibly the girl had been taken completely by surprise. He looked her over as the water drained away. The face was a mess. This one would be a closed coffin, for certain. That was if anyone even bothered to collect the body.

Garner knew that this was probably unlikely, unless she was carrying anything of any value. He glanced at the pouch. It had been carefully hidden among her clothes. It was improbable that anyone would know she had it.

Garner was the top in his field and he had studied under the careful eye of a pathologist called Enrique Simonet. But Garner liked to take Simonet's ideas and concepts even further. Especially on bodies that no one would ever see once they were boxed up. And Doris was likely to become one of those that ended up in a pauper's grave anyway.

He began to cut along the breastbone. He would study the woman's internal organs, looking for signs of her decadent life. Blood slipped away from the cut as though it were a wound inflicted on a living person.

'Doctor?' said a voice from the doorway.

'What is it, Peter?' Garner said, looking up at his assistant.

'Someone's come for the body.'

'Which body?'

'That one,' Peter said.

'Put whoever it is in the waiting room. Then get back in here and help me clean her up.'

Peter went away and Garner began to stitch the wound he had inflicted, and hoped that the grieving relative wouldn't ask to see the body.

After an hour Garner came into the waiting room. There was a tall gentleman there, wearing a black suit and a tall black hat that emphasised his height.

'You've come for Doris Leyland?'

'I've been paid to collect her body, doctor. She is to be interred this afternoon.'

'Who paid for it?' asked Garner.

'I'm not at liberty to say, sir.'

Garner was perplexed. He had been sure this one would be available for his own experimentation.

'I need documentation before you can take this body. Plus, it would have to be a closed…'

The man held out a piece of paper. It was signed, 'A close friend' and endorsed by Doris Leyland's mother.

Garner couldn't argue further.

'We have a coffin. Shall I ask the men to bring it in?' said the man.

Garner nodded.

They placed Doris into an expensive coffin with great respect and reverence, then the lid was firmly nailed down. Garner and Peter watched the whole process with solemn interest.

'Oh, wait a minute. There was a pouch in her possessions. The family will probably want this.' He pulled it out of his pocket and held it out.

'Keep it,' said the undertaker. 'For your trouble.'

Garner watched the bearers pick up the coffin and leave. As the doors of the mortuary closed, he looked down at the pouch. *Strange.* He had never in all his years been told to keep the possessions of the dead. It had been given like a tip and it annoyed the doctor.

He threw the pouch at Peter. 'Here. You have it.'

Garner turned to look at the table. Then his eyes fell on the worn-out boots left on the floor. 'Oh look, you didn't put her boots back on!'

News soon went around that Doris was having a proper funeral in the cemetery, and the local street girls and shopkeepers stopped work and came out to see the spectacle as the horse-drawn glass funeral carriage, fit to carry the body of a queen, pulled in front of the church. The girl was seen off with much crying from the few friends she had.

'I can't believe it,' Enid said. 'She must have known a toff that was secretly in love with her or sumat.'

'Don't talk wet,' said Carly. 'Doris, wiv a toff? Never 'appened. We'd all o' known about it.'

The question was on everyone's mind. Who had paid for the funeral?

Toby returned to the shop as the gravediggers started to cover the coffin. A good Christian burial. He had watched the locals crowd round the hole as they lowered the coffin. This was the most exciting thing to happen to any of them, and he wouldn't kill their illusions by letting them know he was the one who had paid for it.

He didn't know why, but he felt responsible for Doris's death. As though some action he had taken had made it happen. Even the fact that until he heard the shouting, he had not heard the attack itself. And the alley was directly below his bedroom, which meant Doris hadn't screamed. She probably didn't even get a chance to.

He had been shocked and numb when he came downstairs to see what was happening. From his vantage point, he had seen the state of her and thought about the horrible blurred-out image on the photographs he had taken that day.

Even now, on the day of the funeral, he could not bring himself to burn that one picture, having already destroyed the unusable negatives. He kept it upstairs in his room, in the safe space under the floorboards. He went there now and retrieved it. The picture was just like her face. If it had been in colour, he was certain he would have seen blood and bone smeared across it. And every picture had looked the same on every negative. As though they were somehow predicting the future.

Stupid, superstitious nonsense! he thought. But he couldn't push the idea entirely away. It was partly why he had paid for the service and funeral, despite the protestations of the priest that Doris didn't deserve to be buried there. A hefty donation ensured the man's compliance and silence, as it had the funeral director's. Money always talked. Toby had known that. It was why he had been trying to make a success of his business. None of that was important now, though, Toby realised.

Money, success, climbing that unattainable social ladder all felt pointless when some unnameable evil came into your life. And someone very evil had destroyed Doris. He knew it. He just didn't know who that person was.

'Toby? You about?' called Artie from downstairs.

Toby pushed the photograph back in the hole with his money and replaced the floorboard. Dropping the rug back in place, he went downstairs to see what Artie wanted.

'Customers,' Artie said as he came into the front studio. A young couple stood there, eagerly waiting to be photographed.

'I'm afraid we're closed today,' said Toby.

'What?' Artie gasped in surprise.

Toby sent the couple away.

'I'm closing the shop for the time being,' Toby explained. 'I'll give you a week's salary. Take some time off and we'll see how I feel in a week's time.'

'What's the matter with you?' asked Artie. 'Closing shop? Why? What's happened?'

'I'm very upset, Artie. I need a break.'

'Upset? About the death of a whore? You're losing your mind.'

Toby's jaw was set in a firm line. 'I don't wish to talk about this.'

He held out a thick wad of money. Artie looked at it. Then took it. 'You're the boss. But it will set tongues wagging.'

Artie left by the front door and Toby locked it behind him, turning the sign to 'Closed'. He cast his eyes around the studio. It was a little untidy, but he didn't have the strength to start clearing up. What did it matter anyway? He was closed for now and he wasn't sure he even wanted to open again. He knew that Artie wouldn't understand his change of mood. Artie was different from Toby in every way. He was far more materialistic, even though Toby had fallen into that trap himself. He'd wanted wealth for a while. Now the idea of his ill-gotten gains sickened him. All this death – even Gallen's, deserved though it was. It was all so shocking, and Toby had so little energy for it all.

Chapter Twenty-Three

'I'm so happy for you both!' said John Mainwaring to Mitchell and Laura.

They were in Mainwaring's colourful garden. A fine spread of food was set out on a long table covered with a white lace cloth. Among the guests was the local vicar, Henry and Elena Carter, and several of the gentry who were related to both of the families.

'This is a fine day indeed,' said Henry, a smile spreading on his lips for the first time in weeks.

'Thank you so much for all of this, Major Mainwaring,' Laura said. 'You've done us both proud.'

'You must call me Uncle John, now that you're almost one of the family,' Mainwaring said.

'In just a few weeks' time,' Mitchell said, taking Laura's hand.

'It was so nice of the vicar to let us do this quickly. I did have to reassure him that the only urgency is the impatience of youth,' Elena said.

'A donation to the church didn't hurt,' Henry winked.

'What about that awful business with the murder?' Mainwaring asked Mitchell. 'Have you heard any more?'

'Not after you spoke to Stream's boss. He's leaving me alone, and the people in the area were deeply touched by Doris's funeral.'

'I don't suppose we shall ever find out who the kind soul was. Although I have to say, such ostentation would have been better spent on the church-roof fund…' Elena said.

'Oh mother, really. I'm sure the girl didn't want to live the life she did. Mitchell explained to me how these things happen sometimes. Girls fall on hard times, or a loved one is sick. I have every sympathy for her. No one deserves to die like that,' said Laura.

Elena didn't argue with her, but she noted how outspoken Laura was becoming of late. It was some inner strength she had pulled on to help her cope with the awful events that had been happening around them. Elena felt her own equilibrium was still off-kilter, but she admired Laura's vigour. Perhaps it was brought on by the restoration of her engagement, or maybe it was a side she had never shown before, but was always there. Elena didn't know. But this strength, she hoped, would sustain her through the difficult years that life sometimes threw one's way.

Mitchell kissed Laura's hand and glanced up to see Neeraj at the back door of the house. The Indian servant made a small gesture and Mitchell excused himself.

'Is everything all right?' Mitchell asked as he followed the man into the kitchen.

'Your uncle wishes me to give you this.' Neeraj held out a small, strange statue. It was a human body with the head of an elephant. 'Lord Ganesha,' said Neeraj. 'He will protect you as you take this new venture of life.'

Mitchell nodded; he recognised the Hindu god. He wasn't sure what Laura would make of the statue, though.

'Mitchell-Sahib,' Neeraj said as Mitchell took the statue. 'Miss Laura … is she quite well?'

'Yes. Of course. No problem at all.'

'Good,' said Neeraj. 'And the picture. Is it the same?'

Mitchell was surprised to realise he had completely forgotten the photograph. He couldn't even recall where in the house he had put it.

'I … don't know.'

'You *must* watch it,' Neeraj said. 'Any change, and you must burn it in the fire. But keep Miss Laura close when you do, or the soul thief may try to take her with it.'

Mitchell held back the response that almost came to his lips: that Neeraj's superstitions were unfounded. He always tried to respect the man's faith, no matter how absurd it appeared.

'Place this statue in the window nearest the front door. Facing outwards. It will keep evil from entering,' Neeraj explained.

'I will.'

Then he took it outside to show Laura.

'Oh, how unusual!' she said. 'Neeraj, will you pack this carefully and have it sent over to the house?'

'Of course, Miss Laura.' Neeraj took the statue back.

Laura took Mitchell's arm and led him away from her parents and Mainwaring.

'Darling, must we really have that hideous thing in the house?'

'It's for luck,' Mitchell laughed. 'You'll get used to Uncle John's artefacts.'

That evening Mitchell unpacked the statue from a small wooden box filled with straw. He placed it facing the front door, just as Neeraj had suggested. Once it was there, he felt strangely calm. It was all superstition, but he hadn't felt the same since Doris's murder and finding arsenic in his drink. Weeks had passed since then, and life was slowly returning to normal. No more strange things had happened and Laura was in excellent spirits. He was starting to think that everything would be fine. The statue of Lord Ganesha in his hallway gave him the sense of peace he had been looking for, odd though it was that such a false notion could work its way into his British way of thinking. He had been brought up surrounded by these things, though, and had indeed accepted their validity when he was a child. He wondered now if India would ever truly leave his soul.

Mitchell recalled that Hindus believed that God was in everyone, that for as long as you had a soul, then God was always with you. It was a beautiful sentiment but it begged the question: what would happen to the body if the soul were absent?

Mitchell went into his study and sat at his desk, looking through the mounting bills for the costs of the wedding. Mainwaring had increased his allowance, almost triple the usual yearly amount, but his godfather had insisted that having a wife would mean a large increase in Mitchell's expenses. He put the bills together in a pile, tying them with a piece of cord, then began to write a note for his butler to arrange to have them sent to Mainwaring in the morning. The nib of his quill broke before he finished. It was just as well that his godfather never really restricted him with his inheritance, but in just a few more years, total control would come to Mitchell anyway, and his mother's and father's money would be in his own hands.

He opened the top drawer of his desk. His hand fell on the blue velvet cloth. The picture of Laura, Sara and Warren was still wrapped inside. He pushed it aside and searched for another quill, then rapidly removed the broken one and fixed the new one to his pen. He continued writing his instructions, then blotted the paper. Once done, he went to close the drawer.

His hand ran over the blue fabric. On impulse, he pulled out the photograph and unwrapped it.

In the dull light everything appeared to be the same as the last time he'd looked at the image. Then he noticed Laura had moved.

He shook his head. *I'm imagining things. This hasn't changed at all.* He, like everyone else, had to let go of this insane notion that the picture was a problem.

He thought back over the last few weeks. Laura was behaving calmly and rationally. There hadn't been a repeat of her night walking and she was very happy. Very together.

A knock on the door announced Mrs Dalton as she brought in a tray of tea and scones for supper. Mitchell covered the picture again and replaced it in the drawer.

'Thought you might like this, sir.'

'Thank you. Did I hear someone at the door earlier?'

'Yes. There's a letter arrived for you.' She nodded towards the tray as she placed it on the desk before him. Mitchell saw a small white envelope placed on a saucer. He reached for it and, using a bone-handled envelope knife, he cut open one end.

Mrs Dalton closed the door quietly behind her as Mitchell read the letter. It was written in an educated hand, but the writer was clearly in a great deal of distress, because the penmanship flowed as though hurried:

> Mr Bishop,
>
> I'm writing to you as the only person I can think of who may be able to help. We met a few weeks ago at the hospital. I'm Dr Glenister, Warren Carter's colleague.
>
> It is most difficult to put these words on paper, and so I won't bore you with pleasantries. I will, in fact, come straight to the point.
>
> There have been some odd occurrences in the hospital.
>
> Some of the staff, and indeed patients, have said they have seen a ghost. Also, I have discovered who the missing records belonged to. It is these things that I wish to discuss with you at some urgency.
>
> I don't believe in ghosts and so I must assure you that I was incredibly sceptical on this matter. However, one of the nurses, and my most valued matron have sworn on the Bible that what they saw was real. They say that Dr Carter came into one of the women's wards and was doing his rounds.
>
> The nurse was in a state of shock and she ran from the ward, calling for help. Matron was the first to arrive and she returned to the ward with the girl, certain that she was imagining things. All she found was a female visiting a sick relative. They questioned her but the woman says she saw nothing. Matron gave the nurse some time off, convinced that she was delusional because she was overworked.
>
> However, the next night the matron saw Dr Carter entering his office. When she went to the door, unlocked it and walked in, she found the room completely empty.
>
> They didn't tell me any of this until after Dr Carter's office was ransacked, and I have been toying with the idea of going to

the police. Somehow, I doubt that Inspector Stream would believe me.

A few nights ago, I was making the rounds on the very same ward, when I saw the female visitor again. She is the daughter of Mrs Adams, I believe, a woman who has been in a terrible state of catatonia for several months now. Rosie, the daughter, is there every day and she is very dedicated. She feeds the woman mashed-up food, the type a baby could swallow, and she is the only person Mrs Adams responds to.

I don't know why I'm even mentioning them, except to say that when I searched for Mrs Adams's medical records, I found them missing. I suspect these were the ones taken from Warren's office.

After that, several of the patients have reported seeing Dr Carter walking through the ward. I don't know if this is just hysteria brought on by the rumour that someone had seen him, but I'm feeling an urgent need to speak to someone rational who doesn't work here.

If you wish to talk to me further, I am working the night shift this evening. I would be more than willing to tell you everything I've learnt.

Yours sincerely,
Dr Iain Glenister

Mitchell put down the note and closed his eyes. It was only eight in the evening, but he was tired. The letter was absurd, but having met Glenister, he realised the man was not given to practical jokes. He looked down at the page again. *Rosie.* Where had he heard that name recently?

'Of course!' he said, hand slapping his forehead. 'Rosie. *She* was called Rosie.'

Mitchell left his supper untouched, removed his smoking jacket and hurried into the hallway.

'Mrs Dalton?'

'Yes, sir?' said his housekeeper, coming out of the dining room, closely followed by Aggie carrying the tray of newly polished silver knives and forks.

'I'm going out. Don't wait up for me.'

Chapter Twenty-Four

'You can't carry on like this,' Artie said. 'That money will eventually run out.'

Toby shrugged. He was standing in the kitchen, half-dressed, unshaven, hair an untidy mess. Artie had never seen him like this and he had been coming every day to try to talk him into opening the shop again.

'We have to open up and start trading again. I don't understand what's wrong.'

'I can't do it anymore,' Toby said. 'The pictures.'

Artie frowned, confused. 'Why not? You love doing them.'

'They hurt people,' Toby said.

'Look, don't be daft. I can take the custom. You won't have to do a fing until you feel better.'

Toby shook his head. 'I can't. I'm going to destroy the equipment. There's clearly something wrong with it.'

Artie's frown deepened. 'You *can't* do that! This is your livelihood. Look … maybe I should get you a doctor?'

'No!' said Toby. 'Go away, Artie. It is probably best if you find yourself a new job.'

Threatening to return with someone to help, Artie left.

Toby sat down in the chair by the kitchen table and looked around at the discarded remnants of his life. Camera parts and frames were left all over. There was barely any room to manoeuvre. He had been studying the pictures carefully, though. And apart from Doris's pictures, he could see nothing that would cause the strange event that had happened. He was convinced he was right, though. Something was very wrong here.

'Hello, Toby.'

Toby looked up to see Rosie stood in the doorway.

'I'm not doing it anymore,' he said.

'I know. I just saw Artie.'

'Then you know there's no point in you being here?'

Rosie nodded. She came inside and closed the door, running the bolt across.

She said nothing but began to busy herself tidying the sink, which was filled with unwashed crockery. After she had washed it and cleared it away, she put a kettle on the stove and began to prepare tea.

'Go upstairs and get shaved. You've been unwashed for too long and you smell like a dead cat.'

Toby looked up, shocked that she could talk to him like that. He didn't know what to say, because he realised it was true. He hadn't washed or changed his clothing for days, maybe weeks. He thought of arguing, of shouting at her until she too abandoned him to his own self-pity, but he couldn't do it. Nothing in the world would ever make him raise his voice to Rosie. So, like a drugged patient in an asylum, he obeyed her and went upstairs to shave.

When he came down, she had pulled the tin bath out and was filling it with hot water.

'Get those clothes off. This is almost ready,' Rosie said.

She had pulled the curtains across the glass panel on the door and across the window above the sink, plunging the room into darkness, with only a small oil lamp and the fire to light it.

'I can't strip with you here…' he objected.

'Why not? You've seen me naked more times than I can count. No time for that nonsense now.'

Toby couldn't explain the difference between seeing her naked and him undressing in front of her, but her voice brooked no argument and so he began to strip, throwing the soiled clothing into a wash-bucket she had left there for the purpose.

She was looking away when he removed his long johns and so Toby quickly stepped into the hot water and sank down before she turned around. She began washing his back with carbolic soap. The smell reminded him of hospitals.

'Bend your head,' she said. Then she proceeded to tip water over his head and began to scrub the greasy, matted mess of hair until it was clean.

The water was soon tainted but Toby began to feel better. It was as though her cleansing was somehow cleaning the fear from his heart and soul.

He stepped out of the bath while she held up a huge towel and he wrapped it around himself. Then she pressed him down into the chair by the fire and began to comb his hair back from his face. It had grown longer over the last few weeks, but she tied it back with a piece of ribbon, then rubbed his neck dry with another towel.

'That's better,' she said, bringing him a cup of tea. 'I always liked the way you shaved your face and didn't hide it under those mutton-chops like some men. It's not a look I've ever cared for.'

Toby sipped the tea. He felt at peace for the first time in weeks.

'What's been ailing you?' she asked.

Toby looked into the fire. He saw no dancing demons lurking there, only clean flames.

'It sounds insane,' Toby said.

Then he poured out the fears and thoughts he had been considering for the last few weeks. As he told Rosie his troubles, it was as though they just disappeared. By the end he was feeling very light-hearted in a way that confession had never given him.

He looked at Rosie, marvelling at how angelic and calm she was. She didn't react at all to his fears, only listened, and Toby felt a true unburdening of the soul.

'You need to understand that you haven't done anything wrong,' she said. 'Humans are animals. They seem to be civilised but then they do the most terrible things. You have only acted exactly as is in your nature. If anyone has a soul, Toby, then it is certainly you. What you did for that girl was a kind thing, and I doubt that she would ever consider you responsible for her death. That crime is on someone else's conscience.'

Rosie took the teacup from his hands and replaced it with a bowl of stew. He swirled the spoon around the bowl, then began to eat slowly, but, as his hunger got the better of him, he ate faster: eating like a starving dog until finally, he resorted to drinking the last drops down, instead of trying to negotiate it all with the spoon.

Rosie passed him a hunk of bread and he mopped it around the bowl.

'That's the best stew I've ever had,' Toby said.

'Any stew is the best when you've starved yourself.'

'You seem to be much older than your years today, Rosie,' Toby said. 'Why is it you're different every time I see you? You are like a hundred people in one body.'

'I'm just me in here, Toby, and I'm nothing special.'

Toby looked around the kitchen: she had managed to tidy everything up while he was upstairs. The lack of chaos aided the new calm he was feeling.

'You're amazing,' he said. 'You come in here and you make everything seem better. Even my worries feel … unimportant.'

'I have a great fondness for you,' she said.

She took his hand.

'I have a great fondness for you too,' he answered.

They looked at each other for a while until Toby could no longer maintain eye contact with her. He wasn't used to women being so direct, even with his dealings with the street girls.

Rosie leaned forward and kissed him. He felt warmth flowing from her and when she stopped, he felt cold in comparison. It was natural to let her lead him upstairs and for the first time, despite the many times he had seen her naked, he watched her disrobe, even helping with the tight corset that hugged her waist.

They lay down on the bed holding each other in the way that Hansel and Gretel may have done in a fairytale, as they huddled together, exposed and afraid under the stars: innocent and loving and protective. Toby wasn't afraid anymore, though, despite his previous mania. Rosie had washed it away and purified him. He was clean and his mind was clear; clearer than it had ever been. He thought he could see the future. The possibilities with Rosie in his life were endless.

She took his lips again and pulled him closer, pressing her small breasts against his chest. The innocent warmth changed to passion, and he followed his heart and body until they were joined.

Rosie groaned beneath him, a mixture of pain and passion, and he knew then that she had been innocent until that moment, just as he had always suspected. Afterwards, he rolled his weight away, propped himself up on his arm and admired her face in the light that filtered in from the landing.

'I love you,' he said.

'I know,' she answered. Then she turned away and promptly fell asleep.

Toby lay beside her happy, but confused. He felt guilty again. Perhaps he had hurt her after all? In her sleep Rosie turned again and placed her hand on his arm. A calm sensation rushed over him. It was as though she had the healing power of an angel. Toby's eyes closed as his mind and body let go of the pain and fear he'd been carrying for some time. Then, for the first time in days, he slept a dreamless and restful sleep.

Chapter Twenty-Five

Once Mitchell was stood outside Glenister's office he considered turning back. He had promised Laura he wouldn't investigate further, but the truth was, the investigation had dried up, and with so many dead ends, it had been impossible to pursue it anyway. Now the doctor's letter promised possible new leads. He could come to some resolution, that might in the future help Laura and her parents understand what had happened to Warren and Sara. Still, there was the guilt of breaking his promise to contend with, but Mitchell tried to convince himself that this was for Laura's greater good.

Making up his mind, he knocked on the door.

'Come in,' Glenister said.

Mitchell found the doctor sitting at his desk in much the same way as the previous time, with the exception that now Glenister didn't look well. He looked frightened.

'Dr Glenister … your note…'

Glenister stood and ushered Mitchell to the chair in front of his desk.

'Since I sent it to you, even stranger things have happened.'

Glenister ran a hand through his hair. Mitchell noted a new streak of white, which had not been there the last time he had seen the doctor, a few weeks before.

'Carter is alive,' said Glenister.

'Doctor, we buried him. I saw the body myself.'

'It can't have been his body. He was here! Not more than a few moments ago. You must have passed him as you came down the corridor.'

'I saw no one,' Mitchell said. 'No, that's not true … there was a young nurse in the corridor.'

'I'm telling you, he was here. I was talking to him!'

'What did he say?' asked Mitchell.

'He told me his death had been faked. That he had to do it because someone was trying to kill him.'

'That's insane,' Mitchell said, but his mind was already beginning to accept the possibility that Warren was alive. The reasoning was strangely plausible. Warren had been afraid that his reputation was going to be sullied after his contact with the girl, Rosie. Mitchell knew that, but … no. He had *seen* Warren's body. Warren was dead. He *really* was.

'I can only tell you what I have seen with my own eyes. I touched him. He was very much here and I didn't imagine it, nor was I hysterical,' Glenister said.

'I believe you *think* you saw Warren. What else did he say?'

'It was all so sudden and confusing. He said I could tell you he was alive and all right, but that you mustn't tell Laura or his parents, as the truth would be devastating for them. I suppose he thought his actions had been very cruel. He mentioned something about not thinking this through properly.'

Mitchell was silent and thoughtful. He wasn't sure how to respond at this point. Again, the reasoning was logical. But it was impossible, wasn't it? If Warren was alive, then whose body was fished out of the canal, and why did he look exactly like Warren?

'Did he say where he was staying?' asked Mitchell.

'No.'

Glenister could tell him nothing more about Warren and, confused by this revelation, Mitchell was about to take his leave of the doctor, when he remembered Rosie.

'Doctor, can you take me to see the patient whose records were missing?'

'Mrs Adams?'

'Yes,' Mitchell said.

'Of course.'

~

Glenister opened the door of the women's ward and nodded to the nurse on night duty.

'Good evening, doctor,' she said.

She glanced at Mitchell then looked down at her ledger as though looking for something very important. Mitchell promptly forgot about her as he followed Glenister down to the bottom of the ward.

'We keep Mrs Adams in a side room of her own,' Glenister explained in whispered tones. 'Her daughter pays for it because she feels it's better for her mother.'

He pushed open a door at the bottom of the room and they went into a small side-room with a single bed, a bedside table, and a chair.

Glenister went over to the bed and began to examine the woman lying there. Mitchell noticed she was a frail, thin shell, as though she had been sucked dry of all nourishment. Her eyes were half open as she stared at the ceiling, but he was certain she was seeing nothing. Glenister checked her pulse, lifted the half-open eyelids, and looked down into her eyes as though he could see her very soul. Then he listened to her faint breathing.

'What happened to her?' Mitchell asked.

'The daughter told me she suffered a blow to the head some months ago and that she has been like this ever since. But I don't know what Warren was doing to treat her, because the records are all gone.'

Mitchell experienced a strange sensation as he looked at Mrs Adams. There was something about her that reminded him of someone else, though he didn't know who. A surge of anger threatened to overwhelm him. It was irrational and reminded him of some past moment when he'd almost lost control and given in to a darkness that he feared somehow lurked inside him. But the emotion fell away as soon as it occurred, leaving Mitchell feeling breathless and weak, as though staring at Mrs Adams had somehow sucked some of the life from him.

He stepped back, turning away from the emaciated figure.

'How often does the daughter visit?' he said, bringing his mind back to the present.

'Twice daily, from what I've been told.'

Mitchell took the details of the times when the girl usually attended and he left Glenister, promising to be back the next day.

'But what about Warren?' Glenister said.

'Did he give you any indication that he would be back to see you?' asked Mitchell.

'He just said he'd be back in touch.'

'If he does get in touch, tell him I need to see him. That I understand his reasons, but it's important that he gets back in touch as soon as possible.'

Glenister nodded and Mitchell left him with the strangely silent Mrs Adams.

As he reached the door of the ward, he saw a girl wearing a brown coat and a brown hat enter. He barely glanced at her as she approached the nurse's desk.

'How is she?' asked the girl.

Mitchell stopped and looked around. Even from behind there was something familiar about the girl. She was around five foot four, with long dark hair worn loose over her shoulders. The hat was familiar, as was the coat. It was tweed and looked as though it had once been an expensive item but was now becoming threadbare. He saw a patch on one of the elbows where it had been repaired.

'The same. Dr Glenister is with her now, if you wish to see him,' said the nurse.

'Rosie?' said Mitchell, coming back.

Rosie turned and, coming face to face with Mitchell for the first time, she frowned. 'Yes?' Her voice was wary. 'Do I know you?'

Mitchell couldn't believe what he was seeing. Without doubt she was the same girl he had seen in the photograph card that Stream had found in the burnt-out room of the thug, Sean Gallen. He was also certain that she was the woman who had been standing in the street the night that Doris died and his brandy had been poisoned. He tried not to let the recognition show, while he looked for signs that she already knew him.

'I'm a friend of Dr Carter's.'

Rosie nodded her head. 'Poor Dr Carter. He was so kind to my mother … but I still don't see how you know me…'

'I'd like to talk to you, if I may?' Mitchell said. 'Perhaps you will come with me?'

'Certainly not. I don't know you, sir!' She pulled her brown reticule up to her chest in a very defensive manner.

'My name is Mitchell Bishop. I've been hired by Miss Carter to investigate the death of Dr Carter and his sister, Sara.'

Mitchell watched her closely as he delivered this information, but her expression remained confused.

'Dr Carter's sister is dead as well? How awful for his family! Of course, I can talk to you, but I don't see how I can be of any help at all. I barely knew the doctor, and I didn't even know he had a sister. He was very kind when I brought my mother in, but … I rarely saw him after that.'

Mitchell walked back to Mrs Adams's room with Rosie. He had been expecting her to run away, guilty of involvement, but her rational responses did not correlate with someone who had something to hide. Glenister was just coming out as they reached the door.

'Miss Adams. We were just talking about your mother,' Glenister said.

'Yes. We were wondering what had happened to her?' Mitchell asked as they entered the room.

'I don't know. I think she hit her head on something. She wasn't feeling well for a few days – dizzy spells, losses in memory. Then I came home one day and found her lying on the floor. She wasn't moving. I've been trying to save money to help… Dr Carter said he knew a doctor in London that might be able to help, but it would cost a lot to get him to come. I don't suppose that will happen now.'

Rosie's explanation of her mother's condition sounded rehearsed to Mitchell's ears, as though this were a story she had decided on, but didn't really believe.

Warren had mentioned a girl called Rosie to him, but he hadn't said she was a patient's daughter, but was a nurse working in the hospital. She was definitely the girl in the photograph, but Mitchell decided not to mention it. It was obvious now why she had done it. She was trying to help her mother. But was she the girl that Warren said he made love to? Or was there another girl, fitting the same description, also called Rosie? Somehow the coincidence was unlikely, but Mitchell really wasn't sure how to broach the question.

'You say ... you really didn't *know* Dr Carter?' Mitchell asked.

'Not at all. I saw him around the hospital on occasion. Gave him the money to save up for the surgeon he knew ...'

'You gave him money, you say? Can I ask how much?'

Rosie blushed then, as though the idea embarrassed her. 'It doesn't matter.'

'But of course it does. You must have your money back, Miss Adams.'

Rosie glanced down at her mother as though she would be able to hear the conversation. 'I only wanted to help her. Nothing else matters now.'

A small amount of spittle dribbled down from Mrs Adams's dry lips. Rosie opened her reticule, removed a handkerchief and dabbed it around her mouth with loving attention. As she went to return the handkerchief to her bag, Mitchell noticed the sketch-pad inside.

'Do you draw, Miss Adams?' he asked.

For a moment Rosie looked confused. Then glancing down, as though realising the pad was there for the first time, she pulled it free.

'Oh no. This is Mother's. She took up sketching a few years ago, just after my father died. It helped her fill many lonely hours, and I keep it with me to remind me how clever and talented she once was.' Rosie held out the pad. 'Please have a look. I'd value your opinion, Mr Bishop.'

Mitchell took the pad. Everything he suspected about the girl could be revealed as true at the turn of the page. Maybe she knew that he had Warren's drawing, or maybe she didn't. Mitchell opened the pad, and began to flick through it. He saw sketches of objects. A vase full of fresh flowers; a chair set at a table with a plate on it, knife and fork positioned as though the person who had once occupied the chair had just left it.

'That was my father's favourite chair,' Rosie explained.

He turned the next page and found an old oak with a makeshift swing hanging from it. Next was a rose bush. The pictures of flowers changed to the scenery at a graveyard, and one particular gravestone, with the name and date of death of Archibald Adams.

'Father's grave,' Rosie said, her voice quiet.

Then there was a picture of Rosie herself, sat by the fire in a dressing gown, hair down, an ornate silver brush sweeping down the length.

'She was very talented,' Mitchell said. 'I'm sorry to have troubled you.'

He closed the pad, not wishing to see more, and gave it back to Rosie. Despite the similar flow of the charcoal, there really was nothing to connect Rosie to this whole sorry business – other than supposition on his part. He couldn't even imagine how or why he would want to bring this girl to Stream's attention.

'Thank you,' she said.

'One other thing…' Mitchell said, pausing at the door. 'Do you know a man by the name of Toby Naylor?'

Rosie blushed.

'I…'

'Let's go outside,' said Mitchell. 'Just in case she can hear.'

Rosie put the pad back into her reticule, and followed him out into the ward and past the nurse's station.

They found a corner in the empty waiting room and sat down.

'I've seen one of your … photographs,' Mitchell said.

'I did it to help my mother,' she said.

'I realise that. You've also confirmed to me that Naylor is behind it.'

'I didn't…' Rosie blustered. 'What are you going to do? I won't admit this to the police … Toby Naylor is the kindest man I've ever met.'

'You're having a relationship with him,' Mitchell said, but it wasn't a question, more a statement of fact.

Rosie nodded. 'Not until … recently, though. It was all about work until … then.'

'What about Dr Carter?'

'I told you, I hardly knew… Wait, you think I was having a … relationship with Dr Carter?' Rosie laughed at the absurdity. 'Good grief, what type of person do you take me for? I went to Naylor to do those … pictures for the money, to get a London surgeon here to look at my mother. Carter took the money for it. I gave him nothing else, nor did he ask me to.'

'Thank you,' said Mitchell. 'I now know that everything else you've told me is the truth.'

'How?' Rosie said. She looked frightened and shaken, her whole calm completely dispersed.

'Your emotional reaction when confronted with an obvious truth, and the honesty with which you explained yourself.'

'What are you going to do?'

'Nothing,' said Mitchell. 'The way I see it, you have just

been doing what you can to help your mother. That shows great love and courage. But … what were you doing outside my house three weeks ago?'

Rosie looked surprised. 'I don't know what you mean. I've only just met you, Mr Bishop. How would I know where you live?'

Mitchell could tell she believed it was the truth, but he had seen her there with his own eyes.

'St John's Street, off Deansgate,' he prompted.

Rosie thought about it. 'I don't recall being there at any time. But I think I know the street you mean.'

'You'd remember being out at three in the morning, though?'

Rosie shook her head. 'I would never be out at that time of night.'

Mitchell studied her but could see no sign of a lie. He began to wonder if he had just imagined the girl in brown outside his house was Rosie, or whether there was another girl, who might have been dressed similarly and had happened to pass through his street. It wasn't unreasonable to feel paranoid, with the unusual circumstances that had haunted him and Laura over the past six months, but he realised that he might be looking for clues where there were none.

'I swear I don't know anything about your home or you, Mr Bishop. How could I?'

'I'm sorry. This must all seem so peculiar to you.'

'Yes. It does.'

'I'll take my leave of you now, Miss Adams. Thank you for your honesty.'

Mitchell bowed his head and turned to leave, but she caught onto his arm. 'What about Toby?'

'Mr Naylor is running an illegal operation,' Mitchell said. 'I should really inform Inspector Stream that I know about it.'

'What if I promised he would stop? That his business would be nothing more than legitimate photographs from now on?'

'You can guarantee that?'

'Toby has asked me to marry him. He has already told me that he won't be taking those pictures anymore. He only did it because he owed someone money.'

'You seem to know rather a lot more than I suspected.'

'Only because he told me everything last night, when he proposed. He wants to have no secrets between us, Mr Bishop, and I came here tonight to … tell the hospital to put mother in an asylum. I can't do this anymore…'

Mitchell was surprised by her words, because the love she had for her mother was so evident.

'I have to start living again. This isn't living. And I want to be there for Toby. He needs me now. Mother never really has…'

'If Naylor has ceased his criminal activities, Miss Adams, then I won't feel any legal requirement to tell the police anything about it.'

Rosie took his hand and kissed it. 'Thank you, sir. You're a decent man. I promise he will stay out of trouble from now on.'

Although he felt sympathy for her, and planned to keep his promise and his new knowledge a secret, Mitchell was still left in a quandary. He had believed that Warren was seduced by a strange girl called Rosie. This part of the puzzle was far from being resolved. If it hadn't been for the drawing, Mitchell might well have believed that the whole thing was in Warren's disturbed imagination. After all, Warren had clearly been suffering from a great deal of remorse regarding his abandonment of Sara to the sanatorium. Mitchell was sure that Warren's guilt had been heightened by her subsequent death. But what of it? What did it all mean? And, if Warren had hallucinated the whole thing, then it might stand to reason that Rosie, an attractive and vulnerable girl, could become the face for that vision. This explanation didn't work when it was juxtaposed with the drawing – which *was* real and not imagined.

As Mitchell took his leave of Rosie, his mind filled with more questions that he knew might never be answered.

Dr Glenister stepped out of the shadows as Mitchell and Rosie walked away. He watched the girl go and a plan formed in the back of his less-than-honest mind. The girl had given Mitchell some interesting information and Glenister knew just how he would use it.

<h1 style="text-align:center">Chapter Twenty-Six</h1>

Dr Glenister closed his office door only to find that Warren Carter had returned and was sitting by the fire.

'Oh good, you're back. Mitchell Bishop was in the hospital. Let me send for one of the orderlies to see if they can catch up with him. I don't think he believed that you were really alive. I think the man thought I was losing my marbles.'

'He was here?' said Warren.

'Yes. I sent for him, as you told me to.'

Warren turned in his chair. Glenister didn't notice the bloated flesh that was slowly rotting from his face: a sure sign of drowning. All he saw was Warren as he had always been – young and handsome.

An odour wafted from the decaying skin. On some level Glenister noticed it, but he gave no sign as he returned to his desk and lit a cigar. The smoke filled the room, masking the rank smell somewhat, and Glenister breathed in the smoky air as though it were as fresh as the atmosphere at the seaside.

'Cigar?' Glenister said.

'Don't send for Mitchell,' Warren said. 'I'm not ready to see him yet.'

Glenister nodded. 'Very well. But you're going to have to come clean to your family at some point.'

They passed some time talking pleasantries. Glenister offered Warren a drink, which he refused, and during this time, he told Warren everything he had overheard Rosie and Mitchell discussing.

'Looks like you were stringing her along – eh, old man? Some fake doctor from London that could help…'

Warren said nothing. He listened to Glenister waffle.

'I suspect you even turned your own room over…' Glenister said. 'Missing records, taking the money you'd hidden in there…'

'You have some point you are trying to make, I assume?' Warren's corpse said.

'Where's the money? The girl isn't bothered about recouping it. I suspect we could probably persuade her to come up with a bit more. I want a cut.'

Warren's smile was crooked. His lips crumbled as he stretched his mouth wider across his face, but Glenister only saw the familiar handsome face. He tried to ignore the feelings it invoked. He had always felt drawn to Warren in a way that made him feel uncomfortable. There was something about the man that Glenister found attractive. Part of him had hopes that this new development – this secret he shared with Warren – meant that Warren had more than a business interest in him too. But that secret side of his nature could never be openly expressed.

'I knew I could count on you,' Warren said.

'Of course, old boy. I'm here for you anytime,' Glenister said, taking a drag of his cigar to cover this strange surge of hope that made his heart lurch a little and gave him a slight butterfly sensation in the pit of his stomach.

Warren stood, and moved away from the dying embers of the fire, which was just as well, because the heat made him rot faster.

'I think maybe you should bring the girl in,' Warren said. 'We should have a little chat with her and try to come to an arrangement.'

'Good idea!'

Glenister watched as Warren pulled the call bell. He felt tired. He placed the cigar in the ashtray on his desk and closed his eyes for a second.

~

'You wanted to see me?'

Glenister's eyes shot open. Rosie Adams was in the room, standing before his desk.

'Yes. Erm…' He looked round her. Warren had gone. *Blast it! Where had he disappeared to now?*

'Dr Glenister?' Rosie prompted.

'I believe you had an arrangement with Dr Carter.'

Rosie frowned.

'Please sit down,' Glenister said. The girl sank into the chair before him.

'Your mother is … very sick … I think I can get in contact with…'

'That's all right, doctor. I've changed my mind about that now. My mother is perfectly happy where she is. I believe it will be impossible to cure her…'

'Quite so. But your financial donations will continue. I will take them in the future.'

'*Excuse me?*'

'You will continue to bring me fifty pounds a week. As you did Carter.'

'I … can't. I don't have that kind of money…'

'Then you have to persuade your boyfriend to continue taking those filthy pictures of you.'

Rosie gasped, a bright-red blush covering her cheeks. 'How…? Doctor… I can't… I promised…'

'Bishop? He won't know anything if you're both careful. I'd also like to see some of those pictures,' Glenister said.

Rosie burst into tears. 'Please, doctor. I can't…'

'I'll leave it with you,' Glenister said heartlessly, leading her to the door. 'Fifty pounds by Friday, or I may just have to tell the police everything I overheard.'

Rosie stumbled from the room. Outside Glenister's office she bumped into a woman wearing a brown coat, much like her own, but her eyes were so blurred with tears, she couldn't make out who it was. She hurried away down the corridor, fear and anxiety eating at her heart. This was the worst thing that could ever have happened to her. She couldn't force Toby to start doing the pornographic photographs again, not without explanation. She would have to tell him everything now. Even what was *really* wrong with her mother.

'Why are you back?' asked Glenister.

Rosie stood in the doorway. She was no longer crying. Glenister sat back in his seat and smiled.

'I've been thinking,' Rosie said.

She locked the door, then turned, and began to remove her coat. She dropped it down over the chair she had been occupying earlier. Then she began to unbutton her blouse, pulling it free from the skirt.

'I mean, why have pictures when you can have the real thing?' she continued.

Underneath she was wearing a white chemise and a tight corset.

Glenister coughed.

Rosie's skirt fell to the floor. She stepped out of it and leaned over the desk. He could see the soft curve of her breasts swelling up above the corset, hidden by just the thin fabric of her shift.

'I mean … there are many understandings that could be reached,' Rosie said.

'I want to see you naked,' Glenister said.

The corset dropped, and Rosie began to unbutton the top of the chemise. Her pert bosom fell out and Glenister rose to his feet, reaching for her. Rosie backed away, forcing him to come around the desk.

The chemise fell to the floor: Rosie wasn't wearing anything underneath.

'Little slut,' Glenister said.

Rosie laughed. She danced naked near the hearth like a nymph or witch casting a spell in a forest around a campfire. Glenister began to remove his clothes. What she was offering appealed to him far more than the potential money, which would have been spent on prostitutes anyway.

She was on all fours, waving her bare buttocks at him, daring him to take her. Glenister was excited. He kneeled down behind her. He closed his eyes as he reached for the girl, pulling her back towards him. Then he heard laughter and opened his eyes. Warren was kneeling in front of him, not Rosie.

Glenister half-yelled, half-gasped. He pulled away, saw the naked man turn to look at him. Warren's taut body was beautiful, just as Glenister had already imagined. But the guilt of those feelings brought a shudder to his spine and he backed away from him in horror.

'But isn't this what you really crave, Glenister?' Warren's awful mouth said.

Glenister stared at the blackened teeth, the rotted face, the white irises of a dead man, seeing him as he really was for the first time. A walking, decaying corpse.

'Horrible,' Glenister gasped, trying to get away, but he found his back was against the desk.

Warren advanced, snake-like tongue slipping between his lips, flicking from side to side.

'What are you?' Glenister cried.

The rotted corpse of his colleague crawled over him, rancid breath hissed into his face, and the blackened tongue licked at his cheek.

Glenister was paralysed with fear. He felt as though he were in the middle of some horrifying nightmare.

At some point the shallow framework of his mind broke, and Glenister was insane long before the corpse began to tear the flesh from his chest. He was laughing as the terrible fingers tore into his abdomen. His crazed mind barely registered the way Warren's face changed back to Rosie's, nor the hundreds of other faces that crossed its features, even those of Toby Naylor and Laura Carter. Glenister didn't understand any of it. He went inside himself, hiding from his own torturous death in insanity.

Part V

Chapter Twenty-Seven

'Please sit,' Mitchell said as Inspector Stream glanced at the generous platter of eggs and ham on the table.

'Don't mind if I do…' said Stream.

'Why are you here?'

'There's been a very unpleasant occurrence,' said Stream.

Mitchell stopped eating and sat back in his chair.

'Dr Glenister is dead,' Stream said.

'I was with him last night…' Mitchell said. 'He appeared to be in perfect health.'

'I know. Someone at the hospital told me you were there.'

Stream described the circumstances in which he found Glenister. 'His intestines were wrapped around his throat and his hands were holding them, as though he'd cut himself open and tried to strangle himself to speed it along.'

'That's utterly…'

Stream continued to eat his breakfast, taking a slurp from the teacup beside him.

'Horrible?'

'I was going to say … impossible. I just can't imagine a man like Glenister killing himself.'

'He didn't do it to himself, that I'm certain of. But there was the strange circumstance of the bolted door that had to be broken down in order to get to him. Bolted from the inside.'

'The killer escaped through a window?'

Stream looked thoughtful. 'Possible, but they were all locked from the inside as well.'

Stream went on to explain how the screams issuing from Warren's room had alerted the night staff that he was in trouble.

'One of the witnesses said he thought he saw Dr Carter's ghost sitting at Glenister's desk. Just for a second. He was shocked after finding Glenister, so I'm not taking that very seriously.'

Mitchell recalled what Warren had told him of Sara's last moments. She had also died screaming in a locked room, her body found like a mangled doll.

'Glenister said he had seen Warren,' Mitchell said, realising that he would have to share some of what he knew with Stream now.

'Carter is dead, how is that possible?'

'I don't know. I had identified Warren for the family at the morgue. It was definitely him and he was dead.'

Omitting Rosie as much as possible, Mitchell explained what Glenister had told him.

'So, Carter is possibly alive,' Stream said. 'It's possible he faked his own death.'

'The story is plausible, but I believe that Warren is dead. As I said, I saw his body.'

'There's only one way to confirm this. We will have to exhume,' Stream said.

'The family have been through so much… Will you let me explain this to them?'

Stream nodded and took a bite out of a freshly buttered piece of bread.

'I'll speak to Laura about it, then. I was hoping to spare her all this, but under the circumstances, I will have to tell her everything.'

~

'You didn't have to come,' Mitchell said as the bearers carried Warren's coffin out of the crypt.

'He's my brother. If there's any chance that he is still alive, then I must know about it and find him before anything else happens,' Laura said.

Mitchell wrapped his arm around her shoulders as the bearers placed the coffin down in front of them.

'Perhaps you should look away,' Mitchell said.

Laura shook her head in refusal but couldn't speak. She was still in black; the wedding in just one week's time would be the only acceptable opportunity for her to wear another colour for many months to come.

'Open that up,' said Stream brusquely to one of his constables. The man stepped forward with a crowbar and began to prise the lid off the coffin. It had only been interred for a few weeks, but already the wood was warping with the dampness of the crypt.

Laura turned into Mitchell's chest as the lid lifted, at the last minute her bravery dissolving.

'Mr Bishop,' Stream said. 'Can you come here, please?'

He left Laura where she was and stepped forward. There was a body still inside the coffin, and Mitchell was certain it was Warren Carter, despite the obvious decay that had occurred in the interim.

'It's definitely him,' said Mitchell. Then he turned to find Laura by his side, staring down at the rancid remains of her brother.

'Oh God!'

Mitchell caught her as she began to fall, shock and disgust taking its toll on her frayed nerves.

Stream nodded at the bearers and they began to hammer new nails into the lid, placing it firmly back where it belonged.

Mitchell helped Laura back into the carriage.

'I'm sorry. That was so weak of me. I detest women who constantly swoon,' Laura said.

Her hands were shaking as Mitchell offered her a flask.

'What's in it?'

'Gin. It might help,' he explained.

She took a tiny sip of the liquor. The taste was strong, but pleasant, and so she drank a little more, feeling the alcohol dull her senses.

They sat in the carriage while she revived. Once Mitchell was certain she was all right, he went back to the graveside to speak to Stream.

At this point they had returned the coffin to the crypt and Father Radley flicked holy water over the coffin, genuflected and said the words of interment again to help resettle Warren's soul.

'Glenister must have been insane,' said Stream. 'It's the only explanation.'

'Then insanity is catching,' said Mitchell.

'Whatever do you mean?'

'Warren was insane. Sara was insane. Glenister was insane. It doesn't add up.'

'No. It doesn't,' said Stream. 'And I think you know more about this than you're letting on.'

Mitchell didn't answer. He couldn't break his promise to Rosie. He knew deep inside that she wasn't responsible for what had happened to any of these people, but he couldn't deny that she was somehow connected with Warren and Glenister, at least. Then there was Naylor's link to it all…

Damn it!

He took his leave of Stream, not wanting to impart any other information for the time being. In the carriage, heading back to Laura's home, Mitchell's mind was full of Toby Naylor. He realised once more how Artie had foolishly distracted him on the day he visited. He hadn't managed to question the man about what he saw the day Warren died.

As he walked Laura into her house, he recommended that she take a rest, and promised to be back later.

'Where are you going?' she asked.

'I just have some business to attend to.'

'Mitchell…'

'Yes, darling?'

'Promise me you won't get any more embroiled in this awful business. I'm frightened.'

Mitchell couldn't promise, but he kissed her and held her close, hoping to offer some reassurance. 'Everything is going to be fine.'

He didn't believe, however, that it was. His heart told him that something unnatural was happening, even as his mind refused to believe it. His thoughts flew to Neeraj and the advice his old friend had given him. He believed the man's sincerity. He was afraid also, but not for himself, for Laura. On impulse he removed the necklace with the talisman that had remained close to his heart ever since Neeraj gave it to him. He placed it around Laura's neck.

'What is this?'

'Don't take it off, all right?'

'But…'

'It's a good-luck charm. From India.'

Laura smiled. He knew she would indulge him on this. She thought his birth in India somewhat romantic and was very curious about the beliefs of the people.

Laura tucked the charm away under her blouse and kissed him again.

'Really, you two!' said Elena Carter from the drawing room. 'You shouldn't carry on like that with the servants around.'

'Sorry, Mother!' called Laura. Then she kissed him again – a quick peck this time.

'Go and rest. I'll be back in a few hours.'

He climbed back into the carriage feeling more reassured that Laura would be safe for now, but he couldn't shake the overwhelming fear that something bad would happen if he didn't open his heart and mind to explore the impossible, as well as the possible.

'Thank you,' said Toby to the young couple whose picture he had just taken. They took their receipt and left, smiling and holding hands.

'Another satisfied customer?' Rosie said from the doorway.

'Darling! You're here!' said Toby. He hurried over to her and lifted her in the air with his excitement.

Rosie giggled as he put her down, but not before planting a warm kiss on his lips.

'I missed you last night,' he said. 'I thought you were going to come back after visiting your mother.'

'I was. But she'd taken a turn for the worst. The matron said it is best if … I let her go.'

Toby pulled her into his arms. 'I'm so sorry, Rosie. That must be awful for you.'

Rosie took the comfort he offered. His arms around her made her feel safe. They strengthened her resolve for what she might have to face in the future.

She had spent the evening in her small flat in Prestwich, mulling over the awful conversation she'd had with Dr Glenister, and she had come to the conclusion that she must never return to the hospital. No matter how difficult it was for her to no longer see her mother. She wouldn't let Glenister blackmail her. She reasoned that, if he went to the police, then his knowledge of the events would be questioned, and so would his involvement with Dr Carter's death. This might be enough to retain his silence. If, that was, he was smart enough to realise he was implicating himself.

At that moment, Artie came into the studio from the darkroom. 'Oh, 'scuse me!'

Rosie and Toby separated. 'That's okay,' Rosie said, smiling.

'Didn't know you two were … an item,' Artie said.

'We're getting married,' Toby said.

Artie frowned. 'That's a bit sudden, ain't it?'

'Yes,' said Toby. 'She saved me.'

'In that case, I have you to thank for the reinstatement of me job.'

'Yes, you do,' said Toby. 'So be nice to her.'

Artie nodded. 'Cuppa tea, then?'

'I'll get it,' said Rosie. 'Might as well make myself useful.'

She left the room and for a moment there was an awkward

silence as Artie tried to find the words to say what he was thinking, but without offending Toby. In the interim, Toby began to tidy up the studio area.

'You … erm … sure you know what you're doing?' he asked finally.

'I've never been happier in my life,' Toby said. 'Or more certain.'

'But she … she's a…'

'A what?'

'Well…'

'What are you trying to say? If you mean Rosie is a street girl, then you couldn't be more wrong. She was innocent until I…'

Artie looked down at his feet and flushed, but a big grin covered his face. 'Sorry, it's none of me business … but seriously … if you and her have … well done, you!'

The tension defused and Toby began to laugh. The two men were slapping each other on the back when Rosie returned with the tray containing teapot and cups. She eyed them nervously, then broke out in a smile when they noticed her.

'I made some cake this morning. Want some?'

'It's going to be nice having her around,' said Artie, grabbing a piece of the cake from the tray.

'I know,' Toby smiled at Rosie. Shyness returned to her expression and she blushed a little as she recognised the love and desire in his eyes.

'Artie, look after the shop. I'm taking Rosie out to buy her a ring. We also have to go and speak to the priest.'

'Priest?' Rosie said.

'Yes. I want to marry you as soon as possible.'

Rosie blushed again. 'I'll get my coat.'

Chapter Twenty-Eight

Rosie and Toby walked through the church grounds holding hands. Father O'Shawnessy had been very accommodating when Toby had produced a donation large enough for a dock worker's yearly salary. He hadn't even minded that Rosie wasn't Catholic.

'A small formality. We'll baptise you the morning before the wedding and everything will then be in order,' O'Shawnessy had said.

Rosie and Toby were happy when they left, but fear still clouded the excitement for Rosie.

'You okay?' Toby said after she had been quiet for a while.

'Yes. Just … sad that Mum won't be around to enjoy it.'

'Will you have time to get a dress?' he asked.

Rosie laughed. 'Now that should be the thing on my mind right now, shouldn't it? We're getting married in a few days and I haven't got anything at all, and you know what? It doesn't matter. Not one little bit. I have my mum's dress, as it happens, so at least I'll feel she is with me in spirit. I'll need to alter it a little, though. She was a bit wider than me in those days. A bonny lass, my dad always said.'

'What happened to your dad? I assume he's not around anymore now?'

'Oh, look!' Rosie said, pointing to a group of people gathered around a crypt further up in the graveyard.

Toby stopped walking and pulled Rosie behind another crypt when he recognised Mitchell Bishop and Inspector Stream standing beside the open door of the Carter family tomb. They watched them remove a coffin from inside.

'Damn! That detective fellow. What's he up to, then?' he said.

'You *know* him?' Rosie said.

'Yes. He came with the police last week to talk about… It was after Gallen died. They found one of your pictures at the crime scene.'

Rosie couldn't bring herself to tell Toby that she had met Mitchell at the hospital. Or that she had promised him that Toby would give up the pornography sideline. He had already said he was done with it. He didn't want to give the local thugs another hold on him, and he wanted no more to do with the girls that walked the streets. Their lives were too precarious and he needed to feel his conscience was clear if anything happened to any of them. So, Rosie believed this was a promise she could easily keep without mentioning anything to Toby. Even so, she hated having secrets from him: it was a bad start to a marriage.

'Why are they removing that coffin?' Rosie whispered, trying to distract herself as much as Toby.

'I don't know. That woman with him is Miss Carter. Her brother and sister died recently. Mysterious, it was. I suspect that's their crypt.'

'I suppose a lot of men have those pictures of me. I might consider changing my appearance a little,' Rosie said suddenly.

Toby looked at her surprised. 'I'm sorry, darling. It's all my fault.'

Rosie hugged him. 'Of course it isn't! I came to you.'

They watched the scene pan out in front of them until finally Mitchell took Laura to the carriage when she became faint.

Toby frowned as they put the coffin back inside.

'Oh no!' Rosie said suddenly. 'I left my reticule back in Father O'Shawnessy's office.'

'We'll go back and get it,' Toby said.

'That's okay. You stay here, I'll only be a moment.'

She was back quicker than he expected, but her hand was cold when she pressed it into his fingers.

'Where's your reticule?' he asked.

Rosie looked back at the church and frowned. 'The door was locked. There's nothing special in it. I can collect it another time. Let's go.'

They walked back through the graveyard.

'You didn't tell me about your father,' Toby said. 'Is he dead?'

'Yes.'

'Was your mother widowed for long?'

'Not long.'

Toby stopped walking and turned to look at Rosie, but it wasn't Rosie holding his hand. It was Doris, and her face was all caved in. Just as it had been after the attack in the alley behind his shop.

He tried to pull his hand free, a scream choking in his throat.

The face before him altered. It became the laughing corpse of Warren Carter, the sensual seductress Sara Carter, and then it turned back into the vile parody of his future wife. Only this Rosie's eyes weren't blue, they were black. In fact, the blackness filled them, blotting out any sign of white. *Reptilian eyes*, Toby thought as he saw his own reflection in them.

He couldn't pull away. What manner of creature had he fallen in love with?

'Toby? Toby, where are you?'

He heard her voice as though it were coming to him via a tunnel.

'Rosie?' he said to the thing holding his hand. 'Ouch!'

He looked down as the creature gouged his hand. Yanking hard, he managed to free himself.

He backed away, then tripped over a low tombstone, falling backwards onto what appeared to be a freshly dug grave.

Toby let out a scream as the changeling approached. It was holding something out to him now. Toby registered that it was a piece of charcoal, but didn't understand the significance at all. The thing swirled it around as though measuring him up.

'What are you?' he yelled.

'*Toby?*'

He saw Rosie running towards him. The thing between them changed again: the face of an old woman ran across the fast-smoothing features, and then it was Sara Carter again. It jumped over him, more agile than a corpse should have been, and ran into the trees at the side of the church.

'Toby!' Rosie gasped as she reached him. 'Who was that?'

She reached for him but he shrank back. The sight of her looking so normal frightened him almost as much as the creature that had worn her face.

'What happened? You're hurt.'

His racing heart beat so rapidly in his chest that he felt as though he would keel over at any moment.

'Darling?' Rosie said gently. 'Let me help you.'

Pushing back his revulsion, Toby let her help him to his feet. At that moment a bobby, rapidly followed by Stream, rounded the corner.

'We heard a yell. What happened?' asked the bobby.

'There was a woman,' Rosie said. 'She attacked Toby.'

'Is that true, Naylor?' asked Stream.

Toby nodded. He could barely breathe, let alone speak. He felt as though the creature had sucked the breath from his lungs.

'What happened?' asked Stream impatiently.

Toby looked at Rosie. Her features were steady, unchanging, just as they had always been, but he couldn't help wondering why that thing had looked so like her. He met her blue eyes – no hint of the soulless black there. They were pleading with him, but he didn't know what she was pleading for.

'Some … crazy woman attacked me…' he stammered.

'Did you know her?' Stream said.

Toby shook his head, then glanced back at Rosie.

'She … no … I've never seen her before.'

Stream looked at Toby's hand. 'Better get a doctor to tend to that,' he said. 'Come along, we'll give you a lift to the infirmary.'

The accident room at the infirmary was busy. Rosie kept her head down and cast concerned glances around at the doctors and nurses on duty. She didn't wish to be recognised. The last thing she needed was Glenister strolling in right now. He was sure to realise that Toby was her boyfriend, and he may just be indiscreet enough to say something about the photographs and the money.

'You'll have to wait your turn,' said one of the nurses. 'We're two doctors down now.'

'*Two* down, you say?' asked Rosie.

The nurse looked pointedly at Inspector Stream.

'Dr Glenister was found dead in his office last night,' Stream explained. 'There's some weird goings-on in this hospital.'

He looked directly into Rosie's face and for the first time, a prickle of recognition formed in his otherwise bumbling brain.

'I know you from somewhere. Never forget a face,' he said.

Rosie looked down. 'I don't think so, inspector. I've never had dealings with the police before today.'

'Glad to hear it,' he said. Then he frowned as he tried to recall where he had seen her.

'Inspector?' Sergeant Grimes said. 'Can I see you for a moment?'

Stream went away as Toby gripped Rosie's hand for the first time since the attack. 'Go back to the shop. I'll be fine.'

'I'm not leaving you,' she answered.

'Stream will remember eventually. He's seen your photo, remember. I'd rather he didn't pull you in for questioning.'

Tears sprang to her eyes. 'What's happening, Toby? Who was that woman?'

'I don't know…' Toby said.

'But she was … wearing my coat. I mean, a coat identical to mine, even down to the patch on the elbow. I could see it as I ran towards you. I sewed that patch on myself. There can't be two like it.'

Toby looked down. 'It was so strange. You had just gone, and then you came back. But it wasn't you, Rosie. I thought it was. It looked like you. It really did. And I was fooled for a while…'

Rosie's face turned a vivid red. She looked frightened.

'Why didn't you tell *him*?' she said. Her voice was barely above a whisper.

'*Stream?* I wasn't going to say anything that might make him look at you more closely.'

'What's happening?' Rosie said, fear in her eyes as they darted guiltily around the room.

'Go back to the shop. Tell Artie I had an accident, but no more detail than that. Say I fell in the churchyard… I'll get a cab back when I get this fixed.'

Rosie nodded. Stream had gone somewhere with his sergeant, but it was likely he would be back and he was bound to want to question her more. She kissed Toby on the forehead and walked out of the emergency room.

Chapter Twenty-Nine

The front door was unlocked, but no one was in the studio when Mitchell arrived at Naylor's photography shop. As he opened the door a bell rang above his head. Almost immediately Artie came out of the darkroom. He was wearing a thick apron over his clothes, and a pair of clear-lensed spectacles perched on his nose. His face dropped when he saw Mitchell near the desk.

'Can I 'elp you?' he asked.

Mitchell placed the photograph of Laura, Sara and Warren on the counter. It was still wrapped in the blue velvet cloth. He noticed Artie glance at it, but didn't offer to unwrap it or explain what it was.

'You can start by telling me what you saw, the day Warren Carter died,' Mitchell said.

'I already told the police everyfink. Why you bothering me about this? I never want to see nuffink like it again.'

'You told the inspector that Warren threw himself into the canal.'

Artie nodded.

'Just talk me through this. When did you first meet Warren Carter?'

'You know the answer to that already. He came to the shop a few months ago. Him and his sisters. Toby took the picture while I was in the back. I came through as they were finished, took the money and gave Mr Carter a receipt.'

'So, you weren't present when they posed for the picture?' Mitchell asked.

'No. I 'ardly ever got involved then. I take a lot of the pictures now, though.'

Mitchell walked around the room, looking at the pictures on the walls.

'When did you see Warren again?' Mitchell asked.

'When he came back to collect it. Then he paid for another one, I fink. For his sister's wedding. But he came in an' cancelled that a bit later... So probably a couple of times before...'

'And on the day he died?'

Artie's mind flew back to his relationship with Warren. He was considering just how much he could tell Bishop without getting himself and Toby into more trouble.

A few weeks earlier...

Artie loved his job. He enjoyed it most when Toby let him take the photographs. Sometimes he would sketch the people into the poses he wanted, just to show them how it would look. He had always had a talent for that, but lately the sketching had become easier. He felt it was because he had a clearer idea of how he wanted a picture to look, and he put that down to his interest in photography.

At first the job at Naylor's had been *just* a job. Then something happened one day when Toby was out of the room. He peered down the lens of the camera and he saw the world in a different way. It was a captured moment. The picture would never change, or age, even though the people in it would. It was a piece of immortality that could, as Artie saw it, go on and be there in years to come.

It had been Artie who had suggested Toby take pictures of the local doxies and sell them as a sideline. Artie had even passed the word around to get some of them to come to the studio. It was, after all, not something Toby, as a good Catholic boy, would have ever come up with on his own.

The benefits, of course, outweighed any risks when they first started. It was a secret. Something Artie shared with frustrated husbands and single men he knew. The postcards sold far better than expected, and word of mouth spread. Artie made some real money for the first time in his life, and he started to branch out a little on his own. Taking the cards out of the shop and passing them to local businessmen. People with the money to spare. Even Dr Warren Carter had bought a few…

Artie had dealt with Warren a lot. He never came on the open nights, for fear of being recognised by the other punters, so Artie had taken care of it all privately. That's why he had been down by the canal that morning. It was why he was the last person to see Warren alive.

He had been looking downriver, watching one of the cargo barges making its way slowly through the still water, a huge cart-horse pulling it along, walking the path at the side of the canal. He had always liked this place, found it soothing. Very few people loitered in the area, so it was a perfect place to sell the picture cards.

He spent a few moments looking at them. Rosie was definitely the most interesting of the models, and he had added some of the latest ones of her to his pile. He was sure someone like Warren would appreciate her far more than the street-girl pictures that were more graphic but had little class. It was a risk, though; Warren had only ever bought the really dirty pictures before. The ones of the girls together, doing things to each other, for example.

But Rosie was something special, Artie could see that, and he had noticed that her more artistic pictures were selling better on the open nights than all of the others combined.

Artie had heard raised voices. It sounded like a lovers' spat. He glanced around but couldn't see anyone for a moment. Then he realised that Warren was under the bridge about 250 feet away. He peered into the darkness, noticed a female shape by Warren's side, and grinned.

Maybe the doctor had finally acted on his frustrations and had taken a whore under the bridge to get some satisfaction? Whatever he had done, though, there certainly was a disagreement about price. Warren wasn't happy and neither was the girl.

Artie wandered closer in the hope of picking out the details of the argument. He was naturally voyeuristic, but also thought it important sometimes to know things about people. You never knew when information would come in handy.

'I'm losing my mind. You shouldn't be here!' Warren said.

He sounded tired, frightened. Artie recalled that Warren had recently lost a relative. A sister, perhaps. He glanced over to the bridge, but tried not to bring attention to himself. There was definitely a woman there.

'You're so naïve, Warren. I can be anywhere … anytime.'

'What are you?' Warren said. 'I know you aren't *her*. She's dead.'

There was laughter. A cruel female sound that resonated in Artie's soul on a level he couldn't understand, but terrified him nonetheless.

'I'm everything you ever wanted,' said the woman. 'I can be anyone, anything. All you have to do is relax and enjoy it. All you have to do is stop fighting me… Your soul is already mine.'

'Get away from me!' Warren said. He sounded genuinely frightened, and disgusted. Artie forgot about discretion and stared at the blackness under the bridge.

'You want to know what I am,' said the woman.

Then through the corner of his eye, Artie saw the strange transformation. The woman warped. Her height, clothing, face and hair all changed. He turned his head to look directly, to see if his mind was playing tricks with him, but she had stepped back further into the shadow, as though she were aware that someone else was looking in. Artie squinted but couldn't make out who she was.

Warren could see her, though, and he began to scream, running from the tunnel as though the very devil was after him.

Artie dropped the picture cards he was holding as Warren ran full pelt towards him.

Warren gasped. 'Monstrous…'

He was purple in the face and looked as though his heart was about to burst in his chest. Artie was scared, but didn't know why. He looked back at the bridge: what he saw almost drove him out of his mind. The thing that stood there was neither man nor woman, and he turned away in horror. He pushed the memory of it down and away into a safe compartment in his mind, excusing it as his overactive imagination. It couldn't be real. Nothing could live and look like that.

Warren screamed again. White foam around his mouth, he looked like a madman, but Artie knew why, even though he refused to accept it. The sight of the thing he had been talking to was enough to turn the sanest man into a lunatic. Warren grabbed Artie's arm.

'Did you see it? Did you?'

Artie shook his head: he refused to acknowledge seeing anything, though his eyes were drawn back to the bridge and his head turned, despite his efforts to look away.

A woman now stood where the creature had been. She was *beautiful*. This woman was a lovely blonde, with long hair over her shoulders and sea-green eyes that had sucked him in. Artie had been unable to move. The sight of her drove the other thing he'd seen deeper into his subconscious until he completely forgot ever seeing anything but her.

She came out from under the bridge, but the morning light didn't find her and she remained half in the shadow. Cool fingers touched his arm and long-nailed fingers tickled his palm as she gave him something. Artie didn't look at what it was. He couldn't pull his eyes away from her striking face. She was a siren newly risen from the water, a model taken directly from the paintings of Michelangelo, a nymph from the depths of mythology.

'I like how you see me,' she said. Then she kissed him and Artie forgot everything else around him.

A few moments later he came back to reality. He was

staring down into the canal; Warren was in the water and so was something else. He thrashed and screamed but a black shadow moved beneath the surface. Warren gasped as though the air was being squeezed from his lungs. Artie saw the black thing swirling around the doctor's body, and then Warren was pulled down.

Air bubbles broke the surface. Warren stayed down.

Artie snapped out of his trance and began to yell for help then. Warren was drowning, he had to get assistance, and he couldn't go into the water himself as he had never learnt to swim. He stopped shouting for help when he spotted the pornographic cards, now trampled in the dirt at his feet. He scooped them up, stuffing them quickly into his pocket.

He had forgotten the girl in his fright, but he remembered the monster again, the awful thing under the bridge that had scared Warren so much. As a bobby and one of the canal boat owners came running, Toby looked down into the water, trying to see if Warren had resurfaced. Artie saw something black, like a giant slug, swim away down the canal. He stared after it and he knew that no one would believe him if he told the truth.

'What happened?' asked the bobby.

'A man just threw himself in the water. I can't swim,' Artie said.

'Where is he now?'

'He went under. Hasn't come back up.'

'The current probably got him,' said the barge owner.

'Current? The water looks pretty still to me,' said the bobby.

'There's a current that runs along the bottom. It's how the barges get pulled along to the sea,' the owner explained.

Artie was surprised that the bobby accepted the

explanation without further question. He stepped over to the bridge as the bobby blew his whistle.

'Don't go anywhere,' the bobby called. 'You're an eyewitness.'

Under the bridge the beautiful woman hid. She began to whisper to Artie, telling him exactly what he was to say. By the time they fished Warren out of the canal, Artie believed every word of the story he told.

Back in the present, Artie was staring away into space, remembering the horrible thing, but uncertain what to tell Mitchell. He was sure the man would think him insane and he was afraid to tell the truth. Even though it was irrational, he feared the creature that had taken Warren would somehow know what he had done.

'I can't tell you what I saw,' said Artie. 'Because I don't believe it meself.'

'You'd be surprised what I would believe. I've seen some very strange things recently and I'm convinced that my fiancé, Laura Carter, is in serious danger.'

Artie looked away. He felt guilty but didn't know how to help. Part of the problem was that if he admitted to himself what he had seen the day that Warren died, he would have to face again the horrors that sometimes resurfaced in his nightmares. He hadn't seen that – what was it, anyway? – that thing … monster … creature … since that day. Nor had he seen the beautiful woman that kissed him.

'I can't stress enough how important it is I know the truth,' said Mitchell. 'I'm truly afraid for Laura. Can't you *see* that, man?'

Artie shook his head. He didn't want to become involved with Mitchell, particularly as the man was clearly working with Inspector Stream.

'I can't help you, Mr Bishop,' said Artie. 'I don't know nuffink.'

'Who are you trying to protect? If it's Naylor, then your loyalty is misguided. I don't wish you any harm, but I know about his little sideline and I have no intention of telling Stream or anyone else. All I want to do is protect Laura. I don't care what else you've been up to.'

Artie couldn't meet his eyes. Part of him wanted to help, but the other side of him was so afraid that he couldn't bring himself to utter another word. No matter how hard or how much Mitchell pleaded.

'I want to show you something,' said Mitchell. 'This is the photograph that was taken of Sara, Warren and Laura six months ago.'

Mitchell walked up to the counter and picked up the blue velvet cloth. Opening it, he held out a framed picture to Artie. Artie made no move to take it from his hands.

'Look at it!' Mitchell said. 'Is this the picture you developed?'

Artie turned away. But Mitchell would take no refusal. He pressed the picture into his hands.

Despite himself, Artie let his eye drop to the picture. The colour drained from his face. He tried to make Mitchell take the picture back, and when he refused, Artie just dropped it on the floor. The thin piece of glass covering the photograph shattered as the frame hit the ground. The cheap wood split in two and the photograph ripped, tearing a line across Sara's face.

'I'm so sorry, Mr Mitchell,' said Artie. 'It just slipped from me fingers.'

Mitchell bent and carefully retrieved the picture from the broken glass. He stared at the damage. Then gasped as he realised Laura's image had moved. And this time he knew he wasn't imagining it.

Mitchell clasped the picture to his breast. For the first time since this whole nightmare began, he believed that some supernatural element was responsible for all the strange happenings. He looked up at Artie, his eyes pleading.

'For the love of God man, help us!'

Artie backed away. 'I can't. I can't even help myself. Please leave me alone.'

They stared at each other across the room until finally Mitchell decided that he was wasting his time. Artie would not help him, even though he was certain that he knew more about what was going on than he was admitting. Mitchell only wished he knew what. He backed away to the door, opened it with one hand without looking, then he hurried out, leaving the door wide open behind him.

After he had gone Artie closed the door and turned around to look at the mess Mitchell had left behind. Toby would be angry if he came back to find this.

He went into the back room to get a broom and when he returned, he found Rosie in the shop.

'What's this?' she asked.

Artie was shaking but he made a half-hearted attempt at clearing up the mess.

'What's wrong with you?'

'Nuffink…' he said.

'There is something wrong, I can tell. You're shaking.'

Rosie took the broom from Artie's trembling fingers.

'That private detective was here again,' Artie said.

'You mean Mr Bishop?'

Artie nodded. 'He knows too much.'

'What does he know?' asked Rosie.

They stared at each other for a long time, as though they both knew a deadly secret but neither of them could express what it was.

Chapter Thirty

M itchell's frustration overwhelmed his dread. Outside the photography shop he hailed a hansom cab and told the driver to hurry to Laura's address. All he could think about was getting to her as soon as possible. He was convinced that she was in terrible danger, though he was at a complete loss as to what to do about it. One thing he was sure of, if anything happened to her, he would never forgive himself.

The day had grown more peculiar. He had failed to learn anything from speaking to Artie, except that the man was terrified, which could only mean one thing: he was hiding something.

He thought again of Neeraj. His godfather's butler and old friend could possibly be the only person who could help him right now. Mitchell was no longer having trouble accepting what his heart believed to be true: there was a soul thief in England and it was somehow manipulating people he knew and cared for. He still did not understand how it was possible, or why this monster had come to be here, or why it would single out people that Mitchell knew. But he had to keep Laura close now, no matter what.

The cab pulled up outside of the Carter's house and Mitchell hurried to the front door.

It took an unusually long time for Stevens, the butler, to answer the door. By the time the door opened Mitchell was in a state of severe agitation.

'I need to see Miss Laura immediately,' Mitchell said.

Stevens had no time to answer before Mitchell hurried past him and into the drawing room. He found Elena Carter doing needlepoint by the fire.

'Where's Laura?' he asked.

'She's still in her room. Resting.'

Mitchell hurried from the room to the stairs, taking them two at a time. Elena and Stevens were both at his heels as he reached the top.

'Where is her room?'

'This one,' said Elena.

Mitchell knocked on the door. When there was no answer, he tried the handle. The door was locked. He glanced over his shoulder at Elena. 'Do you have a key?

Stevens began to search for a key on the thick keychain that was attached to his belt. He quickly found the one to Laura's room and handed it to Mitchell, but when they tried to insert it in the lock, they found that Laura had left the key in the other side. Mitchell tried to manipulate the other key out, hoping it would fall to the floor, but it was twisted into the half-locked position.

'Laura!' he called. 'Please open the door.'

There was no answer from inside and so Mitchell knocked harder. He called her name over and over, hoping to rouse her from her possibly deep slumber.

'What's going on?' asked Elena.

Elena remembered all too well how Sara died. She feared the worst, and the thought of losing Laura as well as her other two children horrified her. Even so, she managed to maintain her dignity and although the panic rose in her chest, creating physical pain, she tried to make herself appear calm.

Mitchell stepped back from the door and ran towards it, bracing his shoulder against the hard wood. His shoulder was bruised on the first attempt, but he couldn't give up.

The noise from above brought Laura's father, Henry, out of his study and into the hallway.

'What the devil is going on up there?' he called.

'Laura's locked herself in her room and we can't get in,' Elena called, her voice an octave above her normal register.

Henry Carter's face was ashen as he began to climb the stairs.

'Stevens? Get an axe,' Mitchell said as he threw himself at the door a third time.

Even as the butler went to complete his instruction, Mitchell continued to throw himself at the door. His efforts were rewarded as a crack reverberated along the landing and the hinges on the door began to give. Though exhausted, Mitchell hurled himself forward one last time and found himself falling into the room as the door collapsed to the ground.

It took a moment to regain his breath as he stumbled back up to his feet. By then Henry and Elena were in the doorway behind him and Stevens had returned with the axe.

Laura was lying on the bed. Mitchell reached her quickly, but what he saw made him take a small step back. Laura's skin glowed with perspiration. Her face had taken on a strange yellow hue. She was mumbling in her fever-induced sleep.

Stevens moved aside the broken door and Elena and Henry entered the room and came to their daughter's bedside.

'Send for the doctor,' she ordered, and Stevens nodded.

Mitchell went to Laura's dresser and poured water into the bowl from a china jug. He looked around for something to use to wipe her face, and found a piece of muslin in the top drawer of the dresser. He swirled the fabric around in the water, squeezed it out, then walked back to her bedside. He patted her face and neck with the cool cloth.

'My God, what's wrong with her?' asked Elena.

Mitchell didn't know what to say. He had no explanation for why Laura was ill. Or at least none that sounded rational or believable.

'You knew there was something wrong, didn't you?'

Mitchell nodded. 'I had a feeling.'

'Whatever do you mean?'

'Elena, you know how I feel about Laura. I would never do anything to hurt her. Perhaps it is time I told you that Laura asked me to investigate the death of Sara and Warren. There have been some strange events taking place around us, from which we have both shielded you.'

'What are you saying?' Elena asked.

'I'm saying that there are things that I cannot explain to you right now. But I will as soon as I have the answers I've been searching for.'

'I think it's high time you explained yourself, Mitchell,' Henry Carter said.

'Laura's ill,' said Elena.

'I can see that. I do have eyes in my head,' Henry said.

'Sara …' Laura murmured. 'Her… face…'

'Oh, poor girl!' Elena cried. 'She's pining for her sister.'

After a few hours, when the doctor had been and gone, Mitchell sat alone with Laura. Elena and Henry had long forgotten propriety where he was concerned. He had refused to leave even when the doctor had examined Laura. It was a pity that the medic had not been able to give them any reassurance or answers as to why she had such a high fever. All they could do was try to keep her cool, and so the window was left open to allow the summer breeze to waft through the room, and they were to apply cool cloths to her forehead at regular intervals.

Every hour or so, Mitchell used the muslin cloth to wipe down Laura's arms as well as her face. He hoped that this little extra would help take the temperature down.

As the afternoon and evening disappeared Mitchell couldn't bring himself to leave her side, even though his presence did nothing to alleviate her symptoms. He was afraid that if he left her, something dreadful would happen.

In the evening, Stevens brought up a tray of food and a tall glass of red wine. Mitchell didn't feel very hungry, but he picked at the thick stew and fresh bread, knowing that if he lost his strength he would be of no use to Laura. After sipping the wine, his eyes became heavy and he could no longer fight back the intense tiredness. He nodded, then jerked himself awake, but despite his resistance, he fell into a deep and dreamless sleep, almost as though someone had given him a sleeping draught.

Sometime later, Mitchell woke and found Laura sitting up in the bed. He was drowsy and dazed. As he roused himself, he looked around the room, noting that a small oil lamp remained lit on the dresser. It was still completely dark outside and Mitchell guessed it must be around two or three in the morning.

There was a vacant and confused expression on Laura's face. It worried him. He reached for her hand. Her fingers were cold; the fever appeared to have gone.

'Darling, are you all right?'

Laura stared at the open window, then she turned her head to look at Mitchell, but even in the gloom he could tell that, despite her open eyes, she was still asleep. It reminded him of the time when she had somehow found her way into his house and bed in the middle of the night – the night they had almost made love. He tried not to think of it now because it was inappropriate under the circumstances.

Instead, he began to whisper words of reassurance that he hoped would reach inside her subconscious mind and give her the comfort she needed. He laid her back down and pulled the blankets up to cover the curves of her breasts. It was then he noticed that the charm he had given her was no longer around her neck. He cursed himself for not noticing this sooner. Although her hands were cold, her head was still feverish. He placed a damp cloth back on her forehead. She settled once more.

He began to search the room for the pendant. He opened her jewellery box and rifled through the many trinkets, brooches and rings inside, but there was no sign of the necklace. It didn't help that the only light came from the small oil lamp on the dresser. He considered turning on the light above the fireplace, but then recalled the doctor's comment that it was important for Laura to get as much rest as possible. He didn't want to wake her. He picked up the lamp and wandered around the room, looking in various obvious and unusual places to try to locate the missing charm. This was not something that he had ever thought he would have to do, and it embarrassed him somewhat to be opening Laura's drawers, looking at her undergarments like some perverted suitor.

Laura was sound asleep, her breathing comfortable, and she did not appear in any immediate danger. Maybe Elena and Henry had seen the necklace? Elena's room was just next door. It wasn't as though he would be gone far or even for any length of time, and so he made the decision to leave Laura for a few moments.

He passed through the now permanently open doorway and out onto the landing then walked towards Elena's room. He listened at the door to her soft snoring issuing from the room. Mitchell wasn't sure what to do. Perhaps it would be unfair to wake her right now; she was no doubt exhausted with all she had been through. He realised he was panicking unnecessarily. Why would the charm even make any difference at all? But somehow, deep down, he believed it would.

He returned to Laura's room, replaced the nightlight back on top of the dresser, and was about to settle once more in the chair when he noticed she was no longer in her bed.

Panic rose like bile in the back of his throat. His eyes darted around the room. Where had she gone? He had been outside the whole time on the landing and would have seen her if she had left. He searched the room, looking behind the dressing screen, under the bed, and even pulled back sheets to prove she was absent.

A gust of wind made the curtains billow at the open window. Mitchell pushed aside the curtains. Outside he saw Laura walking in her nightdress, barefooted, down the street. How could she possibly be there?

Not wishing to alarm her parents, or to wake the entire household, he hurried from the room, downstairs, and snatched up a set of house keys from the small cabinet by the door on his way out. Then he opened and closed the front door and set off after Laura.

Once outside, he saw her turning the corner of the street, and he pursued. It surprised him, how agile and quick she was. Every time Mitchell thought he had reached her she somehow managed to elude him. His feet felt as though they were stuck in mud; no matter how hard he tried to run, he was never fast enough to catch her. It was as though he was living a nightmare.

After a few blocks he realised where she was going and paused to get his breath back.

It wasn't too much of a surprise to find her in the grounds of the graveyard. As she approached the Carter tomb it occurred to him that her subconscious was desperately mourning the death of her siblings. Perhaps some latent remorse lurked behind her pale-blue eyes, brought on by the horrific sight of Warren's body that morning? He was overwhelmed by immense guilt at allowing her to accompany him. This was all his fault and he should have been firmer in his refusal, but he had found it impossible to say no to her. Now he couldn't help wondering if the fever had come on because of stress.

He called her name but she didn't answer. He was so exhausted from running that he was forced to slow down. He was shocked when she ran past the tomb and through the graveyard like a spirit left in limbo. He had been certain that she would stop there.

'Laura!' he called again. 'Darling, wait!'

Laura ran on, her feverish dreaming mind refusing to hear him.

Gaining his second wind, he gave chase, jumping over tombstones like a champion hurdler.

Meanwhile, Laura was swallowed up by the trees surrounding the church property. As Mitchell entered the woods, he caught a glimpse of her pale pink nightdress glowing in the light cast by the full moon. She weaved in and out of the trees as though taunting him. He marvelled at her energy. It was frightening how someone so sick could suddenly be so very strong. He found himself gasping for air and took refuge against a large oak tree. His lungs burned as though he had breathed in fire. He was just about to give up and return to get help when he discovered Laura standing beside him.

'Laura,' he gasped. 'What are you doing?'

Laura smiled. She no longer looked ill. In fact, she looked more beautiful and more vital than she ever had.

'I'm feeling much better,' she said. 'I just wanted to get out of that stuffy room.'

She wrapped her arms around him, pulling him close. Warm lips pressed against his neck as she placed small kisses on his skin. Her touch made him forget where they were. Cool hands stroked his face, even as her mouth pressed against his. Every muscle in his body ached to be touched. His shallow breathing slowly recovered as her hands ran over the front of his shirt, down over the buttons of his breeches. He gasped.

'Darling…' Mitchell groaned against her lips.

Laura chuckled, a deep throaty sound that vibrated through her chest. Excitement coursed through his veins, a feeling he was all too familiar with when around Laura. He loved her so passionately, and since the other night, when she had somehow found her way into his bed, all he could think about was holding her in his arms and making love to her. It was why he had pushed so hard to bring the wedding forward. He didn't feel he could wait much longer. But he had so much respect for her that nothing would induce him to overstep the boundaries before then.

But now, his resolve vanished as her hand slipped over him. He shuddered, pushing aside the surprise that Laura would do something like this – would even know how to.

'Oh God, Laura…' he gasped. He felt he would burst any second but couldn't pull away.

'I love you,' he said. 'Oh, Laura…'

Then, he opened his eyes and looked into the face of Sara Carter.

'I'm not Laura,' Sara said.

Mitchell yelped, falling back against the tree once more.

Sara's face was a grimacing death-mask. Horrified, he pushed her to one side as he stumbled back to his feet.

The black holes that had been her eyes, burrowed into him as Mitchell lurched away from the woodland and back towards the churchyard. Her laughter was hollow, harsh, a dark rattle in a dead throat.

Pulling his breeches back together, Mitchell staggered around the graveyard, calling Laura's name. He felt drunk or drugged. The strange fugue that had forced him to sleep in Laura's room now threatened to consume him once more. He refused to give in to it this time. She had to be there somewhere and he couldn't return without her. Whatever that thing was, it wasn't Laura. And even though it had taken on the appearance of her sister, he didn't believe that Sara had risen from the grave either.

He found Laura outside the tomb, lying on the cold stone step, sleeping the sleep of the innocent. For a moment he did not want to touch her, afraid that she was really the Sara creature. But her face was so serene that he knew it was her. How could he possibly have been so mistaken? Guilt consumed him. He'd almost had sex with some changeling creature. He tried to push his feelings aside as he bent down and placed his hand on Laura's arm. He stroked her cool skin gently.

'Laura?' he said.

She woke sluggishly, as though coming from a drugged slumber. She rubbed her eyes like a sleepy child.

'Mitchell?'

'Yes, darling, I'm here.'

'Where am I?'

Relief flooded him: the fever had broken and Laura was, at least for now, quite lucid. He only hoped she would stay that way. He helped her to her feet and led her from the graveyard.

'What's happened?' she asked.

'It doesn't matter, darling,' he said. 'Let me get you back home…'

Chapter Thirty-One

'What did the doctor say about your hand?' Rosie asked.

Toby held up his bandaged hand and grinned. 'It's just a few scratches.'

When Toby had returned from the hospital Artie had already left, the shop was closed, and Rosie had prepared a delicious supper in anticipation of his return.

He tried to hide the fact that he was more than a little scared and confused about the events that had happened earlier, as he accepted her hug. Then he sat at the kitchen table with a jug of ale and a plate of mutton and mash.

He noted how easy it was to fall into a comfortable domesticity. He liked the feeling of security it gave him. It felt normal and was so far removed from the strangeness of the day that he almost believed he could forget what he had seen in the graveyard.

Now he ate as Rosie moved around the kitchen, cleaning and tidying. In his absence she had done some washing and now pieces of his clothing were hung over a concertina rack by the fire. They weren't even married, and already she was turning into a first-class wife.

When he had finished eating, Rosie sat down at the table, eyes wide, as though she was waiting to be told some great secret.

'Dinner was wonderful, Rosie,' Toby said.

'Thank you,' she said. 'Toby, we need to talk. About today…'

Toby gazed into the fire, not knowing what to say, or even where to begin. The flames danced before his eyes, swirling into shapes of people and things until finally they resembled a stooped, ape-like figure. Arms and claws trailed on the floor.

'What is it?' Rosie asked.

'I can't talk about it.'

'Something happened today. We both saw *it*, Toby.'

'Can you describe what you saw?' Toby said. 'Only … I can't. I don't know what I saw. I don't know what's going on. I just know something strange is happening, and it started when I first took those photographs.'

'Don't be ridiculous. The camera has nothing to do with this. That's just superstitious claptrap. I know it's weird, but it feels to me like we are all being haunted.'

Toby gave a half-hearted laugh, but her words did not seem so bizarre when he thought about it. After all, it had been a very peculiar few months and he wasn't sure he could explain it all in any other way.

'Perhaps we should speak to the priest?' he said. 'I mean, Father O'Shawnessy or Father Radley would know what to do in these circumstances.'

Rosie came to him and wrapped her arm around his waist. She rested her head against his shoulder until Toby responded and pulled her closer. They held each other in silence.

'I think that's a good idea,' said Rosie.

'I'm tired,' said Toby. 'Let's retire early.'

They lay in bed side by side, Rosie in a blue nightgown, Toby in an old nightshirt. He made no move to touch her, even though he knew she was awake. Toby was lost in his own thoughts.

He closed his eyes to shut out the darkness in the room, then stretched a hand to his side to take her hand. Her fingers wrapped in his and Toby turned onto his side, cuddling up to her until the warmth and comfort helped them both sleep. But Toby's dreams were full of distorted people, who were warped like poorly developed negatives. Or looked like pictures that had been exposed over each other.

During the night, Rosie held Toby. His face was wet with tears shed in his sleep. She watched the shadows cast by the light from the streetlamps outside, moving as though they had a life of their own; as though she could keep some evil at bay.

At first Artie wasn't sure what to do when he saw the woman turning the corner onto his street. She was wearing a pink nightshift and was barefooted. Her long dark-blonde hair flowed over her bare arms and down her back. Then he recognised her.

Artie stepped back into the shadow of his doorway as he saw Mitchell Bishop following her down the street. Although he was doing nothing wrong, he did not want them to notice his observation.

Seeing Laura again reminded him of the day he took her photograph, and now he thought back to the first time he had seen the Carter twins and their sister Sara. Even now he wondered why he had lied to Mitchell about who had taken the photograph. It had been the first one that Toby had ever allowed him to do alone, and at the time he had been extremely proud of his work. Toby had praised him when he had seen the developed negative. The family looked beautiful in the original print. Particularly Sara; she was stunning.

She had flirted with him a little and, though it was against his flirtatious nature, he had tried so hard to retain a professional distance. Artie had never seen a fine lady behave as she had and it had intrigued him. Artie knew that Sara was out of his league and never expected to see her again, though he frequently enjoyed looking at his handiwork. When he developed the original picture, he made a small one for himself to remember it by. In fact, this had become a habit following any photo shoot that he had particularly enjoyed or was proud of.

Artie remembered the day for another reason also: it was the first time Rosie had come to the back door looking to earn money by posing for the backroom postcards. Toby had been distracted by her. It was the only reason Artie had been given a chance to use the camera on the customers in the front of the shop alone, and he would never have met Sara if Rosie hadn't turned up that day.

Artie had an eye for the ladies, that was true. But sometimes those ladies had husbands. Some of them gave him 'the look' behind the backs of those fuddy-duddy men they had been married off to. Others were attractive, but cold and distant, barely acknowledging his presence. Even so, nothing stopped him enjoying looking at those photographs. He enjoyed them far more than the pornographic photos Toby took. Sometimes he would imagine the prim and proper women behaving like streetwalkers. It was a fantasy that he enjoyed and indulged in, sometimes even masturbating with it.

Artie well remembered the second meeting he'd had with Sara. It had been the fulfilment of his ultimate fantasy.

He was alone in the shop that day because Toby was out buying supplies. They'd had a very busy week and because of the new sideline, they were using far more frames than usual. He was sat on the two-seater sofa, sketchpad in hand, while he drew from memory one of the women he had seen that day. He didn't draw her looking prim and proper as she had been sat next to her future husband; instead he drew her semi-naked, lying back on the sofa alone like a whore waiting for her next client. This woman had been particularly cold towards him, and he imagined warming her up, making her scream with excitement as he made love to her.

As the door opened, the bell rang and Toby jumped guiltily to his feet, putting down his sketchpad and charcoal on the sofa. He covered the picture with one of the cushions, concerned she might notice it and be offended.

'Hello,' Sara said.

Artie nodded and mumbled a greeting in response. Then he stood behind the counter, waiting to hear what it was she wanted.

'I was very pleased,' Sara began, 'with the picture that you took a few days ago. My brother brought it home and I was wondering if I could have a portrait done.'

'I'd be happy to help you with that, Miss,' Artie said. 'When would you like it taken?'

Sara smiled. 'Right now would be good.'

Artie was caught by surprise. He began to stutter excuses in his confusion.

'I think we're out of frames … well, we only have one left…'

'That's okay, I'm sure you'll get it right the first time,' Sara said.

Artie didn't argue. Instead, he changed the set, removing the two-seater sofa he had been sitting on, then he replaced it with a single comfortable chair. He placed the table and a plant beside it. In the meantime, Sara removed her hat and coat, and underneath she was wearing a bold evening gown in bronze satin that showed off her décolletage.

Artie found himself staring at her, and instead of being embarrassed by his scrutiny, Sara gave him an open smile that was both knowing and lascivious. It made him feel uncomfortable and aroused all at the same time. It also reminded him of the sketch he had done of her after the photo session. He bustled around the room, trying to hide the blush that came to his cheeks.

When the camera was set up and Artie could no longer avoid looking at her, Sara took great advantage of the situation. She sat down in the chair, carefully positioning the hemline of the dress around her feet, and then posed with an audacious smile. Artie took his position behind the camera, throwing the black cloth over his head. He gazed down the lens and once more fell into that world of perfection that only he could see through the camera. He looked at Sara as though he were a Peeping Tom capturing her in a private moment in her own home. He could almost see the drawing he would do later. It unfolded behind his eyes, taking on a life of its own. As though responding to his mental image, Sara leaned forward, looking directly at him, and Artie felt as though she could see into his very soul.

He felt extraordinarily guilty. As he watched her through the lens, Sara's hands moved over her breasts. Her fingers slid around the point where Artie thought her nipples must be. He was used to fine ladies trying to get a meagre amount of attention from him, but none had ever gone quite this far before. He raised his head from behind the camera and looked directly at her. Sara was sitting primly on the sofa, waiting for his instruction to remain still. There was no provocative smile, her hands were resting in her lap as though they had always been there, and her dress was certainly not as low-cut as it appeared to be when he gazed through the lens.

Artie glanced through the camera again. The image he saw of Sara was so different from the one he could see in the shop that he wasn't sure what to do or say. He realised he must be imagining it. His fantasies were realising themselves through the lens. He stopped, scratching his head in confusion.

'Is something wrong?' she asked.

Artie shook his head. The Sara in front of the camera had raised her skirt up at the front and was exposing her bare legs. She wasn't wearing any undergarments and as the dress slid further up, Artie could see the blonde down of the hair between her thighs.

He fell back from the camera, staring at the girl, shocked, but she was still sitting primly, doing none of the things that the lens showed him.

'I … don't feel too well…' Artie said.

'Oh, really?' said Sara, showing no real concern for him at all. 'Shall we do this quickly, then?'

Artie dropped the cloth back over the camera. 'I just need to get a glass of water,' he said.

Then he left Sara and went into the back room. He poured water from a jug and swigged it, wishing it were something stronger. His head was spinning. He felt strange – not in his right mind at all. He placed the empty glass back down on the kitchen sink and then turned.

Sara had followed him into the back room.

The kitchen was still set up as though it were another studio, and Artie realised that the door to the dressing room used by the girls was still open. Sara's eyes wandered around the room with a knowing expression.

'Why, you have another studio here too. And it's far more private than the one at the front of the shop,' she said.

'Erm … yes … this isn't for…'

'I think I prefer it back here,' Sara said. 'Far more personal…'

'I have to be in the front of the shop when no one else is here…' Artie said.

'No problem. I took the liberty of locking the door before I followed you.'

'Why did you follow me?'

'You said you weren't feeling well. Besides, I felt a little responsible for you.'

Artie was confused. He didn't understand why on earth the woman would feel anything for the likes of him at all.

'Well,' she said, 'I was giving you rather too much to look at down that lens.'

Sara laughed, then she glided around the kitchen as though she were floating.

A strange calm came over him as he watched her move. She was ethereal, a spirit that had somehow seeped under his skin. As she stroked the table top, he felt as though her fingers were running over his arm.

He couldn't take his eyes away from her. He noted that the dress she was wearing had slipped from one of her shoulders; then the fabric fell away from her breasts and the garment slid to the floor.

She was completely naked beneath it. Not even a chemise or corset – so unlike a lady in her position. Not even the Manchester whores dressed like that. Artie didn't know how to respond until her hand touched his forehead – then he knew exactly what to do, as if she had given him some unspoken command.

Artie fell into her embrace, his mouth latched onto one of her pale-pink nipples, and he suckled until faint groans issued from her. Naked, she lay back on the table and pushed his head downwards towards her pubis.

Sara's hair began to come free of her neat coiffure: the tresses, pale blonde, almost white, were fine and soft. It covered her like a shawl. Artie looked up her body to see that she was gently stroking one of her own breasts while his tongue pleasured her. He couldn't help being reminded of the whores that frequented the studio. But Sara wasn't doing this for a photograph. It was personal and for him alone.

He pulled back from her, his senses returning. Although he felt lust coursing through his veins, there was also fear in his heart. He knew he shouldn't be in this position, with such a woman as Sara, but he couldn't help himself. It could lead to all sorts of trouble. He had heard of women like her, whores every last one, who liked to accuse a man of taking liberties when they had shown a complete lack of judgement. But Artie knew she was the one really taking liberties with him, and he couldn't resist her at all.

She pulled him up onto the sturdy table, wrapping her legs

and arms around him as though she feared he would escape. She used obscenities to goad him on.

Artie had never heard words like that coming from the mouth of a lady, and he should have known better. He really should. But he knew that no virgin would be begging for it this way, anyhow. She had done this before, probably many times. He wouldn't be going anywhere that some other man hadn't already explored.

A short time later, Artie fell forward onto her breasts.

'Well done,' Sara said.

Her laughter was sexy and Artie felt aroused again, but he withdrew from her and reached down to pull his breeches back up, suddenly embarrassed by the whole thing. What if Toby returned and found them like this? Sara climbed off the table, scooped down and picked up her dress. When Artie turned around, she had left the kitchen.

He found her fully clothed, hair re-coiffured, sitting once more in the chair before the camera.

'Are you okay?' she asked. 'You were gone a long time.'

'I'm wonderful…' he said, then he realised that she wished to play the game that nothing had occurred between them.

'You can take my picture, then?' Sara said.

Artie nodded. He gazed down the lens. Sara appeared to be formal now, as though she were two completely different personalities. Artie took the photograph, knowing that it would be beautiful, but proper.

'Will I see you again?' Artie said as Sara put on her hat and coat.

'When will the picture be ready?' Sara said, ignoring the implied question. She frowned slightly and Artie realised that despite what had occurred between them, he had somehow overstepped a mark. She clearly didn't want commitment. He felt somewhat affronted and used. He was a toy to her, a thing she could use to pleasure herself.

As she left the shop Artie felt sick and confused again. He wondered if he had imagined everything after all. He returned to his sketch-book and drew the picture of the naked Sara stretched out on the table, one hand cupping her perfect breast.

Now as Artie watched Laura running half-dressed down the street, he was reminded of Sara. He realised that he had never been alone with the girl again. Though he had later heard of her confinement and suicide in the asylum. Her odd, multi-personality tendency was probably to blame. Artie suspected that Sara's behaviour, in a family like hers, could well have been considered insane. Especially if her parents had become alerted to her sexual tendencies.

Artie followed Laura and Mitchell through the streets and on to the graveyard, from a safe distance. Much to his surprise, Mitchell ran past the girl as she lay down before the tomb, as though he didn't see her at all.

Artie hung back. He was afraid to leave Laura alone. Anything may happen to her, left behind as Mitchell ran off into the woods beside the graveyard.

He waited by the side of the tomb watching over Laura until, a short time later, Mitchell returned.

Mitchell looked dishevelled, his breeches were unfastened, and Artie wondered if the man had just been desperate to relieve himself. But even if he had, why was he with Laura out in the middle of the night, half-dressed?

Artie watched Mitchell help Laura to her feet but could not hear their whispered conversation from his vantage point.

When Mitchell and Laura finally left the graveyard, Artie was alone. But he was used to that. He had trouble sleeping at night, which was why he had been on his doorstep taking air when Laura and Mitchell passed. He didn't know what to think of seeing the two of them out so late, and it made him feel such sadness for Sara.

What was with that family, anyway? Trouble appeared to be following them around like a bad smell.

'I've been looking for you,' said Sara. She was standing in the doorway of the tomb, holding out her hand to him.

She was wearing the bronze dress again and Artie let his mind slip back in time as though that day were still here. He forgot that Sara was dead. He couldn't resist her any more now, than he could before.

The tomb doors closed behind them as they entered, but a small oil lamp was lit inside and Artie's eyes ran over the coffins, old and new, but his mind refused to recognise them as such. What he saw instead was Sara's bedroom. A large double four-poster bed in the centre of the room was surrounded by red curtains. It was the focus of where she led him, and Artie dutifully climbed up and lay down beside her.

They made love, slower and more passionately than the last time. Afterwards Artie fell asleep in her arms. He was contented, loved, and his mind never questioned their surroundings, nor the suddenness of Sara's appearance.

~

It was late morning when he woke. He felt Sara's arms around him, but the satin of the bronze dress smelled dusty and old. An awful smell assaulted his nostrils as he took his first morning breath. It smelled like rot, decay, a sickening smell of old and new death.

Artie rubbed his eyes and sat up. He looked around, confused, barely remembering the evening before. He stared blankly around at the dark tomb, then covered his nose, and began to breathe through his mouth.

With horror he realised he was lying in a coffin. And although he could not see the body beside him, the realisation dawned on him that somehow, he had walked in his sleep and found himself in the grave of the woman he had been obsessing about ever since that day in the studio. He climbed out of the open coffin and backed away towards the crypt doors. As he reached the door, he felt sure that the body in the coffin moved. He pushed at the door but it would not open.

He heard the scraping of bones against stone flags. He heaved at the door, rattling and banging. *What madness had led him to this?*

Artie pulled and tugged but the doors would not open. He closed his eyes, pressing his forehead against the sturdy wood. Behind him he felt the flow of air, as though a ghostly hand had reached out to touch him.

Artie turned slowly to face whatever demon was with him in the tomb. Light filtered in from underneath and around the doorframe, and through the small window at the side of the crypt. He could see nothing behind him, even though he had been convinced that something was there. His paranoid eyes darted around, looking in every shadow. The dead remained in their coffins. There was no demonic lover waiting to give him a fatal embrace. Leaning back against the doors, Artie wondered how he had become trapped in here and how on earth he was going to escape.

He considered shouting and banging on the door in the

hope that someone passing would alert the proper authorities, but he knew he couldn't explain why he was there, or how he had become trapped. It smacked of perversion, and he didn't need the likes of Inspector Stream looking too closely into his life, not with all the strange occurrences that were somehow linked to Toby's photography shop. Not with all the unexplained deaths, and the spate of family-related murders he had heard of too. Artie had spent months recognising many of his customers' names appearing in print.

A dark phobic fear crowded into his thoughts. On some level he had understood Toby's sudden closing of the shop, as bizarre and irrational as he had claimed it to be. There was something wrong. Artie knew it, just as Toby did. But how? Why? What? That he didn't know, and Artie was smart. He was good at making links. You didn't survive long on the Manchester streets without being a good observer of people and things around you.

A flash of Sara Carter's beautiful face, her bare bosom, her leg bent and wrapped around his hip as he pushed into her, burst into his memory. He stared at the open coffin and knew without a doubt that her remains lay within.

But what was the connection? What was it about Sara, about the day he first saw her and the photograph he took that had somehow changed their lives?

Something lurked in the periphery of his memory. Another figure: old, stooped, long ape-like arms, knuckles that drooped to the floor. He saw again leather-like skin, tanned and stretched over sharp, grotesque and distorted bones. It was like the remnants of some horrible nightmare that haunted his days as well as his nights.

He sank down onto the floor, head in his hands, trying to

remember, but for the life of him he couldn't. It was crucial, but still evaded him.

He closed his eyes, hoping that he was lying in his own bed, dreaming after all. The stink of the grave was less beside the door and Artie turned his face towards the slight gap and breathed deeply. His conscious mind slipped back into a slumber, as though it was the only way to escape the memories that threatened to rise. Somehow Artie knew that the day he remembered the whole truth, the day he put the entire puzzle back together, might indeed be the last day she – no, *it* – let him live. Until then he was being kept in storage, like a side of beef in a meat locker, ripe and ready to eat, but perfectly preserved.

Artie shuddered as this analogy slipped through his mind. He felt like a mouse staring out at the cat waiting on the other side of a hole in the floorboards. To remain inside meant starvation; to try to outrun the cat was certain death. It was a lose–lose situation, whichever way he looked at it.

He pushed himself further into sleep to escape the reality. Then he floated on a dream of love and lust as the dream Sara took his hand.

Part VI

Chapter Thirty-Two

Mitchell wiped the mud from Laura's feet. Then he helped her back into bed and pulled the blankets up over her chest. He removed his own dirt-covered shoes and placed them outside the broken door for the butler to find and clean. He sat back in the chair that he had occupied earlier. He was afraid to take his eyes away from Laura now, afraid she would dance away once more like a moth attracted to a flame.

He was riddled with guilt over his liaison with the Sara-creature. He was beginning to feel that he was losing his mind. What other explanation could there be for his bizarre behaviour in the woods? To even engage in that sordid sexual contact with Laura would have been degrading for them both, let alone to find it hadn't been her at all.

He could not have seen Sara, unless it was her ghost? In which case, had his near infidelity really happened at all? He shook his head. He recalled Neeraj telling him that phantoms were echoes of memories: people created ghosts in their own imagination. It was a way of convincing themselves that there was more to their mortal existence.

But it had been real.

Mitchell was lost. Completely alone with this sinister fantasy. He couldn't deny that the thing he had met had almost given him sexual release, like a waking wet dream. It felt like a betrayal of the woman he loved, and he knew that, no matter what, he could never tell her what had happened.

Perhaps his mind was becoming unhinged because of his worry for Laura? He certainly was tired and needed sleep, which was enough to unsettle anyone.

He closed his eyes, but sleep wouldn't come. Deep down he feared that she would leave the bed again and vanish into the night. So, he took Laura's hand, knowing that at least if she moved, he would feel it and wake. Her hand was warm but not feverish. It comforted him and, taking a slow breath, he forced himself to relax. It would be so much easier if the door were repaired. He could at least lock it and put the key somewhere on his person, making it difficult for her to leave.

He felt a rush of anxiety at the thought of losing her again. Then, as though it had a will completely of its own, his mind began to float and he felt the calm drug of sleep pushing at the edges of his exhaustion. He tightened his fingers, intertwining them with Laura's as he finally let slumber take him.

The next morning Mitchell opened his eyes and found Laura fast asleep in bed. Despite her apparent brief lucidity, the fever had returned. He placed a cool cloth on her forehead and wiped away the perspiration. Her eyes flickered open and Mitchell thought he saw her return to full awareness. She groaned, eyes blinking rapidly.

'In the tomb,' she said.

'It's all right, darling, it was nothing. Just a dream.'

He raised her head, placed a glass of water to her lips, and encouraged her to sip some of the tepid fluid. The water splashed her lips and Laura's tongue licked on reflex. He did this several times until he was sure that she had consumed at least a few drops.

Looking at her now, Mitchell was certain that things were as bad as they were ever going to get. He had never seen Laura sick in all the years he had known her, and now he began to fear that it would be fatal unless he could somehow find a cure.

He heard movement as the rest of the household began to stir. Stevens appeared with a fresh tray of food and water, and one of the servant girls came to change the water in the wash jug. She offered to bathe and change Laura, and Mitchell, realising that it would indeed be inappropriate for him to be present, used that time to take his own ablutions. When he returned, the maid was brushing Laura's hair. Mitchell couldn't help feeling that this was like the preparation of the dead. She looked as though she had been laid out for a wake. The thought horrified him.

As he walked around the bed to return to her side once more, his eyes fell on something glinting on the floor. He bent to pick it up. It was the charm! As he touched the flat silver and the coloured eye, he felt an immediate calm. He glanced at Laura, recalling how Neeraj had giving him the charm to protect him from evil.

Once the maid had finished grooming Laura, he placed the chain over her head.

'This is not to be removed, under any circumstances,' he told the girl.

He sat down in the chair once more, determined to remain by her side.

'Mitchell?' Laura said. 'What are you doing here?'

His head turned. He found Laura struggling to a sitting position.

'You've been sick,' he said, surprised that she was awake. 'Very sick...'

'Water...' she said. Her throat was dry and she was pale, but Mitchell felt some modicum of relief that she was awake and talking.

He held the glass to her lips; this time she sipped at it herself until she felt better. He saw a rapid return of colour to her cheeks.

At that moment, Elena came into the room, wearing a dressing gown over her night clothes.

'Laura, you are looking much better!' Elena said.

And indeed, she was. It was an extraordinary and sudden improvement, only moments after he had replaced the charm around her throat.

Throughout the next few hours, Laura made a remarkable recovery, and Mitchell could only put this transformation down to the return of the necklace. He stressed on her, and those around him, that she mustn't remove it under any circumstances, and when he went down to the drawing room while Laura insisted on getting up and dressing, he was nervous and concerned that she wouldn't listen to him. He paced up and down the room until he heard the maid come downstairs, with Laura only a few seconds behind.

She was wearing a smart day suit.

'Let's go out for a walk. I have an urge to get some air,' Laura said, putting her arms around him.

'Absolutely not,' said Elena. 'Stevens has set up the garden furniture and you can sit out for a little while, but under no circumstances are you going anywhere else. Mitchell dear, why don't you go home and have a rest? You can see she is much better, clearly out of danger.'

Mitchell held Laura close for a moment. His mind skipped over the awful parody of her that he had met, or imagined, in the forest. He was sick with remorse. And something nagged in the back of his mind about other times when he had not always been himself, perhaps not in complete control. Times of darkness, some of which had been during Laura's absence from his life, and he couldn't help but acknowledge that she was always a positive influence.

The thing he had seen was a changeling, a monster, or maybe he was feverish and delusional himself. Either way, he felt bad and uncomfortable.

Now, the thought of returning home, bathing and changing his clothing was very appealing, even though he was still afraid to leave Laura alone.

'Will you be all right?' Mitchell asked Laura.

She frowned with concern as she noticed the dark shadows under his eyes.

'Yes, darling. You're exhausted. Please go and take some rest. Then come back to me this evening and we'll have supper together.'

'I'd love that,' Mitchell said. He placed a kiss on her forehead. 'I know it's silly, but promise you won't take the necklace off.'

Laura smiled. 'I haven't removed it since you gave it to me. Why would I take it off now?'

Mitchell said nothing; maybe she had removed it when the fever was at its worst?

'All right. I'll be back this evening.'

As he sat back in the carriage Mitchell began to feel the whole weight of his concern weighing down on him once more. The past few months' events began to roll around his mind, making him feel sick and dizzy. Too much had happened since the death of Laura's siblings.

He pushed aside what had occurred with the changeling … he couldn't think about it without utter disgust. Whatever that monstrous thing was, real or imagined, he would never let it inside his head again.

Mitchell felt his nerves were on edge and wondered if perhaps Neeraj could prescribe him something. He had often taken his bizarre cures while growing up in India.

The thought of Neeraj and India made him feel strangely homesick. He suddenly wanted to see Mainwaring and Neeraj, and talking through the events might just help him begin to make sense of them.

On impulse he told the driver to take him to St Anne's Road in Prestwich – to his godfather's house instead of his own home.

Mitchell followed Neeraj into the conservatory, to find John Mainwaring sitting at the table with a light breakfast.

'Will you join us?' Mainwaring said. 'You look *tired.*'

Mitchell took a seat next to Mainwaring and Neeraj soon returned with another plate of bread, cheese and ham, which he placed before him. Neeraj then took a seat on the other side of the table and the three of them ate together.

'Laura was sick yesterday. It's taken a lot out of me,' Mitchell explained.

Mitchell was surprised at how hungry he was, but then recalled that he had barely touched the food he had been given by Stevens at Laura's house that morning because he had been too concerned and distracted. Now he ate with enthusiasm.

'Neeraj told me about the photograph of Laura and her siblings,' Mainwaring said, pushing his plate away. 'He also told me the soul-thief story.'

'I feel like I'm somehow losing my mind,' said Mitchell.

He began to tell them the sequence of events since Sara and Warren's deaths, expressing his concerns about Toby Naylor and his photography shop.

'Also, there is Dr Glenister,' Mitchell continued. 'He said he saw Warren, and then he was found dead.'

Neeraj stood and moved around the table, gathering the used plates into a pile. As he approached Mitchell, bending over him to reach for his plate, the old Indian drew back.

'What is it?' Mainwaring asked when he noticed Neeraj's revulsion.

'Mitchell-Sahib has not yet told us everything. He has been … corrupted.'

Mitchell sat back in his chair, surprised. 'What do you mean, I…?'

'I can smell the sulphur of demon on you.'

'Sulphur?'

The colour drained from Mainwaring's face as he pushed his wheelchair back from the table.

'I think we need to tell him the truth,' Mainwaring said. 'But first you must tell us what happened to you last night. All of it. Omit nothing.'

Mitchell began his story again. This time he told them everything, even about Laura's sleepwalking, the poison in his brandy, and the changeling that had tried to seduce him in the graveyard.

'There is a link, it seems, to the photography shop, which you know about already,' said Neeraj. 'But you are right that Dr Glenister doesn't make sense. Why would this thing go after him, unless of course his soul was corrupted – his image captured somehow by the creature?'

'Why does it do that, anyway? What gain?'

'The mystery of the soul thief's life has long been a concern of my people. Why it takes some souls, yet leaves others. It is believed that the creature at first used the people whose image it took, making them act and behave differently to their nature. Like a puppet master, manipulating its marionettes for *entertainment*. But through the years this creature has evolved. I have seen it appear many times through my own lifetime,' Neeraj explained.

'You have?' Mitchell said.

'Yes. You see, I am beginning to believe that this thing did not originate in the photography shop, but merely found its way there. I think this story began in India. With Bhakti.'

'What do you mean?' Mitchell asked, but he was fearful that Neeraj would confirm what he had always thought, that he was somehow responsible for Bhakti's death. That he was evil and beyond redemption.

'It's not possible,' Mainwaring replied to Neeraj's suspicions. 'Bhakti was Mitchell's nurse. She did not ever, that I'm aware of, have her image taken.'

Neeraj glanced at Mitchell. 'Not voluntarily. But some evil could have stolen it nonetheless.'

Mitchell hung his head. His guilt was overwhelming. He had caused Bhakti's death – he'd always known it, but now Neeraj was confirming it.

'But I think that Bhakti was not meant to die,' Neeraj said. 'She merely got in the way.'

'But … you mean…?' Mainwaring looked at Mitchell hard. 'Mitchell was the target?'

'Me?' said Mitchell, looking up.

Neeraj nodded. 'I suspected it at the time. But taking you from India may well have spared your life, until now. Somehow the creature followed you. Or it is exacting a misguided revenge by attacking those you love.'

'Why on earth would this demon be after me? Was it all because I drew something in the sand?'

'No, of course not. Only the soul thief can capture another's image and use it. But it doesn't mean that the creature hadn't already taken yours. It may have used you to draw Bhakti's death, as a kind of prelude to coming for you,' Neeraj said.

'But why?' Mitchell asked again. He was drowning in confusion, fear, doubt.

Mainwaring wheeled his chair over to the conservatory window and gazed out onto the perfect English lawn, but his mind was elsewhere.

'This is my story to tell,' Mainwaring said. 'But before I do, I need you to know one other truth that I have wanted to share with you for many years.'

Mainwaring stood up and pushed the wheelchair back, then he turned to face his godson and friend, taking a few steady steps towards them.

'You can walk!' Mitchell gasped.

'Yes. Neeraj saved my life on the battlefield. He also used some powerful potion that healed the wound. Over time I steadily regained the use of my limbs. But by then, I realised that being a cripple made me appear far more harmless to those around me.'

'What are you saying? Why would you need to appear harmless?' Mitchell asked.

'It made it easier for me to excuse myself from the army, come back to England. I had to sever ties there and bring you here to safety. For that reason, my improved state had to remain a secret. Even from you. Mitchell, haven't you ever wondered where the money came from?'

'Your army pension ... my parents' estate...'

'Your parents never had an estate, Mitchell. Your ... *father* gambled away his entire wealth and your mother's inheritance. The house you live in was bought back from the creditors by me. I put the money into your estate.'

'Why? Why would you do that for me, Uncle John?' Mitchell said. 'Not that I'm ungrateful ... I just need to know.'

Mainwaring joined him at the table once more. This time he sat on one of the regular chairs. Mitchell frowned. He had mixed feelings about his godfather's revelation. He was thrilled he could walk, but felt a sense of betrayal at never being brought in on the secret until now. After all, Mitchell would never have betrayed Mainwaring. And now, years on from his days in the army, what would it matter if his uncle's condition had improved and he showed others he could walk again? Would anyone care, beyond thinking this was a wonderful miracle?

'It's a long story,' Mainwaring said. 'Firstly, let me apologise for keeping this secret from you. It was a difficult lie to admit to, Mitchell. I hope you can forgive me for not telling you the truth sooner. I had planned to, but I became what everyone expected me to be. The longer the lie went on...'

Mitchell nodded. 'Yes, I do forgive you. But I need to know why and how this all happened.'

'Before you were born, I fell in love. I loved the woman at a distance because she was married to my friend. I knew that he was no good for her. But there was nothing I could do but be there, waiting in the sidelines. Her name was Elisa. Yes, Mitchell, I'm talking about your mother.'

Chapter Thirty-Three

India: Twenty-eight years ago

'This is Elisa,' Colonel Damien Bishop said. 'My wife.'

John Mainwaring found himself stuttering like a fool as he looked into the eyes of Elisa Bishop. His young servant, Neeraj, placed a glass of gin and tonic in his hand and the major sipped it, grateful for the distraction.

Elisa had dark-brown eyes and hair that was as black as night, with a pale English-rose complexion. She appeared strong and vital. Full of life in a way that Mainwaring had never seen in a woman of breeding. She held none of the qualities that would make her appear fragile or weak. And Mainwaring wanted her to stay that way. He had seen lesser women crumble under the intensity of the Indian sun. The life was hard here, though it shouldn't be so bad for a colonel's wife.

Elisa and Damien had arrived a few days earlier, and Mainwaring had given them time to settle into the old plantation house next to his, before he invited them over to a welcome party at his home. The previous colonel, sick with malaria, had returned to England to retire. Mainwaring had been glad to be shot of the old fuddy-duddy, but was feeling rather nervous and wary of the new one who, he had heard, had risen through the ranks, despite his youth. Damien was little more than thirty and Eliza couldn't be older than twenty.

'You must get into the habit of drinking this,' Mainwaring explained. 'It will help prevent the fever. I assume your servant has told you to sleep with the net over your bed at night? Blasted mosquitoes will eat you alive if you don't.'

Mainwaring, almost forty by then, hid his confusion in exposition and advice while he introduced the newlyweds to the rest of the officers and the few English wives that resided in the colony.

'You're not married then, old chap?' asked Damien. 'Must be lonely for you out here.'

'Widowed,' Mainwaring explained. His tone implied that he didn't want to talk about it, and so Elisa began to ask him questions about the area and the people instead, showing a great sensitivity that Mainwaring appreciated.

Mainwaring noticed how fresh and excited she was about the adventure she had undertaken with her husband. He hoped she wouldn't fall foul of the intensity of the heat, or the change of pace that was so different from England.

'It's a shame your wife is no longer with us,' Elisa said. 'I was hoping for some female company that I could relate to, but I will just have to settle for yours instead, John.'

Damien didn't notice or object to his wife's familiarity with Mainwaring. In fact, he encouraged it. He saw the slightly older man as no real threat.

'As long as she's happy, I'll be happy,' Damien said.

Mainwaring and Damien fell into an easy friendship. And

it wasn't long before Mainwaring involved him in the small export business he had started to give himself an income when he left the army. He only brought Damien into the periphery of the business at first, telling him as little as possible until he was certain he could trust him. The selling point being that there were many galleries and customers for the artefacts his sources found. It wasn't strictly legal. There were busybodies who believed that artefacts should remain in the country they came from. But Mainwaring had made many thousands of pounds by bending the rules, and it didn't hurt to have his colonel involved to give the order for crates to be shipped unopened back to England. So, Damien proved his worth from early on, and the partnership became very lucrative.

'I've found something really special,' Damien told Mainwaring one day.

Mainwaring had called in to see Damien on some pretext, but really he hoped to exchange a few words with Elisa on a surprise party she was planning for Damien's birthday.

'Where?' asked Mainwaring.

Damien tapped the side of his nose. 'I have my sources too, you know, old bean.'

'All right, show me,' Mainwaring said. 'I'll tell you if it's worth anything.'

Damien rang a bell and gave an instruction for his manservant to bring something in. A few moments later the man returned and placed a small wooden crate on the lounge table.

As the servant left Elisa came in. She was wearing a sari of purple and gold. She looked every bit the wife of a wealthy Indian rajah. Damien barely gave her a second look, but Elisa sat down beside Mainwaring and began to pour tea for them all.

Mainwaring loved to see her in the kind of sari that showed her flat smooth midriff. Although her skin remained fair, her dark hair and eyes lent themselves to the look beautifully. She was obviously extremely happy in her new-found freedom, as Damien never told her she couldn't do something. Nor did he ever comment that her attire was inappropriate. Mainwaring wondered about this; sometimes he considered that Damien must really love Elisa. But deep down he knew this wasn't the case. He didn't love her, but she was a possession he was fond of, and at other times completely indifferent to. It was an observation he had made about their marriage from early on. Even so, Elisa didn't seem to be concerned or unhappy about it. Few women had the freedom she did.

Damien opened the lid of the box, then impatiently pushed aside the straw that was covering the item.

'That's beautiful!' Elisa said.

Mainwaring could see it was a medicine jar, and the top was sealed on with wax to keep the contents from leaking out. Elisa picked it up and walked across the room to the large picture window that overlooked the grounds. The sun streamed in and she placed the jar on the table by the window in direct sunlight.

'I think it should go here,' she said.

Mainwaring went over to the jar and examined it. It had strange markings. Symbols: circles, triangles and eyes carved into it that he had never seen before.

'Old medicine bottle,' Mainwaring said. 'If Elisa likes it, it's worth keeping for your own private collection.'

'I do like it, John,' Elisa said. 'Damien, can I keep it?'

Damien shrugged. 'I don't suppose us keeping it will make much difference in the scheme of things, John. But tell me, how much is something like that worth on the black market?'

Mainwaring knew that the item would be worth a lot. It was certainly unique, but he saw the interest in Elisa's eyes. She twisted and turned it, looking closely at all the symbols.

'I love it!' she said.

'Not worth much, I'm afraid,' Mainwaring lied. 'I think it's just an attractive bauble, really.'

Damien was satisfied with the response and so allowed Elisa to keep the jar.

'But that's not to say your source won't come up with something else that is valuable,' Mainwaring continued. 'I'd say, let me see anything else that you find.'

Damien was pleased that Mainwaring hadn't completely dismissed the jar, or his sources, and so he agreed.

A few days later, though, Bhakti came into the lounge and found the jar smashed on the floor, contents leaking onto an expensive rug. She was tutting as she cleared up the mess, concerned that the Memsahib would be upset. Then she noticed Elisa sitting on the sofa, staring into space.

'Memsahib?' Bhakti said.

'It was an accident,' Elisa said. 'I was just looking at it and it slipped from my hands.'

Bhakti cleared up the mess and took it out to the back of the house to throw away. But as she was placing the broken pieces into the rubbish, Neeraj came around the corner of the house. He was carrying a crate of fresh fruit that Mainwaring had sent round for Elisa.

Neeraj saw the jar and frowned.

'Where did you get this?'

When Bhakti explained what it was and what had happened, Neeraj insisted on coming into the house to see Elisa.

'Don't throw the jar away,' he said to Bhakti. 'Wrap the pieces in paper and then keep for me.'

They found Eliza sleeping on the sofa. They tried to wake her, but a terrible fever was on her. Bhakti let Neeraj pick Elisa up and take her to her room.

When Damien returned, he discovered Neeraj talking to an Indian doctor in his hallway.

'Malaria,' the doctor said. He gave strict instructions on how to use the medicine he had left with Bhakti.

Later Neeraj placed all the broken pieces of the jar in front of Mainwaring.

'You have seen such jars before?' asked Mainwaring.

Neeraj nodded. He was reluctant to speak because he wasn't sure of his facts. 'I think … this is … a funeral jar.'

'A funeral jar?' Mainwaring prided himself on knowing and understanding Neeraj's Hindu faith, but he had never heard of them using anything like this during a funeral. As far as he was aware, all bodies were cremated within a day of death. The soul freed from the earthly form would travel for thirteen days before finally passing on to another realm.

'It is not usual in my faith,' Neeraj said, almost as though reading Mainwaring's mind. 'Once I heard of a holy man who exorcised a demon from a small child. The demon was hiding inside him, making the boy do terrible things. Once the demon was removed, it was caught and sealed in such a jar as this. The symbols mean imprisonment. The eye is for protection, a ward against evil.'

The two men reviewed the remnants. A smell of burnt matches wafted up from the foul ichor that still clung to the pieces of pottery.

Neeraj said, 'The scent of a demon is always that of sulphur.'

Mainwaring gave instructions for Neeraj to dispose of the jar in the best way he felt fit. As Elisa soon recovered, and was showing no signs of any illness, they both decided that the contents may have been vaguely poisonous, or the doctor had been correct and she had suffered a bout of malaria. Either way, Mainwaring soon forgot the incident.

A few weeks later Mainwaring accepted an invitation to meet with Elisa for lunch. He had often spent time in her company alone, something that would be unsuitable in the polite English society they had all come from, but was not considered inappropriate in their new life. Mainwaring enjoyed the freedom that this lack of propriety gave them. Even though they all pretended they had brought British values with them, behind closed doors the formalities were often ignored.

Elisa was wearing a formal sari when he arrived. It was in red, a colour often worn by the bride at a Hindu wedding.

'You look beautiful, my dear,' Mainwaring said as he took her hand and bowed over it. He placed a kiss on her knuckles, and allowed his lips to linger there a little longer than was respectable. But it was the only contact he allowed himself: Mainwaring would never have made advances on Damien's wife, even though he had strong feelings for her.

Displaying a strength that her small frame belied, she pulled him close into her embrace. Mainwaring tried to resist, but his will was not his own. He noticed something strange, though, before he became hers: her eyes were wrong. The dark brown had bled into the whites, but Mainwaring couldn't stop her as she pressed her blood-red lips on his.

Chapter Thirty-Four

'What are you telling me?' Mitchell asked.

'I may be your father. Though I don't know for certain.'

Mitchell took this in. He studied Mainwaring's face, but couldn't hate him for what had happened with Elisa, especially as Mainwaring had been more than a godfather and had fulfilled the role of parent so admirably for all of Mitchell's life.

'You had an affair with my mother? How long did it last?'

'Only a matter of weeks. I knew, you see, that deep down it wasn't really Elisa in there. In fact, the woman I was making love to, was nothing like your mother.'

'Then where was my mother?' Mitchell said. 'Was this a … changeling? Like the creature that I met in the graveyard?'

'No,' Mainwaring said. 'This is difficult to explain.'

'Perhaps allow me?' Neeraj said. Mainwaring nodded. He took a seat at the table while Neeraj took up the role of storyteller once more. 'The creature was Elisa, it was also itself. The soul of it had gone inside her and begun to manipulate her. Your mother's soul was suffocated, pushed down. Maybe the creature could sense that she had the same feelings for your godfather that he had for her? Or maybe it fed on his emotions, using her to have access to him. In my country, this parasite that feeds on human energy, has no other name, but in your culture, I have heard it called a succubus.'

Mitchell squeezed his eyes shut: his head hurt and he massaged his temples as he tried to bring everything together to show him why this was relevant to the here and now.

'But what has it got to do with this soul-thief creature?'

'I believe they are one and the same,' explained Neeraj. 'Perhaps the merging of the creature with a female gave it a new desire.'

Mitchell was quiet as he tried to take the information in.

'Eight months after I began my affair with your mother,' Mainwaring said, 'she gave birth to you. Not long after, she tried to drown you in a bathtub. By then her mind had deteriorated. Her behaviour was, to say the least, irrational. Damien had no choice but to send her back to England. She was institutionalised.'

'Just like Sara.'

'It wasn't a decision he took lightly. I tried to persuade him not to send her away. I still loved her. But she caused havoc among the servants. She took to drawing them and invariably their personalities changed. When their behaviour was out of character, Damien had to fire them. She was left alone with only Bhakti, who for some reason was immune to her,' Mainwaring continued.

'I was told she was dead…' Mitchell said. 'So was that a lie?'

'The day that Bhakti died we received a letter saying that your mother was in a coma,' Mainwaring said. 'I know that

Damien responded, expressed the wish that he would rather they stopped trying to wake her. That they let her die. He told me some months later that she was dead. I think he was relieved. But by then he was a shadow of his former self. He was drinking heavily and that was when the gambling started…'

'I just don't know how a dead woman can affect us now?' Mitchell said.

Neeraj shook his head. 'I'm afraid I am out of answers. All I know is, the demon that was inside your mother is still alive. That's the only explanation I can think of. It's possible that when she died, it was freed and it went into another body. But who and where that body is, I don't know.'

Mitchell's head was still aching as he walked up the small row of steps to his front door. All he could think about was bathing and changing. He felt as though he could smell the stench of the soul thief on his body and soul. So many questions remained unanswered, not least the one that made him wonder about his own soul. From what Mainwaring and Neeraj said, all of this could be happening because of him. If his mother was this creature, or had it inside her even as she carried him, then what precisely did that make him? Was he too a soul thief, capable of stealing the life from others?

Of course, he'd asked Neeraj this very question.

'No, Mitchell-Sahib. You are not evil. There is no darkness inside you beyond normal temptation. I would know,' Neeraj reassured.

But despite this, Mitchell couldn't help but question everything he'd done, especially in the last few months. Why, for example, was he so drawn to solving mysteries, if not for the fact that he was drawn to evil?

'Mr Bishop, sir! You look exhausted. How is Miss Laura doing?'

Mrs Dalton helped him off with his coat.

'She's much better. I am exhausted and I'd really like to bathe...'

'Of course, sir.'

Mitchell was soon in his bath, and after washing away the stink he imagined clung to his flesh, he felt less contaminated.

He lay down in his bed to try to get a few hours' sleep, but his mind was reeling. He couldn't be angry at Mainwaring for his revelations, even though it meant that potentially Mitchell's whole life had been a lie. It wasn't too difficult for Mitchell to think of Mainwaring as his 'father'. The man had fulfilled that role anyway, ensuring that he was always safe and well, giving generously of his wealth and his time. He understood now, more than ever, why Mainwaring had managed to persuade his father to let him bring Mitchell back to England. Only there did Mainwaring feel his child would be safe, particularly after the death of Bhakti. Of course, the thing that was in his mother was also here, biding its time. But if this was all true, then how could Toby Naylor even be involved at all? Had the creature somehow gained access to the camera and taken part in capturing the images, and the souls, of Laura, Sara and Warren? And who knew how many countless others were in its thrall? But why? What did it gain from using people? Was it merely for sport?

Mitchell turned over in the bed. His mind, body and heart were thoroughly exhausted and he embraced the floating sensation that accompanied the first wave of relaxation.

It was late afternoon and the sun was high in the sky. For a moment Mitchell was confused, not knowing where he was. He staggered from his bed, sweat-drenched, as tremors rippled through his entire body. His heart pounded in his ears and ragged breaths tugged at his lungs, as though all the air had been sucked from the room.

He'd been having a nightmare. One he didn't wish to relive, now he was awake. But he'd seen Doris, falling as if by his own hand, as the wolf's head cane came down on her.

Reaching the nightstand, he poured water into the wash bowl and splashed it over his face.

'It was only a dream…'

Neeraj had warned him as he left Mainwaring's house that the creature had some connection with him. Mitchell thought on his words as he fastened his shirt and pulled on his breeches with still-trembling hands. Did this connection mean that he could somehow see the guilty culprit's deeds? If this was so, then maybe he could also track the monster back to whatever lair it resided in. He just needed to know how.

He reached for the door handle and once more fell into an outlandish vision.

He was looking up at himself in the graveyard, then glanced down at his hands, female hands, undoing the buttons on his breeches as though he were no longer in his own body, but was in hers.

He shook the images away. But it was suddenly apparent that he was tapping into the memories of the creature.

He stumbled back towards his bed, hand reaching blindly for a glass of water on the side table as he slumped back down onto the mattress.

Once more he saw female hands. A bottle unscrewed and poison poured into his glass.

He heard a sinister laugh and realised he was seeing the assassination attempt on himself. Seeing it through the monster's eyes.

It hurried towards his door, hand on the door handle as it looked back at the brandy glass…

The image dissolved and Mitchell found himself clutching the water glass in shaking hands. He sipped the water, splashing a little over his clean shirt. But slowly his nerves steadied and Mitchell found he was in a better place than he had been earlier that day. If what Neeraj had told him was right, he *did* have a connection with the creature and he had just learnt how to use it. He was going to find out all he could about the soul thief and why it wanted to kill him.

Chapter Thirty-Five

'here is she?' Rosie demanded at the nurses' station. 'Where is my mother?'

'I'm sorry, Miss Adams, but Dr Glenister left instructions to have her moved to an asylum. She went yesterday.'

'I never said goodbye!' Rosie said. 'There wasn't time.'

'I'm sorry,' said the nurse. 'That's how these things are sometimes. Best to try and put it all behind you now. You'll be notified when she's passed. That's what you wanted, wasn't it? To let her go?'

Rosie stared at the nurse. Her words were so cold and cruel – so unfeeling – that Rosie couldn't associate them with her own decisions.

'No. It wasn't like that… Dr Glenister said…'

'Ah, well. Unfortunately, Glenister is no longer with us. Evil man, you know…' said the nurse in hushed tones. 'Forced himself on a comatose patient once…'

Rosie backed away as the woman smiled at her as though she had just told her the most pleasant story in the world.

Then the nurse's face took on a cruel expression, one that

Rosie recognised from her past. A face she hoped never to see again.

'It can't be!' she gasped.

Rosie turned away and hurried towards the door. A strong smell, like burning matches, filled the ward.

Outside, Rosie breathed in fresh air but she was trembling. It had all been so awful. And now, just when she thought the whole thing was finally over, her mother had been taken away and she hadn't even had the chance to say goodbye. Or to tell her that she was going to get married.

'Tell me. What *did* happen the day she bumped her head?' asked the nurse. She was standing beside her in the doorway.

'Who *are* you?' asked Rosie.

The nurse smiled, then she turned back and went inside.

Rosie hurried down the street and made her way back towards the photography shop. She was shaken, afraid. The memory of that day swirled around in her head like a fish in a whirlpool. She was trapped: she knew she couldn't drown, but she also couldn't swim away. It was all so confusing and horrible.

By the time she reached the shop she was overwhelmed by memories. None of them good.

Twelve months ago

'Mother?' Rosie called, coming into the house.

She had completed her first week at the dress shop. A job that her friends envied and her mother was proud of. First salary in hand, Rosie had hurried home. There was only the two of them, and so she knew that her new good fortune would change the standard of their living. Their life was on the up, and Rosie was enjoying the new job too. It made her feel like an adult and gave her some real independence.

'Mum?'

She entered the kitchen first, the usual location of her mother at this time of day, but the room was empty. Half-chopped vegetables were strewn on the table, a pan was overturned onto the floor. Rosie picked up the pan and placed it back on the table. For a minute she remembered this. It was as though this sort of thing had happened before, like some awful *déjà vu*.

In the sitting room, she found a man lying face down in front of the fire, a pool of blood soaking into the carpet around his neck. Rosie stared at the body, afraid to move, afraid to make a sound. It was such an irrational reaction that she forced herself to kneel down and turn him over.

The man was dead, eyes open, staring, blood seeping from a gouged wound at his throat.

Rosie yelped and jumped away.

'*Mother?*' she called. Afraid now that something dreadful had happened to her. That she was hurt or worse.

She ran through the house, up the stairs and into her mother's room.

Mother was sitting at her dressing table brushing her long, greying hair. Rosie remembered a time when it had been thick black waves. She was wearing little more than a thin shift.

'Mum! Thank God! Are you all right?'

She met Mother's eyes in the mirror. 'Of course. Why wouldn't I be?'

'There's a man in the sitting room! He's dead!'

'Don't be concerned about it,' Mother said.

'*What?*'

'He came in and attacked me. I killed him. It was self-defence.'

Rosie saw the blood-covered dress that was cast aside as though it were only slightly soiled.

'What happened?' Rosie asked. 'We have to send for the police.'

Mother stood up. 'No, my dear. That won't be necessary. We will just dispose of the body somewhere it won't be found. And if it is, it won't have any connection with us.'

'What are you talking about?' Rosie said, shocked. 'Mother, if he attacked you, then we have to tell someone.'

'It's time you grew up,' Mother said. 'There are things about me you don't know.'

Rosie looked into Mother's eyes and didn't recognise her.

'The man downstairs fathered you,' Mother said. 'In an asylum, nineteen years ago.'

'You said my father was dead…'

'He is … now.'

'Oh my God!' Rosie sank down onto the edge of Mother's bed.

'There's no need to worry. It was a bit of a surprise that he found me after all this time. He served his purpose and you have my blood in your veins. I needed another child, you see. The other one was lost to me. I realised too late that it was a mistake to try to kill him. It was only later that I learned how useful he could have been. Just as you have been.'

'Other one? What are you talking about?' Rosie said. She felt as though the bottom had fallen completely out of her world.

'I became trapped in this body. The woman who once owned it, broke a jar that held me. I don't remember how I was captured there … but … she breathed me in. I bonded with her.

Stupid, really, to become trapped in a mortal like that. But … it has had its advantages. I can feel inside here, not just send out my toys and watch them play. I can be part of it, experience what it feels like to live. The connections are so much more intense. And the structure of this body is so easy to change.'

'I don't understand…'

Before her eyes, her ageing mother altered. Rosie found she was staring at herself, as though she were looking into a mirror image.

'Don't…' Rosie had gasped.

'We have to get rid of the body. I've already prepared the cart outside,' Mother said. 'You're not a child anymore, Rosie. You're going to help me from now on. You're going to feed them to me, and I'll grow stronger for it.'

Shocked and numb, Rosie followed her mother back downstairs. A feeling of unreality overwhelmed her fear and confusion. She felt as though she were watching herself from a great distance. She had no control over her own actions. She was one of her mother's toys, being manipulated and controlled.

Mother rolled the spoilt rug around the body. She looked different: like the man that lay dead inside the rug. Mother had said he was her father. She surveyed the features, saw the familiarity of her own face in there. Was it true? And if so, who had her father been?

After a while Rosie began to believe that she was dreaming. She slipped back inside herself and watched the scenario unfold like a moving-picture sequence, only in colour.

Mother/Father put the body in an old cart in the back yard. Then she deposited more junk on top. Rosie stood by in a daze.

'Stay here,' Mother/Father said.

Rosie nodded. She went back into the kitchen and began to

make dinner. She felt like a marionette whose strings were being pulled and manoeuvred. Every movement felt contrary to what her mind wanted. But she couldn't fight it.

She slipped from her mind and found herself looking through other eyes.

The cart was in front of her and a male voice, coming from her own throat, was making the call: 'Rag… Bone…'

Rosie tried to stop the movement of the cart but had no control at all over the body she appeared to be in. It was as though she were merely a passenger inside her own head.

A woman came out of a nearby house and placed a bag of rags on the cart, right on top of the carpet. Rosie watched the fake man fish coins from his pocket and move on.

Then, she found herself back in the kitchen, peeling knife in hand, poised over a soil-covered potato. She felt faint and swayed against the table, dropping the knife and vegetable down onto the roughly carved surface.

'That's done,' said Mother as she returned to the kitchen. Rosie noted that Mother looked normal again. At least, like the woman she knew.

At night in bed, Rosie had terrible nightmares. She saw the creature that was using Mother's body doing awful things. Somehow, she believed that she was accessing the mind of the creature at these dreadful moments. She didn't know whether it was because she was being allowed to, or whether it was purely unintentional. All she knew was, the woman she had always known and loved had changed. There was no sign of her inside the body that clearly looked like her. She was now openly drawing things and people, no longer disguising her true nature from her daughter.

'You should try this sometimes. See if you have the gift,' Mother said as she sat by the window looking out onto the street. She was drawing a picture of a small child as he played hopscotch alone.

Rosie came to the window and watched as the child suddenly ran out into the road in front of an oncoming carriage. At the last moment a passer-by threw himself into the road, knocking the child aside. The good Samaritan was trampled immediately, whereas the little boy was completely unharmed.

The driver of the carriage was in a state of shock.

Rosie turned to look at Mother: her brown eyes had bled to black and now filled the entire eye, eradicating all trace of white. She was a monster. The thought of using her mother's wicked gift horrified her. She decided then that she would never even attempt to copy someone's image, for fear that it would consume her soul and cause harm to the subject. But she continued to fear that she too was evil.

When she looked back at the scene outside, the little boy was sat on the kerb, smiling at the carnage he had caused.

'Who was that man?' Rosie asked. 'How did he become my father?'

Mother stopped drawing. 'It pleases me to tell you.'

She put down the sketchpad.

'The asylum was a terrible place. They drugged me with laudanum. I realised I could escape if I starved this body. Let it die. It's a vessel, after all, like any other, and could be broken. But they wouldn't allow it to die. They force fed me.'

'That's horrible,' Rosie said.

'It took a few years before I could strengthen this body from the effect of the drugs. Then, I started to get visions of my son. I knew then I could use him. Manipulate him from afar. And I did so, but the connection broke…'

'I don't understand, Mum…' Rosie said.

'The man who fathered you was an orderly. I used my wiles on him. After some persuasion, he helped me escape the asylum. But I didn't meet up with him outside, as I promised. I came away from it with you inside me. A bonus. And it is, Rosie, for your image has always been mine to use. I've never even had to draw you.'

Rosie shook her head in a subconscious attempt to deny what her mother was saying.

'I've not been a bad mother to you, have I?'

Rosie's mouth was dry. Her mind flashed back to all the loving moments of her youth. The care she'd been given, the protection. The money her mother spent on her education. She had never questioned the love behind it, but if what her mother now said was true, how could such a monster feel anything?

Mother returned to her drawing.

'What about the boy … my … brother? Can you use him too?' Rosie asked.

'Yes… But I have other plans for him.'

'Have you ever loved me?' Rosie said, her eyes full of unshed tears.

'I don't feel anything for you,' Mother said. 'But I can mimic what this crushed soul inside me might have felt. Now, would you like to see what I'm drawing? I'll share this chaos with you. I'm sure you'll find it entertaining. After all, Rosie, you are your mother's daughter.'

Rosie swallowed her fear. She could not allow this evil to continue.

She walked calmly to the fireplace and began to stir the coals with the poker, even as she heard the charcoal scratching across another piece of paper. She glanced over her shoulder. Mother was absorbed in her latest game.

Without thinking, Rosie walked back and immediately swung the poker. It connected with the creature's head. The Mother-thing crumpled. Rosie lifted the poker once more and brought it crashing down again.

After that Rosie went out, walked for an hour in a daze. Her mind refused to accept everything that had happened. By the time she came home she had completely forgotten about the evil creature – blanked it from her mind as though it had never existed.

In the sitting room she found Mother's body crumpled in the chair, sketchpad and charcoal still in her hand. Rosie ran outside, calling for help.

Now, almost twelve months on, Rosie remembered everything. It was as though a light had turned on in the back of her brain. Everything she had done to try to sustain her mother's life had been because some dark force persuaded her to do it. Now the woman was gone, and she was manifesting herself in others, just as she had always done. Rosie knew it and she realised she'd failed to stop her.

With the memories came the skill her mother said she had. She was connected to her: she *saw* the creature in the graveyard, wearing her own face and clothes, sketching people, an evil smile curving her lips. She *saw* the hateful attack on Toby: knew without doubt that had she not returned, the thing would have killed the man she loved. Then Rosie saw it wearing the face of Bishop as it struck down a prostitute. Somehow, she even knew the girl's name: Doris. She saw her own face again as Dr Glenister died in agony.

And worst of all, the terrible decaying form of Dr Carter.

It was all too horrible, and this time Rosie's mind refused to let her escape back into her fantasy world. She was forced to face what her mother had done, along with the realisation that, although she'd stopped her for a while, the evil spirit inside her had begun its deadly work again. Death wouldn't be the end for this creature, it would be its beginning. It would be free to wreak havoc on the world, and it would most certainly finish what it had started with Mitchell Bishop, Laura Carter, Toby and … *oh God!*

As the memories and visions rushed back into her mind, Rosie staggered, almost falling into the road. She held onto a streetlamp, sickness churning her stomach. She saw in her mind's eye the charcoal drawing that Mother had been working on just before Rosie had struck her. It was a young man: *Artie.*

After her mother had been taken to the infirmary, Rosie had burnt all the sketches that contained people, except for one. Some impulse had made her keep Artie's image. It was folded in the bottom of her mother's trinket box.

'Oh God, what have I done?' she murmured.

'Mother…' she whispered.

Her mind hated to think of the woman she had loved in this light. But it was true. She had been lied to. Every tender moment had been fake, and why? What was Rosie's role in all of this?

She saw a hire cab approaching and held out her hand. Only one person would know what to do. She had felt from the beginning she could trust him. She had to go and see Mr Bishop, and as she stepped into the cab, his address came to her lips as though she had always known it. Even though she had never been to that part of the town before.

As the cab pulled away, Rosie chewed at her thumbnail. She was searching inside herself for some other information. Mitchell was important and she knew why, but didn't dare accept it.

Chapter Thirty-Six

'I don't know what you're talking about,' Toby said.

'I need to see her. I know she's part of this,' said Mitchell. 'I saw her. Through this thing's eyes.'

'Artie, get the police. I think Mr Bishop has lost his mind,' Toby said.

Artie put down the broom he was using to sweep the studio and began to remove his apron.

'You must burn all of the negatives. Destroy everything. I know this sounds insane, but it manipulates people by using their images.'

Artie tossed the apron aside and took Mitchell's arm.

'All right now, Mr Bishop, what do you say we take a walk outside and find a nice friendly copper to talk to?'

Mitchell slumped as Artie touched him. His mind slipped into one of those weird visions. He felt as though he had lost touch completely with reality.

He saw himself entering the shop some weeks before, his favourite cane clasped firmly in his hand. He had removed his hat, and propped the cane against the reception desk as Toby had greeted him.

The vision jumped.

He saw Artie sitting on the chair, head between his knees as he recovered from his moment of dizziness.

Another jump, and he was leaving with Inspector Stream.

As the door closed his perspective changed. He saw through Artie's eyes. Artie picked up the cane and walked to the door. Instead of calling Mitchell back, he placed the cane in the umbrella stand.

'You…' Mitchell said. He pulled his arm free. 'You had my cane. I left it here that day.'

Artie looked genuinely confused as Mitchell pointed at the umbrella stand.

'You *killed* her!' Mitchell said.

His mind jumped again.

Glenister smoking a cigar. The eyes Mitchell looked through were watery. He looked down at his own hands and found hooked claws, skin falling from his flesh. One of the hands lifted towards his face. Slime covered his cheeks. And the putrid smell of decay wafted under his nostrils. As the head of the body Mitchell occupied turned, he found himself gazing into a mirror. A deathly grimace covered the features of the rapidly deteriorating body of Warren Carter. Inside it, Mitchell screamed.

'What's wrong with him?' Toby asked.

Mitchell came out of his weird episode to find himself sitting in a chair in the photography shop. He couldn't recall how he had arrived there. Then, his immediate memory slowly returned.

'I know this sounds insane,' he said, 'but I've been having visions. I'm somehow connected to this thing and I think Rosie is too.'

'That's nonsense,' said Toby.

'*It* attacked you in the graveyard,' Mitchell said. 'I saw it.'

'*Saw* it?' Toby said.

'Then Rosie came and scared it away. I don't know how she did … but…'

'That's crap,' said Artie. 'He could have been told all this by Inspector Stream…'

'True,' said Toby. 'But … how do *you* know Stream was there, Artie? I never told you the truth about my hand.'

Artie smiled. 'Rosie told me. She said some crazy woman attacked you.'

Toby frowned. 'Well, we'll soon know. Rosie should be back soon. I'll go and fetch him some water.'

Leaving Mitchell and Artie alone in the front shop, Toby went into the back kitchen. When he returned Mitchell was alone.

'Where is Artie?'

Mitchell took a deep breath and then pushed at the corners of his dulled memory. It was as though time had slipped by, while he was unaware of its passing.

'He said he … needed to do something,' Mitchell said, recovering his short-term memory again. He couldn't understand why he had let Artie leave the room. 'Has he … been behaving differently?'

'What do you mean?'

'I mean … *would* Rosie have told him what happened if you had asked her not to?'

Toby looked away. 'I told her to tell him I fell. Nothing more. She wouldn't have told him anything else. I'm sure of it.'

'Then how did he know? I *saw* him put my cane in your umbrella stand. That was the weapon used to kill the girl I found behind your shop.'

Toby shrugged. 'Artie often knows stuff. He keeps his ear to the ground. May even have a source in the police. Probably didn't want to admit where he'd heard about it. Anyway, what do you mean, you "saw" him?'

As his mind cleared Mitchell tried to explain the visions again, but knew it made him sound even crazier. He had to agree that Toby's explanation of Artie's sources all sounded plausible. But he couldn't shake the images he had received when he touched the man. It was as though he were directly linked to the creature Mitchell was searching for. Just as Mitchell was. But how was it possible?

'Why do you think Rosie can help you?' Toby asked.

'I… I feel … a connection with her. This thing uses her image, more than any other.'

Toby said nothing. He knew Mitchell wasn't insane, which was why he hadn't sent for the police. He had seen the Rosie-changeling himself. The idea that Mitchell was having visions sounded every bit as believable to his ears as what he had seen himself in the graveyard.

'You feeling better?' Toby asked.

'Yes. Thank you for the water,' Mitchell said. He stood up. 'I'm now more than ever convinced that Artie is involved with this creature too.'

'Let's go and see what he's up to, shall we?' Toby frowned.

Mitchell looked over at the darkroom door. He had a bad feeling that whatever Artie was doing, it wasn't good.

As Toby reached the door Artie came out. He was holding the box of negatives, and his sketch-pad.

'What are you doing?' Toby asked.

'Thought I'd burn these … they are six months old now,' Artie said. 'I'll take them out the back.'

'No you won't. Let me see what you have there,' Toby said.

'Why?' asked Artie.

'Because I asked you,' Toby said.

Artie looked angry for a moment. He let Toby take the box but removed his sketch-pad from the top.

Toby placed the metal box on the counter. He was aware that something was very off about Artie. He had arrived early that day, keen to take pictures, and he had also caught him sketching again; something he did from time to time when the shop was empty. But this time it had been Toby he had been drawing, not the customers, and he had been watching him so intently, it had made Toby feel quite uncomfortable. Like the man was trying to see right into his soul.

'What have you been drawing?' Mitchell said.

'It's nuffink,' said Artie. He held the pad close, as though he didn't want anyone to see the contents.

'Why are you so shy all of a sudden?' Toby asked Artie. 'Let Mr Bishop see it.' Then he turned to Mitchell. 'He's rather good, you know…'

'How do you know?' asked Artie.

'I had a look at your sketch-pad the other day.'

Artie frowned.

'Well, if you will leave it lying around, people are going to look…' Toby said.

Artie said nothing.

'I'd like to see,' said Mitchell.

'No,' said Artie. 'It's private.'

Toby went over to the box of negatives and began to look through them. At first, he didn't notice anything wrong, but then he found a picture of Rosie. One that he hadn't taken. She looked startled, and from the clothing, it was a photograph taken on the very first day she came to the shop. Toby knew every picture he had taken of Rosie. He had studied them all carefully, and he knew immediately that this wasn't one of them.

'Artie, when…?'

Both Mitchell and Toby turned to look at Artie, but what they found in his place was anything but the young man. Instead, they found a face so old that it almost appeared to be mummified. Hooked claws, attached to stick-like arms, pointed at Mitchell accusingly. Filthy rags hung from an emaciated frame.

'You had to interfere, didn't you?'

Mitchell jumped out of his seat and backed away towards the shop front.

The thing was neither male nor female. Its voice – cracked and harsh – resonated in a bulbous chest joined to crooked and twisted hips.

'You're not Artie,' Mitchell said. 'You took his place, though.'

'Oh my God, where is he?' asked Toby with genuine concern for his young assistant.

The creature gave a twisted grin. 'Safe – for now. I rather like him. He sees me in a way that nobody else does, and so I think I'll keep him. At least until I tire of playing with his emotions.'

'What are you?' Toby gasped.

'A soul thief…' Mitchell answered. 'A demon that captures the souls of humans and uses them and their images for its own entertainment. What I don't understand is why it does it.'

'You know rather a lot,' said the thing. Its visage changed before them, turning into the rotting corpse of Warren Carter. 'Hello, old bean. Have you broken my sister in yet? She's gagging for it, you know…'

The creature cackled.

Mitchell felt a surge of bile in the back of his throat, as

though being close to the thing brought about a physical reaction of revulsion.

'Tell me,' he said, drawing on some inner strength, 'what do you gain by toying with people?'

The soul thief sneered. 'You mean you don't know, Mitchell? With all your instincts and the connection with me you so openly admitted to?'

Mitchell stared at the creature. His mind reached out, searching for the answer, and then it presented itself as though the soul thief was telling him the secret directly into his mind.

'You need them to live. They give you energy. You enjoy using them, but you must hold onto their souls in order to…'

Mitchell stopped dead as more information poured into his mind. The sneer fell from the creature's vile lips. The face that looked at him now was one of pure hatred.

'Toby,' Mitchell said. 'Burn those negatives. Burn them now!'

Toby reached for the matchbox, as the creature turned towards him. Warren Carter's features fractured and rotted skin fell from its skeleton as a vile-smelling ichor dripped down onto the hardwood floor. Rosie stood in its place now, looking beautiful and fresh. But the tar-black eyes gave her away. Toby saw himself reflected in them, as though she owned his very soul and he was already held inside her.

'Toby…' she said softly. 'Don't burn the negatives. You'll hurt me if you do.'

Toby's expression smoothed out. At that moment Mitchell realised that the creature was somehow controlling him. He didn't know how, but he snatched at the sketchbook that the Rosie-changeling was still clutching. The pad fell to the floor, and Mitchell saw the image of Toby loading a frame into the back of the camera. The soul thief had captured him in its usual primitive way, and now Toby was under some kind of spell.

Mitchell snatched the pad from the floor, but the Rosie-thing laughed at his efforts and made no move to stop him.

'What do you plan to do with that?' Sara now stood before him. She was wearing a see-through shift much like the one that Rosie had been wearing in the picture-card Mitchell had seen. 'Come on now, Mitchell. You and I both know what you really want from me. Your desire was obvious. Like most men, you were desperate to get back inside your own mother's womb.'

Mitchell gasped at the reference to his mother. He could not imagine this thing to have any association with him at all. But just as his mind denied it, Elisa Bishop's face, exactly as she appeared in the only picture Mitchell had of her, now took up residence in the soul thief's features. The body, formerly slender and willowy, now filled out into a beautiful and curvaceous woman. He knew without doubt this was his mother's form. This was the thing that had seduced Mainwaring. This was the creature that had given birth to him.

Questions as to how the soul thief had captured her spirit rose into his mind and the creature read them there. For once, it answered, and Mitchell knew what it said was true.

'We are both using this body,' Elisa said. 'I am your mother.'

'No,' Mitchell denied, shaking his head. 'You may have given me life, but you are not the woman who should have been my mother.'

Elisa laughed. 'My child, don't you want to greet me? Come into my arms, Mitchell. Haven't you a hug for Mummy?'

'You mock me with your pathetic words,' Mitchell said.

'But don't think you can fool me. Why have you done this? Why have you hurt Laura and her family? If I am your child, why do you wish so much to destroy me?'

The smile fell from the creature's lips.

'Because I can,' she said.

'No … it's more than that,' Mitchell said. 'I'm immune to you. Therefore I'm a threat.'

Mitchell glanced down at the pad in his hands, then he tore off the picture of Toby. He knew without a doubt what to do. From his pocket he pulled a box of matches.

'What are you doing?' demanded Elisa.

'You will no longer control this man…' Mitchell struck the match and pressed it to the paper. The picture caught immediately and rapidly burned until he was forced to let it fall to the ground.

Elisa screamed; the visage of his young mother fell away. Mitchell could now see the soul thief's true image. Not the hook-clawed creature it showed to terrorise its victims, but the figure of an ageing woman. The same one Glenister had shown him in the hospital: Rosie's mother! He could recognise his mother's face now, and he knew that the creature had a terrible weakness.

A flash of shared knowledge came to him in a rush. He saw Rosie and his mother, a dead body lying on the floor, and then, Rosie taking up the poker. Suddenly he knew everything there was to know about this thing. Bonding with his mother's body meant that it aged. Just as any human did. It was fatally flawed by her weakened body.

'Your body is dying,' he said. 'What use is all of this to you now?'

The old woman stared at him as though his words made no sense at all. 'I can be anything I want.'

'What's going on?' said Toby.

The picture was burned and although her control on Toby was loosened, Mitchell noted that the destruction of the picture had not really harmed the creature at all.

'I'm not so easy to destroy,' she said.

Mitchell suddenly knew why. Her thoughts drifted to him as clearly as if she had spoken them aloud. *I have control of so many souls. All in that box…*

The creature screamed like a harpy as it realised its thoughts were open to Mitchell. He felt a barrier slam down over its mind.

'I underestimated you,' the young Elisa Bishop said, appearing again. 'You have more of my power than I would have suspected. It will only take a push to make you like me. Pick up the charcoal … draw him. Use your inheritance, Mitchell … be of actual use to your mother.'

Mitchell gazed down at the empty page on the pad in his hands, and then followed the soul thief's gaze to Toby.

'I'm not like you,' he said.

She held out a piece of charcoal. Mitchell shook his head, stubborn in his denial of his origins, but his fingers hurt. It was a pain he instinctively knew would ease if only he reached out and took the charcoal. Then he could draw, then he could unleash the evil in himself. An evil he had been fighting his whole life. Deep down he had always known he had this in him, but had fought to never free the darkness that tainted his human soul: the evil given him by his demon mother.

As these thoughts burned into the back of his mind, Mitchell knew they were untrue. No. He had denied himself nothing. He may be her child, but that did not make him evil, or demonic. She was merely manipulating him, and he had to find the original Elisa's body. It was the only way to end this once and for all.

Elisa threw back her head and laughed as Mitchell stared into her eyes and tried to force his own will into her.

'Foolish boy. You cannot read my mind now that I have blocked you, but I can see into yours. I own your soul already.'

But as this battle of wills continued, the soul thief's control on Toby lessened and, out of the corner of his eye, Mitchell could see Toby reaching for the tinder-box on the counter.

Toby struck a match and dropped it into the pile of negatives in the tin box. The film was highly flammable and the box went up with a whoosh. Toby stepped back as the flames burst over the contents.

Elisa crumpled now. Her image began to wane. Hundreds of faces flashed over the visage of the soul thief as each negative burned, and the souls flew away from the creature as though they were being released from some hellish dimension. Some of them floated upwards or hovered around her, while the rest snapped away as though they were being pulled by some invisible force. Mitchell saw the face of Sophia Mobley among them, and her story, involving the murder of her husband, presented itself in his mind. He knew the woman was free now, as were all the other souls the demon had held, but would Sophia recover from what had happened to her?

A cloud of white surrounded the creature until finally there was nothing left of her but one shallow image. This one was of Artie. Mitchell threw the notepad into the tin box, and it burned along with the last remains of film. The soul thief twisted and screamed as the final image was taken from her.

At the last moment Mitchell saw Laura. Her form struggled with the creature but was still hopelessly intermingled with it. Warren and Sara were there too. But even as their faces burst out onto the creature's features, Mitchell knew that Laura was still in terrible danger and souls of her siblings were still held by the creature. It could only mean one thing: the negative of the Carter family photograph was not among those that had been destroyed.

'Where is it, damn you?' Mitchell said, throwing himself at the creature in a fit of rage. But as he propelled himself forward, the thing faded and was gone, leaving a thick miasma of burnt flesh in its wake.

Toby stared at the empty space. The shop was full of smoke from the burnt film. Mitchell hurried to the front door and opened it up to let the smoke out and some fresh air in.

'Where did she go?' Toby said between coughs as the smoke burnt his lungs.

'She was never really there,' Mitchell explained.

'But she was. It was Artie. I touched him…' insisted Toby.

'I know where she is,' Rosie said, entering through the open door.

Chapter Thirty-Seven

'**I** saw it in my mind as though I were watching from inside her,' Rosie said as the carriage sped through the Manchester streets, carrying the three of them towards their destination. 'I saw what was happening in the shop too.'

'So,' Mitchell said, 'as she blocked me, she let you in. It seems she can't keep us *both* out.'

'You're my brother,' said Rosie. They looked at each other for a moment.

'I know,' he said. 'I think I've always known.'

They both felt that overwhelming connection and a deep-seated love for each other. Mitchell realised a missing part of himself had been there in the background, probably since the day Rosie was born. He also knew, that no matter what happened, from now on he'd be her big brother, there to protect her, and he was glad of it.

Rosie knew everything now too. Or at least as much as

Mitchell did, and she was in a state of shock. 'My whole life has been a lie.'

Although Mitchell could say the same of his own life, he knew he had not suffered as much as Rosie had. All those years being brought up by the creature, never seeing its dual personality, only to learn one day that her mother was evil, must now feel like such a betrayal. Yet he could still feel Rosie's love for her. Something he didn't share and didn't quite understand. Mitchell found it difficult to comprehend his own connection to his mother because of this, but believed wholeheartedly in the supernatural creature whose existence he had tried to deny just a short time ago. It wasn't hard to distance himself from the idea that this thing was his birth mother, but no matter how hard he strived, he couldn't truly dismiss the idea, because it was a fact. She *had* been his mother, and yes, Rosie was his half-sister. He couldn't accept one of those things without accepting the other, and he wanted to know Rosie.

Mitchell's previous instinct to protect Rosie from Inspector Stream now made total sense. Somehow, through some primal instinct, he had known she was important. He just hadn't been able to recognise why, until now.

'What do we do now?' asked Toby.

'The hospital sent her to an asylum,' said Rosie. 'It's a few miles from here. I can ... sense the place ... if you know what I mean. But first, we must go to my home. Artie's image is there. He was her first link in this awful chain. He won't be free until...'

'We burn it in front of her...' said Mitchell, finishing her sentence.

Rosie nodded.

'I need to find the negative of Laura, Warren and Sara's photograph too,' Mitchell said to Toby. 'Can you help me?'

Toby went into the darkroom and looked, but when he came out he shook his head.

'If it wasn't in that box, then it's not with my others.'

'It wasn't,' said Mitchell.

'How do you know?' asked Toby.

'You didn't see her releasing those souls?' Mitchell said.

Toby's blank expression confirmed that he hadn't.

'Rosie? Do you know where it is?'

'No,' she said.

'We're going to have to hope that the picture itself will be enough, then,' Mitchell said.

Outside they hailed a hansom cab. Despite their proactivity, Mitchell was still afraid. The soul thief must still have Laura's image, and unless they burnt it in front of the creature, she would never be free.

'Rosie, tell me everything you know,' Mitchell said.

Rosie took his hand and opened her mind to Mitchell. The charcoal drawing of Artie was in her other hand, having been retrieved from her mother's trinket box. Now they were following a trail to the asylum, where the body was being held.

The journey, seen through the eyes of the ambulance driver, unfolded from the city. Already the soul thief was controlling the man.

Now they passed the same road signs that led them from the city centre. After a while the driver turned them north, out towards Salford, onto Prestwich and Whitefield, and then turned towards the industrial town of Bolton. But before they reached the Lancashire town, Rosie instructed the driver to turn off the main route.

They passed through a village called Little Lever and went

out into the countryside again. Mitchell felt a blink of connection with the soul thief once more. They were getting closer.

The cab driver turned into a private, tree-lined road which demarked a huge, expensive estate. They travelled for about half a mile before reaching the tall iron gates. A huge house lay beyond and it looked every bit the insane asylum. A wall, some twenty or thirty feet high, surrounded the building. Tall gothic towers stood either side of a formal castle-like structure. Its windows had iron bars across them. The light was fading now and the panes were all lit up by gaslight. It was as though demonic eyes watched their approach.

'Visitors for one of your patients…' called the driver and, without question, the gatekeeper opened the gates and let them pass.

The driver pulled the carriage in towards the front steps, halted the horses, climbed down, and opened the carriage door. Toby, Mitchell and Rosie alighted and looked up towards the imposing building.

Thick, heavy doors barred the way at the top of a short flight of stairs. Mitchell felt a spark of fear but realised the emotion was not his own. It came from Rosie. She feared what they would find, and was terrified of the confrontation that must happen.

'Perhaps you should wait here?' Mitchell suggested.

He felt Rosie consider this option. 'No.'

Toby took her arm and then Mitchell sensed the deep love she had for him. He understood why she had to see this through. None of them would be safe until Elisa's body was destroyed. And those they loved would be perpetually in danger too. Neither he nor Rosie could allow this to go on.

Mitchell led the way up the steps and he pulled the doorbell.

The ring was piercing but not as loud as the wails and cries that followed inside the building. The insane were disturbed as they heard their arrival. Rosie's fear spiked again, but Mitchell would have realised how she felt by the way she drew closer to Toby, even if he wasn't connected to her.

It took some time for one of the orderlies to arrive at the door; by then the noise inside had ceased.

'Visiting is over for today, I'm afraid,' said the man.

He was tall with white, wispy, blond hair.

'We need to see our mother right away…' said Mitchell.

The orderly folded his arms and shook his head.

Toby withdrew a wad of notes from his inside pocket. 'This is a matter of urgency,' he said.

The orderly weighed up the three people.

'Who've you come to see?' he said, reaching out to take the money.

'Elisa Adams,' Rosie said, her voice low. Mitchell could feel she was torn between loyalty and the need to end all of this. He hoped that Rosie wouldn't prove to be a liability once inside. Her fear was making her resolve waver.

'We want to see the doctor in charge as well,' said Mitchell. 'Mrs Adams … has been sent here to … fade … not to be…'

He couldn't say the words for a moment.

'She's beyond help,' explained Rosie. 'We are her children. We need to say goodbye.'

'Well,' said the orderly. 'I'm sure Dr Simmons will want to see you too, in that case.'

The man took Toby's offered money and slipped it casually into his pocket. Then he led them inside.

'Dr Simmons's office is this way,' said the orderly.

'Could we see Mother first?' Rosie asked.

Mitchell glanced at her. Her emotions were chaotic and he was worried about her. How much hold did Elisa have over Rosie? After all, she had used her image over and over again.

Rosie frowned as though she could hear his doubts and feel his concern.

'I have to say goodbye,' she said. 'You understand?'

Mitchell nodded.

The orderly led them through a ward of inmates who lay quietly in their beds. None of the female patients moved.

'Laudanum,' the orderly said. 'They won't move 'til mornin'.'

At the end of the ward, the orderly took them into a side room. Elisa Adams lay strapped to a metal bunk inside.

'She got a bit excited when she arrived. Scratching and biting. We don't put up with that sort of thing,' the orderly explained, but he was unapologetic.

'She woke up?' said Rosie.

'Well, no. It was all a little…'

Elisa looked frail and aged, her frame thinner and more wasted than the last time Rosie had seen her. She appeared harmless, though they all knew this was not the case. She was a very dangerous person indeed.

'You've drugged her?' Mitchell asked.

'It's hospital policy. None of them are allowed to carry on like that. And night-time means they sleep, even when they don't want to.'

'Good,' said Mitchell. 'Let me speak to Simmons now.'

'I'll stay here,' said Rosie. 'She shouldn't be left alone.'

Mitchell could feel her inner torment. Seeing the woman through Rosie's eyes made him more aware of how dedicated and loyal she had been to the creature. Despite everything, this *thing* brought Rosie up. He understood that now, more than ever, Rosie needed to say goodbye to the lie that was her childhood. A lie that would end when the soul thief was dead.

'I'll stay with you,' said Toby.

'It's all right,' Rosie said. 'I need to be … *alone* with her.'

Toby reluctantly agreed, but only when the orderly explained that Rosie would be safe. All the patients were strapped into their beds and soundly asleep. Nothing would change that.

As Mitchell and Toby approached Dr Simmons's office a high-pitched yell echoed through the hallway from one of the wards upstairs.

The orderly took off at a run, taking the stairs two at a time. Mitchell and Toby were left outside the doctor's office, wondering what to do.

'Don't let this distract us from our mission,' said Mitchell. He felt a growing sense of alarm, that he wasn't sure was his own emotion or Rosie's. 'I think … you should go back to Rosie.'

Toby looked at Mitchell long and hard. 'I don't know much about these things, but I can tell there's some kind of connection between you.'

'Yes,' Mitchell said.

'You're her son, as Rosie is her daughter,' Toby said.

'Yes. I'm certain of it,' Mitchell answered.

'Yet, she's never used your image…' Toby observed.

At that moment Mitchell felt a surge of fear again. 'Go to Rosie *now*! I'll get the doctor. We finish this tonight!'

~

Toby reached the ward a few seconds later, and found Rosie sitting calmly beside the bed of her mother.

'Are you all right?' he asked.

Rosie nodded but her eyes were sad and serious. 'I'm scared. But I don't know why. She hasn't moved. And … I don't believe she would hurt me if she did.'

Toby pulled up a chair and sat down beside her. 'I don't think you should delude yourself on that score. From what I saw today…'

'I know,' said Rosie. 'It's irrational. I know everything she's done. She even tried to poison Mitchell. Her own son. Did you know? And to drown him as a baby. She didn't hurt me. Ever. Maybe there is something human left in there.'

Toby said nothing but he was afraid for Rosie and for himself. What they were planning, what Mitchell hoped to achieve, was the death of a frail and dying woman, anyway. His faith didn't allow for that, even though this thing was the most vicious devil any religion could have imagined. He had always believed in good and evil, but perhaps not in the idea of a devil. Now he knew such things existed, Toby was brought to a juncture that opposed everything he had ever understood about the world.

He stared down at the face of Elisa Adams. She had a look of Rosie, but he couldn't imagine his future wife ever turning into such a decrepit creature. Evil emanated from the thing, even as it lay helpless in the bed. But they had beaten it. Taken down the devil, as it were, just like the Bible stories he had heard at Sunday School.

The fight, in the end, felt too easy, though. He tried hard to imagine Rosie, or Mitchell, being capable of matricide. Surely such a sin would weigh heavily on any soul, wouldn't it?

He considered that this thing wasn't human, despite how

helpless she appeared now. She was evil and they were the good people, weren't they? Surely that would be enough to save their souls from damnation. Despite his quiet rationalisations, Toby wanted to spare Rosie as much pain as possible. Even if he finished the job for her.

'When Mitchell comes with the doctor, I think you should leave. I don't want you to be here at the end.'

Rosie was silent for a moment and then she said, 'I have to stay. I have to make sure it's finally over. I know you don't understand … but I didn't know what she was until the day she killed someone in our home. Then, I saw inside her and I knew everything. Before that, she was just my mother.'

Toby nodded, and then, completely out of the blue, someone struck him from behind. He heard Rosie scream as he slumped forward, tumbling from the chair onto the polished wooden floor.

'The easiest and most humane way to end this, is to give her some kind of lethal injection,' said Mitchell.

'Mr Bishop, it is not for us to decide who lives and who dies,' Simmons said.

'Surely your notes say that she is to be "left". That no attempt should be made to revive or feed her?'

'Letting her go is a far different matter than what you are asking of me,' Simmons said.

'I'm asking that you *help* my mother. We don't want her to suffer.'

Mitchell had realised that telling Simmons the truth about Elisa would only make him sound insane. Elisa had to die this night, no matter what. Now he hoped that the doctor would take this plausible explanation of his somewhat strange request and agree to it.

'My sister and I are very willing to make a substantial donation to the hospital…' Mitchell said. 'Is there an amount that might help you?'

Simmons sat upright at the mention of money, but his reaction was not what Mitchell expected. 'Mr Bishop, lives cannot be *bought* and *sold*!'

'I'm sorry. I meant no offence, doctor.'

'Indeed,' Simmons said. 'To be honest, I'm surprised more families don't ask for this, though. Most don't care enough, I suppose. They put them away, and that's the last you see them.'

Simmons was thoughtful for a moment.

'I saw this patient earlier. My feeling is that she will never recover from her substantial brain injury. She is incapable of feeding or washing herself, and will take significant care while we wait for her to pass on naturally.'

'Precisely,' said Mitchell.

'I really don't have the manpower to devote to her, if I'm honest,' Simmons continued. 'The authorities cut our budget a few months ago and I'm down to a skeleton staff as it is. Even so, the hospitals keep sending cases like this to us because these kinds of patients, hopeless as they are, suck up their resources too.'

'Will you help my mother, then?' Mitchell asked.

'I'm reluctant,' Simmons said. 'But I can think of no valid reason why I should let her suffer.'

'Thank you!' said Mitchell. 'Please, let's hurry. My sister is sitting with her and the sooner this is done, the sooner she can begin to move on with her own life.'

'All right,' said Simmons. He picked up his brown leather

medical bag and took out a bottle of clear liquid from a cabinet behind his desk. Then he followed Mitchell out into the corridor.

'There's one other thing,' Mitchell said.

'What's that?'

'We need to wake her up first.'

Simmons had no time to ask why, because as they reached the ward, Toby was coming out. His head was bleeding and he was distressed.

'What happened?' Mitchell said.

'Someone hit me. Rosie is gone and so is your … mother!'

'Rosie hit you?' Mitchell asked. His mind began to search for her but she was closed to him, as was Elisa.

'No … someone hit me from behind. I didn't see who.'

'What the devil is going on?' asked Simmons, but neither of the men answered.

'They can't have gone far,' Mitchell said.

He turned back towards the main reception, only to find the front door open. Then he recalled the hansom that was waiting outside for them.

'Quickly!'

Mitchell hurried outside with Toby and Simmons at his heels, just in time to see the hansom driving towards the gates of the asylum.

'Can you get a message to the gatekeeper?' Mitchell yelled. 'Tell him to stop them!'

Then he and Toby ran after the carriage.

The gates remained closed as Mitchell and Toby caught up with the cab. Though breathless, Mitchell yelled to the driver to stop. As they reached the cab, they threw open the door but, much to their chagrin, they discovered that the cab was empty.

'Sorry, sir, but the young lady told me it was no longer needed,' said the driver.

'We've been duped,' said Toby. 'Where are they? How else could she escape this place with a patient who is unconscious?'

'They wouldn't,' answered Mitchell. 'They are still inside.'

'Stay here!' Mitchell told the coach driver. 'Don't take anyone from here other than us. Is that clear?'

The driver nodded and placed the brake on the carriage.

Then the asylum became everything that a sane person might dread. Yells, screams and madness ensued, as patients woke from their drug-induced sleep and began to cause havoc.

Mitchell and Toby ran back towards the insanity.

Chapter Thirty-Eight

Back inside, they met with a confused Simmons. The orderly who had shown them in hurried down the stairs to speak to the doctor.

'What's happening?' asked Toby.

'This is most irregular! They each have enough medication to keep them under all night, but somehow … it hasn't worked. We will have to sedate them all again.'

Mitchell paused in the hallway. He cast his mind out for any connection with Rosie, but her mind and emotions remained cut off from him.

'I have to find her,' he said.

'Simmons, we need help to search this place,' Toby said.

'Get them quiet and drugged, then I want all spare help down here,' Simmons said to the orderly.

The man hurried away again to complete the doctor's orders. Simmons examined and dressed Toby's head wound. The injury wasn't too bad, but Toby had a mild concussion.

'Do you have a telephone here?' Mitchell asked.

'Yes. In my office,' Simmons said.

'I need to use it,' Mitchell said.

Mitchell was concerned for Rosie, but for some reason the image of Laura flashed into his mind. Only when his mother's body was destroyed did he feel Laura might finally be safe.

While the asylum inmates were being settled, he used Simmons's telephone to call Inspector Stream at the police station.

'Stream is off-duty, sir,' said Sergeant Grimes. 'Can I help?'

Mitchell quickly filled Grimes in on the problem at the asylum.

'I know this will sound strange, but I'm concerned about Laura Carter. Can someone drive to the Carter home and check on her?'

Grimes was reluctant but there was something in Mitchell's voice that persuaded him to agree. When Mitchell put the phone down, he felt certain that Grimes would not only call Stream, but someone would call in on the Carters.

After that, he called Mainwaring's residence and spoke to Neeraj, filling him in on everything he'd learnt.

'Don't do anything until I get there,' Neeraj said. 'We can't just end this. The demon must be recaptured.'

'But how?'

'I think I know,' Neeraj said.

By the time Neeraj arrived at the asylum an hour later, Toby was feeling stronger and all the patients were quiet again. Mitchell noticed that Neeraj was carrying a box. He didn't ask what was inside, for fear that somehow the soul thief would hear their conversation.

Leaving orderlies at the exit points, Mitchell, Toby, Neeraj, Simmons and the first orderly began a room-to-room sweep of the premises, starting with the bottom floors and working their way upwards.

They passed through the now-silent wards, along corridors of single locked rooms, where the doctor and the orderly checked on the patients by opening a sliding panel on the doors. After each room was cleared, the orderly locked them, allowing for no one to exit or enter afterwards. Finally, they reached the top floor, and there they found the attic door open.

'Upstairs,' whispered Simmons.

'It's a trick,' Mitchell said, 'they aren't up there.'

'How can you know that?' asked Simmons.

Toby and Mitchell exchanged a glance.

Mitchell felt *her* then. His mother – the soul thief – was in one of the rooms across the hall. It wasn't a clear rush of memories or thoughts or visions like previous times, though. It was a burst of incoherent energy that projected from her out into the atmosphere. He doubted that anyone but himself and Rosie would even feel it or know it was there.

He hurried forward, leaving the others to follow sceptically behind. As his hand reached for the doorknob, the door slowly opened.

'Come in, Mitchell,' said a husky female voice.

The room was in complete darkness. Mitchell hesitated, but he felt the pull of her hypnotic voice and he plunged forward.

'Mitchell!' called Toby.

Mitchell glanced around to see the door slam shut behind him, locking him inside, while Simmons, Toby, Neeraj and the orderly remained in the corridor.

Mitchell heard Neeraj shouting and there was hammering on the door behind him. 'You are a thorn in my side, child,' said the voice again.

Mitchell's eyes began to adjust to the gloom. He could now

make out shapes in the room. A chest of drawers, a wardrobe, a double bed in the centre. Somewhere in the distance he could hear his companions banging on the door, trying to get inside, but his focus was on the shadow that stood beside the bed – a tall female shape that was both familiar and alien. He couldn't make out her features but imagined that the creature had somehow regained the use of the body she inhabited. Maybe the head injury had finally healed, in which case, would she now be harder to kill?

'Where is Rosie?' he asked.

The woman laughed, her head moving as though disembodied. Mitchell took a step closer to the bed. Then he noticed another shape lying on top of the duvet. A small shaft of light leaked through a gap in the curtains. Mitchell heard activity outside the building as well as in the hall, and the courtyard below was suddenly lit up by gaslight. The light was enough for him to realise that the body on the bed was his mother.

'Rosie?' he said to the woman beside the bed.

Laughter again.

'Fight it. Fight her. She may be our mother, but she doesn't control us.'

'You're rather slow on the uptake,' the woman said again.

She stepped forward into the light and for the first time Mitchell saw Laura standing beside the bed.

'No…' he gasped.

'She's such an easy body to manipulate,' the Laura-thing smiled. 'Didn't struggle at all when I gave her soul a final push.'

'Get out of her!'

'She's mine, Mitchell. She's mine and I'll make her do anything I feel like.'

Laura's lips moved, but Mitchell knew the words were not coming from her mind at all. Her body was a puppet for the monster that lay helpless in the bed. For the first time in his life, he wasn't sure what to do.

But he did know one thing. The reason the soul thief was using Laura was because it couldn't control Rosie, any more than it could control him. After all, it had only ever used her image, and not her. But now it couldn't use her at all, or it would have kept her close.

'Mitchell!' called Toby from outside. 'Are you all right?'

'For now,' he replied.

The Laura-thing turned her head to face the door. 'Your reinforcements can't get in.'

'Mother?' he said finally.

Laura's head snapped back to look at Mitchell as he approached the bed.

'*Mother*,' he repeated.

The thing inside Laura watched him closely as he knelt beside the prone figure. Mitchell stared at the worn features but could not recognise himself or Rosie in them.

'I'm sorry this happened to you,' he said. 'I suspect you would have been a proper mother to both Rosie and myself, if only you hadn't been tainted by this creature.'

'I was a proper mother to Rosie...' the creature said through Laura. 'I was the best mother any daughter could wish for.'

'Then you wouldn't hurt her?' he asked. '*Would* you?'

Laura's brow frowned. The soul thief's grip on her was intense and Mitchell had no idea how to sever it. If he killed the woman in the bed, would that be enough? Or would that just mean the creature would remain inside Laura?

'I want to talk to my *real* mother,' Mitchell said.

'I am all there is,' said Laura.

'No … I mean I need to hear the truth from her lips.'

Laura gazed down at the old woman on the bed. She shuddered as though the thought of entering this creature, breathing through its lungs once more, revolted her.

'This body is damaged. It is best I use Laura to speak,' the creature said.

'But you're still in there, aren't you?' Mitchell asked.

The Laura-creature smiled. 'I'm everywhere.'

Mitchell tried to probe its mind but the wall was firmly in place and he could get nothing from the creature. Where was Rosie? He feared for her, but also knew that she might possibly be able to answer the questions he had.

'Get out of Laura,' he said. His voice was firm and held an undercurrent of threat that showed the level of angst he had at this current scenario.

The creature looked down once more at the body. Mitchell took one of the cold claw-like hands in his.

'You show such tenderness to that body,' the creature said. 'Why?'

'You have no understanding. All you are is a cold, callous thing. But didn't you feel anything when you joined with Elisa? Didn't you experience any of her emotions?'

Laura frowned again and Mitchell wondered if in fact the creature could feel. He dug his nail into the palm of his mother's body until he drew blood. Laura took a step back in surprise. It felt the pain, but had that pain hurt the woman he loved also?

The creature raised Laura's palm. It was unmarked, but the hand he held now bled. Mitchell squeezed the fingers, hard.

'Stop it!' Laura said.

Mitchell now knew it felt pain through this body, which

confirmed that it was still connected to it. But how far could he go with this? Could he perhaps throttle his own mother, and if he did, would the soul thief die also? Making a quick decision, he slapped the body on the bed. The soul thief jerked inside Laura. He slapped again. The barrier blocking her mind slipped. He could see inside her and knew then that the control she had over Laura was only tentative. His original assessment of it had been right: the creature was weak. Laura was being manipulated, but the soul thief was not inside her.

He slapped his mother again, harder.

'Mitchell?' Laura said. She was looking around. 'Where am I?'

Mitchell pushed his thoughts into the mind of the soul thief while its consciousness was still reconnecting with the old woman's body; he could see Rosie now. She was unhurt, but tied up in the attic.

'Toby! Rosie is in the attic. In a trunk,' he called. The banging outside stopped, and he heard feet running away and up the steps.

Now that the soul thief was debilitated by pain, Mitchell lost the will to hit the body. It sickened him to beat a helpless person, even though he knew this was an evil thing. It was still the body that had once been owned by his mother. He couldn't get away from that, no matter how hard he tried to disassociate himself.

He hurried away from the bedside and took Laura in his arms. She was trembling with fear.

'You're safe,' he promised. Then he pulled her to the door and tugged it open with ease, proving once more that the soul thief's strength was failing. He found the doctor still outside with the orderly, who looked nervous and afraid.

He handed Laura over to the orderly. 'Hold onto her. No matter what happens, don't let her go.'

'What the devil is going on?' said Simmons.

Neeraj pushed past Simmons into the room and placed the box he was carrying down on the floor. He knelt and began to chant a prayer in Hindi.

'Get the injection ready now,' Mitchell said to the doctor.

'This is madness…' Simmons said, but he opened his bag and retrieved the needle and the bottle of clear fluid.

'Mitchell, what is going on?' asked Laura.

With trembling hands, the doctor filled the syringe, but as he approached the bed, Laura changed. She became inordinately strong. She overwhelmed the orderly, pushed him back and away. The man fell to the floor and lay still.

Mitchell turned back and saw Laura entering the room once more. He rushed between her and Neeraj, realising too late that the doctor was her target. She back-handed Mitchell and sent him flying into the dresser. His head connected with the wood and a loud crack echoed through the small, sparse room.

Laura glanced at him briefly; confusion, fear and then anger crossed her features. The doctor stared at her from the other side of the bed.

A terrible smile, like a predator stalking its prey, crossed Laura's features as she began to walk around the bed.

Neeraj ignored all that was happening around him as he opened the box on the floor. The chant tumbled from his lips, faster and louder.

'Who are you?' Simmons asked as Laura approached him. He was used to dealing with the insane, who sometimes had inexplicable strength, but his fear of Laura was so acute that he found himself backing away, until he was pressed against the wardrobe and could go no further.

As she reached the doctor, he raised the needle before him, as though the threat of it would be enough to ward off the evil that he could sense was controlling her.

Laura's smile widened. Simmons let go of his bladder. Urine seeped into the crotch of his breeches and dripped down the inside of his leg to form a puddle by his feet. The doctor was completely oblivious to it. Instead, he was captivated by the beautiful woman before him. Terror was taken over by euphoria. The syringe fell from his fingers. It clattered to the floor and skidded across the room, coming to rest under the bed.

Laura's hand shot out and gripped Simmons around the throat. With superhuman strength she lifted him up against the wardrobe door until his feet dangled above the floor. The air choked from his lungs, but other than the automatic twitch of his feet as he died, the doctor felt no fear or pain. He was lost inside a world of lust, the like of which he had never known.

The doctor was long dead when the creature controlling Laura let go of his throat. He slid downwards into the pool of his own mess. The room stank but she didn't notice, she merely turned and looked back to where the body she still owned lay.

Mitchell was by the bedside, the needle poised against the arm of the creature. He pushed it into the skin, and Laura reacted immediately, as though the pain reached her. She gripped her arm and staggered as the pain shook the soul thief from inside her.

Meanwhile Neeraj had retrieved the photograph of the Carter siblings from the box he'd brought and was proceeding to burn it, while he continued to chant. Laura screamed as the picture burned and began to beat at her own skin, as if she were on fire too. As the picture dissolved into ashes, Laura crumpled to the ground. She was now useless to the soul thief.

Neeraj removed an old Indian relic in the shape of a funeral jar. It was carved with ancient symbols that the old mage had copied from the shards of the original jar, whose pieces lay in the bottom of the one he now held.

Mitchell turned his attention back to the body, but he hesitated and he felt life spring into the wasted limbs for the first time since he had seen it. The old woman beneath him moved, the arm wrenched from his grip, while the other claw-like hand reached over and pulled the syringe from her dried-out skin.

Mitchell fell back from the bed. He watched as the soul thief pulled the sagging body upwards, the needle in its left hand pointed downwards towards the mattress.

'Surely you couldn't kill your own mother?' the creature said through a voice cracked with age and lack of moisture.

Laura groaned and began to sit up.

'Laura, get out of here!' Mitchell said.

Laura glanced down at the body of Simmons beside her feet, and then staggered backwards towards the door, as though she were sleepwalking.

'No, Laura,' said the soul thief. 'Stay.'

Laura stopped moving; she was rooted to the spot.

Mitchell backed away from the bedside, pulling himself upwards on the dresser where he had previously hit his head. There was a small bruise blossoming on his forehead; a thin trickle of blood seeped out from his hairline and ran in a thin line down his cheek.

The soul thief pulled the old ravaged body to the edge of the bed, then casually discarded the syringe. It tottered on the edge of the mattress.

'My son,' said the creature. 'You are strong, but my will has lived for centuries. Your humanity is your failing. You have my nature, all of it could be yours. You could use this woman to slake your desires. I see the perversion inside you. You are me … I am you…'

'Be quiet!' Mitchell said. 'I am nothing like you. You may inhabit the body of my mother. But you aren't her and never have been.'

'I can smell the lust in you. You want this mortal, but she'll be no good for you in the end. An easy flame that will be snuffed out as simply as a candle in the breeze.'

The old woman staggered to her feet, the wasted legs barely holding her as she stepped forward towards Mitchell.

He drew back as far from the bed as he could. The sight of her disgusted him, but he forced himself to keep his gaze on her skull-like face.

'Laura,' she said. 'Come and kiss my son. He wants you. Show him how much you love him.'

Laura responded immediately. She passed between them, but Mitchell snatched her away as the creature reached out her gnarled fingers to caress the girl's face.

The point of the syringe scraped the back of his hand. Without him realising, the creature had taken it up again. She had used Laura as the distraction. Mitchell quickly realised that had he not moved her, the needle would have been plunged into the woman he loved.

Now the creature approached with renewed strength that belied the frail appearance of the body. The syringe was raised like a dagger and she swung it at the two of them.

Neeraj's chanting grew louder.

'Be quiet, old man!' the soul thief said, casting him a look of disgust. 'Your gibberish has no power here.'

Mitchell pushed Laura aside. She fell towards the bottom of the bed, and he grabbed the soul thief's arm.

She was so strong that Mitchell felt the muscles in his arm hurt as he struggled to wrestle the syringe from her fingers. He smashed back against the dresser; his shoulders screamed as he was yanked back towards his mother. They struggled together in a bizarre tug of war.

'Mother, no!' yelled Rosie from the doorway. She ran inside, pulling and tugging the soul thief from behind.

Neeraj continued chanting, unfazed by the struggle that was happening, though he was aware that the siblings' dual strength was beginning to overwhelm the worn body the soul thief inhabited.

Then Mitchell felt his strength leave him. The soul thief pulled him forward once more, expecting a resistance that Mitchell couldn't give. The creature tumbled backwards on momentum caused by its own strength. The fall pushed Rosie backwards also, and she fell away.

Mitchell and the soul thief rolled back onto the bed; the syringe twisted beneath them. Then suddenly the creature stiffened. Mitchell felt the death-like grip on his arms release. He pulled back, stood and gazed down at the figure.

The syringe was protruding from the stomach of the creature. The plunger was fully down. She was still alive, but shocked.

Mitchell pulled the syringe free. It was empty. The contents had clearly gone into the body of the creature. He wondered for the first time, what the solution was, and how quickly it would work.

The creature's face contorted with pain. The body twisted and writhed on the bed.

'My God!' said Rosie, getting to her feet. '*Mother...*'

Mitchell glanced towards her, then back to the creature inhabiting his mother's body. He saw Laura begin to walk forward, trying to reach the dying figure.

'Stop her!' yelled Neeraj. 'All of you, back away. She can't have another vessel to enter as she dies.'

Toby grabbed Laura, but she struggled fiercely until both Mitchell and Rosie waded in to help remove her from the room.

The soul thief was alive and its cackled laughter rang out from Laura's throat. 'She's still mine,' it said.

Then Rosie saw something on the ground by the bed.

'Hold her!' she said to Toby and Mitchell, and she ran into the room, retrieving the negative. 'It's the negative of Laura – she had it on her all the time!' she said.

Rosie pulled the sketch of Artie from her pocket.

'Burn it. Now!' Mitchell said.

Rosie cast her eyes around the dark room, looking for fire.

'Here!' yelled the orderly, coming into the room with a lantern. Until then, he'd remained at the door, paralysed with fear. Now he opened the front of the lantern, burning his fingers on the hot glass.

Rosie wasted no time in dropping the negative into the flame, and she let the corner of the sketch paper catch alight, holding it until the last embers almost reached her finger before she dropped the last piece inside the lamp.

The body on the bed began to squirm and twist, screaming with abject agony as it tried to hold onto its life. Mitchell pulled Laura into his arms as he watched the white mist pouring from his mother's body. Laura's image finally fell free, and he saw Sara and Warren rising up, their ghostly forms pausing momentarily as though to look at Laura and Mitchell in the doorway before they dispersed. Then the likeness of

Artie was the final one to break free. The white shadow's mouth was open in a surprised 'O'.

Still chanting, Neeraj pushed the jar closer and backed away.

The figure was no longer moving and the frail shell began to calcify. The eyes glazed over like the white sightless gaze of a marble statue, as the skin turned as white as desert-bleached bone.

A grey blur rose from the body and was drawn, as though caught in a net, towards the jar. As the haze disappeared inside, Neeraj ran forward, placing the lid on top. He bound the jar with string and then placed it carefully back inside the box. From there he sat and diligently heated a wax stick using the fire from the lamp, and he smeared it around the edges of the lid to ensure that nothing could ever leak out from the jar. The soul thief was trapped once more.

Both Mitchell and Rosie swayed on their feet, as though the death of their mother somehow took the strength from their limbs.

Mitchell was vaguely aware of Toby moving, and he caught hold of Rosie as though he thought she was about to faint, even as Laura gripped Mitchell to stop him falling.

Rosie recovered sooner, and she extricated herself from Toby's arms after placing a loving kiss on his cheek. She went back into the room, then bent down. Her hand reached out to touch the cold white flesh of her dead mother, but as her fingers brushed lightly across the corpse's cheek, the face began to crumble. The features fell inwards, like lime on flesh. It burned through the remains, setting off a domino effect on the rest of the face. The body soon followed, collapsing down until nothing but chalky dust remained of the old woman's body.

Rosie wiped her hand against the skirt of her dress.

Mitchell came back to his senses as the room erupted in a crazed bustle of activity. The orderly was checking Dr Simmons's body and many more of the staff came running to see what the commotion was. There would be some palms to grease, maybe some explanations to be made – all of which, Mitchell knew he'd deal with, as long as he knew everyone was safe.

Epilogue

'You have a lot of explaining to do,' said Inspector Stream.

'Not now,' said Mitchell. 'My sister is getting married in a few minutes. I have to escort her down the aisle.'

They were standing outside the church, waiting for Rosie to arrive with Laura as her maid of honour. Since the death of the soul thief over a week ago, Mitchell, Laura, Rosie and Toby had been spending a lot of time together. They were becoming a family, bonded in their joint experience, and Mitchell and Rosie had fallen into easy familiarity. They were brother and sister now, as though they'd always been, because they had a link that no one else could ever share.

The wedding, previously booked by Rosie and Toby, was going to take place. It was important to all of them to resume a normal life as soon as possible.

'We found Artie where you said. Can you at least tell me how you knew he would be in the Carters' tomb?' asked Stream.

'Was he all right?' Mitchell asked.

'Yes. Dehydrated, hungry. Very confused. He, apparently, didn't know how he got there.'

Mitchell glanced towards the graveyard. He couldn't see the tomb from here but he knew it well. He had seen it in the mind of the creature in those last few moments before it died. He didn't know how to explain it, though. Nor could he ever tell Stream the truth about the death of Dr Simmons, no matter how much he asked.

The orderly had been paid for his silence and no one else had witnessed what had happened. All they said was, a patient had gone after him. The patient in question was missing; a hunt had failed to turn up the escapee. Mitchell hoped that Stream, although a dog with a bone, would soon forget about the incident in favour of another crime that needed solving.

At that moment the open-topped carriage approached. Mitchell's eyes fell on Laura. She looked beautiful and normal. She was whole again. It had reassured him to see this. He now felt certain that Warren and Sara were finally at rest, and Laura, his beloved, was safe from the poison that had contaminated her soul.

The carriage pulled in by the door and Mitchell stepped forward to help Rosie and Laura down.

Inside the church the organist began to play the wedding march. Rosie's face lit up as Mitchell offered her his arm and Laura took up the long train on the ornate ivory dress that Mitchell had paid for.

As Mitchell led Rosie past Stream, the Inspector nodded politely, but Mitchell saw that familiar look in the Inspector's eyes: he wanted answers. Perhaps Mitchell would one day give them, when he'd thought up something plausible to say. But then, perhaps he wouldn't.

It occurred to him that he could make their problems go away with the swirl of charcoal, but that darkness was locked inside him, just as the soul thief was locked inside an elaborate jar. Hidden, he hoped, where no one would ever find it.

Acknowledgments

My agent and friend, Camilla Shestopal, for always believing in me and being my guiding light. My editor, Jennie Rothwell, who has been a delight to work with and whose enthusiasm for the book has been so uplifting. Steven Smith, PR Guru and friend, cheering me on at every opportunity. My husband David, who is always my rock and supports everything I do with patience and grace. To Emma and everyone working tirelessly behind the scenes at One More Chapter to help make my books a success.

The author and One More Chapter would like to thank everyone who contributed to the publication of this story…

Analytics
James Brackin
Abigail Fryer
Maria Osa

Audio
Fionnuala Barrett
Ciara Briggs

Contracts
Sasha Duszynska Lewis

Design
Lucy Bennett
Fiona Greenway
Liane Payne
Dean Russell

Digital Sales
Lydia Grainge
Hannah Lismore
Emily Scorer

Editorial
Simon Fox
Arsalan Isa
Charlotte Ledger
Bonnie Macleod
Jennie Rothwell
Caroline Scott-Bowden

Harper360
Emily Gerbner
Jean Marie Kelly
emma sullivan
Sophia Wilhelm

International Sales
Peter Borcsok
Bethan Moore

Marketing & Publicity
Chloe Cummings
Emma Petfield

Operations
Melissa Okusanya
Hannah Stamp

Production
Denis Manson
Simon Moore
Francesca Tuzzeo

Rights
Vasiliki Machaira
Rachel McCarron
Hany Sheikh
Mohamed
Zoe Shine

The HarperCollins Distribution Team

The HarperCollins Finance & Royalties Team

The HarperCollins Legal Team

The HarperCollins Technology Team

Trade Marketing
Ben Hurd

UK Sales
Laura Carpenter
Isabel Coburn
Jay Cochrane
Sabina Lewis
Holly Martin
Erin White
Harriet Williams
Leah Woods

And every other essential link in the chain from delivery drivers to booksellers to librarians and beyond!

One More Chapter is an
award-winning global
division of HarperCollins.

Sign up to our newsletter to get our
latest eBook deals and stay up to date
with our weekly Book Club!
<u>Subscribe here.</u>

Meet the team at
<u>www.onemorechapter.com</u>

Follow us!
@OneMoreChapter_
@OneMoreChapter
@onemorechapterhc

Do you write unputdownable fiction?
We love to hear from new voices.
Find out how to submit your novel at
<u>www.onemorechapter.com/submissions</u>